Captain James Lockwood

Captain James Lockwood

A Novel

by

Mark Bois

www.penmorepress.com

Captain James Lockwood by Mark Bois
Copyright © 2015, 2019 Mark Bois

ISBN: 978-1-946409-96-6(paperback)
ISBN: 978-1-946409-97-3(Ebook)

BISAC Subject Headings:
FIC032000FICTION / War & Military
FIC002000FICTION / Action & Adventure
HIS018000 HISTORY /Europe/Ireland
Editing: Chris Wozney.
Cover work by The Book Cover Whisperer:
ProfessionalBookCoverDesign.com
Please address all correspondence to:

Penmore Press
920 N Javalina PL
Tucson, AZ 85748

Revews

" again Mark Bois is spot on with his accurate portrayal of the life of an army officer. Bois is able to seamlessly tie in the importance of the role of a military spouse and all they do to hold down the fort while their loved ones are deployed. Bois also has the unique ability to transport you to that time and place and make you feel as if you are a member of Lockwood's own company. Bois is an author for all generations; I'd love to see Lockwood on the big screen!"
-Brad Luebbert, Colonel, US Army

"Bois captures the true essence of life of a military spouse. He focuses on the strength and independence necessary to deal with the whims of the military and the rigor of maintaining a household with an often absent and/or deployed spouse. He accurately displays the challenges military spouses face as they cope with loneliness and frustration. Bois has brilliantly captured the unique bond military couples have shared since the time armies first marched off to war."
-Sarah B. Luebbert, military spouse who endured multiple overseas deployments and tour combat tours

Dedication

To Dr. Mark Wurster, my lifelong friend

Acknowledgments

Michael James and the staff at Penmore Press have been helpful, supportive, and demanding, and I owe them a great deal. My friends and colleagues at the Cincinnati Writers' Project are a constant source of inspiration, and a necessary check on my passion for semi-colons. Malcolm Nye, esq., was kind enough to share details of early 19th century swords, Dr. Wayne Lee made me a historian, and several friends in the US Army, especially Colonel Brad and Sarah Luebbert, have given voice to the realities of the lives of soldiers and their families, in peace and at war. The internet is of course a great tool for all authors; Ask About Ireland's support of Griffith's Irish Valuation Maps is invaluable, while the staff and readership of The Napoleon Series have saved me from several errors. But in the end I owe all I am to my family: Jon, Kevin, Catherine, Genevieve, Patrick, and the meaning of my life, Charmin.

Our thanks to David Higham for the cover art.
'More examples of David Higham's work can be found on the www.printsforartssake.com website'

Chapter One

A foggy dawn, and as the last notes of reveille sounded from the castle below, an officer of the Inniskilling Regiment strode purposefully down Queen Street. He was a very tall man, though not so heavily muscled as he once had been, as twenty years in His Majesty's service had worn him, and on more than one occasion, had nearly killed him.

His name was James Lockwood, a captain of the regiment, though one still unaccustomed to his rank. He had purchased his captaincy only two months before; the previous sixteen years he had served as a lieutenant in Spain and France, against the French, then against the Americans, and then again against the French at Waterloo.

His destination was his regiment's headquarters at Enniskillen Castle, a low, crumbling structure that stood on the banks of the River Erne in the center of Enniskillen Town. At the castle's front gate a red-coated sentry paced a relaxed guard.

At the approach of the captain, however, the soldier drew himself up and studied the officer with keen attention. He smiled a bit as the officer drew closer, then halted to deliver his salute. He knew his trade and sharply shouldered his musket at the prescribed twenty yards' distance.

Captain Lockwood

James had not been to the regimental headquarters for many years and was surprised to find that the man at the gate looked familiar. He had always considered it an officer's duty to know the names of any man who served under him, and he was fortunate in having a good memory. Though it took him a moment, the name came to him: O'Boyle. Nearly eight years earlier, Patrick O'Boyle had been drafted from the regiment's Second Battalion and served in James's company at Waterloo. While more than half of the men of the Inniskilling Regiment were killed or wounded on that Sunday in June of 1815, O'Boyle had survived the day unscathed. Lieutenant Lockwood had not been so fortunate, as a French musket ball had passed through his arm and lodged deep in his chest. Every doctor who had examined him on that day, and for some time afterward, was amazed that it had not killed him.

James returned the sentry's salute and said, "Good morning, O'Boyle. I trust I find you well."

O'Boyle, pleased to be remembered, said, "Good morning, Lieutenant Lockwood, sir." But then, noting the fringed bullion on Lockwood's epaulette, he went on, "Oh, but a captain now? May it profit you, sir. Faith, it has been a very long time."

"It has indeed." They were both quiet for a moment; that day had shaped their lives and the lives of thousands of others. With some trepidation James recalled how, at one point, the young O'Boyle had frozen in horror, and how he had grabbed the private by the back of his collar and shaken him like a dog.

O'Boyle evidently did not hold a grudge, as he gave Lockwood a grin and said, "We held them, sir. We held them."

James gave him a reassuring nod and said, "We did indeed. You did well there, soldier. Now, where might I find Major McLachlan?"

In a voice that betrayed a hint of delight, O'Boyle exclaimed, "Oh, the headquarters office, I think, sir."

Passing into the courtyard, Captain Lockwood found twenty or more men lounging about, none properly dressed, equipped or directed. A cloud crossed his face and he thought, "It looks as if O'Boyle is the only soldier in the God damned place."

He crossed the yard to the office, where a fat, sleepy sergeant sat behind a desk. The sergeant coughed, waved at the stairs, and offered, "The major is not yet available." He then sniffed and added, "He is entertaining."

Captain Lockwood swelled and told the sergeant, in the kindly manner he reserved for God damned slovens, that if the sergeant did not make a proper salute and a proper response he have would have the stripes, the hide, and the God damned insolence off him before breakfast.

The sergeant leapt to his feet, but was saved from any more of the captain's attentions by the sound of heavy footsteps coming from the major's quarters. The source of those heavy treads proved to be a thickly rouged woman of imposing girth, one who was in no hurry to lace her impressive bodice.

From the bottom of the steps she struck a massively busty pose, and, eyeing the captain, she coyly asked the sweating sergeant in Irish, "Ah, now, *Lacha*, who is the *ispín?*"

Sadly, the lady did not know that the captain was married to an Irishwoman, that his five children routinely spoke Irish amongst themselves, and that the captain had picked up enough of the language to realize now that the sergeant's nickname was "Duck" and that he himself was now being referred to as "a sausage."

The sergeant did not dare reply, and only widened his eyes and discreetly tossed his head toward the door. Lockwood silently

3

glared at her and, though she was a whore of long standing, the woman had rarely met with such a wall of disdain as that emanating from this towering captain. She raised her eyebrows and hems in wounded umbrage and brushed out of the room with not a little style.

James had nothing against whores *per se,* as they had followed every army since Solomon's host. There were times that he had found them positively useful, as men on garrison duty required something to distract them from boredom and thoughts of desertion. He was, in fact, a man of some appetite, but never allowed himself to partake of their charms. He was far from perfect, but for the past twenty-three years he had remained wholly devoted to Brigid O'Brian Lockwood.

The slamming of the office door was evidently the signal for Major McLachlan to come downstairs, unshaven and pulling on his uniform coat.

James made his salute, but McLachlan waved him off with a smile, shook his hand, and said, "Ach, no formalities, Lockwood. This is our end-of-the-earth depot battalion, nae bloody Horse Guards."

James had always liked McLachlan, and was pleased to hear that he had not lost his heavy Highland accent. He'd not seen him in ten years or more and was saddened to see that the major had not aged well. He was nearly as tall as James, but his belly had swelled, his limbs were thin, and his graying hair was wildly combed over his balding pate.

McLachlan motioned James to follow him into his private office, and as they both took a seat the major said, "I knew you were coming up to take command of this draft, but I had nae expected you for a fortnight. You always were keen, Lockwood."

"My orders state that the transport is already waiting in Derry." He pronounced it *"Daire,"* as would Brigid, but he hurriedly added, "I beg pardon; I meant Londonderry."

"Bugger the navy; let 'em wait." Then, eyeing Lockwood, he added, "You've had an interesting year or two, have you nae? I had heard your Waterloo wound flared and nearly did for you, though you look well enough now. And then dismissed the service! A vile political job, that. How we bombarded Horse Guards and Dublin Castle! I wrote two letters myself, and gave 'em some very direct language, I can tell you. That'll teach them not to mess about with His Majesty's officers. Damned bureaucrats."

James gave the major a pained smile and a nod. "Thank you for your support, McLachlan. You and the others ... Well, it was most touching, how you all rallied to me."

Leaning forward and looking intent, McLachlan said, "We are old comrades, Lockwood, and so I feel I might impose, and ask about Barr. The papers were full of how he went mad—he always was a foul *ainmhidh*—and made an attempt upon the life of your own daughter, and her firing a pistol in his face! I know he escaped the law, and rumours still fly of where he might yet be hiding."

Lockwood, his face a mask, said only, "The matter has been tended to."

McLachlan made as if to ask another eager question, but, meeting James's stony face, he caught himself, went silent, and leaned back in his chair, studying Lockwood.

James had tracked Barr to a distant corner of Clare and had fought a duel in a remote, frost-covered field. He had left Captain Charles Barr lying dead there. James preferred, however, not to make that news public. Dueling was common enough in Ireland, but even then, the magistrates would have insisted upon a murder trial to ensure that the duel had been conducted according to accepted codes. James Lockwood had recent experience with the uneven application of justice in Ireland and had no desire to risk another such encounter. Charles Barr would no longer pose a threat to his family's safety, or to their reputations; that was all that mattered.

McLachlan nodded, a quiet acknowledgment between two soldiers, and deliberately changed the subject. "It was old Mainwaring who started the campaign to support your reinstatement, you know, and then Colonel Nelson got half the army to wring the castle's tail."

James coughed awkwardly; McLachlan waved his hand dismissively and went on, "Still, no obligation, Lockwood, no obligation. Band of brothers, Saint Crispin's Day and all that, you know."

James coughed again, and McLachlan added with a kindly tone, "You will pardon me for mentioning that your breathing seems a bit... ragged? Are you quite sure you are up to a foreign posting? Gibraltar is very far from home."

"I feel quite well, thank you."

"Well, just know that being a Waterloo veteran will nae longer carry much weight these days. You had best watch your health, brother; indeed, I am surprised you are willing to go at all."

"You know as well as anyone, McLachlan, how much leave I have taken to allow my wounds to heal. At this point I believe that honour requires me to go wherever the regiment is sent. Our men, after all, do not have such luxuries as deciding whether to go or no."

"Hoot awa, you and your ideals, Lockwood. If you are not careful someone will confuse you with a republican; such nonsense is floating around Ireland in a most dangerous fashion. You are a gentleman, and thus entitled to consider your options. But it is too late for you now, I suppose." McLachlan flipped through some papers on his desk and went on, "The draft will consist of one hundred four men. There were more, but last week I allowed a few outside the walls on a work detail, and six deserted as quick as kiss my hand. I've done what I can with them, but most of this rabble is fresh off the bog without a word of English and no more sense than God grants a rabbit."

"I met one of my old Waterloo men at the gate—O'Boyle. Is he amongst the draft?"

McLachlan let his finger drift down the list, finally saying, "Aye, here he is: O'Boyle, Patrick. He's one of the few who knows one end of a musket from the other. It seems he re-enlisted after finding civilian life less luxurious than he recalled. You might count on him, I think, and your NCOs—you'll have just one sergeant and one corporal—but no more. And won't you have a merry time of it, trying to get your one hundred four sheep up to Londonderry with so few shepherds."

"Oh, come now, sir," said James, his official voice rising, "you might loan me another NCO or two? I shall be herding cats all the way to the sea, else."

McLachlan waved a hand in surrender, and said, "Ach, keep the heid, man! Do not look so put upon. I might, at great inconvenience, mind you, send another reliable corporal or two. But you must send them straight back."

"Thank you, sir," James said, mollified. "We shall march the day after tomorrow, with your permission."

"Certainly, certainly. The men have been aware of the move for some time, though we need to determine the question of wives. The men know the regulations, but of course, we have far too many on

7

the books, and there will be tears aplenty when you march. How many will you allow?"

"Three, I think. This is a company-sized draft, so we shall take a company's allotment of wives."

The question of wives and children was a difficult one. While the army was typically hesitant to allow too many of its men to marry, married men who enlisted were permitted to bring their families into the barracks, where they lived in cramped squalor. But it was now up to James to determine which of the wives and children would follow the battalion, and which would remain in Ireland. He had done so once before, just before Waterloo, and he had found it exquisitely painful.

"Now, Lockwood, as to the march. After breakfast I shall take you over to see my quartermaster sergeant, who will lay out the logistics. And to show there is no ill will over your petulant insistence on stripping this depot of every man worth his salt, I shall loan you a saddle horse so that you need nae walk all the way to Londonderry. My corporals can lead it back."

James smiled and nodded his thanks as McLachlan continued with a deliberate change of topic and mood, "I suppose you came in on the mail last night?"

"Yes, we got in late and stayed at Mrs. Noble's."

With a sudden delight, McLachlan sat up straight, and said, "We? You dinnae mean Mrs. Lockwood is in town, as well?"

James took no offense at the reaction his wife's name provoked, as he heard it with marked regularity. While the men of the regiment, in fact every sensible man who met her, had an appreciation for her beauty, it was her compassion and genuine goodness that bound her to them. She had a kindness for the enlisted men, especially their wives and children. Among the officers she was a perennial favorite, as she enjoyed the company of men, and while always a lady, she did not look down her nose at a man who enjoyed a drink, a cigar or a ribald story.

Some years before, at an informal regimental dinner for twenty officers and their wives, the gentlemen had sampled Major McLachlan's cherished Lagavulin single malt whiskey, and declared it fit only to tar a boat. Brigid had then reached across, taken a sip from her husband's glass and confidently declared it full of God's peat smoke, and a fine drink indeed. The officers roared their approval, and when James turned to speak to the officer on his right, Brigid made as if to set the glass back down, but then, with a sneaking smile and a glint of mischief in her eye, she first took another full swallow. The officers once again roared with laughter, every one of them delighted with Mrs. Lockwood, though some of the other wives were not quite so enchanted. As for McLachlan, after Mrs. Lockwood's first taste of Lagavulin, he thought very highly of her; after the second, he would have walked through fire for her.

"Yes," said James. "Brigid came up with me from Clonakilty, and she will go on to spend a week with Colonel and Mrs. Nelson at White Hall. We brought Doolan along as well, to see her safely home. Before I forget, Brigid asked if you should care to dine with us before she leaves Enniskillen."

"And so Doolan is still with you! Ach, and so does Mrs. Lockwood indeed recall me? How good in her. That's a braw lass you have there, Lockwood, a braw lass. I shall have the Maguire Arms reserve us the upstairs room; fine trout there, but a pity I'll nae have time to send across to Islay for a Christian haggis. But for now, let us go across for breakfast. You may recall me as a man who values a good meal, Lockwood."

Captain Lockwood

Early that afternoon McLachlan ordered the draft to be paraded for Captain Lockwood's review. If James had been in command, he would have called for the parade later in the day, after the men had been fed their dinner. Instead, the hungry men were drawn up in a misty rain, subtly eying this towering captain with his prying ways. It was customary for an officer tasked with taking out a draft to check every man's kit for completeness and quality. Some officers would not bother with such details, but Captain Lockwood was not such an officer.

Though McLachlan had made himself unavailable, Captain Lockwood hunted down the reluctant quartermaster sergeant, a sly-looking fellow named Mulvaney, and had him join in the review of the men's equipment. With the sergeant in tow, James strode out to the yard, where the draft was drawn up in a thoroughly shabby manner. Ranks and files were ragged; few held their musket in any way approaching the prescribed manner and their dress ranged from ridiculously ill-fitting to something resembling a disreputable stage company.

It should be mentioned that Private Darby Rooney had come down to Enniskillen from the most remote corner of Donegal. He had never spoken a word of English in his life, and when he found no work in town, enlistment had become his only alternative to starvation. His three weeks as a soldier had filled his belly and taught him a bit of his duty, but had not given him more than a nodding acquaintance with the English language. A conversation with this mountain of a captain was thus well beyond him, being such a small, shy fellow himself. But Rooney was the front rank man in the first file, so he was the first man to meet Captain Lockwood's discerning glare. When the captain asked Rooney, in a

10

harsh tone, why he appeared bareheaded on parade, Rooney turned to Sergeant Mulvaney in panic, hoping for support.

"*Whist, ye Bostoon,*" said Mulvaney, "don't make a beast of yourself before the captain."

The soldier gasped something in Irish to Mulvaney, but the sergeant ignored him and said, "Captain, this man carelessly lost the shako that was issued him, and is having the cost of a new one deducted from his pay."

James, long familiar with garrison quartermasters, ignored Mulvaney and instead, pointing to the soldier's head, he said something approximating, "*Áit a bhfuil hata do bhFiann, fear?*"

Rooney was puzzled for a moment—the tall Saxon so gruff, and him speaking like a Mayo lunatic, until he discerned that he was being asked about his great tall hat. Rooney pointed to his head and rattled off a long, pleasant, conversational answer that was, in turn, well beyond James's understanding. Mulvaney, looking smug, made no effort to translate.

The captain looked frustrated, Rooney looked wounded, and for a long awkward moment no one knew what to do. Finally, from the supernumerary rank behind Rooney, a young corporal boldly said, "He says the shako was rotten, sir." The quartermaster sergeant shot him an angry look, but the corporal returned a defiant glare, and then, to the captain, he added, "The shako fell to pieces the first day, Captain. Sure, it's not the man's fault."

"Your name, please, Corporal?"

"Shanahan, please, your honour," said the corporal, wondering if he was about to lose a stripe.

"Thank you, Corporal Shanahan." Then with a nod of understanding to the private, James took a deep, angry, breath that made Mulvaney turn pale, and made a note in his orderly book. Up and down the ranks the stories were the same: shoddy equipment, weak excuses, poor instruction, and lax discipline.

At the end of the review, he turned to Mulvaney and said in a tense voice, "Sergeant, you will please draw your ledgers and meet me in the Major's office. The three of us will then see what stores are at hand, and attempt to equip these men like soldiers rather than a pack of God damned castaways." Then to his draft sergeant, a soft little man named Maguire, he said, "Sergeant, I believe that Major McLachlan would agree, the men of the draft merit an extra tot of rum to make up for their tardy dinner." He did not say it loudly; he would not overtly curry the men's favor. That was a weak officer's ploy. But later, word would pass through the draft that it was the captain who'd got them those extra articles of clothing and equipment, him railing against that corrupt Mulvaney like a Sligo shrew, but they especially treasured their extra tot, one of the few things that made army life bearable.

That evening in the barracks, Private O'Boyle's company was especially sought after. He had stories about the tall captain, and O'Boyle told them of Waterloo, and the captain walking that field like Fionn Mac Cumhaill, a giant amongst men, fierce and fearless, but he also told of how the captain kept his men true to their duty, and in turn cared for them like his own sons. And he told them of the captain's wife, an Irishwoman, an O'Brian, and her said to be kind and good, and the most beautiful woman in all Munster. O'Boyle also shared the nickname Lockwood had long carried amongst the men of the Inniskilling Regiment. The next morning, but only amongst themselves, the men of the draft began referring to their captain as 'Daidi.'

*****

Brigid O'Brian Lockwood had grown up with four sisters in a small house in Clonakilty, her father clinging to a few Irish acres, a man fond of telling his daughters, in pride and bitterness, of the thousands of acres once held by the clan O'Brian in the happy years before the English came.

She thus grew up with very simple possessions, and while her marriage to the handsome young Ensign Lockwood had given her some social standing, it did very little to supplement her wardrobe. A junior officer's pay allowed for no luxury, but they were deliriously happy together, even if children came to them with much greater frequency than promotions. But then came the wholly unexpected day when James had inherited his father's estate, when his elder brother and his father alike, had died in a fire at Lockwood House.

And now, Brigid sat in her shift in the finest room in Mrs. Noble's rooming house, a lovely new gown draped across her lap, trying not to cry.

James was leaving again. As a soldier's wife she would never say it aloud, but she thought he had done enough, that the army should have no further claim on his life, on their lives. He had been gone from 1811 to 1815, and now, six years later, the notion that he would be gone again, likely for several years, nearly broke her heart. She had passed her fortieth year, and was coming to realize that every year of health and happiness was a true gift, and precious.

Of course, James would leave her now in much better straits. The Lockwoods of Clonakilty were not truly wealthy, as his late father had been a poor steward as well as a mean-spirited old fool. But their eldest daughter was well married now, and their three youngest attended good schools. Brigid worried about their second daughter, Brigit, known as Cissy since her birth, who had suffered

13

as a child and was now grown to womanhood, but was still finding her way. James had his captaincy, new uniforms and, finally, some money in his pocket, while Brigid had several new gowns and the opportunity to travel a bit, but when she returned home she would return to an empty house, her only hopes hinging on Cissy, if she might yet stay at home. Still, that future seemed for them both without much purpose or promise.

When Brigid was younger, such melancholy thoughts would have loosed her tears, but she now gathered herself, still blinking and sniffing a bit, and began to dress. They were going to dinner with Major McLachlan, and she was expected downstairs at half three. She would not be late, she would look her very best and she would not show tear-filled eyes to the man she loved.

*****

They were just stepping out the door of Mrs. Noble's stylish house when the messenger found them, an orderly dragoon on a lathered horse.

Our Dear Captain Lockwood,

The First Battalion, 27th Regiment of Foot, has been ordered to immediately depart Gibraltar for Georgetown, Guyana.
With the greatest urgency you are requested and required to gather the draft consigned to you under previous orders for Gibraltar, and instead depart for Guyana in the hope that your detachment might reach that colony as quickly as is possible, as there is rumour of a Slave Revolt, and additional forces may be required to ensure order.

14

This letter in duplicate is dispatched to Admiral Eli Boyd, Port Admiral, Londonderry, who shall expedite your departure on the merchant brig hired for your transport.

In the event the detachment under your command should arrive in Guyana prior to your Battalion, said detachment should operate as an Independent Company, answerable to the Governor of the Colony, in consultation with Mr. Gordon Read, His Majesty's recently dispatched advisor to the Governor.

So ordered, this day, 14 June, 1823
Major General Sir Lowery Cole

James shook his head in disbelief. Seeing the questioning look on Brigid's face, he silently handed her the order and then opened an informal personal note that had been attached. He checked the signature at the bottom; it was also from General Cole, under whom James had served in France after Waterloo. Cole was now military secretary to the Colonial Office, and James was flattered to see that Cole addressed him with some familiarity.

Lockwood:

In the greatest haste I write in the hope these orders reach you before you take ship to Gibraltar.

I know this move to Guyana comes as a surprise to you, and likely a damned unpleasant one. Following a review of your record, and my personal recommendation based upon your conduct at Waterloo, the Colonial Office has opted to place a considerable burden upon you, and anticipates your speedy arrival in Guyana, as the full battalion may well be weeks behind you.

Make no mistake, the situation in Guyana is an ugly one. The slaves grow discontented, thinking, in some cases thinking correctly, that the slaveholders are withholding certain privileges enacted by Parliament.

The First Battalion of the Royal Scots Fusiliers is in Guyana, of course, but, in the strictest confidence, I might mention there are those in the Colonial Office, myself included, who fear that some officers of the regiment are too close, financially and socially, to owners of the great plantations, and will act in their own interest more than the king's. Our Mr. Read may be of some aid to you; you shall consult him, but you may not disobey the Governor's direct orders. All this is being arranged on the fly, so Read may or may not sail with you from Londonderry. He is a gentleman of some years, and perhaps not as quick off the mark as he once was.

It is the intent of the War Office to dispatch the full battalion from Gibraltar as soon as possible, but transports must be gathered, and a man of your experience will understand the delays such moves typically incur.

In anticipation of your immediate and urgent sailing,
Cole

Brigid knew as well as James what the order meant. Assignment to the Caribbean was often little better than a death sentence for British troops, as yellow fever, dengue, filariasis and malaria decimated the ranks.

In horrified astonishment she quietly said, "An Irish battalion in Guyana, on the Demerara itself—" For an instant, she thought to beg him not to go, that she could not bear to lose him, but she knew it would be in vain, so she threw the orders down and ran back into the house.

James stood alone, turning helplessly to watch her run off, not knowing what to say to her, even what to think.

Chapter Two

Cissy Lockwood had a bit of a reputation in Clonakilty, indeed across much of the County Cork. The stories surrounding her did not impugn her virtue, as she kept the many men who had come to admire her at a very determined distance. Instead, she had been given, and largely earned, a reputation as a hell-cat.

On that particular afternoon she was riding across the fields north of the River Arigideen, cantering with considerable skill and a barely contained joy. She was one of thirty riders who had gathered for one of the area's carefully organized fox hunts. She did not much care for hunts, particularly the unpleasant, if rare, death of the fox; she did, however, revel in riding, and doing so in a fashion that bordered on the reckless. The manner in which she rode across those fields would have worried her parents, but it left the young men in her wake staring with something like rapture.

She had no horse of her own, but news of her father's recent inheritance had given her hope of one. She was well aware of the old Penal Law that decreed that no Catholic could own a horse worth more than five pounds, but she was determined to one day buy Abby, this beautiful young hunter, from Colonel Simon, though the mare would likely bring thirty pounds in any horse fair in Ireland.

Cissy, intent and enjoying herself immensely, rode alongside her friend Lizzie Fitzgerald, and in a steady canter they came upon a low hedge. Lizzie reined in, as riding sidesaddle rendered such obstacles not a little daunting. Cissy, however, was not deterred, and though Lizzie called, half in warning and half in glee, "Oh, Cissy Lockwood, don't you *dare!*" Cissy flawlessly guided her mount over the hedge with room to spare.

Ladies of breeding, particularly attractive young ladies, did not ride in such an aggressive fashion, and they most certainly did not learn to shoot. But Cissy did both, largely out of necessity. Some months before, she had defended herself against the crazed Charles Barr with a pistol in her hand, and the local press had hailed her as beautiful, brave, and resourceful.

That praise aside, it was shocking to the conservative elements in Ireland that this young Catholic woman (the papers had been deliberate in pointing out her affiliation, as religion was the defining factor in that society) had access to a pistol at all, as the Penal Laws also restricted Catholics from owning firearms. But, strictly speaking, the firearms upon which Cissy practiced were from Colonel Simon's gunroom, as it was the colonel and his servant, Corporal Archibald M'Vicar, late of the 10th Hussars, who had taught that ardent young woman first the basics and then the finer arts of horsemanship and shooting. Cissy Lockwood had become one of the more capable riders in the county, sidesaddle or no, and her marksmanship made her a threat to anything that crawled, walked, or flew.

It is true that the Colonel's interest in Miss Lockwood was not entirely altruistic, as he had been an ardent admirer of the female form for many years. Some years previous, in fact, he had made a few leisurely casts in the direction of her mother, the elegant Brigid Lockwood. Brigid, however, had long experience in gently rebuffing unwanted attention, experience she passed on to her daughters. Thus gently rebuffed, the colonel remained a friend to the family, and at no point during his foreign service did James Lockwood feel compelled to return to Ireland to put a hole in Colonel Simon.

To everyone's advantage, the colonel had reached the age where his admiration for attractive women in general, and the Lockwood women in particular, was no longer tainted by base impulses. He was pleased to spend long hours with the sparkling Cissy Lockwood, with only the occasional sigh for his lost youth.

*****

The fox hunt concluded as the afternoon grew cool, with a threat of rain in the distant west. Cissy and Abby, tired but content, returned to Colonel Simon's small but fashionable home south of Clonakilty. His stables were extensive, as were the paddocks beyond, and it was there that Cissy dismounted and, after an affectionate farewell, left Abby with a stable boy. Cissy then reported to the stable office, where Corporal M'Vicar was well into his rum ration.

M'Vicar shot Miss Lockwood an evil glare and growled, "Make your report, trooper."

Cissy suppressed a smile, snapped a salute which would have satisfied the most demanding martinet, and gave the corporal a succinct, informed account of the mare's behavior and condition.

20

The corporal returned an appreciative nod and said, "To my personal knowledge, miss, the 10th Hussars have a recruiting party in Munster, and I'll be damned if you wouldn't make the best recruit they'd find, if they should search for a year."

"That is high praise indeed, Corporal. And how I should treasure a hussar's uniform; the fur-edged pelisse would make me the envy of every woman in town."

M'Vicar returned something approaching a grin and asked, "Shall I see you back on Tuesday, then? That mare needs her workout, or she'll go ill-tempered as a Spanish mule."

Cissy replied that she would report as ordered, then walked up to the house to thank the Colonel for allowing her to take Abby out.

Her approach to the house was carefully observed from a window of the drawing room, where the frail Colonel Simon hung on his nephew's arm.

The colonel pointed out Miss Lockwood and said, "Yonder comes the loveliest woman of my acquaintance."

"She appears rather too slender for my tastes, Uncle."

"You shall change your tune, sir, when she steps into the room. To see her smile is to see the sun rise."

"And I wonder, too, Uncle, if she is, perhaps, not the ideal gentlewoman? From what I know of her reputation, she is, after all, painted as—how shall I phrase it?—a most *active* young person."

Simon flared a bit and said, "Since when, sir, is courage not the trait of a gentlewoman? That fellow Barr had long been an enemy to her father, them both officers of the 27th. In the end it seems this Barr was crazed by the French pox..."

"Syphilis!" cried the nephew. "How very disreputable!"

"...and when her parents were forced out of the country by Barr's false denunciations, he stalked Miss Lockwood and brutally rode down her servant, an old soldier named Doolan in the family's employ. That set her off, I can tell you! She rode like hell and fury, tracking Barr into an officers' mess—an officers' mess, sir!—and had it out with him. She got a shot off in Barr's face and received a sabre cut across the arm for her trouble. Good Lord, what a woman!"

The nephew made an appreciative tilt of his head and closely eyed Miss Lockwood. Not a tall woman, she was, indeed, rather slender, but as she neared the house her perfect complexion shone, and locks of dark hair slipped in charming disarray from beneath a jaunty riding hat. Her eyes shone with intelligence and what was an obvious joy in life. He unconsciously licked his lips as he noted her riding boots; he was privately a close student of women's boots.

Shown into the drawing room, Cissy was surprised to find the colonel entertaining. To the best of her knowledge the colonel had only two friends, the very aged Colonel Parker, a comrade of long standing, and one Mrs. Kennedy, whose exact relationship went unexplained.

The colonel's nephew was introduced as a young clergyman, newly arrived from Cambridge, en route to his new living in Kinsale, where he was to shepherd the Anglicans of the area. His name was Cyril Babcock,; moderately handsome, polite, and confident. Cissy, though, found him rather too handsome, polite and confident and was prepared to dislike him. She attempted to make her escape, explaining her muddy boots and riding habit as unfit for the drawing room, but Colonel Simon would have none of it.

The Colonel ordered tea, and as they chatted, it soon became clear to Cissy that Mr. Babcock had some notions regarding her adventures. While he was obviously bursting to know more, he was sufficiently wellbred not to enquire, and Cissy was contrary enough not to speak of it. She deftly diverted the conversation, saying, "I imagine, Mr. Babcock, that you have been introduced to the Anglican minister here in Clonakilty, our Reverend Butler. The Butlers are good friends to my parents, in fact to our whole family. We hold them most dear."

"At the risk of being importunate, Miss Lockwood, might I humbly suggest that I might properly be addressed as 'Reverend Babcock'? I know it is a minor point, but now that I am in orders, it is technically the correct form of address."

Cissy did not reply, giving the gentleman only a slight, icy, nod.

Colonel Simon, too, seemed displeased with his nephew, but Babcock went on, "Yes, the Reverend Butler is an esteemed colleague, but sadly out of tune with the current themes in theology. Reverend Butler's position in the community is sadly static in nature, while mine, miss, shall be boldly evangelical. Regarding Catholicism, Reverend Butler's credo is evidently 'live and let live' while my every action shall be aimed to strike a blow against the crumbling façade of Papism!"

Babcock was growing heated, and his uncle attempted to stem his flow by saying, "My dear Babcock, I ought to have mentioned—"

But Babcock would not slow, declaring rather more forcefully than courtesy allowed, "Schools, Miss! Schools shall be my weapon against superstition and false piety. Amongst the ways to convert and civilize these deluded people, I am convinced that a sufficient number of English Protestant Schools must be erected, wherein the children of the Irish natives might be instructed in the English tongue and in the fundamental principles of the true religion!"

Colonel Simon winced, turned to see Miss Lockwood's reaction, and did not appear at all surprised when she sat upright and said in a very decided tone, "I beg your pardon, sir, but your opinion of

Reverend Butler is incorrect. He is a kind, wise gentleman, whose every breath does credit to himself, his family, and his faith. Further, I might point out that there are government schools aplenty, but the majority of the Catholic population, which I may point out comprise the vast majority of the people of this island, refuse to attend them. They are no fools; they recognize the government schools' intention to proselytize, and to anglicize Ireland. There is a hedge school, maintained by a Mr. MacDonagh, a renowned poet, which meets just a mile from this very house, the only place where Catholic children might learn their own language, their own history, and the value of their own culture. Lastly, Mr. Babcock, I might be so bold as to point out that I myself am an adherent of the Catholic faith, and while I cannot defend its every tenet, I will not deny it my loyalty."

In truth, Cissy Lockwood had not attended Mass in many months, but she felt no need to explain her deep-seated issues with the Catholic Church, and her loathing of the local priest, to this strutting fool.

Normally, Colonel Simon would have taken control of the situation—this was his own house—but his age bore him down, and so he went silent, disappointed in his nephew. Thus Babcock felt free to retort, "Ah, a Catholic woman who has been granted some education? And some status, it seems. My uncle, indeed, appears to be quite taken by you, grants you the honour of an acquaintance, and invites you into his home, and yet you are not, Miss Lockwood, fully schooled in the niceties of Christian conversation. I am surprised you have not yet berated me with talk of tithes."

Cissy answered very quickly, "You raise the issue, sir, and so I shall share my opinion. Pray, sir, are you indeed content with the notion of your living being wrung from the meager earnings of thousands of poor people, all of whom are forced to pay ten percent of their few pennies to maintain your comfort? And that for them not to pay means eviction from their property?"

In a condescending tone, Babcock said, "My living is prescribed in scripture, miss. Leviticus 27:30-33 tells us, 'all the tithe of the land, whether of the seed of the land, or of the fruit of the tree' is to be used 'that thou mayest learn to fear the Lord thy God always' per Deuteronomy 14:23. Surely, Miss, even the most devout papist cannot argue against God's own commands?"

As a Catholic, Cissy had had little direct experience with the Bible, but her falling out with the Church had prompted her to make occasional forays into the copy that her father owned but rarely opened. She had culled one phrase and memorized it in order to throw it in Father McGlynn's face at St. Brigid's, but she now found it useful with this Mr. Babcock. "And yet, sir, Paul tells us that, 'Every man according as he purposeth in his heart, so let him give; not grudgingly, or of necessity: for God loveth a cheerful giver.'"

She saw that shot go home, and she went on, "If you ever should step beyond the walls of your church, sir, you might see that a man whose family is hungry does not willingly give to any church, particularly one foreign to him. A true Christian might argue that God's intention was for tithe to help the poor and crippled, rather than to maintain churchmen in luxury."

The air was very tense, and Babcock was on the verge of a gross violation of decorum when M'Vicar stepped into the room, growling to his master, "Beg pardon, Colonel, but I wonder if I might be of any service." Cissy saw that the corporal had changed from his stable jacket into his uniform coat; as a cavalryman he was not an especially large man, but his scarred face bore a look of veiled authority.

The old colonel, hurt, tired, and confused, muttered only, "Yes, Corporal, I wonder if perhaps ..."

Cissy quickly stood and said, "Yes, thank you, Corporal, I was just leaving."

M'Vicar nodded and said, "I have an errand in town, so I shall walk with you, then, if I may, miss."

Cissy gave the corporal a smile, ignored Babcock, and bent to gently take Colonel Simon's hand, saying, "I do thank you, my dear sir, for your very great kindness." The old man said nothing, but his eyes flashed with real affection.

Cissy and M'Vicar then walked out of the room and down the hall, unconsciously falling into military step.

Chapter Three

The dinner with McLachlan did not go especially well. James and Brigid were both tense, in their own minds and with one another. Munro sensed it and could think of nothing to say, eventually launching into a lengthy monologue on the dangers of a posting in the West Indies.

The Lockwood's last night together went no better; they were both tired, anxious and unhappy, and after some missed signals and simple miscommunication, they fell asleep, fitfully, thinking and dreaming and despondent.

The next morning Captain and Mrs. Lockwood breakfasted at the Officers' Mess, and then stood together at the long windows, looking down onto the castle parade ground. They had said nothing more of Guyana. Instead, they watched as the married men of the draft gathered, together with their wives and children, so that Captain Lockwood could determine which three wives and their children would sail with the draft and which would stay behind.

With a break in her voice, Brigid said, "They look so frightened."

James straightened his jacket and turned to check himself in a mirror. "They have reason to be. They know what is at stake here." He grimaced at his reflection and added, with frustration in his voice, "There is a great deal of ill-will over this question of wives. The problem lies with the God da... rather, the foolish recruiters, who take in far too many married men and happily omit any mention of them going on Foreign Service and leaving their families behind."

Brigid tried to put a laugh in her voice, but she sounded almost accusatory, saying, "I am sorry, sir, that wives should prove such a burden."

He did not respond, only stood silently at the window, eventually saying, "They have been told that our destination is Guyana, but still they wish to stay together."

With some bitterness she said, "Well, of course they do. The women left behind will be forced from the barracks, their wee children in tow, and given—what, two pence a mile?—to travel 'home' to family or friends who may or may not want them."

James exhaled sharply and said quietly, "Please, my dear, do not make this harder than it already is."

She reminded herself that in just a few hours they would part, and tears started to swell. But she blinked them back, stretched up to kiss his cheek, and gently straightened his epaulette. Her hands were shaking.

He tried to sound dispassionate, but failed. "The pity of it is, if they were wiser with the bounty, the families left behind could make a new start of it. But the moment they get some gold in their pockets they live like Bob's-a-dying, and then, hey presto, two weeks later they are back on army rations and living like cattle in the barracks without tuppence to their name, some even in debt.

Fools. And now it is left to me to break their hearts, split up families, and see people thrown aside. Christ."

She took his hand, and said, "I am sorry this falls to you, *a grah*. But I am certain there is not an officer of the regiment who would handle the matter with greater kindness."

"Thank you, love. There is O'Malley. I must go."

Brigid looked out the window to see the drummer standing below. She tried to brighten her husband's mood and her own, saying, "Is he not rather ancient to wear a king's coat?"

James picked up his shako and distractedly said, "O'Malley is a fixture here. He first saw action at Agincourt, I think, but he is very popular in the barracks, so they keep him about. I need his drum for the ceremony, and I also hope that, if he is standing next to me, the disappointed wives might not tear me to pieces." Then, with a half-smile, he asked, "A kiss for luck, please?"

The large, severe-looking man who walked down the steps of the Officers' Mess did not look like a man who had just gotten a kiss. He reached the bottom of the steps, placed his shako on his head, and was every inch an imposing presence.

Drummer O'Malley, however, had known that imposing figure as a young, nervous Ensign Lockwood, and so felt confident in stepping up to the Captain, tossing his head toward the crowd and quietly saying, "There's a storm brewing, young fella."

"Good morning, O'Malley. Yes, I thought this process might prove difficult."

"Mrs. Sergeant Maguire has got them all stirred up, hasn't she? Oh, my, yes."

"She has three children, has she not? So she stays. She and Maguire must surely know the rules; no more than two children."

The old soldier hitched up his drum, stood at attention beside the massive, and added under his breath, "Well now, son, knowing is one thing, and doing is another."

James nearly grinned in response, but only muttered, "Forward," and as O'Malley tapped out the step, they approached the crowd, all eyes on the captain, their looks suspicious, hopeful, angry and afraid, in equal measure.

As was his custom, James had gone over this speech in his mind a dozen times, and so managed to sound confident and very much in control, though his inner man was far less composed.

"Men, ladies, and children! I am Captain James Lockwood, and I command the draft that departs for Foreign Service on the Demerara Coast tomorrow morning." He heard a female voice from the back of the crowd say something about "being in a great bleedin' hurry," but he pressed on. "Regulations allow three wives to travel with the draft. Those wives must be on the Married Roll, be of good moral character, and have no more than two children."

He saw a very young woman weeping into the chest of a very young soldier. Most of the children were dirty and dressed in rags, but he pressed on, some harshness slipping into his voice. He had to turn to harshness or pity and pain would creep in, and he could not allow that, or there would be chaos. "As there are sixteen wives who qualify, the traditional method shall be used to determine who will go, and who will stay. Drummer, come forward."

O'Malley stepped forward, unslung his brass drum, and set it at the captain's feet. Lockwood dropped two dice onto the drumhead and said decisively, "God, or chance, will decide. The wives with the three highest rolls may go." Those were the same words he had used at the draft at Gosport barracks eight years before, just before Waterloo. The words had steadied the crowd then, and they worked

30

again, now. The attention was turned to the dice; the power lay there, and no one argued about the rules or blamed the captain, the same captain who had to clasp his hands behind his back to keep them steady.

Many of the men from the Gosport draft had died at Waterloo; some of the wives and some of the children had died in Belgium and France, as well, not in combat, but in the misery of following a battalion at war: of exhaustion, exposure and disease. Their memories were part of the burden he carried, a burden he could not share, or ever shed. The women quietly formed a line, many praying their rosaries, some giving their husbands and children nervous, tearful smiles. Eager, hopeful, fearful, faces; above all, a knife-edge anxiety gripped them, and James was afraid he could lose control of the crowd. But then he saw many of the people point and look up past him, and when he turned, he saw Brigid standing in the door of the Mess, looking kind and brave.

Some of the women in the crowd called out to her in Irish, and while James could not understand all they said, he heard her addressed with kindness and respect. And so Mrs. Lockwood came down the steps and joined the women of the draft, many of them smiling in welcome and gesturing for her to take the first place amongst them.

Brigid O'Brian Lockwood took up the dice. "God's own luck to you, gentlewoman," whispered the worn little woman behind her. Her Irish was of Donegal, sharp and quick.

Brigid dropped the dice onto the drumhead, but before they stopped their bounce she covered them with her hand, and taking them back up she said in a strong, decided voice, "My husband shall journey far, but I shall stay in Ireland, with my children."

A wave of approval rolled across the crowd. Brigid handed the dice to the woman behind her, closely clasping, then kissing, the woman's dirty hands. From the crowd there were murmurs of, "a soldier's wife," and Brigid stayed at her husband's side, offering blessings and hope and condolence, as each of the wives steadily took her chance.

*****

Before Waterloo, he had written to her, and sworn that he would one day come home. Sitting close together in the carriage that would carry her away, he swore that same vow again: he would come home to her, though hell should bar the way.

Then it was time for her to go. Following anguished, heart-wringing farewells, the carriage bearing Brigid Lockwood clattered out of the yard of Enniskillen Castle, rolled onto the old stone bridge over the River Erne, and then turned left down Henry Street, following the river to the south and west.

James pushed himself to hurry across the yard, then up the steps of the Water Gate Tower, gasping for breath by the time he reached the narrow window at the top, but well in time to see the carriage cross the bridge, so that he might wave like a fool. Brigid, too, waved madly, until her handkerchief was a white dot in the distance.

And then she was gone. They had said farewell so many times—the fate of a soldier's family. They had long before vowed to keep the other's feelings at the uppermost in their minds. Thus, there were wet eyes but no weeping, commitment but no demands, passion but no hysteria, love but never foolishness. And Christ, how he did love her.

*****

James fell into the foul humour that gripped him at every separation, and while he tried to maintain a steady composure, he largely failed. While the draft was forming up to march, his mood was not improved when McLachlan showed him to the stables. James had some doubts regarding the major's ability to judge horseflesh, and his fears were quickly confirmed. He declined McLachlan's favorite, a wild-eyed stallion of ill temper, then also passed on a tall, sway-backed mare that looked at him with pleading eyes. He eventually settled on an ancient gelding, which slept even while being saddled.

The gelding had a good soul, but the draft's march had scarcely reached Drumcoo before the old horse decided not to advance at any pace above a grudging walk. James restrained a furious urge to spur and whip the beast, instead sitting quietly while his heart tortured him for once again parting from his love. At one point his eyes misted over, and he cursed himself for such weakness.

The men proved equally unwilling to exert themselves. James was again tempted to rage, but opted not to push them. He needed time to get to know them, and for them to know him. He soon surmised that Maguire, the draft sergeant, (who, it turned out, was none too distressed at the thought of leaving Mrs. Maguire behind) was neither here nor there; he was not cruel, but neither did the men pay him much heed. The two corporals on loan from McLachlan were stupid, brutal, and tough, but they served to dissuade any thoughts of desertion. James had some hope, though, for the draft's corporal, the bright young Shanahan.

The first leg of the march was an easy nine-mile move to Irvinestown. Some of the men had never worn shoes in their lives and few had ever carried a pack or a musket. Blisters and sore backs would need tending, and while he would make soldiers of them, he was content to do so slowly. This was his life's work, and, his personal misery aside, he was determined to be a professional.

*****

A man named Conchobhar O'Donnell was part of the draft. That, at least, was the name he had given a few weeks before, when he had taken the bounty in Derrylin, thinking he could desert quietly, the next morning.

O'Donnell's real name was Joseph Flaherty, but he had not used that name for five years or more, as he had made such a practice of enlisting and absconding with the bounty that there were days he had trouble remembering which name he had taken.

O'Donnell was well aware that his was a capital offense, often repeated. More than once, he had vowed that he would take one last bounty and then return home to Dublin to work in the family tailor shop. But temptation was everywhere. Endless recruiting parties scoured Ireland looking for men, and a healthy young specimen like O'Donnell was viewed as a prize beyond measure. Seasoned recruiting sergeants would ply their tricks—them in their glowing uniforms—buying strong drinks and telling stories about glory, and women who adored soldiers. O'Donnell, in turn, would play hard to get, feigning indecision while getting some good meals and plenty of drinks in the bargain. Then he signed up, swore his oath, took the golden bounty, and in a day or two he was gone without a trace.

But this time he had, perhaps, grown too confident and strayed close to Enniskillen. This last recruiting sergeant, a knowing old veteran of the Inniskilling Regiment, was no fool. He took O'Donnell by the back of the collar and marched him the thirteen long miles to the confines of Enniskillen Castle.

For the first time, O'Donnell was handed a red coat and a musket. He was introduced to the basics of army life, and was not surprised to discover just how much he hated it. This was no life for an intelligent man of a mobile nature; as long as the walls of the castle kept him penned in he would bide his time, but at the first opportunity he would slip away; this time, he vowed, it was back to Dublin and a tailor's life.

*****

O'Donnell found his chance on the draft's night in Irvinestown, where the tired men were quartered in a stout stone barn. After a scant supper and a tot of burning rum, Sergeant Maguire had the men bed down, blankets in the straw, while he and the two thugs of corporals rolled out their blankets in front of the great swinging doors that faced the farmyard. A lantern burned above them, and no man would get past them that night.

What O'Donnell had discovered, and what the sergeant and his friends had not, was that a tack room in the back of the barn had a small window, blocked from sight by rows of hanging harness. He kept that happy knowledge to himself, and dutifully rolled out his blanket beside his comrades, but very near the back.

The effects of the march and the rum soon had the draft sleeping hard, snoring, sighing, farting and snorting in the darkness. O'Donnell was patient, lying awake until the old gods walked in the deepest waves of the night. He then slipped back to the tack room, glided through the tangles of harness and silently climbed out the window. He dropped the few feet to the ground below, the free moonlit beckoning fields in the distance beyond.

There then came a sharp click; a dark lantern was opened, its light sudden and dazzling, and there stood the massive captain, Lockwood, and in the shadows behind him Corporal Shanahan and

Private O'Boyle, muskets in their hands, their bayonets fixed. They both grinned and cocked their hammers.

The captain casually said, "Ah, I am pleased you could join us, Private..."

O'Donnell, ashen, agape, stared in wordless terror and said nothing.

Helpfully, Shanahan said, "That, sir, is our Private O'Donnell."

"Ah, yes, O'Donnell," said the captain. "We were just discussing the term 'pear-making' and wondering its origins. I do not doubt, Private, that you are familiar with the term?"

O'Donnell managed to hoarsely gasp, "Christ and His nails, no... no, please, Your Honour."

The captain seemed to swell in the darkness, but he only nodded and said, "An unusual term, 'pear-making,' I grant you, a rude term, but it seems to refer to men who repeatedly take the king's enlistment bounty and quickly desert. They defraud a different regiment each time, abusing His Majesty's generosity, taking Dutch leave like thieves and craven cowards."

"Oh, dear God," croaked O'Donnell.

"Yes, shocking, is it not? That a man would steal from his king ... a capital offense, without benefit of clergy. Such fellows will never see heaven. I am told that a man nicknamed 'Tom the Devil' holds the record, as he enlisted under various names forty-nine times, making off with nearly four hundred guineas before he was caught. A fortune!"

"Oh, dear God," again croaked O'Donnell.

"They hanged him, of course. Or is it 'hung'? I can never recall. Corporal Shanahan, is it 'hanged', or 'hung?'"

Without taking his eyes off O'Donnell, the corporal said, "Oh, now, sir, I am not a man to consult in such matters, not being a man of letters such as yourself."

"Well, in any case, they put a rope around this fellow's neck and dropped him. Rumour holds it, however, that the hangman was less than careful in doing so, as the army was determined to get its four hundred guineas worth. Oh, yes, all quite shocking."

O'Donnell's hand went slowly to his neck, and he turned an even bluer shade of pale.

"Yet such wretched fellows still ply their tricks," continued the captain. "In fact, I had an opportunity to flip through the bulletins in the castle's headquarters, each citing the description of these felons. One fellow had the benefit of being of very average appearance; average height, average weight and no distinguishing features at all, which seems to be a great advantage for a man who opts for that type of career. Just think, men of such description can be found on every corner. You, for example, Private, fit that description. So very average; you could easily be taken to be that man."

Lockwood studied him for a moment, then looking over his shoulder he said, "Corporal Shanahan, I wonder if I might beg your opinion. Will this man, this O'Donnell fellow, ever make an acceptable soldier?"

Shanahan gave the private a long, appraising look, then finally offered, "Well, sir, he's as ignorant as a new-born babe, sure, but not as stupid as he may currently seem. He may prove useful, in a decade or two."

A long pause, as the captain again studied O'Donnell. Then, the tension broke as Lockwood said, "Private O'Donnell, until we are aboard ship, in fact, aboard ship and well clear of the land, you had best cling to Corporal Shanahan for dear life. If anyone was to see you more than six feet from him they should certainly take you for a deserter, and any man might shoot, stab, or hang you without a second thought."

"Six feet, sir, oh, yes, certainly, sir."

"You are a soldier now, O'Donnell, and you had best get used to that notion. Private O'Boyle here will surely advise you on some of the finer points." Then, over his shoulder, "Corporal Shanahan, Private O'Boyle, please see the private back to his billet. You may find the barn doors more convenient than this window. And, Corporal, you might mention to Sergeant Maguire that I shall have some words with him in the morning."

*****

James returned to his billet, once again pondering the ways of the men under him. Maguire might well lose a stripe if he didn't show that he was up to his responsibilities, especially once on Foreign Service. On the other hand, Shanahan might one day gain a stripe, though James was unsure if he could read and write, a necessary prerequisite. "I must remember to ask him in the morning." Shanahan might learn to read, though the battalion had never, in its long history, ever filled the slot of "schoolmaster sergeant," so optimistically allowed by War Office regulations. Perhaps, once they were in garrison, Shanahan might find some bored soul to help him.

Since it was nearly dawn, James opted not to go back to sleep, instead digging some magazines from his trunk. Upon learning of the draft's diversion to Guyana, McLachlan had thoughtfully sorted through his library and given James what little he had on the distant colony. In the past James had given little thought to such

Mark Bois

places, and was now determined to learn as much as possible about South American colonies.

The topmost publication was a year-old copy of *The Gentleman's Quarterly* which carried a population study of the colony, written by a Guyana planter, a Mr. Rowland. He stated the colony's population as 2,500 whites, 2,500 freed blacks, and 77,000 slaves. James was never proud of his arithmetic skills, but still calculated the slaves outnumbered their masters by thirty to one. While much of the article caused James to shake his head, he visibly winced as he read:

> In addition, the Aborigines number on the schedules 7,500. The Registrar-General gives 10,000 more of this race is estimated to be wandering about the interior of the colony. The numbers on the schedule show a decrease in the figures from 1818, when 8,000 were returned. This race is of little or no social value and their early extinction must be looked upon as inevitable, in spite of the sentimental regret of Missionaries. At the same time, it is unnecessary to hasten the process in any way, for in this manner, nature, as ever, is gentler than man.

He swore softly and muttered, "And so, in Christian kindness, we are to allow the Indians to starve and die of disease rather than murder them? I shall retire to Bedlam." He tossed the *Quarterly* aside, and flipped open a Parliamentary publication. Page 147 held a summary of the colony's recent governors.

2 May 1813–17 May 1813 Edward Salmon (1st time)
17 May 1813–24 August 1813 John McAllistair (1st time)

Captain Lockwood

24 August 1813–9 December 1813 Edward Salmon (2nd time)
9 December 1813–25 July 1815 John McAllistair (2nd time)
25 July 1815–3 October 1815 Edward Salmon (3rd time)
3 October—current John McAllistair (3rd time)

So, two men were playing political football with the governorship. A brief article in another periodical listed Salmon and McAllistair as owners of the two largest plantations in the colony. They had recently expelled a Methodist missionary who had derided the colonial government as a "plantocracy," a term James thought fitting. It was no wonder the Colonial Office had dispatched this Mr. Read to consult.

The last of his resources was a recent newspaper which carried an account of the conditions borne by the slaves of Guyana Colony. Missionaries and abolitionists hoped that new legislation, implemented by a new governor, one dispatched from beyond the colony, and a fresh garrison of disinterested soldiers might in some way shield the slaves from their murderous, vengeful, masters.

James was an officer of great experience, and was qualified to imagine what might await him in Guyana. He anticipated something just short of hell.

Chapter Four

Brigid Lockwood was fond of Mary Nelson, though they differed in nearly every respect. Brigid was the daughter of a struggling Irish Catholic farmer, while Mary had been raised in Northumberland, the only child of a prominent Anglican minister. The Colonel's wife was much taller than Brigid, prone to plumpness, and not especially pretty. She was younger than Brigid and far younger than Colonel Nelson, and while Mrs. Nelson was not always very wise, she was a kind woman and Brigid enjoyed her company.

A year before, Colonel Nelson had been a key supporter when James had been dismissed from the service, and James's reinstatement was, in no small measure, due to the Colonel's efforts. The Lockwoods had spent weeks at the Nelsons' Dublin town house, and Brigid was very conscious of the debt they owed.

Brigid had arrived at White Hall two days before, and while she was, in most ways, the ideal guest, she had sometimes come downstairs with red eyes and only a thin veneer of self-control. The weather did not help her spirits, as cool rain drummed against the windows for hours at a time. That afternoon, the two ladies sipped their tea as the wind got up, as well—as bleak a summer day as Ireland could muster.

They sat quietly in the ornate room, idly watching the storm wash over the surface of Lough Nilly below. Mrs. Nelson, looking displeased, set aside a letter from Colonel Nelson and asked, "Mrs. Lockwood, I hope your post brings you more pleasure than my own."

Brigid gave her hostess a mild smile and replied, "Oh, yes, thank you. I am in proud possession of two letters from my children. Joseph and Richard write from Sussex. They have seen Lucy safely to school at Richmond Academy and have finally found their way to their own school, Barron House Academy in Mitcham."

Brigid then raised her eyebrows, and giving Mrs. Nelson a knowing look, she went on, "It seems, however, that my two young gentlemen spent an inordinate amount of time in reaching the school; I imagine they allowed themselves an unauthorized diversion, along the way."

Mrs. Nelson nodded and replied, "I have three older brothers who attended public school. Now that they are grown, they tell my mother stories that make her cringe... though I am certain your sons would never do such things. I very much look forward to meeting them and your lovely daughters, in the very near future."

With a rueful grin Brigid said, "Oh, I have no doubt my sons are capable of mild shenanigans, but, yes, they are good souls, the both of them. Handsome to a fault, but kind, and thoughtful—every bit their father." She hurriedly changed topics with, "This second letter is from my daughter Brigit, whom we have called Cissy since she was a tiny thing; she writes from Clonakilty. She misses the company of our eldest daughter, Mary, who is married now and living in France. She also misses her father. She is such a dear girl, but I fear she will also miss his influence. One of the more prominent local families is to host a ball, and while her friend Lizzie has already received an invitation, my Cissy has not, and I fear she waits for it in vain."

They were quiet for a while, until Mrs. Nelson turned to Mrs. Lockwood and asked, with some hesitation, "I am unsure how to best phrase this question, but as I do hold you to be my dear friend, I trust you will not think me importunate. Might I enquire as to how... how you manage to cope with your husband's lengthy absences?"

Brigid's face nearly crumbled, and Mrs. Nelson quickly, apologetically, went on. "Oh, pray, Mrs. Lockwood, I trust I do not injure you with such a question." Then Mrs. Nelson's eyes also grew pained, and she continued, "I ask your advice, you see, as you seem to handle your life with such skill, while I... Well, I wonder if I expect too much from Colonel Nelson. Do not mistake me, he is most kind, but in three years of marriage we have been under the same roof for perhaps three months, and I confess, I grow lonely. If I had a child of my own, how happy I would be, but there is so little chance of that." Then quickly going on, she said, "I had so hoped to make new friends here. But it is twenty miles to Enniskillen, and there are so few local families on whom I might properly call. I was looking forward to your visit for the longest time."

Brigid was nonplussed for a moment, until with a soft smile, she said, "Oh, my dear Mrs. Nelson, I wonder if—"

She was interrupted by the housekeeper who slid into the room and primly told Mrs. Nelson, "I do beg your pardon, madam, but there are number of peasant women at the kitchen door."

"Very well, Mrs. McNulty, a penny each, and a pound of potatoes."

"Actually, please, ma'am," said the servant, shooting a critical glance toward Brigid, "the women are very insistent on speaking with Mrs. Lockwood."

Mrs. Nelson and Mrs. Lockwood traded looks of surprise.

"I was not aware, Mrs. Lockwood, that you knew anyone in Fermanagh?"

In her surprise, Brigid's Irish accent grew sharp. "And so I don't, sure. And who would come out on such a miserable day?"

"Shall I send them away, ma'am?"

Brigid set aside her letters and said, "Oh, I shall see them, of course. Mrs. Nelson, will you join me in greeting my callers?"

Mrs. Nelson was not accustomed to dealing with anyone who called at the kitchen door of White Hall, but she happily set her tea aside and said, "Oh, my, yes. At last, something interesting to do!"

The three women working in the kitchen curtsied as Mrs. Nelson came down the stairs, and, while the lady of the house was usually kind with them, they seemed concerned that they might somehow be blamed for the odd group at the kitchen door. Mrs. Nelson, however, glided past them, escorting Mrs. Lockwood back. The cooks stole long glances at this Mrs. Lockwood; dark hair and perfect skin, so beautiful, and one of their own. They took pride in seeing her treated as an equal by their mistress.

The housekeeper opened the kitchen door with some drama, and Brigid was taken aback to find a pack of women and children, soaked and shivering, standing in the rain. Most held shawls over their heads, while some had babies in their arms or children clinging to their skirts, all wet through and exhausted. She then recognized a few faces from the muster at the castle; with a start, she realized these were all families of men who had sailed with James.

Mrs. Nelson looked shocked; her housekeeper wore a look of disapproval on her old face. Brigid was surprised, then she flared with anger. "Why have these people been left to stand in the cold rain? For God's sake, these children will catch their deaths!"

Mrs. Nelson secured her place in heaven by rallying and saying, "Well, of course, they must come inside. Come, all of you, come into our kitchens. These children really must stand by the fire."

While the housekeeper clucked and shook her head, the kitchen staff was instantly helpful, and soon loaves of bread and a cheese were produced, the fires were stoked, and some semblance of considerate order restored. Mrs. Nelson helped to tend the children, allowing Brigid a moment to think. With the tip of her tongue ticking the count against the back of her teeth, she counted her visitors: seven women and eleven children, three of the children not yet walking. Several were obviously ill, and they all looked exhausted. One young woman with blonde hair, who might have been pretty in other circumstances, shuffled—ill, alone and ignored —into the scullery, where she lay on the floor and quietly wept.

As they warmed, the tongues of the battalion wives loosened, and a low murmur of Irish, English, and in one case Castilian Spanish, filled the kitchens of White Hall.

One of the women separated herself from the others, stepped up to Brigid and roughly curtsied. She was short and sturdy, older than the others, and Brigid saw an intelligent glint in her eye. She said, "I am Eileen Goodwin, please, ma'am, wife of Private Peter Goodwin, who is gone with your husband to fight those terrible men in the jungle. We beg pardon for disturbing you, please, mistress, but we are in dire straits, sure."

"I am sorry, Mrs. Goodwin, but whatever brought you here? Have you walked all the way from Enniskillen in this miserable rain?"

"Oh, aye, every inch on foot, but being who we are, that is no great story. Yesterday's march wasn't so bad, was it? But last night the rains came, and all this day has been a misery." With a flicker of anguish in her face she went on. "We had to leave Fiona Blackburn behind, as she and her baby were sick and could not go on. We offered to take her baby with us, but she clung to him so. We built a wee shelter for them in the ditch, and God forgive us, we went on without them."

Mary Nelson had been listening and asked, "Where? Where did you leave them?'

"Perhaps two miles, two Irish miles, please, Mistress, short of Belcoo on the Enniskillen road."

For a moment, perhaps even a long moment, Mary Nelson was torn, finally saying aloud, "So that is twelve or fifteen miles from here. Must I not send my coach to fetch them? Well, of course I must. What was I thinking?" She hurried out into the yard, into the streaming rain, calling for her coachman, Duncan Heaney.

Eileen Goodwin's son called to her from beside the fire, and turning to Brigid, she said, "One minute, mistress, please, so that I may attend to my Anthony."

But Brigid caught the woman's sleeve and quietly asked, "First, Mrs. Goodwin, if I may, who is that young woman who went alone into the scullery? I don't recall her being one of the wives at the parade ground."

Eileen raised her eyebrows, and hesitantly said, "She's not really with us, is she? But she came down from town, the dear, when we left the Castle. Some of these hens wanted to turn her away, willing

46

to cast the first stone, but most of us voted to keep her, as she's in kindle, the poor child."

Brigid went to the miserable figure who lay on the slate floor of the scullery, brushed a strand of sodden hair from that delicate face, and kindly said, *"Is mise Brigid Bean Uí Lockwood."* My name is Brigid, wife of Lockwood.

In a half whisper came the reply, *"Is mise Margaret ní Hanahan."* I am Margaret, daughter of Hanahan. She was not married.

"Come, child, you mustn't lie on the floor. Come and warm yourself, and have a bite to eat."

While some of the other women looked on from the kitchen with pity on their faces, they were clearly cowed by one of the older wives, a fierce-looking creature with dark features who glared at the sick girl with something like disgust. None of the wives came to help Brigid get the girl to her feet, though a kind-hearted kitchen maid hurried over, set a stool by the stove and got the shivering girl a plate of bread and cheese.

Brigid was unhappy with the women, and on the verge of asking them what the hell they were about when Eileen hurried back over to her and furtively explained, "Now, please, Mistress, don't be upset with us. But Mrs. McGunn, there, is as devout as a bishop, and as unforgiving. Her brother is a priest, her two sisters are nuns, and she puts up with nothing in the roving line, not if it's ever so. And Christ, what a sharp tongue she has—none of us dare cross her." Then, with a bit of pride in her voice, Eileen added, "Though we did stand up to her when we allowed Margaret to come along, didn't we?"

"That was good of you, sure, but if Margaret is so unwelcome with the wives, why did she not go elsewhere?"

"Oh, that's the problem, Mistress. Her Kerry McIlhenny, a young soldier gone with your husband, is a good lad, but the Hanahans are prideful folk—they own the Fermanagh Arms in Enniskillen town—and would never stand for their Margaret taking up with some soldier. So, Margaret, for fear of her family, wouldn't marry him, nor tell him about the baby, and so away Kerry sails, broken-hearted, for he did love that girl so. When her family finally did hear of the baby, they turned her out, didn't they? Foul people they are, spitting at her feet and calling her a whore with a soldier's bastard in her belly, and her only seventeen years of age."

Mary Nelson hurried back into the kitchen, and shaking out an umbrella to the obvious annoyance of the housekeeper, she called to Brigid, "Mrs. Lockwood, dear, I am going out with my Heaney to find this Mrs. Blackstock and her poor baby."

There ensued a hissing, pointing disagreement between the housekeeper and the fierce Mrs. McGunn, as the housekeeper had made some unkind remarks regarding the cleanliness of the army wives and their children. That disagreement soon escalated into something resembling a feminine Waterloo, with Irish accents. As only Mrs. Nelson held any sway over her housekeeper, Brigid volunteered to take Mrs. Goodwin in the coach to search for the lost Fiona Blackburn.

In the yard, they found that the rain had not lessened, and the heavily-cloaked Heaney looked displeased, as did his four sullen horses being harnessed by a pair of stable boys.

Mrs. Lockwood, however, had some experience in dealing with men. As Eileen Goodwin climbed awkwardly into the coach, Mrs. Lockwood paused, and from under the umbrella, queried the coachman, "Mr. Heaney, you know where we are bound?"

"Yes, ma'am."

48

Under the lady's unflinching eye, he went on, rather more helpfully. "Up past Belcoo the road is as bleak as you'll find in Fermanagh, ma'am." Still, Mrs. Lockwood looked at him, not unpleasantly, but with her head cocked a bit, and he felt compelled to go on, "That is O'Neil territory: cattle thieves and sodomites, to a man, and so your lost lamb shall find no charity there. Still, we shall find her, fear you not, ma'am, fear you not."

Mrs. Lockwood climbed into the coach, and as they set out Heaney's left-hand wheeler pulled sideways, out of pure petulance. A snap of his whip beside her ear recalled her to her duty, Heaney telling her, "Mildred, you quit your nonsense, damn you. We're on an errand of mercy, us." But shortly thereafter he muttered, "Feckin' rain…"

In the coach, Eileen sat wide-eyed, running her fingers across the fine leather seats. Brigid got her attention and said, "Mrs. Goodwin, we have a few quiet minutes. Will you tell me now, how it is you and the other ladies came to seek me out?" She almost added, "And how I might be of service?" but she withheld that, for now.

When she'd first sat in the fine coach, Eileen had felt out of place, nearly overwhelmed, but she was no fool. She gathered herself, nodded, and calmly explained, "You'll know, mistress, that the wives who were forbidden the ship were paid our marching money, and were to be out of the barracks the next day. Tears and cursing the army in plenty, I can tell you, but we were all making plans on where to go, what to do, some of us old friends casting our lots together, like."

On a downhill stretch the coach picked up speed, and as the rain drummed on the roof Eileen turned to look out the window and with an exhilarated smile, she said, "This is traveling, now, is it not? Sitting like queens, dry as our own beds, and how we fly!"

49

Brigid let her enjoy the moment, until Eileen pulled her face from the window, smoothed her skirt, and went on, "Well, now. We had our marching money. Not much, the army being miserly devils, beg pardon, mistress, but it is so. Most of us had some other money set aside, and we were determined to set about our lives as best we could."

Eileen's face hardened, and with pain and anger building in her tone she said, "As we knew there were thieves in the barracks, we gave all our money to Mary Maguire to hold, didn't we, she being a sergeant's wife, and she having a separate room, all safe, like. What fools we were, to trust her, the *bitseach*. The next morning we were packing up our things, but was there one sign of Mary Maguire? No, Mistress, there was not. She and her foul brood had slipped away in the night, every penny of our money in her pocket, and us with no idea as to which way she may have gone. We complained to Major McLachlan, sure, but did he care? No, mistress, he did not. He told us it was our own foolishness, no business of his, and he wished us to be out of the barracks before dinner. So out we went, penniless."

Brigid scowled and said, "Well, I shall write to Major McLachlan at the first opportunity. Honestly, how could he be so very callous?"

Eileen sniffed, and for the first time Brigid saw the older woman look at her with a flash of disdain. "Oh, that is very good of you mistress, I'm sure." But then with something like pleading in her voice, she added, "We had nothing. Some few had people nearby to whom they might turn, penniless or no, but most of us were destined to starve or play the whore. But then I thought of you, mistress, a soldier's wife and an Irishwoman, and how kind you had been with us. We had heard of how you were going to the colonel's great house, and so we voted to stick together and turn to our captain's lady."

Brigid reached over and took Eileen's hand and said, "You were quite right to do so. We shall get this settled, sure." She'd intended to pitch her voice with a ringing confidence, but she detected her own tone of uncertainty.

Outside, the rain and wind both dropped suddenly, in that unique Irish way. Heaney halted his team, reached over to thump the side of the coach, and called down, "Woman! Where did you leave your friend?"

With her head out the window, Eileen could not recall the exact place, and so the coach slowly rolled on until Eileen called out "There! Yes! There, in that hedge!"

Heaney dismounted, handed the two women down and then helped them across the water-filled ditch beside the road. In the hedge there was a dry little hollow, but there was no sign of Fiona Blackburn or her baby. They did, though, see a wizened old man with a shovel on his shoulder walking across the next field, evidently intent on speaking to them.

Heaney stepped forward, and as the old man approached, the two eyed one another. The old man halted a few steps away, eventually gave a subtle nod and said, "Heaney."

Heaney gave an equally noncommittal nod, and said, "O'Neil."

O'Neil gestured toward the edge of his field and said, "You'll be looking after the woman from my hedge?"

"Aye."

"You'll be tardy, then. I just buried her, yonder."

Eileen gave a wail of grief, and as Brigid held her she asked the old man, "Her baby, what of her baby?"

"It's well enough. I took it up to the cabin for my wife to see to."

Through her remorse Eileen called, "And so you bury the poor woman in the corner of a field, with no priest?"

51

O'Neil snorted and said, "A priest, woman? And who would be paying for a priest's motions? Not Ken O'Neil, I tell you." Then, softening his tone, he added, "Besides, I laid her in a proper *cillin*, where my own son is buried, and no man can say fairer than that."

O'Neil led them down a narrow path that led to his lowly home, a filthy hovel cut into the side of a hedge. Brigid was all too familiar with Irish poverty, but the dark, smoky interior of the cabin was so horrid as to make her catch her breath. In a dark corner sat O'Neil's invalid wife, who was slow to let the baby go. Even after Eileen pulled the child away from her clinging, claw-like hands, the hag still whispered, "So much like my little Jimmy. Precious boy, precious boy."

As they hurried away from the cabin, Brigid kept her head down, her hand to her mouth. Eileen ran a hand over the baby, as if she might exorcise any lingering shadow of such squalor. Heaney trailed, spitting and muttering "Feckin' O'Neil trash..."

When they returned to the coach, Heaney snapped his reins and turned the team back toward White Hall. Eileen gently rocked the sleeping baby and said, "We shall have to hurry to find him a wet nurse, sure. After all he has been through, and still perfect as the Christ child."

The coach bounced along, Brigid's face soft as she idly watched the lovely child, but her mind was awhirl with thoughts of what to do next. She was completely at a loss. A handful of money would not resolve such a tangle of want. Still, she was aware, and a bit ashamed, of a deeply buried flicker of happiness; it was good to be needed.

Chapter Five

The brig *Dispatch* made her living carrying every class of material and humanity between Europe and the Americas. She had sailed that profitable circuit for years, in all manner of seas. Having off-loaded her latest cargo of rum and sugar at Belfast, the *Dispatch* sailed next to Londonderry, to fill a lucrative army contract: she would carry redcoats to Gibraltar.

There, on Ireland's forbidding northern coast, the *Dispatch* did not attempt the awkward passage down the River Foyle to Londonderry town, instead anchoring at the foot of Lough Foyle.

Her crew, a mate and ten sailors, were anxious to be underway, but they were to be disappointed. In the manner typical of such arrangements, they were left waiting for two weeks, their boredom interrupted only by a letter from the ship's owners, altering their destination. The crew were not pleased; the soldiers were now to be carried to Guyana, where disease and pirates haunted every foot of that lawless coast.

That cool, misty afternoon, most of the crew were ashore, as they were now regulars at Miss Hardwood's establishment on

Glendermott Road. Only a harbour watch was aboard, when they saw a boat being rowed out to their berth. A very tall infantry officer clambered up the side, looking as if he had done so many times before. The soldier looked fit enough, but he seemed out of breath when he reached the deck.

The *Dispatch's* master, Joshua Clapsaddle, was comparatively young to have his own command, but years in the Royal Navy had prepared him for the soldier's intimidating countenance. It looked as if the gentleman was prepared to be displeased. The master made his salute and said, "Joshua Clapsaddle, master of the *Dispatch*, at your service, sir."

The officer returned the salute, offered his hand, and replied, "Captain James Lockwood, 27th Foot."

"You are a welcome sight, Captain. My crew and I have been most anxious to set sail, though perhaps not quite so anxious once we learned of Guyana as our destination."

Clapsaddle eyed the big soldier with some interest, curious to learn if he, too, knew of the change in destination, but Lockwood said only, "We do as the king commands. I desire to have my men aboard before the day is out, Captain Clapsaddle, but I should first like to see the ship. I will not conduct them aboard a coffin ship."

A flash of displeasure crossed the master's face. He was not often challenged aboard his own ship, but he said only, "Very well, sir, if you should care to follow me below, I have nothing to hide. I captain a sound vessel; I have my own son aboard. As regulations demand, we have engaged a surgeon for the voyage. We are no Indiaman, but we are dry and clean, and as we sometimes carry two hundred immigrants, your one hundred soldiers should have elbow-room aplenty."

The soldier suddenly eyed him and asked, "Immigrants, Captain Clapsaddle? I trust you do not carry slaves."

In a firm voice the seaman replied, "Certainly not, sir. Not on any ship of mine."

The soldier gave a conciliatory nod, and as Clapsaddle led the way below, he went on, "By the way, sir, I imagine you have been informed that a Mr. Read of the Colonial Office is to sail with us. He is ashore just now with his servant, buying provisions and such, but he is anxious to sail. I have given my cabin over to Mr. Read, as he is an older gentleman. My son and I will sling our hammocks with the crew; I do not put on airs. I have had my carpenter fashion a rough cabin for you below, and while it is not Covent Gardens, you shall have some privacy and some degree of comfort."

Lockwood's examination of the ship was thorough. The water was fresh, the ship's beef and biscuit were at least edible, and the hold clean and dry. At his signal, the draft was rowed out in loads of twenty, the NCOs staying ashore until the last boat so they might prevent any last-minute changes of heart regarding the benefits of army life and the charms of the Demerara Coast.

*****

The next day the *Dispatch* rounded the northernmost point of Ireland, then slanted south and west toward the blue waters beyond. James had a great deal to do in getting his men settled aboard. The winds were mercifully kind, the weather fair, and there was, thus far, only a moderate amount of seasickness amongst the soldiers.

James was, thankfully, immune to that malady, a trait in which he took some pride.

Mr. Read did not share his good fortune. That gentleman, who had returned aboard just before they sailed, had retired to his cabin while James was busy below deck. He had left a note with Captain Clapsaddle.

My Dear Cap<u>tn</u> Lockwood,

Pray accept my heart-felt apologies for not allowing myself the pleasure of an introduction, but long experience with sea travel has taught me to prepare for a most violent bout with the sea sickness. Even the boat ride out to our dear Dispatch was nearly enough to render me inhuman.

Still, my long experience informs me that this malaise, while wholly debilitating, is a passing indisposition. In three or four days I shall recover my sea legs, but until that time I am not fit company for a dog.

I thus retire, braced for the worst, trusting to my servant's ministrations, consoled only by the prospect of your company in the very near future and our discussion of the tasks which await us.

Please believe me to be your most devoted servant,
Gordon Read

As Mr. Read remained *hors de combat* and Captain Clapsaddle was typically occupied with the ship, James could concentrate upon making his men's lives a misery. Twice a day, for hours at a time, he drilled them. Their drill ground rolled and pitched more than was typical, some of the men became horribly seasick and the sailors were forever complaining about the Lobsters being in the damned way. Captain Lockwood calmly persevered, and the men of the draft were gradually instructed in their new trade.

As part of their indoctrination to army ways, Captain Lockwood organized the men into messes of six. He did so deliberately, after consultations with Corporal Shanahan and, for form's sake, Sergeant Maguire. He also asked the opinions of Private O'Boyle, though only as quick asides; neither Lockwood nor O'Boyle desired to have the men view O'Boyle as a favorite. Eventually Lockwood posted his list, trying as best he could to put friends together, but also attempting to put the hard cases and grumblers into messes with a strong man who might keep them in line. The mess was the first building block in any army's structure. A man who was closely tied with his messmates would be less likely to desert. More than that, once in action, a man who valued the opinion of his friends would not abandon them when faced with the stresses of battle. The Inniskillings were known for close bonds among the men, and between the men and their officers. At Waterloo not a single man had run from his brothers, no matter how terrible their suffering.

They drilled by mess, six men working with Shanahan, six with Maguire, the balance being drilled by their very demanding captain. First, the basics: how to form, touching elbows with their neighbors, then the basic step, even on a pitching deck in the North Atlantic, then weapons, endless bayonet drill and long hours of handling their muskets before they were trusted to fire a single round.

The three regimental wives proved useful. James hired them as cooks, and while they would never gain employment at Kildare Street Club, they gave some life to the army rations. Their four children were young enough to stay close to their mothers until they grew accustomed to life aboard, although he assumed they would be out exploring and likely becoming a damned nuisance before long.

Captain Lockwood

Ten days out of Londonderry they hit their first patch of heavy weather, with a strong swell and driving rain. When Sergeant Maguire asked if the drill would be cancelled, the captain replied, "The French do not wait for good weather, Sergeant. I have personal knowledge of them being so ungentlemanly as to attack in quite miserable weather. The men will stand to, please."

Soon, however, the wind grew so severe that the master forbade the soldiers the deck. Captain Lockwood would not dismiss his sodden men, instead gathering them in flickering lantern light below deck to show them the correct way to sharpen a bayonet, and how best to knap a flint. Sergeant Maguire showed some promise when he showed the men how best to load a knapsack and then how to adjust the shoulder straps, so they would not rub a man's shoulders raw.

During that stowing of their packs, Private Carr found that his prized St. Brigid's cross, a gift from his mother, was missing. After a short investigation it was found in the pack of Private James Hogan, who had already been given the nickname Rógaire, "Rascal," amongst his fellows. Hogan managed only a weak defense, and the Captain quickly pronounced him guilty of theft. Much can be tolerated amongst soldiers, but never a thief.

Hogan was sentenced to six lashes. As the draft had no drummer, the bosun of the *Dispatch* laid them on the next day, as the draft stood at attention to witness punishment. Hogan had few friends, and no one had much sympathy for him, even after the bloody strokes made him cry out. In some respects army life was not much different from the lives they had always lived.

*****

As is typical with life at sea, the crew and the passengers fell into a routine. Their voyage was not an especially long one, so no one involved had occasion to grow bored. There was little diversion in their routine, though the antics of the ship's goat, a creature addicted to tobacco and rum, were much appreciated. The captain's twelve year-old son, David, was cherished by the crew, and soon by the soldiers as well. He was kind to the soldiers' children, playing the role of veteran seaman and pointing out the various parts of the ship, though he and his young charges were forbidden to go aloft. David's mother had died some months before, so he had gone to sea, and had proved himself an uncomplaining, companionable boy.

Every man aboard, no matter his character, had at one time loved his mother, and knowing that the wee boy had lost his own so young, they treated him with affection. James was pleased to see that the boy did not top it the knob, but respectfully strove to learn all he could.

James thought of his own children, convinced that they, too, would behave in such a fashion. He was desperately proud of them, and that night wrote to each of them to tell them so.

*****

The heavy weather kept Mr. Read in his cabin, but the next day was nearly calm, allowing him to make a shaky appearance on deck. James was prepared to meet an older gentleman, but Mr. Read, terribly pale and unsteady, bordered on the ancient and walked with a severe limp. James was surprised that the Colonial Office would dispatch him on such a mission. Further, the exact scope of Mr. Read's powers was still a mystery; James assumed he would consult, advise and report back to the Colonial Office. However, there had been instances when such an envoy had been granted extraordinary powers, up to and including supplanting the governor, until another could be dispatched from London.

Their first formal meeting was held two days later, when Mr. Read was more recovered. James, Read and Clapsaddle gathered in the cabin, where two maps had been spread out across the table. The first was a current nautical chart that showed only the coast and the off-shore hazards. The second, James was pleased to see, was dated 1823, newly issued, with a wealth of detail on the colony's settlements. He had a moment to study the map: for twenty miles along the Caribbean coast, then twenty miles up the Demerara River, plantations had been cut out of the jungle. Most of the holdings were only a quarter mile wide, allowing access to the water, but then ran four or five miles deep into the interior. Beyond the land along the water, the map showed only solid jungle. Each strip of land was neatly marked with a number; only one of the larger tracts was given a name: Plantation Friendship. James snorted in disdain and turned to face the young seaman and the elderly bureaucrat.

James opened by asking, "Captain Clapsaddle, as Mr. Read and I have never set foot in Guyana, I wonder if you might share what you know of the colony and its people?"

The seaman grimaced and said, "I know precious little, I'm afraid, gentlemen. The nearest I've been is a hundred miles off the coast, and, I confess, I was precious glad to get further off. There are pirates based on the Isla de Margarita, here," he continued, tapping the nautical chart, "some 500 miles to the northeast, who would cut a man's throat for a shilling. Scuttlebutt at Barbados holds that those devils are setting up a base here, at the mouth of the Rio Orinoco, only 250 miles from the Guyana colony and those fat plantations."

Clapsaddle went on with a detailed explanation of the navigational hazards of the coast, until James interrupted him with, "Yes, yes, thank, you, Captain, but if I may, what have you heard of the conditions in the colony itself? What does your 'scuttlebutt' tell you is happening there?"

Clapsaddle gave a slight shrug and said, with not a little bitterness, "I say only this: once we touch, I intend to see you gentlemen ashore and I shall then stand off with all sail set. None of this crew will go ashore there; I will not allow my son to see such a place. So, in answer to your question, Captain, I hear that Guyana is every bit the slave colony, with the usual veneer of silk and a heart of horror."

James was intrigued to hear Clapsaddle speak with such passion, until the bent Mr. Read, who had availed himself of the captain's chair, waved a hand and said with a cultured tone, "If I may, gentlemen, insert myself at this point. While I have never had the—I shall not say pleasure—of a posting to Guyana, I might yet boast a knowledge of the pertinent issues, gathered in my extensive experience with the Colonial Office."

James wanted to asked Read what powers he carried in his portfolio, but only joined Clapsaddle in bowing to the old gentleman. After taking a moment to gather momentum, Read went on, "It is the policy of His Majesty's Government that the slave trade is now abolished. The slaves currently in bondage, however, are to remain in bondage, a condition that many of them find—objectionable. Government has, however, introduced some regulations to ameliorate their condition, including no labour to be carried out on Sundays, and access to church services."

Read smacked his mouth in an odd manner, nodded toward a bottle in the corner, and in a different tone, asked, "I wonder if I might beg a taste of your rum, if you please, Captain Clapsaddle? I developed a taste for it on a passage aboard *HMS Leopard* en route to Sumatra, back when the world was young."

Clapsaddle poured a tall glass for Read, and then looked to Captain Lockwood with a tilt of his head. James shook his head; some years before he had learned to avoid neat rum before dinner. Read, however, had no such compunction.

After a long swallow and a sigh of pleasure, that gentleman went on with new vigour. "Now, where was I? Oh, yes, Sundays. Well, the planters have largely ignored Government's mandates, and a number of abolitionist clergymen, primarily Methodists—say what you will about their unorthodox ways, one must admire their selfless, one might say self-destructive, determination to point out society's failings—have managed to slip into the colony to rail against such cruelty, and the poor souls in bondage are an attentive audience. Some of the clergymen were turned out with no ceremony, but not before they stirred things up to a remarkable degree. That is all that is known to date. I have no doubt conditions will be much changed by the time we arrive, and likely changed for the worse." Read took another swallow of rum and added thoughtfully, "Another truism gained after many years of government service: No matter the situation, count on it to grow worse."

*****

Mr. Read had kindly offered to have his servant tend to Captain Lockwood's washing, and so it was some time into the voyage before James had need to dig very far into his trunk. But near the bottom he found a surprise; Brigid had hidden a handkerchief into which she had elegantly stitched a monogram with both their initials, and a lock of her hair sewn into a heart.

He was fortunate to have discovered the gift when no one else was about, as any man aboard would have been amazed to see the towering captain clutch the kerchief to his face with tears in his eyes.

*****

Weeks passed, and they steadily grew closer to Guyana. With every degree of south latitude they passed, the air grew warmer and the sun more oppressive. As a man born and raised in Ireland, James enjoyed the warmth for a few days, allowing it to sink into his damaged frame, and then began to suffer: his uniform coat became a burden. So, too, did Mr. Read.

While in most other respects an enjoyable companion, that aged gentleman proved to be an inveterate whistler. At first James took some delight in Read's talent, as the old fellow was remarkably versatile, with an enormous library of tunes at hand. He delighted the crew of the *Dispatch* with sea shanties, and the men of the draft with Irish ballads. After dinner, he entertained the gentlemen at table with Bach and Beethoven.

Perhaps it was the long confinement aboard ship, perhaps it was the pervasive heat, but after two weeks of this whistling, Captain Lockwood was quite prepared to strangle Mr. Read.

James did come across one thing that would silence Mr. Read, indeed drive him back to his cabin. The elderly fellow did not care for the sound of musketry. James found that a full volley would send Read below in short order. They were just a few days from Guyana on an especially still, hot, humid evening, with Mr. Read at the stern rail in what little shade the deck could offer, whistling endless variations of "Greensleeves," a tune which James Lockwood thought worthy of one listening per annum.

Feeling hot, peevish, and contrary, James spotted a log floating nearby and, after an evil glimpse astern, he ordered up the full draft for target practice. He was not cruel about it—for the first time he allowed the men to appear in their shirt sleeves, and with a party atmosphere, the hundred men lined the rail and threw a quite reputable volley against the offending log. Pleased, the captain allowed them each to fire off two more rounds at will. The grinning men took the opportunity to blaze away, without the captain studying every motion.

James, too, took pleasure in the noise and heady smell of smoke, but when he looked at Read, the old fellow was fleeing the deck with a pained look on his face, and in hurrying away, his limp and a lift of the deck nearly did for him. Only a kindly deck hand kept him from a bad fall. James winced and recalled a phrase Brigid had used more than once: "You'll be going to hell for that one, James Lockwood."

As an Anglo Irish gentleman and a king's officer, he had long practice in the suppression of strong emotion, but this instance was an exception. For a moment he was unsure of what to do, then, muttering, "Oh, damn it all, anyway," he turned to follow Read.

As he left the deck, he ordered Maguire and Shanahan to keep an eye on the rest of the firing, adding, "...and for God's sake have Conley cease waving that firelock about in such a fashion. He may be certain it is unloaded, but that will be small consolation if he blows a man's head off."

At the cabin door James hesitantly rubbed his hands together, and then gently knocked. Read welcomed him with his usual grace, mentioning nothing about the impromptu musketry drill. James

64

did not allow himself the easy way out, instead saying, "I wonder, sir, if the sound of musketry is unpleasant to you? I confess that after Waterloo I found the sound most distressing. I have gotten past that discomfort, but I wonder if I have been thoughtless in exposing you to such noise and smoke. Many civilians find it unpleasant."

Read sat down, motioning James to a chair, and with a fleeting grin said, "Would it surprise you to learn, sir, that I was a soldier, once? An ensign, joined in 1775, just as my regiment was ordered to prepare for Foreign Service in America. We arrived in Boston just in time for the Americans to chase us out, then some time later we were landed near New York. I was a complete novice, mind you, and was unwise enough to take a ball in the leg at Brooklyn Heights." Tapping his bad leg, he went on, "It never healed to my satisfaction, so I sold out, after less than a year's service, and took up a post in Government. I do confess that after Brooklyn Heights, I have found the sound of gunfire acutely painful."

"Oh, I do apologize, my dear Mr. Read, but do you say Brooklyn Heights, sir? My regiment, the 27th Foot, was there as well."

"I am acquainted with that fact, Captain. You see, I was an ensign in that same 27th Regiment of Foot."

James's face lit up, and he excitedly said, "You amaze me, sir! I had no idea!"

Read turned a lively pink with pleasure and said, "Oh, honestly, I did not wish to show away. My service is a drop in the ocean in comparison to your own, sir."

With a nearly boyish enthusiasm James asked, "Oh, sir, might you honour me with some reminiscences of your days in the regiment? Just think, you served against the Americans! I tangled with them briefly at Plattsburgh in the year thirteen... I found them to be a decent set, though certainly not Englishmen, poor fellows. Pray, how did they comport themselves in your day?"

*****

James Lockwood was a man of some imagination, and was thus prone to dreams, and occasional nightmares, of vivid reality. As his body rolled to the now-familiar pitch of the *Dispatch's* paces, in his dream he sat atop a hill covered in lovely pink grass. His two dogs, Sergeant and Corporal, were there as well, thoroughly cross with one another. Sergeant argued that Corporal, who was, after all, his own son, was insufficiently respectful, and in evidence Sergeant cited several occasions where Corporal had deliberately snubbed, even insulted, his sire. Corporal offered little defense beyond an occasional bark of "I never!"

This *tête-à-tête* continued at length, the dogs sharing some interesting insights, until a blue and green cat, with whom James was unacquainted, strolled across the pink grass and repeatedly said in a clear boy's voice, "Beg pardon, sir. Beg pardon, sir."

That voice, coupled with an insistent tugging on his hammock, prompted James to jolt awake and ask in a startled, angry voice, "For God's sake, what is it? What o'clock is it?"

"Just dawn, please, sir. Beg pardon, sir, my father's compliments, and he wonders if you might join him on deck. There is a strange sail to windward."

Chapter Six

Miguel Otero did not consider himself a bad man. His work occasionally required him to do some unkind things, but he took no pleasure in them. That, he thought, was a distinction that might yet allow him entrance to heaven. It was, admittedly, a minor distinction, but the Holy Church was capable of such subtle interpretation.

Otero was also certain that God would be pleased that His devoted servant was also a family man. Some years before, one of the women who hung about the Isle de Margarita had borne him a daughter, though she had died in doing so. As he was in port after an exceptionally successful cruise, Otero had decided upon a *Deo gratias*: he would see the child cared for. Further determined to remain in God's good graces, Otero had consulted the Bible for a name. Sadly, the Bible in question was rather slashed and bloody, as it had been pried from the hands of a dead Anglican minister. That gentleman had died attempting to protect his two daughters, a foolish man. Happily, one of the Old Testament pages was still legible, and the name Hadassah was thus bestowed upon the squalling infant.

Thus certain of heaven, Otero commanded the heavy sloop *Halcón* with a clear conscience, a long, low, sleek vessel that cruised every corner of the Caribbean, outrunning anything that might hunt her, and in turn preying upon anything slow, weak, and profitable.

Otero preferred the term "buccaneer" to "pirate." "Pirate" rang of lawlessness, whereas Otero considered himself a businessman, a businessman of dashing style. If pressed, he might grudgingly concede that most of the men aboard the *Halcón* were bad men. A hundred of them were packed aboard; criminals of every ilk who did not serve for wages, only for shares of what the ship could take. The polyglot crew sprang from wildly different backgrounds: Europeans, escaped slaves, Indians from every Caribbean tribe, even two wandering Malays. But more than a few were Irishmen, Irishmen who had an especially keen hatred of the English.

The mongrels he led were not good sailors—their gunnery was poor, and few of them had more than the basic skills required to fight their way aboard a prize. What they did possess, and had learned very quickly, was savagery.

When the brig was sighted at dawn, Otero nodded for the helmsman to close on her; the boatswain called for the deck to be cleared for action and the topsails were raised. Every man aboard contemplated his share of such a fat little prize. The brig had just four gun ports, so she was no match for the fast *Halcón*, her heavy crew, and her eight brass nine-pounders. With any luck, the brig would be packed full of luxury goods intended for the rich planters of Guyana or, better yet, an illicit cargo of slaves, worth a fortune.

Miguel Otero eyed the brig, privately hoping she was English. Otero happily killed every Englishman who crossed his path.

*****

By the time James reached the deck, the *Dispatch* had already swung, to flee downwind, her crewmen scrambling to raise every stitch of canvas she could carry. Captain Clapsaddle had a glass to his eye, staring long and hard at the stranger astern. He eventually handed the glass to James and said, "She's a pirate out of Isla de Margarita, or I'm a Dutchman. Perhaps Señor Otero, or even Mr. Goodsole himself."

The strange ship astern leapt into focused reality when James held the glass to his eye. Low, dark, and threatening, alive with men in her rigging and on her deck. "How many guns, do you think, sir?" he asked.

"As she came about I caught sight of four gun ports. So, eight guns, all heavier than our four six-pound pop guns."

With the glass still at his eye, James muttered, "She looks fast."

"Aye, fast, and she'll steer two points closer to the wind than we might ever dream. In this light wind, it will be an hour or so before she is on us. I'm precious happy to have you and your men, aboard, sir. He could knock us to matchsticks from a distance, but he wants this ship and her cargo whole. As soon as he sees our consignment is nothing more precious than redcoats, he'll spin on his heel. Those gentlemen astern want no truck with soldiers."

James said nothing, only steadily studying the stranger.

"And so, Captain," continued Clapsaddle, somewhat puzzled by the soldier's looming silence, "if you would be so good as to have your men line the rail, I'll wager that damned pirate will be on his way, in search of a less combative prize."

James snapped the glass closed with a predatory gleam in his eye. "I wonder, sir, if I might suggest something."

Captain Lockwood

Captain Lockwood hurried below. It took a moment for his eyes to adjust from the dazzling light of dawn to the gloom below deck. His men, who had been ordered to remain below, gathered around, wildly curious to know what was happening.

James stopped halfway down the ladder, and, trying not to let his own excitement be too evident, he grinned and said, "Well, men, it looks as if you shall find your first action today. That's a pirate to windward, meaning to take the *Dispatch*, and us with her."

Their discipline was still spotty, so several men felt free to voice their opinion of the captain's announcement. Some were pleased, some afraid, some so surprised at the notion of battling pirates on the high seas that they uttered damned foolishness, up to and including a Christian surrender. Sergeant Maguire said nothing, a look of astonishment on his face, so it was left to Corporal Shanahan to roar, "Silence, there!"

They did go quiet, all except Michael Lennon, a weak-minded weaver from Cavan, who whispered to his neighbor in Irish, "Are these pirates bad fellows, Liam, *a grah*?"

"Oh, yes, quite bad, indeed," whispered his messmate.

Pirates had plagued Ireland for centuries. Irish children were raised with the tale of Saint Patrick's abduction by pirates, and stories of Viking raiders and Algerian corsairs were told in every Irish home. Pirates were renowned for savage brutality, and all across the island they were feared and hated.

*****

Otero was amused. The crew of the merchant brig had hove to and launched a boat, which was now carrying her crew briskly to

70

the west. He would take the brig, and determine her nationality. If they were Dutch, French, even Yankees, he would allow the crew to make for Barbados. Two hundred miles—with any luck they might even make it. But if the ship proved to be English he would chase them down and ensure they never saw land again.

When they first spotted the brig, Otero had noted a red coat on deck. Being a man of thorough nature, he duly noted him crawling down into the launch. A very small fellow, perhaps even a boy, but if that was an English officer, Otero would ensure a special death for him. Several children were lifted down into the boat, but he saw no women.

It was working out nicely. It was easy to take an abandoned prize, without any unpleasantness. His crew would be pleased to take a rich prize without a fight, and if the brig was English, his men would enjoy murdering the bastards. It would be complicated if the English had any women amongst them. Christ and His nails, if there were women aboard, what a mess that would make, as a few women could not be shared equitably amongst a hundred men. There would be fighting, and blood on his own deck. Besides, the ensuing rapes were distressing to him. Was he not a gentleman? Gentleman should not witness such things. Their last prize had had several women aboard, and their prolonged screams had absolutely ruined his evening.

Damien Sorhaindo, one of the most vicious men of the starboard watch, saw the boat pulling away and called, "They're getting away! Let's put a sword through those cowardly bastards!"

There were some growls of agreement, and all eyes turned back to see Otero's reaction. No sane man told Miguel Otero what to do. Fortunately for Sorhaindo, Otero proved to be in good humour. "We're here for profit, Sorhaindo! Besides, there were only trousers dropping into that boat; not a single skirt! So, none for you today—though there may be a boy or two, if you prefer that!"

There were howls of ribald laughter, followed by Otero shouting, "Let's see what those cowardly dogs have left us! We may be rich men!" There came a roar of fierce greed, and Otero called to the helmsman, "Acebo, lay me alongside!"

*****

As the long minutes passed and the pirate sloop steadily approached, James had time, too much time, to question himself.

He could have easily followed Clapsaddle's first plan and shown his hand, and allowed his men to be seen, and so driving the pirates off without a shot. He did not know how many were coming for them; and his own men were green. What if they misbehaved? Would they follow him?

He studied the men around him. There was room for only thirty to huddle along the rail, hidden even from the topmen of the approaching pirate ship, while the others waited in the hold, anxiously huddled at the feet of the ladders. One of the men at the rail was whispering to himself as he rubbed the stock of his musket, "We'll show them. We'll show them." James could not remember the man's name.

He was glad the wives and children were safely off in the boat. It had been Clapsaddle's suggestion that the women dress as men, and so pose no risk of distracting the pirate's attention.

More time, more doubts. He admitted to himself that he would take pride in bringing a pirate sloop into Georgetown harbour. If they succeeded, their victory would be the talk of the service: a raw draft taking a lethal pirate sloop. Was he driven by ambition? He had seen enough service to know that his life, and the lives of his men, were at risk. He also knew himself and was privately thrilled at the notion of action. Whatever his motivation, he consoled himself with the knowledge that it was the duty of every officer to battle His Majesty's enemies. It was his duty, in that place, in those circumstances, and he would require his men to do theirs as well.

*****

Several minutes of near-silence followed, broken only by the gentle creaking of a ship under easy sail and a few orders as sail was reduced. The crew of the *Halcón* could make out the brig's name, *Dispatch*, gilded across her broad stern. The two ships thumped together. The *Halcón* had been built for speed, so the side of the *Dispatch*, a wallowing merchantman, towered above her. Otero barked another order, and grapnels were thrown from the bow and stern.

The *Halcón* and the *Dispatch* were pulled together and secured. Many of the pirates set their weapons aside and prepared to scramble aboard the brig. They looked up hungrily at the tall side of the brig, though the morning sun was in their eyes.

Otero had a flickering premonition. He absently crossed himself, and then reached to draw his sword. He was on the brink of calling a warning when the brig came alive with a flash of red.

*****

Captain Lockwood leapt to his feet and roared "Inniskillings!" in a voice that brought blood to his throat.

None of his men—they proved themselves his men—flinched. In an instant every man on the rail was on his feet, the rail a steady line of red-coated Irishmen, many of them calling out in English and Irish, anxious to be at it.

"Ready!" Every barrel was pointed down into the faces of the stunned pirates.

"Fire!"

Fire and smoke spewed from every muzzle. It seemed that every shot struck flesh; the narrow, crowded deck of the *Halcón* was scythed with lead balls. The men at the rail fell back to reload, their places taken by men who scrambled up from below.

"Fire at will!" His orders came loud but calmer in tone, meant to steady them. Too much excitement made for unsteady hands and slow loading. The smoke was dense, but in the brief lull of reloading, the wind cleared his view and he had the opportunity to study the deck below. Dozens dead and wounded. There was pandemonium on the deck of the sloop, most of the pirates scrambling for cover, some few keeping their wits and returning fire. A big man in a light blue coat at the stern was screaming orders in Spanish, pointing to the lines that held the ships together. Before James could say anything, he saw Clapsaddle and the two other seamen who had stayed aboard throwing their own grapnels into the pirate's rigging. There would be no flight; one side would win, and the other would surrender or perish.

Shanahan was standing near his captain. With his sword, James pointed out the officer in the blue coat and called to him, "Shanahan! Pot that fellow!"

Seconds later Miguel Otero dropped to the deck, clutching his head.

James called out, "Keep firing, men! Put them down!" A spattering of musket shots ensued, then a steady pattern of fire, balls striking the deck in a pelting gale. Captain Lockwood walked up and down the firing line shouting orders and encouragement. He stepped over the body of Private Robert O'Neal, dead with a shot to the head. Three men bent over the body, shocked and ashen until Lockwood pushed them back to the rail, crying, "Never mind, now! Pay the bastards back! Load and fire, there, load and fire!"

Clapsaddle and his two men hurriedly loaded one of the four-pound guns and aimed it down into the teeming deck of the *Halcón*. Firing canister at close range, even such a light gun, was murderous. They served the gun like demons, the hail of shot carving paths of bloody destruction below.

The volume of fire was steady—lead, smoke, and fire lashing the *Halcón*, stabbing flames from every shot cutting the dense smoke. Captain Lockwood continued to walk the line. "Fire and step back, men, fire and step back. Take aim, there, Reilly. Don't throw your shot away. Rooney, well done. Steady, McIlhenny, remember your training, son. Well done, Monahan."

James felt the shock of surprise waning; the deck below was covered with bodies, but some of the enemy were regrouping—fierce, violent men. He had to press his advantage.

Another roar from the captain: "Inniskillings! Fix! Bayonets!" The firing stopped as his men hastily snapped the eighteen-inch blades into place. He paused, judging them. A few were obviously frightened out of their wits, but most were flush with victory and bloodlust, panting, wild-eyed and anxious to be at it. Most had never truly injured another man in all their lives previously, but for these few minutes, they were as terrible as men could become.

James waited one more beat, feeling his fury, and theirs, rising, boiling, then roaring, "Across!" as he threw himself over the rail and down onto the enemy's deck. James caught a glimpse of Clapsaddle, a sword in his hand, the first to follow.

Going over the side, several men cried out, "Baltimore! Baltimore!" It had been two hundred years since Barbary pirates

75

had stolen away the entire population of that Cork village to a life of slavery. A pirate was a pirate; these mongrel pirates would pay for the crimes of those corsairs. Fineen O'Driscoll, who had been raised with stories of his ancestors' slavery, was in such a fury that he foully cursed in Irish and howled for the blood of the godless slavers. And so the Irish came, scrambling after their captain, screaming curses.

They found the deck a charnel house. Soft lead musket balls made terrible, gaping wounds, and dead and writhing wounded men lay everywhere, the decks slick with blood. But still the remaining pirates would not surrender, as captivity could lead to nothing better than hanging.

They sold their lives dearly. Those who had run below came surging back on deck with pistols, pikes, and cutlasses. There were more of them than James had anticipated, furious and deadly. And then, they were amongst them, men packed together on the narrow deck, dealing and receiving blows, a reeling melee, slashing, thrusting, sweating, screaming, tripping over the bodies of the fallen. James pushed his way to where the pirates seemed best organized, parrying pikes and cutlasses, thrusting into the mass of teeming bodies. Close to his enemy now, he heard them calling out in Spanish, French, English, and for an instant James was shocked to hear more than a few pirates screaming the same Gaelic oaths that his own men called. Shanahan was now beside him, and O'Donnell, and some others, their bayonets doing deadly work.

It was the type of fierce, merciless close-quarter fighting with which Captain Lockwood was all too familiar. At Badajoz, Waterloo and in the west of Ireland he had seen as much combat as any man in the king's service. The wounds he had suffered in previous battles still hindered him, but his size, skill, and experience made him the deadliest man aboard.

His focus was reduced to flashes of the men around him. One of the pirates, a viciously ugly white man in a red shirt, made a clumsy thrust with a cutlass and made no attempt to recover his guard. James handily parried and reposted his point into the man's throat. A wild-looking pirate—in an instant of distraction, James judged him an Indian—snapped a pistol at him. The ball whistled past James's head, and in turn, James slashed him down and finished him, pinning him to the deck. A black man with some knowledge of sword play lunged at Lockwood with an old-fashioned rapier. James parried the point, and in a flash the man was swept away by a wall of screaming Inniskillings. Darby Rooney, the little fellow who spoke only Irish, dashed past, thrusting his bayonet in a frenzy, wild-eyed and howling Irish profanities.

Finally, there were only redcoats near Lockwood, and he could look up. In isolated pockets across the deck, crowds of soldiers closed in on the surviving pirates, but still the soldiers' inexperience showed. Some of them failed to use the advantage of their long weapons, allowing the pirates inside their guard. A short, bald man, bare-chested with arms like an ape, leapt out from behind the capstan and brutally hacked down Tim O'Mulqueen, a gentle soul, a former weaver from Limerick. Gerald McNamara made a childish lunge at a gnarled old pirate, a lunge which the pirate easily parried, and he, in turn, slashed at McNamara. The soldier was fortunate to take the blow in the shoulder, and his life was only saved by Clapsaddle, who rushed in and struck the pirate down with a back-handed slash of his cutlass.

It was a short, brutal, fight, but the soldiers' superior numbers soon told. The last of the pirates were overwhelmed, fighting to the last.

It was over. James allowed himself to double over, gasping and coughing. Shanahan and O'Boyle rushed to support him, barely keeping him from collapsing to the deck, as O'Boyle cried out, "Ah, shite, sir, are ye hit?"

Gasping, wincing, holding his side, James answered, "No, man." Heaving breaths. "Waterloo wound." A few seconds more. "Damn."

His breath grudgingly returned. Finally upright, looking about, the scope of the slaughter became evident. "Jesus."

The dead were still; the wounded crawled and writhed, groaning or screaming. Some of them were his men. "Captain Clapsaddle! Where is that bloody damned surgeon!"

The redcoated soldiers stood motionless, staring at their captain, shocked, stunned, and relieved. "Sergeant Maguire, secure the prisoners!"

James saw that the big man in the light blue coat was still alive, trying to rise, his head wound dripping blood on the deck. He pointed him out and said, "O'Boyle, I believe that man is the captain of this vessel. Do sit on him, won't you? I shall want to speak with him later."

At his feet, a pirate with his entrails in his hands began to scream. Distractedly, James said, "Oh, be quiet, sir, be quiet." He saw Private McNamara sitting on the deck clutching his shoulder, blood pouring through his fingers. He went to him, and, with Shanahan's help, he eased the soldier back, pushing the wound closed, calling for the surgeon.

A dead redcoat lay near the *Halcón's* rail: Peter Blackburn, whose wife had died a few days before, in a Fermanagh ditch. He would not, of course, have known of his wife's fate, though he might have taken some consolation if he had known that his orphaned son would grow up safe and loved, in a great house.

The ship's launch returned, bearing a concerned Mr. Read and the young David Clapsaddle, still wearing one of Captain Lockwood's massive uniform coats, who anxiously looked up until he saw his father's face at the rail, and then, with a beaming smile, yelled, "Da! Oh, Da, have you won?"

*****

The dead pirates were tossed overboard without ceremony, and the prisoners secured below. The Inniskillings—they now deserved the title—asked their captain if they might stay aboard the *Halcón*. They had taken her and earned the right to keep her. So that night four men from the *Dispatch* joined the few soldiers who had some knowledge of the sea, and crewed the *Halcón* under easy sail, following the *Dispatch* south and west toward Guyana.

Captain Lockwood stayed aboard as well. That night, as the men of the draft waked for their dead on the deck where they had died, he sat alone in Otero's well-appointed cabin, a pen in hand, trying to compose a summary of the action for submission to the Governor of Guyana Colony. In the cold calculus of war, theirs was an astounding victory.

An infamous pirate sloop had been taken, and seventy-four pirates killed. Eighteen more had been wounded and captured, screaming, at bayonet point. Only two prisoners had been taken unhurt. Six of his men—he would not say 'only' six—were dead, fourteen more wounded.

James pondered those totals for a moment. In most any battle, the wounded outnumbered the dead by three to one. But many of the pirates had been determined to fight to the death, and his men had evidently been willing to oblige them. He had not thought them so bloody-minded. He should have known—their cries of "Baltimore!" ought to have told him of their fury. They had been blooded. For better or worse, they were now soldiers, bound to one another through experiences no other man could know.

But he could think of little else but the cost of their victory. Those six soldiers were dead. That would never be undone. Twelve more were in agony: shot, stabbed and slashed, suffering in the relentless, staggering heat. The surgeon was tending to them, aided by one of the wives, young Mrs. McManus, who had clambered aboard the *Halcón* and set to work aiding the wounded and had proven herself a stout soul. The other two wives had flinched; horrified by the blood flowing from the scuppers of the *Halcón*, they screamed across, to learn that their husbands were unhurt, then remained aboard the *Dispatch*.

James found that his hands were shaking. He looked at them in surprise and set his formal letter aside. After a moment, he started another, this one for Brigid. He sat staring at the blank page for long minutes, until finally writing, "All those lives lost, and all the lives lost over these past years! I fear I have lost what little chance I had at heaven. In my heart I wonder if I have seen enough; perhaps I ought to just come home." By writing those lines he felt as if he had shared them, across the endless miles that separated them, and that somehow she could hear him. Consoled, he folded the sheet of paper, held it over the candle and dropped the softly burning paper to the deck. It soon faded to a bit of ash and smoke, and the gentle Caribbean breeze wafted the smoke away.

Chapter Seven

Father Joseph McGlynn of St. Brigid's Chapel in Clonakilty celebrated a well-attended morning Mass. He then directed choir practice, fine-tuning the group's their "Exsultate Justi" to a nearly professional level, and then, after receiving an urgent note from Councambeg, he walked five miles in a pelting rain to give Extreme Unction to Robert Hurley, arriving in time to give the man a guarantee of heaven. McGlynn left the contents of his purse with the widow Hurley, so that she and her six children might not starve, and told her to go see Mr. O'Donnell at the Linen Hall, as the Father was sure that she might secure a position there. He spent the balance of his day, still in the rain, calling on the wretched cabins east of town, giving comfort and blessings to the destitute souls who dwelt there.

He then went to meet Dermot MacCarthy at the ruins of Ballinoroher Castle, where he gave orders for three men to be killed.

*****

Captain Lockwood

The previous year, Cissy Lockwood had nearly been recruited into McGlynn's clandestine rebel organization. The Father was its organizer, director and chief recruiter. He had been disappointed in losing the lovely young Miss Lockwood; he had hopes of molding her into a *femme fatale*, a tool with which he might have garnered marvelous access to government plans. But she had slipped away from him, a loss which he keenly regretted.

At the same time, John Cashman had also left the movement. That was a true loss—there was never such a deft hand with a knife. For a year or more Cashman had handled the more brutal aspects of the movement's work, moving and killing with amazing stealth. He had never been caught, never even been identified, despite Government's relentless efforts to find him.

McGlynn constantly mulled over methods by which he might bring those two, willing or not, back to the cause.

*****

Cissy Lockwood prepared tea, but there would be no fine china set upon the dining room table, only three rough, familiar mugs on the kitchen table. She was aided by Private Diarmuid Doolan—she and her mother were the only people on the planet who used his Christian name—who put out a plate of biscuits.

"Sure and it was kind of you to bake these for him," he said in Irish—it was rare for anyone to speak English in that kitchen. "There never was a man so fond of biscuits."

Outside, frantic barking signaled the arrival of their visitor. Cissy and Doolan watched the kitchen door, and after a moment a man in a rough coat came in without knocking, gleefully roughhousing with Sergeant and Corporal. The dogs were ecstatic, jumping and yelping and licking like fools.

Trying to look cross, but failing, Cissy said, "John Cashman, those dogs are meant to guard this house, not frolic like lunatics every time a known felon wanders into our garden."

Pulling off his coat, John smiled and said, "There never was a dog who did not love me."

"It's your winning personality, sure," said Doolan with a welcoming grimace.

"Dogs are fine judges of character, as every Christian knows," said John as he gave Cissy a kiss on the cheek and traded a thumping embrace with Doolan.

Doolan slipped each of the dogs a biscuit and bade them lie by the fire while Cissy sat John at the massive old kitchen table.

"Come, sit, and have a bite," she said. "Pray, how are Niamh and the children?"

"Smashing, thank you, smashing. Christ, but these are fine biscuits, *a grah*. Do you know those youngsters call me 'Da' now? Who would have thought such a thing, an old sinner like me?"

They chatted in the manner common to old friends, but by any measure, they were unlikely companions. Cissy, the twenty-year old beauty, John Cashman, in his forties, and while at first glance he seemed older, there were occasions when his hard green eyes sparkled like a child's. Diarmuid Doolan, old and ill-tempered, had, in this, his sixtieth year, succeeded in melding his character and his face into the very definition of a curmudgeon.

John looked around the kitchen, smiled contentedly, and said to Cissy, "You know, from the day I returned to Ireland, I have loved this room. My Ma still watches over it, and you, I think, *a stor*." Catherine Cashman, John's mother and the Lockwood's beloved housekeeper, had been waked in that very room, and Cissy smiled at the notion of her spirit gracing the kitchen of Fáibhile Cottage.

John's presence in town was, ostensibly, to work the cod running in Ring Harbour, but he had sailed his curragh to Clonakilty at Cissy's invitation. He now lived his life as John McCarthy, having separated himself from the John Cashman who had once terrorized Government forces. He had married a pretty young widow and adopted her children. He worked hard, made a decent living as a fisherman and reveled in the love of his new family. Still, he carried a double-edged fighting knife in his boot.

Cissy poured more tea, and sitting at their ease, she told her grizzled friends, "To business, please, gentlemen." John and Doolan both snorted at the term. "I have received a letter from my mother. When she returns home from Fermanagh, she will be accompanied by seven women and eleven children. They are the families of the men of the regiment who are with my father in Guyana. They are penniless and have nowhere to go. It is her intention to see them settled here in Clonakilty."

Both John and Doolan sat upright in surprise, John crying out, "What, is the woman picking up every stray cat in Ireland?"

Doolan shook his head and muttered, "A great heart, that woman, but at times it masters her head."

After a moment's consideration, and with a hint of delight in his tone, John said, "I see, Cissy, *a grah*, how this news affects our handsome Private Doolan, as it is certainly he himself who will tend to the homeless urchins." Beneath the table, outside of Cissy's view but well within John's, Doolan made a gesture that had never before been made in that kitchen. After the slightest pause, and a brief glory in Doolan's discomfiture, John raised his eyebrows and went on, "...but I fail to see, *a grah mo chroi*, love of my heart, how this news affects me in any way at all, at all."

John expected to get a smile and a coy answer, but instead Cissy grew serious and said, "My mother intends to work with the Little Sisters of Mercy in seeing the families housed and supported, and the women instructed in a trade."

Doolan, who had an unfortunate tendency to flirt with the Sisters at every opportunity, gave a slow nod of approval and said, "Well, now, that makes great sense, sure. I shall go by that good house and help those dears in any manner I can."

John folded his arms, considered his response, then said, "And so, Miss Lockwood, you are concerned that our Father McGlynn will interfere with the Sisters' efforts?"

"I am. We all know the Father's disdain for the Sisters. Sister Margaret told me just the other day that McGlynn is again complaining to the bishop, as they take such delight in defying him. I am afraid that he will use these poor families as a way to show his displeasure with me."

Doolan flared and said sharply, "That devil will twist things about and try to drag you back to his cause. We shall have to be on our guard."

Despite her youth and beauty, there were instances when Cissy Lockwood could be as hard-edged as any man. Both John and Doolan were thus attentive when she held up a finger and told them, "But more than that, in his dark mind McGlynn might well decide that the Irish wives and Irish children of Irish soldiers are somehow traitors to his damned notions of Cause. They may find themselves at great risk, and we must be prepared to support them. But always remember: we must adhere to our previous agreement. My mother must never learn of my previous affiliation with McGlynn, however brief, and she must certainly never know that Diarmuid and I are your friends, John."

The three were silent for a moment, until John's face took on a wistful look, and he said, "It would be the pity of the world if Joseph McGlynn woke up dead one morning."

Cissy rolled her eyes and said, "I do wish, John, that you would not say such things. What would Niamh say?"

"I would hate to displease Niamh, sure," said John with resignation, "but more important, think of the blood that would flow, avenging McGlynn."

Doolan shook his head and added, "Neither dare we denounce him to Government. On his way to the scaffold he would put a noose around every one of our necks."

Still in charge, Cissy firmly said, "And so we stand: we cannot bring much harm to McGlynn, though he may very well attempt to bring harm to us. And of course, this all must be kept secret."

John said quietly, "As a priest, McGlynn can count on the support of nearly every Irish soul in Cork, and, more to the point, he has forty or fifty men who would do his bidding without blinking. Still, I know who those men are, and some of them I count as friends." He took a sip of tea and added casually, "It would be interesting to see which of them would remain my friends, should McGlynn order my throat cut."

*****

When Fiona Blackburn's baby was brought to White Hall, there was no discussion as to who would care for it. None of the army wives could assume responsibility for another child, and when Mrs. Nelson held the child with such trembling affection, there was instant tacit agreement that she would at last have a baby to love.

Brigid noted a decided turn in Mrs. Nelson's bearing, as if a baby in her arms gave her validity and worth. Thus, Brigid found Mary a strong partner, as they discussed at length the path to follow, and it was eventually agreed that the families would be moved to Clonakilty by sea. To move them by land, two hundred fifty rough, jolting miles, would be expensive and difficult. While Mrs. Nelson had insisted in financing the transportation as her contribution to the families' wellbeing, there was no sense in spending exorbitant funds while subjecting those eighteen souls to the uncertainties of inns, coaches, horses and muddy roads. More importantly, many of the women and children were still in fragile health, even after two weeks of rest and recuperation in the comparative luxury of the White Hall stables. A long journey over rough roads in an Irish winter would certainly be beyond them.

Instead, Mrs. Nelson called upon a Mr. Maddox, a wealthy, if normally standoffish, neighbor, in order to secure transit by sea. Mr. Maddox had made his fortune by exporting Irish grain and livestock to Britain, and initially scoffed at the notion of one of his vessels carrying a pack of peasant women and children. Mrs. Nelson, however, would not be dissuaded, and secured one of his ships through sheer power of personality.

And so Mrs. Lockwood sat in the captain's cabin of the merchant vessel *Warranted Profit*, adding a page to the serial letter to her husband. She had a sizeable stack at hand, as she was a prolific, if somewhat undisciplined, writer. This would be the last page of this letter, as the captain of the *Warranted* had promised Mrs. Lockwood that after he had safely deposited her and the other ladies at Clonakilty, he would proceed to the Cobh of Cork and place the letter in the hands of the Port Post Master himself.

Mary Nelson is such a dear but it is perhaps just as well that she remained in Fermanagh as so many of the wives

find her intimidating. It may be my birth and speech which draw these women to me but I wonder if the differences between us shall ever allow us to be completely frank in our conversation. Both the women and the children take it as a matter of course that I should dress, dine and in every manner be treated differently than they and while they seem to take it in stride I mentioned it to Mrs. Goodwin. You may recall her as one of the older women to whom the others look as leader and it is a good choice as she has a good head on her shoulders as well as a good heart which is equally important. She laughed it off saying as long as she had food in her belly and a roof overhead she was happy with never a thought about tomorrow.

She paused to look over the page, knowing that James would once again have cause to tease her about her lack of punctuation. She had lovely handwriting, and her spelling was perfect, but she did not much care for quibbles like commas and periods, as they tended to disrupt her train of thought. She pictured him, grinning, perhaps drawing his pencil to add punctuation, and she smiled in turn, knowing his hand would soon touch that page.

There was a quick knock at the door, and Eileen Goodwin stuck her head in to say, "Beg pardon, ma'am, but Mary Pat O'Connor has pummeled one of the sailors, saying he's been fresh, and now the sailors are saying that none of us shall be allowed on deck until she says she's sorry. You know our Mary Pat, and she wouldn't apologize to Christ himself if she stepped on His toe, let alone some sailor man with a roving eye and rough manners."

Brigid sighed and said, "Very well, I shall speak to Captain Waite. But do ask Mary Pat to wear her shawl when the sailors are about, please. She is rather too proud of her bosom, I think."

With a grin and a wag of her eyebrows Mrs. Godwin retreated, and Brigid returned to James.

I confess to your ear alone my dear love that I wonder if I have taken on too much. Whatever shall I do with these people all of them looking to me for the answers I have told them a dozen times that I intend to <u>help</u> them but some of them at least think that I shall <u>provide</u> for them which is a different matter entirely.

Poor dear Margaret Hanahan is so ill with the baby just a month or two away and the seasickness I do hope my dear that you shall keep her in mind and I shall do my part in seeing her and her baby secure and God willing happy. Oh, but that Vera McGunn is a judgmental shrew, she is thinking she can hold a young woman in such disdain, when God has given us all youth and love and desire and if she made a mistake with those gifts, who of us has not? I recall us being uncommon lucky ourselves sir, back when we were just that age Christ I was mad for you, James a grah mo chroi, and even now I remain most... what is the word a gentlewoman might use in a letter? I shall say <u>affectionate</u> in my regard for you. Before I further risk my reputation, I close, with my dear, dear love and prayers for your safe return home.

Your most <u>affectionate</u> wife
Brigid Lockwood

Captain Lockwood

*****

Cissy couched her visit to Colonel Simon as a request for advice, but hoped for an offer of even a temporary refuge for the families, as that gentleman owned several properties in and near Clonakilty. As she had hoped, as a former soldier and a decent old fellow, the colonel was sympathetic to their plight, and he quickly offered up a clutch of empty cabins called Doonasleen, which stood north and west of town, in Cloghgriffin Township, near the ruins of Templequinlan Church. Cissy swallowed the question that rose in her throat, only briefly, painfully, wondering what fate had befallen the previous residents. Expulsion had once been a rare tactic for landlords, but it was being resorted to with increasing frequency and heartlessness.

Cissy's next day was spent with the Little Sisters of Mercy. The sisters were experienced in the handling of the poor, and of those without resource, and realized the weight of the project proposed by the Lockwoods. While sympathetic, the sisters begged time to discuss it amongst themselves, and to pray for guidance.

Her spirits somewhat dampened by the sisters' caution, Cissy was walking home along the Western Road when a horse and rider approached. She was displeased to recognize Cyril Babcock, and was further displeased to realize she had no polite way to avoid him.

Babcock reined in, but did not dismount to address her. "Ah, Miss Lockwood. You find me on my way home after calling on my dear uncle."

As he did not address her properly, she did not feel compelled to return more than a noncommittal nod and a muttered, "Mr. Babcock."

Babcock did not catch the slight, as he said, "I sometimes free myself from my pressing duties to allow myself the pleasure, indeed

90

the honour, of calling on my dear old uncle. It is some twenty miles each way, you know, but for a rider of my ability, it is but a minor challenge. As an amusing aside, I might mention that *en route* I was absolutely required to pass through a hamlet named Balinspittle! Sink me, what an apt moniker." Reaching over to pat his mount's neck, he went on, "As my duties include travel to even the most distant corners of my living, I indulged myself in the purchase of Bucephalus here. Is he not magnificent?"

Cissy was still in the mood to be contrary, but she admitted, "He is indeed, sir. He is what, seventeen hands?"

Babcock nodded approvingly and said, "Quite right, Miss. My uncle has instructed you well."

Cissy bristled but said only, "Colonel Simon is most kind. I was just on my way home to write to my mother to inform her of your uncle's generous offer. Good day, sir."

She turned to go, but Babcock held up an elegantly gloved finger and said, "Miss Lockwood, one more moment, if you please. My uncle tells me that you and your mother are determined to aid a number of destitute peasant women and their children. As a beneficed clergyman, I see myself as an instrument of God in such matters, and I wonder, Miss, if you have reflected on the wisdom of such a course? For a private family, especially a family of, might I surmise, respectable but limited resources, the cost will certainly be prohibitive. And who are these people you hope to help? Penniless *wives and children* of common soldiers, and as such, they are likely soon to be rendered penniless *widows and orphans*. As a class, people of this nature are predisposed by nature to take advantage of undisciplined generosity and may indeed prove positively dangerous through the spread of disease and perhaps even physical violence. It is my intention to advise my uncle to have nothing to do with such an ill-advised scheme."

Cissy was growing angry, but she was determined to play the lady, saying, "Mr. Babcock, these families are…"

From atop his mount, Babcock shook his head and said, in an instructional tone, "The Poor Laws, Miss Lockwood, the Poor Laws, are the tools provided by Government in its providential wisdom to deal with such people. If these people have chosen to live in such a manner, they shall then be required to abide by the rules governing such lifestyles. You will please allow me to step in and manage the matter. When they arrive, I shall divert this indigent herd straight to the Cork City workhouse and be done with them."

"The workhouse!" flared Cissy. "There never was such a den of misery in all the world! Would you consign these people to such a place, sir? Young children, Mr. Babcock!"

"My dear, dear, naïve Miss Lockwood. Conditions at workhouses, especially Irish workhouses, are *deliberately* made uncomfortable, sometimes even unpleasant, so that the slothful members of society do not gravitate there, in hopes of a life of luxury at the expense of their betters. And begging your pardon, ma'am, the Irish are much more prone to such thoughts than even the lowest members of English society."

Cissy shook her head incredulously and said, "Sir, it frankly astounds me that you are capable of insulting me, my family, and my people with such complete lack of conscience. I can only conclude, Mr. Babcock," here Cissy paused, an inner voice crying for caution, but it was overwhelmed in a flood as she went on, "that you, sir, are a deliberately wicked man. There is no Christian charity, nothing resembling love, in your soul. You call your rants 'wisdom and religious truth,' but in the end you spout only the fear and bias of a mean-spirited little man."

Babcock, as shocked as he had been in all his life, could only stare open-mouthed.

As she turned away, Cissy added in a tone of disdain, "By the by, sir, I see you are using a Dutch Gag bit; your uncle would be disappointed to see that you are riding such a fine mount with such a bit. It is indicative of a weak rider, sir, unnecessarily harsh, especially when it is mounted backwards. Honestly, it is a wonder you are allowed out of the house alone. Goodbye, sir."

Chapter Eight

"Señor Otero, I am Captain James Lockwood of His Majesty's 27th Regiment of Foot."

Otero lay in the dank hold of the ship he had once captained, manacled hand and foot, his head heavily bandaged. The surviving members of his crew were scattered around him, all in chains, as a handful of Inniskillings stood guard over them. In the flickering lantern light Otero was pale, drawn and in a simmering rage.

"You will address me as *Capitán* Otero. I shall not be disrespected aboard my own ship," Otero spat, in an accent which James could not fully discern—it was mostly Spanish, but echoed another tone, as well.

James snarled, "You, sir, have no ship. You are a pirate, and my prisoner."

The blood returned to Otero's face. "And you, sir, are a dead man. You and every one of these red-coated sheep will be crucified at my command. All of Isla de Margarita shall rally to me. Even as we speak, they fly to my aid."

James scoffed, "You think you can intimidate me, sir? I am a king's officer of twenty years' standing, and I know a strutting fool when I see one. You will lie here in chains and be carried to Georgetown. There, you will be tried for piracy and hanged."

Otero stared at him with hatred in his eyes but said nothing.

Turning to his men, James said, "Sergeant Maguire, you will maintain two men standing over the prisoners at all times. Their bayonets shall be fixed. Two hour watches. Keep the men on their toes." Turning to look at the dirty, bloody pirates, he went on, "If these fellows give you even a bit of trouble, feel free to knock them on the head and save the hangman his fee."

*****

The lingering light breezes made for slow progress toward Georgetown. On that second hazy afternoon, Private James McNichol, one of the few redcoats who had not pled a fear of heights, was posted as lookout atop the *Halcón's* mainmast. The quiet, the heat and the gentle rolling of the sea were soporific, but McNichol had heard Otero's threats and was determined to stand a good watch.

After three hours aloft, he thought he caught sight of a sail in the haze. It took several minutes before he was convinced that his imagination had not deceived him, and he called down to the deck with panic in his voice, "Captain Lockwood, sir! A sail over that way, sir!" Pointing madly to windward, he added, "Ah, shite, it's Otero's mates, sure, and won't they be right bastards!"

At McNichol's prompting, the lookout aboard *Dispatch* saw the stranger as well, and the decks of both ships filled with frantic activity. The redcoats grabbed their muskets, while the Dispatches looked to their cannon. Lockwood and Clapsaddle, separated by

95

forty yards of rolling sea, urgently called back and forth, trying to devise a plan to deal with the stranger.

The ancient Abel Bloxham, one of the Dispatches who had volunteered to help aboard the *Halcón*, did not much care for manning guns, and so found his way up the mainmast to join McNichol. After borrowing McNichol's glass, he studied the stranger for several minutes until calling down, "On deck, there! No sense messing about with them old guns, sir. That's *Dartmouth*, 36, as much a friend as we are likely to find in this dark corner of the world." In a more conversational tone, he went on, "We might as well have our dinner, as it will be a while before she gets down to us. Christ, we might think of our supper as well, as there never was such a foul-bottomed slug as poor old *Dartmouth*." To McNichol he said, "This here *Halcón* could give her topsails in any kind of breeze, and even the dear *Dispatch* could lead her a merry dance."

Slow as she was, the *Dartmouth* made clear her intention to speak to the two strangers by firing a gun. Both the *Halcón* and the *Dispatch* politely folded their wings, hove to, and awaited her lumbering arrival. The *Dartmouth* raised her ensign, to which both the *Dispatch* and the *Halcón* responded in kind; happily, James had found a Union flag in the *Halcón's* signal locker, evidently one of her disguises.

As compliant as the *Dispatch* and *Halcón* seemed, the *Dartmouth* was having none of it, and came down with her gun ports open and her crew at quarters. She arrived ploddingly, her teeth bared, and from her quarterdeck a voice boomed across, "What ship is that?"

From his rail, Clapsaddle roared back, "*Dispatch*! Captain Clapsaddle, out of Derry, bound for Guyana, and our prize, *Halcón*, a pirate out of Isla de Margarita! Taken by this ship, with Captain

96

Lockwood and men from the First Battalion, 27th Regiment of Foot!"

There followed a growl from both the *Dispatch* and the *Halcón*, followed by a puzzled voice from the *Dartmouth's* quarterdeck, "What, merchants and soldiers?"

In the long moment of silence that followed, the frigate mulling over such an unusual turn of events, the voice of Private Peter Goodwin sounded clear across the sea, "Saved you the trouble, didn't we? You're welcome, I'm sure."

There were grins aboard all three ships, followed by cheers from the *Dartmouth.*

The voice from the frigate boomed again, this time more politely, with a touch of a laugh, "Captains, will you come aboard?"

*****

The *Dartmouth's* captain, Josiah Quash, (James briefly wondered if the possession of an involved name was a prerequisite to command at sea) was a short, round, deeply tanned gentleman, who proved a generous host, especially in sharing his considerable wine stores. He also had dozens of cases of books lining the walls of his cabin. As Quash poured the wine, James looked over the titles nearest him, noting that all were pertaining to subjects military.

"Oh, my, gentlemen," said Quash with a laugh, as they sat in his well-appointed cabin, "I thought it the most childish ruse ever devised! A merchant brig with a captive pirate schooner in her lee! Who would have thought such a thing possible! Oh, I assure you, I was quite prepared to blow you both out of the water. Yet it proves true! How very delightful. This shall be the talk of the service, though how the Admiralty will handle the matter, I am sure I do not know."

Captain Lockwood

James, whose dark mood had not fully lifted, was not feeling particularly social, even after three glasses of wine. Thus, he did not offer a reply, but instead raised his eyebrows and looked to Clapsaddle. That gentleman explained, "I imagine it likely, Captain Lockwood, that you are familiar with the Royal Navy's practice of officers and their men gaining financial benefit from defeated and captured enemy vessels."

It would have been a miracle if Captain Lockwood had not been familiar with the practice, as every army officer felt it immeasurably unfair that men afloat could grow rich in the king's service, while men afoot risked their lives for less tangible reward.

There ensued a highly technical discussion between Captains Quash and Clapsaddle over the Admiralty regulation on captures by independent vessels bearing men in the king's service, and whether captures might be bought into the service, and if head money would be paid.

Quash pulled out a pencil and paper to scribble some figures. "*Halcón* will certainly be bought into the service. I shall go over later, if I may, and have a look at her, but she looks a fine little vessel. I have known similar vessels bring £1,100 or more. And then there is the matter of head money ... £5 per man aboard *Halcón* at the start of the action ... say £500." Tapping the paper he went on, "£2,100 pounds, gentleman, a tidy sum, but will the Admiralty pay such a sum to such a non-traditional crew? And then, there is the issue of shares! I assume they shall be split according to army regulations " Springing to his feet, Quash went to a bookcase and ran his finger along the spines, finding and pulling out a slim book. "Yes, Mr. Hood's treatise shall guide us. Here it is... if I may, gentlemen... privates: one share, corporals: two, sergeants: five

98

shares. Now, as to officers, I believe you were the only army officer aboard, Captain Lockwood?"

Trying but failing to appear disinterested, James said, "The only army officer, yes, but I think Captain Clapsaddle certainly merits a share equal to my own. And his men fought well, so should certainly collect the same share as my men." That drew an appreciative bow from Clapsaddle.

Quash looked over at Mr. Read with a question on his tongue, but Read waved him off with raised eyebrows. "Oh, pray, sir, make no mistake. There must be no calculation of my interest in this affair. My role was that of a spectator, and a distant one."

Quash nodded, thought for a moment, tapped his pencil on the desk top, then returned to his calculations. He had extensive experience with such exercises, as did every officer of the Royal Navy.

He muttered as he worked, but finally sat up with an air of satisfaction and announced to his attentive guests, "I beg your pardon, gentlemen, as I have made some gross assumptions as to how this will play out, but the way I see it, each share come to roughly £8 11s 2d. Thus, fifty shares should bring each of our two captains... bring over the one... £446 17s 6d."

James found his mood somewhat brightened by the notion of making the equivalent of two year's pay in an afternoon. More than that, each of his men would be rewarded, as well. He would, of course, send most of his fortune home and he would advise his men to do the same, or at least keep the money in their pay balance. Throughout history, every soldier who had ever marched more than a mile from home had been subject to temptation, and Captain Lockwood had some hope that his men might apply their moderate wealth to something more noble than the squalid pursuit of whores and liquor.

Quash poured them all another glass of wine and went on. "A tidy sum, gentlemen; my congratulations. Moreover, it seems likely that you have taken the only worthwhile prize in these waters. The Admiralty has sent the *Dartmouth* to assist in the suppression of piracy, but she was built to fight other frigates, not to chase nimble, shallow-draft pirate craft across uncharted shoals and up jungle rivers. No, this pursuit of pirates is best accomplished by brigs and cutters. I am a devoted officer of the Royal Navy, but even I must admit we do not much care for such vessels, and such duty. We long for noble ship actions in blue water, but what we need here are longboats mucking about in mango swamps." With a sigh he added, "Trafalgar is a very long way off."

Quash and Clapsaddle went on to discuss numerous obscure naval matters as Read dozed in his chair. James nearly did the same, until he heard Quash mention that the *Dartmouth* had passed through the Cobh of Cork on her way to Guyana. Captain Lockwood quickly brightened and asked, "I wonder, Captain Quash, if you might have picked up mail for Guyana?"

*****

Morning in the tropics came bright and sharp, as the *Halcón* slid slowly south and west in the company of the *Dispatch* and the *Dartmouth*. Captain Lockwood sat at the desk in Miguel Otero's cabin, reading Brigid's letter for the third time. He mused over the seventh page for a moment, then called out the cabin door, "Sergeant Maguire, pray have Private McIlhenny report to me. Bring Corporal Shanahan as well, please. Both our NCOs need to witness this."

McIlhenny rushed in a few minutes later, to nervously make his salute. James studied him and wondered if he had ever been that young. Maguire stood behind McIlhenny, obviously curious. McIlhenny stood at stiff attention while Captain Lockwood quietly made entries in the Company Roster Book, waiting until Shanahan hustled in.

Setting his pen aside, the captain stood, folded his arms across his chest, and scowled down at the young private. "Private McIlhenny, I am informed that you were secretly married before we left Enniskillen, in direct violation of Regimental Orders."

Confusion replaced nervousness on McIlhenny's face, and with the guileless honesty of the young he said, "Married, sir? Me? I had hoped, sure, but..."

"Silence, Private! Do not deny it. You were married to this..." James consulted Brigid's letter, "...Margaret Hanahan woman, without permission. I am most disappointed, soldier. You had been shaping up so well. I saw you board this ship like a good 'un, plying your bayonet like a Christian, but now, this."

Captain Lockwood scowled the scowl he reserved for such instances of vicious felony, but then cursed under his breath, sat down, and returned to his paperwork, resignedly adding, "But what is done is done. I shall enter Mrs. McIlhenny into my records, and so, too, write to Regimental Headquarters to have Major McLachlan update the Married Roll there as well."

With some realization McIlhenny whispered, "*Mrs.* McIlhenny? My Mags?"

McIlhenny was reeling, but his captain was not through with him. Lockwood flipped through the roster book and casually added, "Yes, I have received word that Mrs. McIlhenny is doing well, quite

101

settled with her friends and will have a suitable nest established when the baby arrives."

"A baby!" cried McIlhenny, in direct violation of military courtesy.

"Well, of course there is to be a baby. Women have them at regular intervals." That drew a nod from Sergeant Maguire and a restrained grin from Corporal Shanahan.

Such news is an enormous burden to any sensible man, and McIlhenny looked rather a mess, but Captain Lockwood had decided opinions regarding discipline amongst his men. He pointed his pen at the private and firmly said, "As punishment for such reckless conduct, you shall go one week without rum. And I will witness no more of this wild behavior. You must not marry anyone else, do you hear? You are a soldier in the king's service, and I shall stand no further instances of this mad proclivity toward matrimony. This is all quite shocking. You are dismissed, soldier."

Maguire and Shanahan each had a twinkle in his eye, though Private McIlhenny made his salute and retreated with a churning mix of confusion, wonder, and trepidation, although joy soon joined the mix, in increasing doses.

*****

There was another letter in the bag addressed to Captain Lockwood. While he had read Brigid's first with close attention and a surging heart, he read the second with less anxiety and a dose of boyish delight. Captain Thomas Craddock had been his very close friend for many years.

Gibraltar
18 July, 1823

Mark Bois

My dear James,

You may recall that some years ago you and I spent long hours in Señor Rogerio's establishment (I believe there yet remains a collection of empty bottles to commemorate those occasions) musing as to whether Horse Guards could ever find a posting more miserable than this congested pile of rock. Well, brother, word has finally arrived that we are at last to leave this rabbit's warren, for the disease-ridden heat of Guyana.

While none of us here are enamoured of such a relocation, I, for one, am pleased to hear that you will be joining us there. As it will be weeks before we might even consider taking ship, (you would not conceive such confusion and mismanagement) we all speculate that you may reach Guyana before the rest of us.

Oh, before I forget: Julia has written to tell me that her father is adding a new set of rooms onto the house, and so may go to Clonakilty for a month or so while the workmen are about. I am heartily pleased that she and Brigid are friends, and I hope more time together will cement a friendship as sound as our own, if perhaps not quite so sealed in potent potables.

Returning to the topic of Guyana: Dr. Ennis says that once we arrive, we must stay clear of swamps and other stagnant, fetid places, particularly at night, as they are home to foul airs that breed fever. It sounds a charming place.

To further expand on matters medical, I ought to mention that I have been musing on your tendency to ply me with strong drink (it is not fair you know, for you expect me to keep pace with you—a man of my elegant frame cannot compete with someone of your primordial mass) so I have prescribed myself a course of strong brandy, to be administered prophylactically at regular intervals, in an attempt to brace myself for the coming contest. Even as I put this pen to paper, I find myself remarkably medicated and pleased with you, myself, and humanity in general.

If you do indeed, arrive in Georgetown before us, pray reconnoiter (it is a military term, sir, with which you are doubtless unfamiliar: it means to survey, or to scout) the place and find us a suitable spot where we might sip a beverage. I do so look forward to seeing you again, brother.

With unceasing regards, I remain your most devoted friend,
Thomas Craddock

*****

A gray, windless day, as a steady rain fell over Georgetown—an elderly slave named Scipio Africanus sat on a stool in the steeple of St. Andrew's Kirk with a glass to his eye, as he had done seven days a week for the past twelve years, no matter the weather. He was an old man now—had lost a leg in a wagon accident—and the only use Master Salmon had for him was to watch the sea for incoming ships; Master Salmon liked to know before anyone else in town.

After so many years of study, Scipio knew the sea, although he had not been on it since he had been carried across from Africa as a terrified child. In such still weather he knew he could risk a nap, at least until the tide came in at late afternoon. When he awoke in the afternoon, he caught sight of three ships coming in slowly through the rain, borne by what little wind they could catch and the incoming tide. He studied them closely as they coasted in: a merchant brig, a lean schooner, and a Royal Navy frigate. The schooner was not well handled—hers was likely a small prize crew. Their order of sailing was what puzzled him. Since the brig led them in, the schooner was her prize, not the frigate's. There was a story behind that, he wagered.

The frigate and the merchant ship hove to and anchored at the mouth of the Demerara, though the lean schooner continued well upstream and only anchored after she came abreast of Government House. The frigate and the merchantman were not planning on staying long, but the schooner was there to stay.

Scipio called down the echoing steeple until another elderly slave named Belle came in sight far below and called up, "What you want up there, you old fool? It ain't time for your supper yet." They spoke the involved slave patois, a mix of English, Dutch and words from nearly every language spoken on the west coast of Africa.

"I'm doing what I'm told, ain't I? Fool of a woman, you go now and tell Old John to tell Master Salmon that three ships are coming into port. A brig, a schooner, and a great fine frigate. Say it back to me, so I know you got it right."

"I got it, I got it. A brig, a schooner, and a frigate. I ain't no fool."

"In that order, right?"

"All right, all right," she muttered as she hustled away, while far up in the tower Scipio mused over how a little merchant brig had outdone a frigate for such a prize—the world turned upside down—a notion that pleased him. Scipio knew something that Mr. Salmon did not, something that none of the white men knew. Slaves on many of the plantations were organizing, and there was a rising coming, just you wait and see. Just you wait and see.

*****

105

When Clapsaddle informed the soldiers that Georgetown was just a day or two over the horizon, there was a great deal of activity aboard the *Halcón* as Captain Lockwood and his men prepared for a return to life ashore.

The soldiers had heard that the government might buy the *Halcón*, and did what they could, in their lubberly way, to priddy her up, going so far as to holystone the massive bloodstains from her deck.

The captain also ordered that the broken-head fair be held before they reached shore: the effects of the men killed in action were to be auctioned off. The proceeds would be added to the pay due the dead men and eventually forwarded to their distant families, though those few shillings were subject to the extortionate percentage due the regimental agent.

Deep in the hold, however, the enchanting Caribbean breezes were masked by the stagnant heat and stink of the bilge and the misery of the shackled prisoners. In the sputtering lantern light, Privates Hogan and McIlhenny were standing the guard, displeased at having to miss even a moment on deck with their mates, searching the horizon for the sight of land with something resembling lust.

McIlhenny was no friend to Hogan, the man who had been flogged as a thief. But as the young man was of a talkative nature, he told Hogan of his meeting with the captain. "It does puzzle me," said McIlhenny in his Ulster Irish, "how all this talk of marriage came about, as I'm sure I've never stood before a priest with any woman, let alone my dear love."

Private Hogan replied, "Well, boy, might I suggest that, while you might not have been married by a priest, perhaps you and this girl sometimes *conducted* yourselves as husband and wife?"

McIlehenny's young face looked puzzled, so Hogan went on, "Come, now have you lain across her?" Then, with a leer, he added, "How was she, now? How was she?"

McIlhenny blushed, grinned, and muttered, "Oh, well, it was her lying across me, at first, you know, until I got the hang of things, like."

"A wench with spirit!" cried Hogan. "No man can ask more than that. And now the captain, even if he is an unforgiving prick to me, has the decency to get you and your missus in the books, all neat and legal. A bastard child's life is a misery, sure."

From the darkness beyond the lantern light a voice growled, also in Irish, "It is a lucky man who has a child."

Astonished, Hogan lifted the lantern high to discover the owner of the voice. In the gloom they saw Miguel Otero sit up, his chains shifting heavily. He went on in Irish, his voice a pained rasp. "I have a daughter of my own; may God bless her as much as He has cursed me."

The two soldiers stood wide-eyed for a moment until Hogan gathered himself and scoffed, "Who are you to be speaking to us in God's own Irish?"

While his English was thickened with a Spanish accent, Otero's Irish was that of a man who had just stepped out of Glendalough. "Was I not born Michael O'Toole in the mountains of the County Wicklow, as good an Irishman as ever wore the green?"

"You were not."

"I was."

"But... you turned Spaniard!"

Otero coughed hard, wiped a hand across his mouth and growled, "I had to, didn't I?"

107

Kerry McIlhenny shook his head in wonder and muttered, "This is the oddest day I'm likely to see in all my life, sure."

Hogan asked, "What in Christ's name brought you here, then, man, a pirate and renowned fiend?"

Otero held up a filthy hand as if to take a vow. "You must swear, brothers, not to divulge what I shall tell you. While my life as a buccaneer is forfeit, I will not have my family in Ireland brought to peril should the Castle know of my life as a rebel, and a patriot. I've been lying here in chains for these long days, listening, waiting, and trying to decide which of my countrymen I might confide in. I held my tongue until you two noble spirits were on duty, and at last my chance has come! But you must swear to keep my secret!"

Otero stared at the two redcoats. "Swear it!"

Otero was a masterful speaker, a natural leader. Hogan and McIlhenny exchanged a quick nod, then turning to Otero, they slowly held up their right hands and said, "I so swear."

Otero told the story in a harsh whisper as his remaining men lay by him in chains, the two soldiers mesmerized.

"In 1798, at seventeen years of age, I left my dear family, my parents and four sisters, to join the United Irishmen in rebellion against the unholy tyrant King George." Otero spoke low, his voice seductive. "With only a pike on my shoulder I joined Captain Holt's company. We marched far and long, didn't we, as disciplined as any army that ever strode the earth. No rape, no murder, no robbery of any English we captured. The purity of the Cause guided us, even though we were hungry, soaked, and dirty as pigs. And when we finally arraigned ourselves for glorious battle on Vinegar Hill, it was death or victory for us, boys, death or glory."

Hogan and McIlhenny, who had themselves faced death only days before while battling Otero and his pack of cutthroats, were now glued to Otero's every word.

Otero slowly nodded, cementing his hold over them and then went on, "Well, boys, it was both. Death in plenty, I can tell you, but Christ, the glory! I myself slew a dozen redcoats, but they were too many, and did they not carry the finest weapons that filthy money could buy?"

Hogan nodded and said softly, "My own cousins, the brothers McAffrey, fought in the '98, brave lads both, but dead."

"God bless them!" said Otero with admiration and grief in his voice. "But glorious death was not my fate. No, our company was scattered. Some escaped, while some were captured. But our wounded were murdered where they lay, and many of the other prisoners were murdered as well, but as I was so young, the magistrate took pity on me, and I was given a pardon. I was nearly free! But a foul redcoat officer cried that I might not go, and I was taken up again and given only the choice of death or a red coat of my own."

"They made you a soldier!" gasped McIlhenny. "Like me and Hogan here?"

"They beat and starved me until I signed their papers, then with a few other patriots they threw me into the hold of a scow and carried me off to Barbados, no more than a slave, but one in a red coat. But I showed them, didn't I just? As soon as we patriots had muskets in our hands we killed our officer and broke away into the hills, living as free men once again, even if they called us bandits."

"Jesus! You killed an officer!" cried McIlhenny, shocked, though Hogan looked at Otero with open admiration.

109

"Aye!" hissed Otero, this O'Toole, with fierce glee. "What a grand life we led, free men taking what we wanted, living off the fatted calf! But after a while things got too hot even for us, so we stole a boat and set out for a new life at sea. With my new life, I took the name Otero, so that my family home would not be persecuted in revenge. Ah, what adventure and glory, boys! Kings of the sea, and me working my way to my own ship! Living high and free, while kings and their lackeys pissed themselves just thinking of me."

Hogan grinned and muttered, "Kings of the sea."

McIlhenny, not convinced, said, "But we beat you fair and square, didn't we? And now your adventure and glory is over, and the king's rope as your reward."

"Ah, now," said Otero conspiratorially, "that's why I'm confiding in you lads. My adventure need not be over. Spread the word amongst your brothers, those you think we might trust, good patriots, and we'll take to the sea! We could take the ship! And then we sail off, brothers, free Irishman!"

"Christ and His nails!" whispered McIlhenny in shock, but Hogan grinned and nodded in tentative agreement.

"Think of it, boys," went on Otero, plying Hogan now. "The Isla de Margarita! Rum, gold, and women!" Seeing that struck a note with Hogan, he added, "Oh, yes, brother, the women! Beautiful, plentiful, and horny as goats!" With a grim smile he said, "Join me."

McIlhenny quickly said, "I must tell the captain, sure! This is treason!"

But Hogan stuck a finger in McIlehenny's face and hissed, "We took a vow, damn you, boy! Remember that, a solemn vow, with a promise of hell if you break it!"

The boy was quickly cowed, his face anguished. Hogan turned to Otero and said, "I shall tell a few others. No promises, now, but there may be a few patriots in the ranks."

Otero nodded and grinned. "We are brothers, then. But we must hurry! Land is near—I feel it. For liberty, and freedom, we must hurry!"

Chapter Nine

Cissy Lockwood lay next to her old dog on the kitchen's slate floor. Sergeant had been ill for some time, harsh coughing racking his frail old frame. Cissy and Doolan hoped that he might hold out until Brigid returned home, but he was very weak.

Cissy whispered assurances to the dog she had known since she was a very little girl. Corporal was typically jealous of any attention paid his sire, but on that day he sat quietly behind Cissy, perhaps less a puppy than he had been that morning, allowing Sergeant his moment.

Doolan saw them there and found it necessary to stalk out to the back garden to inspect the lazy beds, pulling weeds and quickly wiping his eyes with the back of his hand, knowing the day was coming soon, muttering, "Ah, that feckin' dog..."

*****

Cissy had her shawl draped over her head in the traditional manner, and Doolan had his musket over his shoulder. They set out that cool misty morning for the patchwork of small fields and meager cabins that made up Cloghgriffin Township. When Cissy questioned his need to bring his musket, Doolan replied, "Half loads of power with a handful of shot, *a grah*, is a sure cure for rats. And mark my words, rats there will be aplenty, vacant buildings in farm country."

It is worth noting that a Catholic civilian carrying a loaded firearm in broad daylight would typically prompt the leading citizens of the town to fear rebellion and murder, with shrill calls for the militia. Diarmuid Doolan was at least nominally a Catholic, though only by the most generous application of the term, and while he still wore his red coat and Inniskilling regimental shako, he had been discharged from His Majesty's service two years before. But across town, Doolan was known as the Lockwoods' man, his status as a soldier was taken at face value, and as such he was allowed outrageous freedoms, freedoms which he believed were only his due after twenty-two years' service.

It was, perhaps, two miles from Fáibhile Cottage to Cloghgriffin Township, but it was a great shift in fortune. The hills east of town were covered with clusters of cabins, people who subsisted on potatoes and milk in good years and bordered on starvation in lean. Some of the cabins were little more than holes in the ground, whose impoverished residents tended their tiny plots and scarcely noted Cissy and Doolan passing. Other cabins were more substantial and carried an air of hope, and Doonasleen had once worn such an air. But now those six homes stood empty, three with their roofs pulled down, populated only by one very old man, who sat outside, smoking his pipe and eyeing Cissy and Doolan as they approached.

As they drew near, the old man pointed the stem of his pipe at the young woman and shrilly said in Irish, "I am Gearoid O'Tuathaigh, the caretaker of this place. You are a daughter of

113

Brigid O'Brian, the girl Cissy grown into the woman Brigit ní Lockwood, and your coming was foretold to me."

"I am she. This is my dear friend, Diarmuid Doolan. You stand guard here, grandfather? What misfortune caused these homes to stand empty as the Saxon king's soul? What fate befell the good people who once lived here?"

"The Devlins and their like, you wonder? Off to Kerry they are, and may I never see their like again."

"Gearoid O'Tuathaigh, did they deserve such a fate?"

"Oh, they were foolish people, sure. They borrowed twelve pounds fifteen, a fortune of money, from the gombeen man, Feardorcha Hurley by name, getting some wild ideas in their heads to give up their potatoes to raise a great herd of pigs! For money! Not one or two in each house, where they might be tended proper, like decent Christians, but a great herd of the snorting beasts. I've never seen the like."

Diarmuid Doolan sniffed in disdain and wandered off to inspect the empty buildings. O'Tuathaigh returned to his pipe, requiring Cissy to ask, "What happened, next, please, sir? Did the pigs not prosper?"

O'Tuathaigh whipped the pipe from his mouth and cried, "Prosper, young woman, prosper? No, they did not. They lived long enough to eat everything the Devlins owned, including every seed potato, and then they died. The pigs, mind you, not the Devlins, though the Devlins might just as well have done so, and good riddance. The pigs died, and so the loan to Feardorcha Hurley went unpaid, and so, too, did their rent to Mr. Kennedy go unpaid. That, of course, meant that Mr. Kennedy could not pay Mr. Murray, who in turn, could not pay Colonel Simon. A terrible mess, sure, all due to a Devlin fascination with pigs. Pigs!"

After a restorative pull on his pipe, the old man went on. "Now, Mr. Murray was content with them being thrown off the place, but Feardorcha Hurley, who is a vengeful fellow when crossed, was after having his toughs break every Devlin skull they could lay hands on."

O'Tuathaigh attempted a smoke ring, failed, and resumed his discourse. "The Devlins did not care to have their skulls cracked, and so took off one night, leaving two cows. Two! Well, the Hurleys swept over here the next morning and made off with the cows, I can tell you. And then the Devlins' neighbors, likely the Callahans, the seditious bastards, threatened to burn the place, in protest of rents and such like, so Mr. Kennedy has posted me here to mind things."

From inside the nearest house came the crack of Doolan's musket, his prediction of rats fulfilled. O'Tuathaigh jumped at the shot, allowing Cissy a chance to speak. "Your vigil is soon to be relieved, grandfather. Hardworking, honest folk, people of my father's own regiment, are coming to live here and make these homes whole again."

The musket barked again, and Cissy rolled her eyes at Doolan's enthusiasm.

O'Tuathaigh stood, sniffed, and pointed the stem of his pipe out at the small plots around the cabins, low stone walls marking plots of an acre, some much less. "You are no farmer, young woman, so I shall tell you that this ground is worthless, fit only for a Saxon's grave. Poor, thin stuff, you might tend it like your own child and yet it would yield only rocks and heartache. So, your army people can come up here and have a roof over their heads, but will they thrive here? No, young woman, they will not."

*****

Doolan's quarters were a small room just off the kitchen of Fáibhile Cottage, and, while they were nothing elaborate, he was as comfortable there as anywhere he had ever laid his head. Before dawn, he quietly slipped into the kitchen to find Corporal awake, lying close beside Sergeant, as the old dog lay half-conscious, panting and coughing in the most pitiable manner.

The old soldier awkwardly knelt beside the dogs, speaking softly; there is little in this world that a dog understands and appreciates more than being told that he is good. After a few moments Doolan made up his mind, and went to fetch his coat and shako. He then slung his musket over his shoulder, gave Corporal an affectionate thump, told him to stay, then bent over Sergeant to gently help the old dog to stand.

Doolan was not surprised to hear Cissy come downstairs, buttoning up her coat as she came into the kitchen.

With a strain in his voice, Doolan said, "I was just taking old Sergeant out for a stroll, *a cuisle*."

"I shall come along, as well, if I may." Then giving Corporal a scratch behind the ear, she added, "I think Corporal will forgive us, just this once, if we leave him at home. This morning it shall be just we three old friends." Sergeant gave one thump of his tail.

They walked out to the kitchen garden, but Sergeant could go no further. He was in such pain that Doolan had to carry him, the dog so thin, and though Sergeant sometimes whined in pain, he once raised his head enough to lick Doolan's face, and the old man wept as he walked out into the fields above the cottage. Cissy followed in his wake, her head down, trying not to let Sergeant see the shovel she carried.

They walked far into the hills as the first light of dawn grayed the sky. On a distant hill there was an ancient *cillin*, a rough graveyard for unbaptized children, a place that rang more holy than the grandest churchyard.

When the time came, Cissy wandered slowly away and buried her face in her hands, trying not to cry, but failing. The crack of the gunshot seemed inordinately loud. They would not bury Sergeant too close to the babies, but close enough that he could keep an eye on them—he had always loved children.

*****

Brigid O'Brian Lockwood had lived in Clonakilty for most of her life, but she had never before approached her home by sea. She had been at sea before, of course, the most memorable occasion being the family's voyage to Marseilles, to see Mary, their oldest daughter, be married. But on that voyage she had come and gone through the Cobh of Cork, the only true deep-water port in the south of Ireland.

Having grown up in Clonakilty, Brigid was well aware of their harbour's shortcomings. A shifting bar lay across the harbour mouth, while Inchydoney Island and innumerable shallows made the harbour itself a nightmare for any but local seamen. In short, no rational sailing master approaching Clonakilty Harbour would attempt to enter without the benefit of a local pilot. Neither would any pilot attempt to guide a ship of even moderate draft into the harbour at any but high tide.

When a pilot was rowed out to the *Warranted Profit* at dawn, he invited himself to breakfast, as he assured the master that the heavy brig could not dare the bar before the very peak of the tide. The *Profit* was thus required to linger beyond Ring Head until late morning, when the sunny morning saw that elegant ship gliding over the shifting sands into the harbour beyond. Even then, the *Profit* did not attempt to round Inchydoney Island to reach Clonakilty proper. The town sat at the foot of the harbour, two miles away at the end of the narrow channel that wound through the shifting shallows. Instead, the *Profit* followed the practice common to larger ships by anchoring at Ring, where only a sordid collection of animal pens, warehouses, and seedy shebeens dotted the shore.

On the deck of the *Profit* the army families eyed the distant town, many with distrust or skepticism in their eyes. Brigid did her best to cheer them, pointing out landmarks with affectionate familiarity. She had been away from home for three months, and she went quiet with misty eyes when she saw McCurtain's Hill in the distance above the town, where Fáibhile Cottage and years of memories patiently awaited her return.

A ship required a quayside berth only if shifting heavy cargo. As their place in society rendered the army wives and children a rather lean group, the *Profit* could off-load while anchored a half-cable offshore, employing her launch to shuttle the families to the foot of Ring's north quay. Brigid was in the bow of the first boat, scanning the people on the shore, searching for Cissy. They soon caught sight of each other, happily waving with broad smiles. When the launch gently bumped up against the quay, Brigid shot out of the boat to run up the steps. There was little pretense of lady-like decorum when she and Cissy ran to embrace each other gleefully.

There followed moderate chaos on the Ring Harbour quay. The two Lockwood ladies were well known in town, and well regarded, but when the battalion wives gathered on the quay the longshoremen bombarded them with hoots and catcalls. Those ladies were not to be intimidated and returned the hazing with an edge acquired through long practice. The longshoremen's lewd suggestions soon ripened into offers, and Brigid had to rush over to keep Mary Pat O'Connor from tearing into them. To add to the confusion, Mrs. McAuliffe slipped while climbing from the launch and dropped her meager baggage into the sea. While it was soon fished out by the *Profit's* coxswain, the sodden bundle was all she owned in the world, and she stood on the quay pitifully weeping.

Several of the wives voiced harsh questions about where they were to go next, and why they had come to such a foreign place. Some of the regimental children, disoriented and upset, commenced to cry, and when it then began to rain Brigid was quite prepared to lose her mind. The families were confused, frustrated and on the verge of behaving very badly, indeed.

Brigid Lockwood, however, was fortunate in her choice of daughter, as Cissy stepped up to give instruction in a decided manner. At first, the wives did not know what to make of that beautiful young woman and, though she spoke Irish, Cissy had an even stronger Munster accent than her mother. That was soon forgiven, as the young woman gained credibility with even the most skeptical of the wives when two of Mr. O'Leary's farm carts came trundling down to meet them. The carts carried a cask of sweet cider, a basket of apples, a wheel of Munster cheese, and two baskets of soda bread, baked by Cissy Lockwood and Private Diarmuid Doolan.

That same Diarmuid Doolan sat next to the driver of the first cart, again with his musket across his lap, as if the private expected swarms of howling miscreants to surge up from the ditch to murder all involved. Those miscreants did not appear, to the evident disappointment of Private Doolan, and so the old soldier had to set his musket aside and content himself with distributing the victuals to the families. He was notably tender in dealing with the younger children, though he would have denied it with his dying breath.

Doolan was a familiar sight to the Ring men as a devotee of the Lurking Banshee shebeen, and a man who could be relied upon to stand his round. So, when he genially told the longshoremen to shut the fuck up, they largely did so. That trick gave the ladies a positive impression of the old redcoat, beyond their initial acceptance of him as a soldier, one of their own regiment, and thus a familiar commodity.

A full belly is the antithesis to ill feeling and disorder. Brigid, Cissy, Doolan, and Eileen Goodwin worked to get everyone ready for the march to Cloghgriffin Township and their new home. Brigid was pleased to see that Doolan did not find it necessary to fix his bayonet when Cissy was confronted by the irate Mrs. McGunn, over who would ride and who would walk. The farm carts were soon loaded, with better humour and some instances of sisterhood, with the regimental children and the less mobile wives. Margaret Hanahan, soon to be re-christened Mrs. Margaret McIlhenny, was now obviously pregnant and many of the wives made her the object of some kindness. She was given pride of place in one cart—Mrs. McGunn be damned.

*****

The Ross Diocese of the Church of Ireland sponsored a Committee for Beneficent Works. The committee had met once a quarter at Reverend Butler's home, but at the suggestion—very nearly the insistence—of its newest member, the committee now met at Clonakilty's Customs House. That new member, Reverend Cyril Babcock, thought the atmosphere of the Customs House lent a greater sense of fiscal responsibility, rather than an air of undue sentimentality.

The committee was made up of leading members of the community, all Protestant gentlemen. Prominent ladies of the community were tasked with visiting those who applied for aid, determining their qualifications and offering advice on how best to economize.

Reverend Butler, who still chaired the committee despite the change in venue, called the eight gentlemen to order. There followed a recitation of the minutes by Mr. Beemish, the tall, jolly secretary, followed by a summary of the financial situation, the very constrained financial situation, by the treasurer, the bovine Mr. Boffut.

Reverend Butler, a large, raven-haired, subtly commanding presence, then said, "Now, gentlemen, to the current business. The committee has been forwarded a petition by our esteemed neighbor, Mrs. Lockwood, who pleas the committee to entertain—"

Babcock interrupted with a toss of his hand. "If I may beg the floor, please, gentlemen, I claim some particular knowledge of the matter. In truth, my uncle, the honourable Colonel Simon, has been imposed upon by the ladies Lockwood and a group—I shall not call them a pack—of penniless vagabonds, without plan or sustenance, brought all the way from Ulster—*Ulster*, mind you—so that the ladies Lockwood might impose upon our generosity, and deposit these people upon my uncle's property, a township legally and ethically cleared of its previous tenants, Papists who defaulted upon their lease. This property has been sitting vacant for months due to the deliberate defiance of the peasantry."

Boffut leaned in and said, "You are new to Ireland, I believe, Reverend Babcock, so I might mention that this deliberate defiance by the peasantry is a growing, and concerning, trend. It started in Limerick with that Captain Rock nonsense, and is now spread down here to Cork. Once a place is cleared of defaulting tenants, the peasants band together so that no one will resume the lease. The Whiteboys post notices threatening death if anyone does so. Even if you lower the rent to nothing, no one will touch the place. It is a deliberate effort to strip the landowner of his rents and rights."

Babcock, thrilled to find an ally, ranted shrilly on. "Praise God for such men as you, sir! I still pray that my uncle's property might be turned by honest Christian labour to profit, but it stands empty, a God-given asset which now seems to be corrupted into a way-station for slothful indigents. These people are the worst kind of scoundrels, the consorts of common soldiers, whose morality is still very much in question. As a minister of the Church and a man of God, I move we dispense with the reading of this petition and apply to the magistrates that these Papist beggars be directed to the Cork Workhouse without delay." Babcock spoke with a malice that was not typical amongst that staid body, but he had appealed to the worst aspect of their natures, and in the face of such temptation, several of them fell.

"Ulster!" cried Mr. Boffut. "Why on earth are they to be brought here?"

"Are common soldiers indeed allowed to marry?" asked Mr. Jeter with disdain. "I did not believe government would allow such things. And what type of woman would marry such fellows? And we are now to see to their every whim? Humpf!"

That comment finally garnered the attention of a Mr. Jackson, who had been distracted by the sight of an attractive young woman in the street below. That gentleman had once served as an ensign in the 23rd Light Dragoons and still held a captaincy in the West Cork yeomanry. He was also a devoted drunkard and so spoke with some bluntness. "Of course soldiers marry, sir! I have never heard such nonsense. Are they not flesh and blood?"

Cowed, Jeter only muttered, "I was given to understand they had special houses…"

There followed a long, foolish, and futile discussion in which Reverend Butler and Mr. Jackson spoke with some notion of caring and understanding, while the other gentlemen did not. It concluded with only a motion that four members of the committee would, at some time, be named to form a sub-committee to determine the value of Mrs. Lockwood's petition, and only then whether it might one day be recommended to the full body.

*****

Father Joseph McGlynn eyed the letter that Brigid ní Brian had sent from Ulster. He preferred to address her in the old Gaelic manner, in acknowledging her father's name rather than her husband's, if for no reason other than the fact that McGlynn loathed James Lockwood and all he represented. He had known Brigid since she was a girl, and it was natural that, as he was her parish priest, she should come to him for advice regarding the homeless families.

In most parishes the priest would have been prompted to help, but McGlynn was not the typical priest. His was a poor parish, and while he had slowly amassed a hundred pounds or more, he had other plans for it. A Glandore smuggler had been engaged to deliver two crates of French muskets. It was the good father's belief that the struggle for liberty was a greater gift to the poor than the temporary surcease of want.

Still, he ran a number of scenarios through his head, musing how he might turn the situation to his advantage. Even without any financial contribution, he would go to see these homeless waifs, to offer blessings and encouragement. If he was to gain control of them, he would need to keep the Little Sisters of Mercy at bay—those artful witches crossed him at every opportunity.

He would also attempt to cull potential recruits to the Cause from among the new arrivals. And better still, being amongst the families would give him a chance to speak with Cissy Lockwood; he was not through with that girl. She had allies in John Cashman and that old soldier, but with just the right snare, he would pull all three of them into his service. He might once have said 'God's service,' but his allegiance to God had deserted him some years before.

*****

Thaddeus O'Malley owned a wallpaper shop in Clonakilty, but he also served as the pastor of the town's small Methodist congregation. The new, very untraditional Methodist faith was eyed with suspicion by both the Catholics and the Anglicans. O'Malley was thus flattered when a letter came from Mrs. Lockwood, addressing both the pastor and his congregation in a respectful tone, asking if they might provide any support or advice for the army families coming to town.

The town's few Methodists were largely middle-class people with limited means, but O'Malley thought he would speak with one of his congregants. John Callaghan, a retired linen merchant, built furniture for donation to the poor. If nothing else, the Methodists would see that the families had beds in which to sleep.

*****

The Society of Friends was known throughout Ireland for good works, but they were no fools. They invested generously, and attempted to contribute not just in subsistence, but, when possible, also in projects where people might find ways to support themselves.

The Friends had no chapter in Clonakilty, but one member of the Cork chapter, a Mr. Mason, received a letter of inquiry from Reverend Butler. Mr. Mason resolved to present the matter at the next meeting of his chapter, but he thought of one member of the Dublin committee, a Mr. Brown, who had business interests in Clonakilty. The linen industry was changing and Mr. Brown had expressed some progressive notions as to how capital and labour might best be managed.

*****

At the far end of Clonakilty's Western Road, the Little Sisters of Mercy kept their house. It was a simple dwelling where the ten nuns devoted themselves to the care of the poor and the sick. Sister Theresa, a daughter of one of the last prominent Catholic families, had founded the house and was thus entitled to dictate the home's direction. But she was at heart a republican, and put all major decisions to a vote of all the sisters.

"My sisters," said Sister Theresa to the assembled nuns, "we are once again tested by God. A decision, an opportunity, is before us. We have all had opportunity to read Miss Lockwood's well-crafted letter and, while she and Private Doolan have long been supporters of this house, we need to rationally consider her appeal. So, I put it to you, my sisters in Christ: our resources are already near an end. Dare we extend ourselves to these military families?"

Sister Margaret was the niece of John Cashman, and like the rest of her family she took a subtle pride in his ability to tweak government's nose, though she would not have been so pleased had she known the violence of his earlier days. She needed no convincing, and none of her sisters were surprised when she heartily extended her hand in favour.

Captain Lockwood

Sister Theresa nodded, and then added, "In all fairness, I must tell you that a number of Protestant gentleman are very opposed to Mrs. Lockwood's project and we are all aware of the power of such men." With a hint of anger and distaste, she went on, "Further, Father McGlynn has spoken to me, and, in no uncertain terms, he has expressed his desire that he alone should act as the Church's ambassador to the poor souls who will be deposited upon Cloghgriffin Township. We have defied him in the past, but he warns of dire consequences if we reach out to these army families."

With some trepidation, but more resolution, the hands of all ten women went up.

Chapter Ten

Aboard HMS *Dartmouth* a grizzled old warrant officer chanted, "If I wasn't a gunner I wouldn't be *here*." With the last word he fired one of his twelve-pounders, the gun firing blank to leeward. Chanting and walking slowly along the row of guns, he eventually fired seventeen times, a steadily paced salute, the number required to salute a governor.

The battery at the mouth of the Demerara replied with the seven guns necessary to salute the *Dartmouth* and a Royal Navy ship's captain. Standing on *Halcón's* deck, James realized that Georgetown was not expecting Mr. Read. They ought to have fired nine guns for a political agent of the Colonial Office.

Dartmouth's launch carried Quash over to pick up Clapsaddle and Read. Clapsaddle had changed his mind and now planned to go ashore, as he was determined to see some reward for himself and his crew for the capture of the *Halcón*. The launch then began the long row against the Demerara current to gather Captain Lockwood.

Climbing down into the boat, James saw they had all dressed for the occasion. Read was resplendent in a bottle green coat that bore several orders, while Clapsaddle, technically a civilian, wore a fine blue coat reminiscent of a naval uniform. Quash was a statement in blue and gold, wearing his hat fore and aft in the modern style, and as a post captain of seniority he wore an epaulette on each shoulder.

James wore his best uniform, glad that the rats aboard *Dispatch* had not been at it. He quickly came to realize that the heavy red wool coat, the finest work of Doyle's of Dublin, was not intended for the heat and humidity of Guyana, especially on a mid-August evening. He suffered silently, his sword across his lap, studying Georgetown as the *Dartmouth's* launch carried them in.

The coast was low, flat and sullen. The town, a collection of small buildings surrounding a few grander structures, clung to the east bank of the Demerara River. Along the riverbank every building was built on stilts, the grander structures further inland protected by drainage canals and low dikes. On either shore, James saw a small battery, though there were no true fortifications. Only a low sea wall faced the Caribbean, behind which stood open ground and a number of low, long buildings. James Lockwood recognized a parade ground and barracks when he saw them.

Battered wooden quays reached out from the shore. The boat's coxswain searched the shore until he spotted a group of redcoats gathered at the foot of one of the quays. After exchanging a nod with Quash he muttered, "Give way," and the crew of the launch laid into their oars. The boat slid across the stagnant waters of the Demerara until the coxswain said, "Rowed of all." The boat's crew skillfully tossed their oars, the launch gently kissed the dock, and James had the feeling that a very different chapter of his life was coming, welcome or not.

As dictated by tradition, the military men were the first to climb the wooden steps up to where the redcoats were waiting. In the complex hierarchies of military entitlement, a senior captain of the Royal Navy was the equal of an army colonel, so Quash led the way, followed by James. Read, now unaccustomed to a surface underfoot that did not heave and roll, leaned on Captain Clapsaddle's arm as he came slowly up the steps.

They were met by ten enlisted men and one ensign, all of the 21st Foot, the Royal Scots Fusiliers, wearing the blue facings befitting a royal regiment. James had been a soldier for a very long time, and was aware of the subtleties of a military salute. The enlisted men were not as clean as they might have been, which hinted at inattentive officers, but the soldiers' salute was well executed, which suggested NCOs who knew their trade. The ensign, who wore an exceptionally fine uniform, made an amateurish wave with his expensive, non-regulation sabre.

Formal introductions followed. The ensign did not address the party with the deference typically shown by, and expected of, very junior officers. His name was Boston, and he showed little interest in the sailors or Mr. Read, but was obviously curious about Captain Lockwood.

"Gentlemen," said Boston, looking only at Lockwood, "I have been dispatched to guide you to Camp House, where you will meet with Governor McAllistair himself! Lieutenant Colonel Leslie and Major Addis of my regiment will join us there."

The walk to their meeting was short, but instructive. James tried not to be obvious about it, but he took careful note of his surroundings. The only white faces belonged to their party. There were dozens of black men and women in the streets, but every one was a slave except their driver. Some wore chains, driven like cattle, the very air soaked with oppression and despair. The relentless heat, the humidity and the brooding skies were mirrored in the joyless demeanor of the colony's inhabitants.

As they walked, James said, "Ensign Boston, I had heard of disaffection amongst the slaves of the colony. The people, though, seem quite... subdued."

Boston grinned a boy's grin and said, "Oh, the governor puts up with no nonsense, sir, and most of the plantation owners have an admirable sense of discipline. We are no strangers to the lash here, and things are run in a proper manner, sir, most proper indeed, though there are a few soft hearts who complain. A couple Methody ministers have been preaching disaffection amongst the blacks. There is one fellow, a Mr. Jones, who is accused of teaching the blacks that all men are equal in God's sight. Can you imagine!" A few more steps, and with a wave of his arm, Boston said, "Here we are, sirs."

In an instant the four newcomers were shown from squalor to luxury. The governor's residence, a rambling building with broad galleries, was built almost on the beach. The interior of the Camp House was beyond elegant. The governor's offices were a study in polished mahogany and plush carpets, and beautiful, silent slave women came around and served an excellent Madeira. Lieutenant Colonel Leslie and Major Addis came in—polite, curious, elegantly uniformed—and, as the introductions were made, James deemed them to be at least mildly intoxicated.

After a glass or two, the party was shown into the inner office. Governor McAllistair rose to greet the four newcomers, while Leslie and Addis took station behind the governor's chair, the picture of deference. The formal introductions required several minutes, highlighted by Mr. Read stepping forward to present his credentials.

His Majesty's governors were typically polished aristocrats, but McAllistair was a planter, one who spoke with the rough manners of a commoner, and one accustomed to having his way. He was balding, heavy, and obviously flustered by Read's unanticipated arrival. He took his time lighting a cigar and James saw his hands quake just a bit, but whether in fear or anger, James could not tell.

"So, Mr. Read," said McAllistair politely, as he returned to his seat, "as I am to be favored by the presence of an official of the Colonial Office, might I ask the nature of your visit to our fair colony?"

"My instructions, Your Excellency, require me to observe, advise and report."

McAllistair's tone turned with remarkable rapidity. "What you will *observe*, sir, is a colony on the verge of open and bloody rebellion. What you will *advise*, sir, is how I am to maintain order in this colony with one battalion of five hundred men in the face of seventy thousand mutinous slaves. What you shall *report*, sir, is a recommendation, nay, a demand, for a permanent garrison of five thousand troops."

Read returned only a restrained, polite, noncommittal nod.

McAllistair then pointed his cigar at Captain Lockwood and said, "Well, sir, I had been assured of a veteran battalion to bolster this colony's defenses against murder and rapine, and yet Colonel Leslie presents me with your returns, and you plead only a hundred men, every one as green as grass? Why is that, sir? Pray, explain yourself, if you can."

Captain Lockwood paused for a breath, exhaled slowly and said, "This draft was diverted to Guyana by the War Office, Your

Excellency, in light of the urgency of your request for reinforcement. The balance of my battalion, my *veteran* battalion, follows from Gibraltar with the greatest haste."

Major Addis scoffed and muttered, "A battalion of *Irishmen*, for Christ's sake."

James quickly turned to Addis. "Yes, Irishmen, sir, men who were key to holding the center of Wellington's line at Waterloo."

Addis flared and said, "After you face a mob of raging blacks you will think the Frenchmen soft fare, *Captain* Lockwood."

In a flash of temper McAllistair growled, "Collect yourself, gentlemen."

"Beg pardon, Your Excellency," said Addis.

Lockwood nodded absently, straightened his coat, and set down his glass. He did not wish to let the wine run off with him. Turning back to McAllistair, he said, "I might mention, Your Excellency, that those hundred new soldiers, in company with the esteemed Captain Clapsaddle and his crew,"—he nodded toward that gentleman, who returned an appreciative smile—"have captured a pirate sloop which had plucked six ships off the coast of this colony in just the past two months."

That brought a smile to McAllistair's fleshy face. He said, "Oh, yes, you remind me. You will please have Otero brought ashore, and I shall have him hanged immediately."

Several of the men in the room look startled, but they left it for Lockwood to say, "I, of all men, wish to see Otero hang, but surely you mean to try him first, Your Excellency?"

"Jurisprudence is not typically the concern of infantry captains."

"Begging Your Excellency's pardon, but justice, at least its formalities, is the concern of any Englishman."

McAllistair, astonished, surveyed the four men sitting before him with wide eyes. Lockwood was composed and immovable. Clapsaddle deliberately folded his arms across his chest. Read said nothing, but was obviously paying very close attention. As Quash was not in obvious opposition, McAllistair looked to him and said, "Captain Quash, you represent the Royal Navy here. You will have the pirate Otero brought ashore and remit him to our custody."

Captain Quash was quiet for a moment, obviously considering the situation, then said with finality in his voice, "My apologies, Your Excellency, but this Otero fellow is not mine to deliver. His capture is owed entirely to Captains Lockwood and Clapsaddle. He is aboard the *Dispatch*, in Captain Lockwood's custody. Otero is a pirate and a rogue, but I can in no way dictate his disposition."

McAllistair's rage nearly slipped. "By God I will not have a pack of..." but he caught himself and pointing at them, a gesture of furious command, he said, "I am the *governor* of this colony. As such, I am the king's representative here. My decisions are binding. You will now withdraw and reconsider this reprehensible defiance, not to say, disrespect. Disrespect, damn it! Now, withdraw, gentlemen. By midday tomorrow I shall have Otero hanging by a noose or I shall have some damned scofflaw in chains."

*****

In the stifling stink of the *Halcón's* hold, Otero spoke in Irish, the four other surviving pirates eagerly looking on. He hissed, "You must make it happen now! Boldness, man! It is now or never!" He lunged to grab Private Hogan, but the chains went rigid and brought him down.

Hogan gestured in frustration and hoarsely whispered, "I want to help, don't I? But Lockwood watches everything!" Then turning his palms out and down, he added, "Now, be quiet, will you? Casey will be back from the head any second!"

Otero sneered and said, "If you do not help me and my brothers out of these chains by morning you are a coward, and a fool. But make no mistake, if the redcoats drag me to the gallows, I will tell anyone who will listen of how you vowed to help me. I will not die alone! Free me, you ignorant prick, or you will hang beside me!"

*****

Only four men in the draft could read and write, Private Patrick O'Boyle being one. As such, some of the others would occasionally ask him to write a letter for them, and, as he was a good-natured fellow and a good comrade, he would often do so, asking perhaps only a splash of their rum ration in return. Writing their letters was not always an easy task, as O'Boyle had become literate in English, while many of the men wanted to write home in Irish. O'Boyle had no idea how to manage the spectacularly difficult spelling of Irish words (an obstacle that tortures any student of the language), but that was difficult to explain to Michael Lennon, who whined, "What good is a letter to my ma in English, Patrick, *a grah*? She speaks only the Irish."

"But Michael, does your mother *read* the Irish?"

Lennon laughed, "My ma? Read? Oh, Christ, no! There is not a reading eye in Ballygawley, only Father McDevitt, and he won't have shite to do with my ma after she caught him lying with Kate McGonagall at the dance at the Annaghilla Crossroads, him being in the drink, and Kate being so taken with men of learning."

"Why then do you wish it written, brother, if no one will read it at all?"

Lennon was puzzled for a moment, eventually suggesting, "Maybe she can keep it as a thing of mine? A keepsake, like? Please, now, Patrick O'Boyle, for Ma's own sake?"

And so O'Boyle labored over a phonetic spelling of Lennon's Irish, and with penny postage, the missive was taken ashore with the *Dartmouth's* mail. It would have given Lennon and O'Boyle some pleasure to know that, months later, contrary to all chance and circumstance, the letter did arrive in Ballygawley, and was duly delivered to the widow Lennon. While it was never read in the many years that followed, it was as treasured as any letter ever written.

Beyond his letters, O'Boyle kept a rough journal in his pack, entries made in pencil whenever opportunity arose.—*Aboard transport Dispatch for Demerara coast. Barney Toon cannot hold his rum, but I like his singing. Wish Da could hear his 'Carrickfurgus.'—Captain Lockwood asked if I wished to be his servant, but I declined, as too rough for such company. I said he should ask O'Donnell, who can sew, and is not a bad lad, since he quit his taking of Dutch leave.*

The next morning the captain did indeed call Private O'Donnell back to the cabin. As O'Boyle had earlier spoken to O'Donnell, advised him of his recommendation and told him, "not to be a feckin' eejit about it," O'Donnell was prepared to graciously accept the position.

"Very well, then. When I get some time I shall detail your duties, and you can visit a few shops in town to pick up thread and wine and such. I can only hope such a place has shops."

*****

Captain James Lockwood was familiar with the traditions of an Officers' Mess. In his own regiment it was customary for each officer to daily contribute 2s 6d of his meager pay (a lieutenant, after all, earned just 4s 8d a day), so that the mess officer, usually a younger fellow who wished to impress his elders, could arrange daily dinners for his brother officers. A number of years before, a newly promoted Lieutenant Lockwood had acted as his battalion's mess officer in Spain, and had executed his role with some skill. The St. Patrick's Day feast he had concocted was the stuff of regimental legend, especially when one considered that the Inniskillings occupied a village in war-ravaged Valencia, while a large number of Frenchmen lingered in the plains below. Lockwood had managed to purchase two hogs that had not yet been devoured by the rampaging armies, though the beasts had to be driven miles through an ink-black Spanish night. The determined young officer was accompanied only by the cursing Private Diarmuid Doolan, with a number of howling wolves slathering in their wake. What had truly endeared Lockwood to his brother officers, however, was the young Lieutenant's daring sortie to procure three barrels of strong red wine from a Franciscan monastery, a monastery that technically stood within French lines.

While mess fees were a sizable portion of an officer's pay, in Guard regiments and a handful of Line regiments traditionally populated by gentlemen of means, the officers contributed considerably more than was mandated, often two or three hundred pounds a year, and so lived very handsomely, indeed. Most Line officers had to content themselves with fare which was far from luxurious, and their wine, while red and wet, often carried distinct notes of lead, wood alcohol, and arsenic.

James's familiarity with such traditions came to mind that afternoon, after he had called upon the Quartermaster Sergeant of the spacious Georgetown Barracks. The First Battalion of the 27th

Foot was to be quartered in the south barracks building. Until the full battalion arrived, the draft would have the building all to itself.

A Lieutenant Hart of the 21st found James outside the quartermaster's office. "I do hope I am not intruding, sir, but as Mess Officer, it is my duty to offer the respects of my brother officers, and to inform you that the First Battalion, the Royal Scots Fusiliers, have unanimously voted to approve your membership in their Mess. The other members of your party will be welcome as guests, of course."

"Well, this is a handsome compliment, Lieutenant Hart, and one I am honoured to accept."

"You are most welcome, sir. We have all been here on garrison, staring at one another like apes in a tree, for so long that any new member is a most welcome diversion, especially one who might share tales of Waterloo itself."

"Pray, Lieutenant, what is the customary contribution to the Mess Fund?"

Lieutenant Hart was young, enthusiastic, and not as strict in military courtesy as he might be. He gushed, "That's the glory of it, sir! In light of our service here, the governor provides our dinners gratis, free and for nothing! He sends his people to cook and wait on us, sir!"

Captain Lockwood, who was neither young nor enthusiastic, studied Hart for a moment, and said in a more formal tone, "By 'his people,' Ensign, I assume that you are referring to slaves?"

"Slaves, sir? Well, I suppose they are. Whatever they are, they cook and serve most wonderfully, and there is one who can make a fellow a new uniform coat, most elegant-like, and all it costs is the price of the cloth and braid, and a few pennies as a tip, like."

Captain Lockwood crossed his arms, looking displeased.

Anxious to please, Hart said, "So, then, if you'd care to accompany me, sir, I'll see you settled at the Officers' Quarters. We'll send a boy—or, rather, we'll send one of the men of the regiment—to bring your trunk from aboard ship.

"As I said, Ensign, I am honoured by the offer to join your Mess, and appreciate the elegant manner in which the invitation was delivered. I am, however, duty bound to remain with my men aboard ship, until I see them quartered ashore."

Hart was discomfited, but made a gracious departure. James stood alone in the street for a moment to watch an elegantly dressed man ride by. His mount was one of the most beautiful horses James had ever seen. His stylish air was ruined by the group of sullen slaves who followed in his wake, trailed by a mixed-race overseer, who slapped a coiled whip against his leg as he walked.

James turned to walk back to the quay. He had long carried a marked sense of right and wrong, and so had always opposed the general principal of slavery. But he was now faced with the reality of the institution. He watched those men and women pass by, heavy with oppression, and realized his hatred, his absolute loathing, for such a practice, and his disgust with any system which benefited from it. He was astonished and disgusted with himself not to have realized it beforehand.

*****

Captains Quash and Clapsaddle returned to their ships, but when James returned to the *Halcón* he was surprised to find Mr. Read settled in the cabin with a case of wine at his feet.

The cabin was lit by a single candle; the night was hot, humid, and achingly still. Read gestured toward the wine and said, "My dear Lockwood, I do hope you do not me mind me inviting myself over for a glass or two. But in light of today's developments, I thought it best we chat before we retire. Shall I pour?"

James peeled off his uniform coat, and the two men sat in their shirtsleeves in the stifling cabin. James took a long drink of wine and said, "You know, I am not known for my discriminating palate, but this is amazing good wine."

"The last of my eighty-seven port, which I should prefer to finish tonight, with your kind assistance. It may sound unkind, indeed unchristian, but I should not wish to share it with those gentlemen ashore. Pearls before swine."

With a wry smile James said, "As a mere infantry captain, I hesitate to refer to Governor McAllistair in such terms. But monikers aside, I confess that I remain in a quandary. Honour requires me to seek something resembling a legal process for Otero, yet it also requires me to obey, and obey without God-damned question the orders of one of His Majesty's governors. For all my pains, in the end I see little option but to transfer Otero to the colonial authorities. Unless, sir, you see any other course available?"

"I do not." Read rubbed his face and said again, "I do not."

James was typically cautious in drinking more than a glass or two with any but trusted friends. He paused for a moment, the mouth of the bottle at the cusp of his glass. He had always depended upon his ability to read most men and the occasional woman. For a moment he looked thoughtfully at Read, and then filled his glass.

"And so," said James slowly, "a man of honour finds himself at a stand."

"After our session at Government House I poked about in town and managed to speak to one or two old contacts—clerks are such overlooked assets—and popular opinion holds that Governor McAllistair is in over his head. He is desperate to keep control, and is willing to grasp at any hand-hold. Otero is one such. Otero's death will please the planters, but will do nothing to enhance his control of the slaves, and that is where his greatest peril lies."

He James asked, "Do you think a rebellion imminent?"

"I shall need more time ashore to make such a prediction," Read responded. "There is discontent, surely, but is there sufficient organization amongst the slaves to make such a proposition feasible? I doubt it. Not a successful rebellion, at any rate."

They were quiet for a few minutes, until James opened another bottle, topped off his glass, and, following a subtle nod, filled Read's as well.

Read sipped his wine and muttered, "This really is quite good," then in a stronger voice he went on "McAllistair needs to find measures which both please the planters and subdue the slaves. One such stroke would be the arrest of Reverend Smith."

"The Methodist?"

"That's the fellow. Typical of his genre in that he possesses the prickly, righteous nature common to zealots, but he is widely admired by the slaves. His arrest would be problematic, as it would either cow or enrage the slaves."

"Then we must tender the question: is McAllistair clever enough to realize the critical nature of Smith's arrest, or will he make the simpleton's decision and fail to realize the repercussions?"

Read raised his glass in salute and said, "Yours is a discerning mind, Captain. You could have a career in the Colonial Office if you ever tire of the soldier's life."

Another bottle was done away with as the two men wandered across topics as varied as family and the cost of grain in Ireland.

Read finally set his glass aside and said, "I must leave you, Lockwood. I am ancient, and in need of my bed."

James jumped to his feet and said, "I shall have the watch hail the *Dispatch* for a boat."

Read rose unsteadily and waved the suggestion aside, saying, "No need, sir, no need. When I first came aboard some of your men offered me a hammock hung on deck, which I took most kindly, especially on a night as close as this. I shall sleep like the dead; pray, do not stir."

James escorted Read to the cabin door. Nearly every man of the draft was spending the night on deck. Privates Mulrooney and McCarthy stirred and showed Read to his hammock with genuine affection.

James returned to Otero's desk and mused upon what portion of Read's demeanor, what particular act, had rendered him so popular with the draft. His thoughts then turned to the situation ashore, and the nature of men, and how such frail brutes might grow to value or loathe one another with evident ease. He cursed quietly, drained his last glass and turned to his serial letter to Brigid.

The Royal Scots are in garrison here, though I believe they have been here rather too long, and have lost a degree of the professionalism that once marked them. That being said, today in Georgetown I absolutely witnessed an officer of His Majesty's army carrying an umbrella in the street. Madness.

The older I get, the more I grow to loathe humanity. (I do hope that confession does not disappoint you, my dear.)

But on the other hand, it is odd to consider that taken as <u>individuals</u> humans are typically likeable beings. You know

141

my social skills are not what my friends might wish, but I honestly believe there are few people I could not sit down and chat with. (The other night I had another one of my dreams about the Devil. He was very generous in sharing a wonderful liqueur distilled in Hell; he said it was filtered through the souls of corrupt attorneys. I am unsure if he was joking. At any rate, I found him an amiable companion, and he had some wonderful stories, though he admits to making some poor choices in his youth.)

I find, however, that exceptions to my fondness for the individual dwell here in Guyana. Tomorrow morning I shall have to present myself to Governor McAllistair and his cronies, and I do not think that I shall be able to disguise my disdain. Godless, soulless, greedy, selfish brutes. I must be careful not to expose myself.

He set aside his pen, uncertain if he would include that page when the time came to post his letter home.

As a soldier of extensive experience James had long before learned the value of a good night's sleep. And though a soldier, he found he slept amazingly well in naval hammocks. While Otero had had his bed in the cabin, after the capture of the *Halcón* James had his hammock brought over from the *Dispatch* and hung navy fashion.

And so, that night James slept well, the stifling heat and humidity countered by the effects of Mr. Read's wine and a night breeze wafting in from the Caribbean.

His sleep was blessed by a particularly delightful dream, and when he woke with a start his first thought was to remember the dream and write it down to share with Brigid. He had to tell her how he treasured her.

But an instant later, the reason for his sudden wakefulness became obvious. Musket shots cracked in the near distance. Church bells began clanging out a frantic peal.

It was still very dark. James threw on his trousers, grabbed his sword, and ran for the door. He bolted on deck, where he was met by Corporal Shanahan, in full rig, and James thanked God that young man had the watch.

"Make your report, Corporal."

"All hell is breaking out ashore, sir. Lots of people running about in town, and now some fires breaking out, in the distance."

James stared into the night, vainly trying to make sense of what little he could see. Frustrated, he hurried back to his cabin for his glass, and then climbed up to the maintop like a boy. Every man of the draft was gathered on deck below him.

Sergeant Maguire called up, "Signal fires, sir?"

Through the glass, the fires took on character. Buildings were ablaze.

James stared for a moment, gathered himself, and called down in a voice like brass, "Sergeant Maguire, form the men!" He climbed down quickly, and as the men scrambled below he found the sergeant and added, "Full uniform, but let us leave the packs below. We will be going ashore; detail two men to stay aboard to guard the prisoners."

Maguire said, "Private Leahy is still battling the wet gripes, sir, and yesterday Private Hogan twisted his ankle."

"Very well. Have them remain aboard, and alternate four hours on, four hours off. Barring a miracle, the governor's people will soon come to claim the prisoners."

Captain Lockwood

From the East Battery three cannon fired, the universal signal for alarm. "Better late than never, I suppose," James told himself, then, catching Shannon's arm, he said, "Corporal, you will please ensure that every man has a full cartouche. It appears that we shall be pressed into service once again, sooner rather than later."

Chapter Eleven

Murtagh Flynn was a bachelor farmer who worked a small plot of land on Templequinlan Road, just down from Doonasleen. His rent was £2 2s per annum, to be paid every All Saints' Day. He had been on that land for forty-seven years; he had been born there, and bragged that he would likely die there. He was, therefore, familiar with the kind of traffic likely to pass his door. His neighbors, many of them related to him, routinely went to and fro on business or visiting. Some days a militia patrol might slog by, or, worse, mounted Yeomen, who would search your cabin and treat you like a dog for no reason other than your breathing. On some nights, groups of Whiteboys passed by like shadows, local boys poking a stick in the landlords' eyes. But lately even the Whiteboys had grown proud, saying that you were either their friend or their enemy, and threatening death if a man crossed them.

But, for all his experience in the neighborhood, Flynn finally saw something that surprised him. He was hoeing the edges of his lazy beds, silently praying that his potatoes would grow, miserable weather or no, when he looked down the road and then stood upright with a start.

Two wagons, accompanied by a mob of women and children, were coming up the road. He had heard that someone had been foolish enough to take up the Doonasleen lease, but he had had no idea it was to be this band of roving spalpeens.

Of the three women who led the way, he eventually recognized Brigid ní Brian and that pretty daughter of hers, the wild one who no longer came to mass, whose name he could never recall.

As they passed he tipped his cap and said, "*Dia agus Mhaire duit, a* Brigid ní Brian."

Brigid turned, gave him a nod and said, "*Dia, Mhaire, agus Padraig duit,* Murtagh Flynn."

The primary cause of Flynn's bachelorhood was his addiction to drink and his inability to moderate his sharp tongue. He thus felt no hesitation in asking, "Is it a brothel you're thinking of, then?"

Both Brigid and Cissy flared and turned to remind him of his manners, but they were bettered by the wives who followed in their wake, as those ladies quickly bent to the road and showered Flynn with rocks, clods, and dung. Flynn beat a hasty retreat, followed by jeers and laughter, but the contest was witnessed by many of the neighbors, and the first impression made by the army families was not a positive one.

*****

At Doonasleen, Gearoid O'Tuathaigh looked down the road, achingly got to his feet, took a moment to pull on his pipe, and coughed an old man's cough. "A feckin' parade it is. It'll be angels flyin' out me arse, next."

The new residents of the farm were variously excited, skeptical, dismissive or appreciative. They were also wildly disorganized, so

146

after a few minutes of stumping about the farm, trying to show the place off, Gearoid tired of their yammering and retired to his stool in the yard. He was accustomed to peace and damned quiet, and for children to be running about was a trial. After an hour of such torment, he went in search of those Lockwood women. He eventually cornered them and said, "Now, then, gentlewomen, I am off home, and won't I have a fine walk of it, the rain coming, and me with these crippled brogans. But my suffering aside, your Colonel Simon came by yesterday and told me he'd have my hide if I forgot to give you this plot of the place. You are to hold the lands marked 3C in this plot, three good Irish acres in eleven fields."

Tapping the various points on the plot, he said, "This field just behind Doonasleen itself is called Buaille, the Milking Place, the only field you'll not find spoiled by Devlin pigs. To your west is what is left of Templequinlan Church, and you'll be knowing its graves put forth three ghosts every new moon."

"Oh, pooh, sir," said Brigid.

O'Tuathaigh was unaccustomed to having his wisdom summarily dismissed, but after making eye contact with Mrs. Lockwood, he quickly returned to the plot. "To your north is the Timoleague Road, and here in this corner is a spot never tilled by human hand, called An Reiligín, the Little Graveyard, dense hollies around a wee cillin." He winced, coughed and then went on, "These other fields here to the north are unworthy of a name, small and churned to barren mud by those feckin' pigs."

O'Tuathaigh then tapped the plan with some relish and said, "And here, plop in the middle of this holding, is the field called Cnoc na Sióg, the Hill of the Fairies, and why, gentlewomen? It's because of this great feckin' fairy fort. A fairy fort!" Doing his best to sound wise, he went on, "The great curse of this place, and the curse

147

facing all these new folk of yours, will be the fairies, as that is a *fairy* fort, and these houses built in its very shadow. Oh, very foolish, that."

"The fairies, Mr. O'Tuathaigh?" ask Brigid. "What might these people have possibly done to offend the fairies?" Brigid was an educated woman, but she was raised in Ireland and thus not one to question the old ways.

"Oh, my, yes, the fairies. The Devlins used that very ring fort as a pig pen, didn't they? That would offend even the most tolerant of fairies, I'm sure. And look what happened to the Devlins, will you?"

O'Tuathaigh then turned away from the two gentlewomen and, in a different tone, feigning indifference, he added, "And you know, of course, that the fairies want a place that has been cleared by eviction to sit empty for two, even three years, and only then to be taken by local folks—to let the good magic return to its balance, you know. And of course, strangers coming from halfway across the world to take such a place might be called spalpeens, and land canters, and violators of our ways."

Cissy tried to mirror the old man's indifferent tone, saying, "I wonder, Gearoid O'Tuathaigh, if these fairies of yours might wear white, and come only at night?"

As he used a stick to dig at his pipe bowl, O'Tuathaigh quietly replied, "Oh, they just might, Miss. They just might. And won't they be foul-tempered if they do!"

*****

In the bustling yard, Caoimhe Leahy stepped up to Brigid and abruptly said, "Chickens, please, mistress."

"Chickens, Mrs. Leahy?" responded Brigid, startled. Mrs. Leahy was perhaps the most quiet, withdrawn woman Brigid had ever met. For Caoimhe to speak at all was unexpected, but that odd sentence left Brigid fully taken aback.

"Aye, chickens, you see..." At that point the flustered Mrs. Leahy's foray into exposition ended, though fortunately Eileen Goodwin stood beside her and took up the conversation.

"It's Caoimhe's notion, sure, but perhaps I might explain it a bit, if you have a moment, please, Mrs. Lockwood?"

"Very well," said Brigid, "but perhaps we might step under the eave?" It was raining again, an endless Irish drizzle, though Doonasleen was busy, nonetheless. Three parishioners from the Methodist congregation had arrived with a wagonload of rough furniture. At first, the army families had been standoffish, not wishing to accept charity, while the three Methodists had been equally reserved, not wishing to offend or be offended, but when the actual work of offloading the furniture began, the activity largely burned away the awkwardness. The ladies decided amongst themselves which families needed what furniture, and Brigid was pleased to step back and let them sort themselves out.

Stepping under the eaves, Brigid took her shawl from over her head, shook it out, and to Mrs. Leahy and Mrs. Goodwin she said, "Now, you were mentioning chickens, ladies?"

Caoimhe looked to Eileen, who nodded, turned to Brigid, and said, "Well, ma'am, you know how every woman on an Irish farm keeps a chicken or two, so that she might sell eggs for a bit of pocket money?"

Brigid nodded, as she herself had grown up with chickens. Before her father had grown into a moderately prosperous middleman, Brigid's mother had kept several birds, and one of Brigid's earliest memories was the adventure of searching their farmyard for eggs. In a society that mandated the man's control of every penny of a farm's business, it was the only way for a farmwoman to have an income, however small, of her own.

With some excitement Eileen tilted her head toward her quiet friend and went on, "Caoimhe here, as bright as she is quiet, thought that is how we can earn our way in this place! No pigs or farming for us, but chickens, for eggs, and for meat! We can sell them in town, and beg no one's charity."

Brigid thought for a moment, and with a flash of a grimace she said, "That is a fine notion, sure, but how are we to keep things from getting all muddled? We can't keep all the birds separated." Irish men were fond of jokes made about women living together, especially farm wives with their mothers and mothers-in-law, and all of them in an ongoing argument about whose chicken laid which egg.

Both the army wives nodded, expecting that objection, and Eileen said, "That's what I said, too, ma'am, me thinking mainly of Vera McGunn and her mean temperament, but Caoimhe here thought that through as well. You see, ma'am, we keep the farm, its work, and the profits as a group, like. It will be like our men in their messes; we share and share alike, and everyone does their share, or gets her arse kicked by the rest, you see?"

Private Doolan walked past and Brigid gave him a brief smile. While one of Doolan's hands steadied a chair he had slung over his shoulder, the other was engaged with the hand of four year-old Michael Murphy, who was explaining to his new Uncle Diarmuid how chairs worked, and how one needn't sit on the cold old floor if one had a chair in their kitchen, oh, no, not at all. Brigid knew Doolan well enough to recognize the delight hidden beneath that grizzled, weather-beaten old face.

With a trace of embarrassment, Eileen went on, "What we're short of, Missus, is stake money. If you can see us a few pounds to start the flock, why, we'll pay our rent, keep ourselves fed, and see you repaid, in time."

Brigid thought for a moment, and then said, "I think it a wonderful idea. But you will have to polish it, you know, so that we might determine how many birds and what type and such. Have you spoken to the other ladies?"

"Just a couple—seeing who knows a bit about chickens. We wanted to ask you first, like, before we got the others worked up about it."

"Yes, please do talk it through." Then, as she turned to go, Brigid looked to Caoimhe and whispered, "Well done, Mrs. Leahy."

Caoimhe beamed as if blessed by the Pope, and before she and Eileen returned to their children and the work of setting up house, they clasped hands and laughed like girls.

*****

The following Friday was market day in Clonakilty. A great deal of buying and selling, from linen to livestock, was done in the town's spacious market square, although for the past few years the price of every commodity save butter had dropped nearly in half. Tithe rates and rents, however, had not made a corresponding drop, and the rural people of Clonakilty were, like most Irish farmers, in deep trouble.

Cissy and four of the ladies of Doonasleen walked to town. The pregnant Margaret McIlhenny, who was quickly becoming a friend to Cissy, felt up to the trip, so they walked side by side into the crowded market, in search of laying hens. The auction was scheduled for two o'clock that afternoon, and a hundred people or more were gathered in anticipation. In the area behind the auctioneer's desk everything from butter churns to plows were lined up for bidding, including dozens of chickens. That day's auction, however, was to open with the sale of the tithe proctor's distrained goods, anything seized from the people in lieu of tithe payment. Reverend Babcock's proctor and his drivers had been active.

The auctioneer took his place, banged his gavel, and called for anyone with business to gather round. Two rough cages containing six beautiful chickens were brought out from the proctor's wagon, and set at his feet, and the auctioneer then chanted, "Our first lot! Six prime hens—who will start…?"

An anonymous voice, stronger than the auctioneer's cant, boomed out, "Those are Marie Hurley's birds! You have no right to them!"

There was a moment of tension, the auctioneer cowed to silence. The tithe proctor, William Twiss, was a thin, well-dressed man with a harsh, sharp face; he walked out from behind his wagon and was greeted by a chorus of hisses and groans.

"None of your foolishness, now! These chickens, and all these other goods, were seized legal! That's a lesson for all of you! Pay your tithes!"

Marie Hurley herself, old and bent, stood in the front row of the crowd, crying, "Please, sir! Those birds are all I have! I am a poor woman, why ever do I have to pay a tithe to support the Proddy minister, and him in his great house?"

Twiss pointed at her, hard, and said, "The law is the law! Pay what you owe, woman, or I'll be back to take your bed and chair!"

The crowd roared insults and jeers, and very nearly fell on Twiss, but the noise had brought twenty militiamen hustling into the market square. Two weeks previously, the proctor's auction had turned ugly, and while Twiss had been knocked about, the militiamen had beaten a number of people. Four men were still in the town bridewell.

Dispirited, the crowd went silent and sullen.

Looking over the furious throng and then over at Twiss, the auctioneer tentatively resumed, "Very well, then, do I have an opening bid... say, three shillings... for these stout hens...?"

Margaret, who had been standing close beside Cissy, moved forward to get a better look at the hens, saying, "They are such fine birds... ."

Cissy quickly put her had on Margaret's arm and said, "Keep your hand down, *a grah*. Be still, now."

Cissy discreetly pointed toward some people in the crowd, people who stealthily moved about, whispering. Eventually one passed near Cissy and her friends, a woman, who hissed, "Do not bid. Anyone who supports these devils and their tithes is a traitor to the people."

The auctioneer went on, begging for something like a bid, while the crowd muttered and glared. Twiss and the militiamen carefully studied the crowd, looking for troublemakers. The militiamen readied their muskets, while in the crowd men clutched their blackthorn sticks and women stooped to pick up stones.

The market was on the verge of exploding. The frantic auctioneer was at the end of his rope, growing shrill, calling for a bid for Christ's sake, when Cissy finally raised her hand and cried, "One penny! I bid one penny!"

In an instant the gavel was down with a cry, "Sold!"

Twiss and several voices in the crowd yelled, "No!" but too late.

"A legal bid, accepted, and done," said the auctioneer, his voice cracking as he made an entry in his ledger.

Captain Lockwood

People in the crowd hissed and groaned in derision and betrayal as Cissy stepped forward and placed a penny on the auctioneer's desk. She picked up the two cages, but she then turned and carried the birds over to Marie Hurley.

Setting the cages at Marie's feet, Cissy said in Irish, "I believe these are yours, please, mother."

Marie bent to whisper to her birds, but then stiffened and said, "I do not accept charity. I am not yet fallen, girl."

Cissy bent toward Marie and gently said, "It is not charity, mother. Please come one day soon to Doonasleen, and teach us about hens and their ways. I wager you have much to teach us. But for now, we hope to buy two dozen birds, and I wonder if you'll please point out some that would serve?"

The crowd watched expectantly, some suspiciously. But a wave of approval went across many faces when Marie hobbled over to stand with the Doonasleen women, pleased to share her knowledge, saying, "Elsie Hurley is selling some fine birds today, but perhaps too dear." As the auctioneer went into his next cant she bent over and quietly said, "I am called Marie Bean Uí Hurley, and I beg your pardon if me or mine gave offense."

"I am Brigit ní Lockwood, called Cissy. And I, too, beg pardon if I gave offense."

Marie patted Cissy's arm and said, "Oh, no need to introduce yourself to me, *a grah*. You and your mother are known to us country people, and held dear by many."

"But not all?" asked Cissy playfully.

"Do not be forgetting the color of your father's coat, young gentlewoman."

*****

Father McGlynn sipped a glass of John Jameson's whiskey and mused over how best the army families could be used as an example to anyone who defied the Whiteboy edicts. He did not wish to alienate Mrs. Lockwood, as her donations to St. Brigid were so beneficial, and so, to her and the rest of those unaware, he would maintain the façade of the concerned priest.

But he would act, oh, yes, he would act.

*****

John O'Leary had long been a neighbor and friend to the Lockwoods, and came to shake his head at the state of Doonasleen's pastures. He kicked at the pig-churned mud and muttered, "It's a bloody mess, this. What brought you to have anything to do with such a place?"

Brigid held up a finger and said, "One must make do, John. These children must have their milk, and the people need their butter. So, tell me, how many cows will these three acres support?"

"You are a good woman, Brigid Lockwood, but you are no dairyman. You must not think in terms of acres, but in how the land is best to be used. So, before I sell you a single cow we must determine if this place has a cow's worth of grass. In my good fields, two acres is a cow's grass, while in the bitter north, it may be four acres to a cow's grass. A fourth of a cow's grass is called a foot, and half of that is a cleat. What I see here in Doonasleen is a cow and a foot. Those mud pits to the north are a cleat, but given a year or two they may grow back to a foot or two."

"And so we are to keep the cow in the front fields?"

O'Leary was a little round man, who finally grinned as he said, "Aye, so long as your fairies are amenable."

Brigid rolled her eyes and said, "If I hear one more word of fairies I shall run mad."

"You must admit, *a grah,* a fairy fort in the middle of a farm is odd, very odd indeed. Still, the wise and the good say that cows and bees can be great friends to the fairies. The young cow I have in mind for you is called Chumhra, 'Sweetpea,' and she is a good, biddable girl, who won't be bothered by grazing in your Cnoc na Sióg. But I beg, please, a Brigid *a grah,* keep her out of those back fields until they recover their grace, after those pigs and their ruination." He shook his head and added, "I am a Christian man, but I cannot bide a pig."

*****

That next afternoon Brigid returned to Doonasleen with a newspaper under her arm. She hurriedly called all the wives together in the yard, but shooed the children away.

Surrounded by those curious, anxious faces, she said, "This morning's newspaper carries news of import to us all. First, the happier news: Major General Sir John Lambert has been appointed military commander of His Majesty's forces in the south of Ireland. Many of you will recall that General Lambert commanded the 10th British Brigade at Waterloo."

Margaret Hanahan looked puzzled, prompting one of the experienced wives to tell her, "The 10th, *a grah*; our Skins were brigaded with the Lions and Exellers."

Margaret shrugged, prompting one of the veterans to whisper, "The 'Skins' are our Inniskilling men. The 4th Foot has a lion on their shako plates, so there are your Lions, and the 40th Foot has the Roman numerals XL on their shako plates, so they are called the Exellers."

156

Brigid waited for the ladies' attention and then went on. "The newspaper carries word of an incident up at Kildorry, some sixty miles from here, up past Mallow. A party of army wives and children, traveling in three wagons were on their way to join their husbands, men of the 95th Rifles who were to be stationed in Cork town after years on Foreign Service."

Brigid's voice broke and she paused, blinking back tears.

In the silence Catherine Murphy said, "I know some of the women of the 95th. When we were in France and I got so sick, they brought me soup, the dears—most kind, they were."

Brigid continued in a strained voice, "The party was stopped by a group of Whiteboys, on a main road, in the middle of the day. When the Whiteboys learned who the women were, they beat and robbed them, cruelly." She caught her breath. "Many of the women were repeatedly raped."

Screams and weeping followed her words.

Brigid waited a few moments, and then continued, more forcefully. "On my way here I called on Captain Moore of the militia, to ask for patrols to be stepped up. Private Doolan will, of course, stay on the farm as long as he is needed. I have also asked my daughter to call on Colonel Simon, a friend of our family and commander of the local Yeomen, for his support. It is Cissy's intention to borrow firearms from Colonel Simon's gunroom. She is very familiar with firearms and can quickly train us in the basics. We cannot know if this assault on innocent women and children is a deliberate new tactic, but if the Whiteboys should come here, they will not find us defenseless."

*****

The next morning, eight year-old Anthony Goodwin woke early to turn the chickens out into the yard. It was all new to him, and he delighted in the responsibility of seeing to the farm's thirty hens. But when he came to the rough shed that served as the coop he quickly stopped, his eyes wide.

The mangled bodies of a dozen chickens had been strung together and hung from the shed door.

Their blood stained the edges of a neatly written letter. Anthony was a bright boy who had learned to read in the barracks at Enniskillen Castle. He quickly read:

To the servants of the foreign cubs of Calvin: Your infidelity and your transgressions against the newly established laws of this land, which were founded on the laws of God, have marked you in conflict with the righteous will of the People.

He read no further, but quickly turned to run, tearfully calling for his mother.

Chapter Twelve

In the swinging lamplight of the *Halcón's* hold, a mass of scrambling Irishmen rushed to dress and grab their gear. Sergeant McGuire pushed his way through the throng to find Private Hogan, who was moving about with an exaggerated limp. "Hogan, you will stay aboard with Leahy. Guard the prisoners, four hours on, four off. Don't you dare slack, now, boyo, or I shall have your arse in a sling the moment we get the darkies seen to. Now, where is that lazy dog Leahy?"

"The head, please, Sergeant," replied Hogan with a hidden smile. "He's been shitting water these two days and more. As he's so sick, I'll take the first watch."

McGuire gave Hogan a nod and went off in search of Leahy. Hogan was elated, seeing the commotion in town as a gift from God. He grabbed his musket and rushed, forgetting his limp, to relieve the guard below. He would share the news with Otero, certain that his path now led to wealth, drink, and women. Oh, the women Otero had promised him!

Captain Lockwood

*****

On deck, Captain Lockwood cursed the darkness as he scanned the town, trying to make sense of the bells, fires, screams, and musket shots. People were running about with torches, for light or to set fires, or perhaps both. One warehouse along the shore was ablaze, throwing light across the rippling ink of the river. In that light James caught sight of a boat putting off, a skiff with two men rowing and one in the stern.

"Corporal Shanahan," he calmly said, "There is a boat approaching. You will please line the rail with a dozen men. There is no telling what they intend. If you see anyone with a flame you will fire into the boat. I will not see the ship burned by some budding incendiary."

The boat grew closer, and in a fierce voice, James cried, "Ahoy the boat! Explain yourself, or we shall fire on you!"

In a steady voice a man, a black man, replied, "A message from Governor McAllistair for Captain Lockwood!"

"Approach, then!" he called, but he turned to Shanahan and hissed, "One flame, Corporal. Just one, and you send them to hell."

The boat bumped softly alongside, and the messenger climbed aboard like a seaman. The deck was illuminated by just one lantern, but the man soon spotted Captain Lockwood, knuckled his forehead, handed across an envelope and said, "With the governor's respects, please, sir."

For an instant James wondered just how sincere the governor's respects might truly be, but he said only, "One moment, please, sir. I shall likely have a reply."

With that, James stalked back to the cabin, and in the gentle lamplight he read:

Lockwood—

For God's sake come quickly. The slaves are risen, and are murdering and burning the colony. Fire on the blacks as you see fit—it is of no consequence. Think only of <u>order</u> and the preservation of European <u>lives</u> and <u>property</u>.

McAllistair

With a shake of his head James muttered, "The fool. No instructions, other than to come ashore and kill any blacks we come across." Still, James found his heart racing, the notion of action as stirring as it had been to the very young Ensign Lockwood.

With a grin he recalled an incident from the march to Waterloo, when his battalion had come across people fleeing from Brussels, wide-eyed refugees who told them of Bonaparte's half-million men and their irresistible advance. James's friend Lieutenant Nicolas Pitts had taken a drag on his cigar and said with his usual elegant nonchalance, "Why do civilians always behave so badly? It is always the same: panic, rumours, and wholesale flight."

James laughed aloud at the memory, then taking up a pen he sat and wrote his reply at the foot of McAllistair's letter.

Your Excellency;

I beg you to forgive the hurried nature of this reply. I read with the greatest concern of the difficulty in the Colony, and per your orders I am mustering my men and will come ashore immediately.

Lacking direction as to the exact nature of my mission, with your permission I shall land at the southern end of the town, in anticipation of the Royal Scots ensuring your

161

personal safety by securing Government House, and thus gaining control of the northern portion.

I am certain that you will agree with my conviction that the honour of professional soldiers will be the unfailing guide to our conduct in these stressful hours. An application of deadly force need only be our last resort when dealing with unarmed civilians.

I shall send word to Government House by midday with an update as to my situation.

I remain, sir, etc.,

Captain J. Lockwood, 27th Foot

As James watched the messenger's boat pull back toward the shore, he allowed himself to finish his memory of Nicolas Pitts. At Waterloo, Pitts had been shot in the face. James had never seen him again; he had tried writing to him, but the last he'd heard, Waterloo had cost Pitts an eye and much of his sanity.

*****

There were nearly thirty redcoats in the *Halcón's* launch. Every one of them was tense and not a few of them were afraid, as the boat pulled through the darkness. They were unable to make any sense of the shadows and noises ashore—when a woman's terrified scream cut across the water, several of the men crossed themselves.

The eight men at the oars did not row especially well, but the boat made steady progress upriver, silent and removed from the chaos ashore. James stood in the bow, trying to look confident, but he was unsure what to do. The heat, the darkness, the water, the relentless insects, even the smell of the place, were far removed

162

from anything he had faced before, and he had to swallow a mad impulse to just go ashore and start tearing the town apart.

A few minutes passed, and finally he pointed the boat toward a quay that seemed quiet. Turning to the men in the boat, he said, "There is no telling what we shall encounter once we are ashore. Keep your wits about you, stay in your ranks, adhere to the voice of command, and we shall get all this nonsense sorted out directly."

James would go ashore with only twenty men. The boat would take a half hour or more to return with another twenty; he would not have all one hundred men at hand until well after dawn. But he would not give voice to his concerns. Confidence was everything.

In a confidential tone, James said to Private John McHenry, who had once served as a sailor and so commanded the boat, "McHenry, once we are ashore you will return to the ship. Tell Sergeant Maguire to get the women and children into the jolly boat with two older, sober men, and deliver them safely to the barracks. Then, get as many men as you can into your boat and come back here straight away. Straight away, do ye hear?"

McHenry nervously nodded his agreement as the first light of dawn greyed the sky far above. The boat thumped against the dock. James braced himself, drew his sword, and leapt up the steps, his men rumbling up behind. They quickly, nearly frantically, formed two ranks across the narrow dock, bristling muskets facing inland.

James was surprised to find his anxiety ill-founded, as precisely nothing happened. He heard the boat pull away, and in the darkness, the twenty-one anxious men of the Inniskilling Regiment stood and stared into the gloom.

Long minutes passed, slowly dispelling the tension. The light gradually filled more of the sky, but the low, dilapidated buildings in the near distance were still dim shadows when a black man's voice asked, from surprisingly nearby, "Are you come to kill us, gun men?"

Captain Lockwood walked forward a few steps and replied in as calm voice as he could muster, "We don't wish to hurt anyone, but have come to see order restored."

From the near distance, a cannon fired, a thunderous boom that echoed in the faint light. Puzzled, Lockwood said aloud, "What the devil is that?"

"The morning gun, soldier. It sounds at five every morning, then again at eight every night to signal every slave's workday, a long day of hell. You and your gun men are new come to Guyana, no?"

"We are. We are the king's men, and honourable."

"You are welcome here, king's men with the blood coats, so long as you see the law gets done, no matter a man's skin. There are new laws that are meant to lighten our burden, but these plantation holders ignore them and abuse us without pause."

Into the darkness turning dawn, James nodded and said, "I understand. I am Captain James Lockwood of the King's 27th Regiment, an Irish regiment."

"Irish? Hey now, our masters hate the Irish near as bad as they hate us blacks. Are you Irish, too, Captain James Lockwood?"

"I was born in Ireland, and my wife is Irish."

The black man laughed and said, "The Fante people say that what a woman is, her husband will become."

James sniffed in acknowledgement, then said, "Now, I need to know your name, sir, and the name of the man who leads your rebellion."

"Hereabouts I am called Scipio Africanus, who first saw you coming here, and I will not tell you that man's name. But I will pass word to him that you are come. We don't mean you boys no harm, so long as you don't give no harm to us."

"That is fair," said James, "but there can be no further burning, and no murder." James could now make out the man he was speaking with; an old man missing a leg, leaning on a crutch.

Scipio scoffed and said, "Oh, there has been some burning, sure, gun man, but not one soul has been knocked about, let alone killed. We are no animals. We are, after all, guided by God's hand, the year of Jubilee as our reward."

They were interrupted by the sound of the *Halcón's* boat returning. James was no longer so concerned with the number of muskets at his command, and evidently neither were the men with him. When one of the newly arrived men hurried into formation beside one of the original twenty, he muttered, "We thought we'd get here just in time to find you bastards cut to ribbons by the darkies."

The man who had been ashore for a while responded, "Oh, shut up, *amadán*. Thus far, the locals seem right civil. They just want to be treated fair, is all."

One of the other men chuckled and hoarsely whispered, "We've been here so long, waiting for you lot, that we've already made some new friends. Cassidy has already made plans with that Scipio fellow's sister."

"Katie Africanus," muttered Cassidy. "Not much to look at, but she sure can scuttle."

There ensued some soft laughter, mostly out of sheer relief, but Captain Lockwood was having none of it, roaring back to his men, "Silence in the ranks, you pack of God damned moon-calves!"

In an instant, discipline was restored, though Scipio had a laugh in his voice when he said, "All right, then, gun man, I'll go and tell my folks that you are come, and have a head on your shoulders. All hell is breakin' free here, and God knows who will still be breathin' come Sunday."

*****

In the *Halcón's* stagnant bilge, Hogan stood over the prone figures of Otero and the three surviving pirates, musket in hand. Leahy slowly crept below, looking ashen and frail, to say, "Hogan, the last boatload just shoved off. The women and kids are gone, too, so it's just us left now, with these God-forsaken sons of perdition. I'm going back to my hammock. Christ, but I'm done in."

As soon as Leahy was gone, Hogan produced the keys and knelt to pull the chains from around Otero. Otero was slow in getting to his feet, stiff and sore, but when Hogan went to unchain the three remaining pirates, Otero sneered and said, "Leave them. They aren't worth shit—sick, weak, and cowardly."

One of the prone pirates rasped, "But, Captain, we can still fight..."

Otero spit at the man and said, "You should have died defending my ship. Now you can rot here and hang like the dogs you are."

Otero climbed the short ladder up to the hold. There, he found a rigging pin, crept over to where Private Leahy was sleeping and savagely clubbed him to death.

When Hogan saw Otero standing over the lifeless Leahy he stopped and stared in horror.

"Christ!" cried Hogan. "What the hell made you do that! He was all right, him!"

Otero spun on Hogan and brutally backhanded him to the deck. "Listen, you ignorant bastard, you work for *me* now. You will *never* question what I do. So shut up, and get that red coat off. You have

166

made a deal with the devil, and it's time you learned that you are *fucked*."

*****

Jack Lancaster was a slave at Success Plantation. He was the face of the rebellion, a handsome, well-spoken young man, though his father, Olufemi, and other senior members of their church group, were primarily responsible for the planning and execution of the rising. The head of their Methodist congregation, Reverend Jones, had been arrested, but his absence did not soften their resolve. Jones, in fact, had never advocated rebellion, but had been a relentless advocate for securing what few rights the slaves had been granted by Parliament, the mildly repentant Parliament.

Though the family of Joshua Hemple, the erstwhile master of Success, had been tumbled into their carriage and sent into Georgetown, Hemple himself had been placed in the stocks in which he had previously punished disobedient slaves. Of all the planation masters, Hemple was renowned as the heaviest flogger, which was saying a great deal. The ascendant Jack Lancaster established his headquarters in the plantation office, using a desk that looked down onto the enraged but silent Hemple.

Runners from other plantations reported to Lancaster, bearing news of their progress and requesting instructions, and for the first time in his life Lancaster could employ his remarkable intelligence. There was no written communication guiding their rebellion; the messengers carried verbal instructions from Lancaster counseling nonviolence and restraint. When a runner came from Friendship Plantation to report that some of the newly freed people were intent on murdering their hated overseer, the greatly respected Olufemi had gone to restore civility.

Captain Lockwood

Lancaster was no fool; he knew the only chance for reform, let alone their emancipation, was to reflect humanity and intelligence in their behavior, and thereby convince government that they were indeed men and women, not chits in a pitiless economic puzzle.

*****

On deck, Otero tucked two knives into his belt, scanned the ship, and then told Hogan, "Listen, you bastard, the boat is gone, so we'll have to swim for it. We head for the west bank, then across the fields and into the jungle. We'll follow the coast until we can steal a boat and head for the Orinoco. I have friends there, and we'll be on Isla de Margarita in a week."

"You haven't asked if I can swim."

Otero did not bother to look at Hogan to say, "I don't care if you can swim."

As Hogan pulled off his coat and shoes, stuffed them into his pack, and made ready to jump over the side. Otero, though, hesitated, swore and hurried below. After a few minutes he returned to the deck muttering, "Take my ship, will they? I'll show those bastards." Otero pulled the bandages from his head, the ugly wound healing but giving him the look of a demon. With evil in his eyes, he gestured toward the western shore and told Hogan, "We had best hurry. I have loosed the devil."

It was perhaps two hundred yards from the *Halcón* to the western shore, and since the tide had yet to change, their swim was not difficult. Once ashore, the two sodden men dragged themselves up the bank and looked about. There was no town on the western bank of the Demerara, and the low, flat fields were barren after the recent sugar cane harvest. A few small houses and clusters of slave huts marked the location of each plantation. A half mile of field was all that separated the river from the edge of the jungle. A road ran

168

alongside the river, and as the light grew, Otero spotted two riders a few hundred yards away. When the riders saw the two white men on the road they galloped toward them.

Hogan's first instinct was to run, but Otero grabbed him by the back of the neck and hissed, "Stand still, and keep your fucking mouth shut."

The two riders were white men, frantic and ashen, who galloped close, reined in, and yelled, "Are you come from town? What in God's name is happening? Are the blacks risen? For God's sake, are we all to be murdered?"

"Ah, it's all hell across the river! We are sailors from the *Dispatch*, and had shore leave, but in the middle of the night, the blacks were everywhere, cutting throats! We had to swim for it, and barely escaped with our lives." Otero did his best to hide his Spanish accent, but his white skin was passport enough. Each of the riders had a shotgun slung across his back and pistols in his belt, but they showed no fear of two white men.

Otero gave them a friendly wave, inviting them down to talk. The two men dismounted, and proved to be the masters of the Bush Lot and Henrietta Plantations. Their position in the closed society of Guyana did them no good—Otero killed them both with practiced efficiency. Then he rifled their pockets, rolled the bodies into the ditch and swung up onto one of the horses, all while Hogan watched in stunned silence.

Hogan had never been on a horse in his life, but he desperately hung onto his mount as it pounded after Otero, who rode the stolen horse with brutal efficiency. They galloped north and west, toward the sea, and Otero's natural element.

*****

James looked back downriver as the first rays of dawn reached the *Halcón* in the near distance, with the *Dispatch* and the *Dartmouth* anchored further out. James was wondering if Quash would land his marines when a flash of light that surpassed the dawn lit the anchorage and the *Halcón* suddenly blew to pieces. In the thunderous explosion, debris was tossed a hundred feet in the air.

Every man of the draft scrambled to watch the explosion. Their captain, as stunned as his men, did not order them back into formation, nor did he silence their comments as they watched the burning remnants of the shattered *Halcón*.

"The darkies blew up our ship!"

"Shite, there was Leahy and Hogan aboard, poor bastards."

"And those pirates, too. A better end than they deserved."

"And now will we see one penny for capturing that ship? No, brothers, we will not."

"Well, fuck me."

"Look at her burn, the poor dear."

After several long minutes Captain Lockwood gathered himself and said, not unkindly, "Form up, men, form up, there. We have lost our ship, so we are once again returned to our natural environment. Give me dry land, and the life of a soldier. McHenry, I am going to have to ask you and the boat's crew to make one more trip downriver, to look for survivors."

Then, pulling his corporal aside, James said, "Shanahan, you will command the boat; try to find our people, but watch for Otero. He is a foul devil, so if he survived, you need not be over gentle in laying hold of him. Take any survivors to the barracks hospital or the gaol and then meet us back at this quay when you can."

The boat's crew had been nearly exhausted when they'd carried the last boatload up from the ship, but now they hurried back to their oars with a purpose.

James had his suspicions regarding the cause of the explosion, but they would have to wait to find out. The light and heat were building, while smoke and humidity hung heavy in the stagnant air. "Sergeant Maguire, column of fours! We are infantrymen once again—let us see what the day brings."

Chapter Thirteen

They were friends, the crumpled old man and the sparkling young woman, though that bond was being tested as they sat in Colonel Simon's elegant drawing room. Their tea was growing cold, sitting untouched, as were the colonel's petit-fours, his favorite, sent weekly from Cork town. Cissy had never before noticed the mantle clock, but now its ticking seemed inordinately loud.

Colonel Simon frowned, waved a spotted hand, and said, "My dear Miss Lockwood, I do wish you would attempt to see this matter from my perspective. I shall mount additional patrols of my Yeoman cavalry, but, pray, keep in mind that these men are volunteers, and cannot be constantly deployed. Beyond that, we are at a stand. I cannot, simply cannot, empty my gunroom to arm a pack of peasant women, especially Catholic peasant women. It will not do."

Cissy controlled her temper, but there was tension in her voice when she replied, "Your offer of the Yeomen is kindly meant, Colonel, but those men rarely serve to protect anyone's interests but their own. As to the weapons, I recall, sir, that you were good enough to supply me with arms, indeed, going so far as to train me in their use when I was in need. Do these women and children not merit equal consideration?"

The Colonel sat back into his chair, shook his head, and said only, "You, Miss Lockwood, are an exception to many rules."

"They are *army* families, sir. Surely you feel some sympathy, some alliance, with such women, and their children?"

Simon sniffed defensively and said, "They knew the risks when they married His Majesty's soldiers. For God's sake, woman, in 1809 every wife and every child that followed my regiment was captured by the French at Walcheren. Theirs is a hard, dangerous life."

"Danger when abroad, from the king's enemies, to be sure! But at home, from those whom they have every right to regard as their own people? No, sir, this is quite another matter."

Simon frowned and tapped the arm of his chair in deliberation.

Cissy studied the old gentleman, and reflected on her motivation. It was true that she was fond of the Colonel, of that she was certain, but she had to admit that she had benefited most from their friendship. He had taught her to ride and to shoot, two skills that had served her when Captain John Tucker had stalked her. His friendship had given her status in the community, status that might not normally be granted a young Catholic woman, even if her father was a serving army captain. And now she was once again asking for his aid.

The Colonel reached over and rang the bell that sat beside the teapot. With an air of finality he said, "Miss Lockwood, I shall not arm your women. I will, however, take some limited measures to aid you, and them."

The bell had summoned Corporal M'Vicar, who snapped to attention at the door. To that rugged figure Simon said, "Corporal, you are seconded to Miss Lockwood's command. Pray draw a week's rations, three pistols, a carbine, twenty pounds of shot and ten of powder." Turning to Cissy, he went on, "Should you like your shotgun, Miss Lockwood?"

"If you please, sir."

Simon nodded.

M'Vicar snapped a salute, barked, "Yes, sir," and turned on his heel. Colonel Simon got to his feet with unexpected vigour, requiring Cissy to do so as well. "That, Miss Lockwood, is what I am prepared to offer." His voice was more sad than angry, and carried a definite sense of dismissal.

Cissy nearly apologized, nearly begged his pardon, nearly reminded them both of her regard, but she could manage only a meek, "I thank you, sir."

*****

Much of the County Cork was peopled by O'Brians, and thus, for better or worse, were kin to Brigid Marie O'Brian Lockwood. She left Fáibhile Cottage that afternoon bearing bread and salt, traditional gifts of mending. When she called Corporal to accompany her, she told herself that he needed the walk, but still, she was comforted by his protective presence. It was nearly six miles to her uncle's home, roads she had known since she was a child, and when she arrived it was as if he had been expecting her—him standing in the doorway with his arms folded.

"Who is this, come to call? I do not recognize this woman." Then, frowning at Corporal, who stood very close to his mistress, he went on, "and what is this, a steer that has strayed from his pasture?" The Irish of southern Ireland is typically soft and fluid, but Michael O'Brian turned it harsh, and challenging.

He was going to treat her roughly, but she remained polite, though, by God, firm. "Certainly you know me, Uncle, for I am Brigid, daughter of your sister Maeve, and the girl who learned *An Bonnán Buí* at your knee. Will you not speak with me?"

"If it is she, does she then recall the first of those lines? Is she yet an Irishwoman? Or is she turned Saxon, one who must turn to books for poetry, Shakespeare and his ilk, verse unfit for any place but hell?"

If someone had asked that morning for her to quote the great poet Cathal Buí Mac Giolla Ghunna she might have stumbled, but to see her uncle's face, to see his home, made the words flow to her tongue as readily as her children's names. Her voice was clear and bright, reciting the old poem that was always popular around Irish hearths, about the death of a yellow bittern, a bird that shared the poet's fondness for drink.

A bhonnán bhuí, is é mo léan do luí,
Is do chnámha sínte tar éis do ghrinn,
Is Chan easba bidh ach díobháil dí
a d'fhág i do luí thú ar chúl do chin.

His tough old face broke into a grin of approval, but still he did not invite her inside. "Well done, Brigid. You are Maeve's daughter, sure, and shall always have my ear. But you live now among the rich and the powerful; how can a simple man such as your Uncle Michael O'Brian be of service?"

Brigid laid her basket of bread and salt at her Uncle's feet, earning herself a subtle nod of thanks and respect.

175

"Uncle, I come to you as your niece, your own blood, one who would never betray you, who *could* never betray you. I beg you to trust me, as I come to beg your aid. The birds whisper that you have some influence amongst the Whiteboys. I come today to ask that you speak to their leaders, so that they might leave the women and children of Doonasleen alone. Innocent they are, Irish as Patrick, and never an enemy to the people."

Michael O'Brian nodded and then, drawing his pipe and tobacco pouch from inside his jacket, he carefully loaded the pipe, speaking slowly. "From what I understand, what I hear from casual conversation at the pub—mind you, there is no deliberate animosity toward those people, or against you, thank God. But you, of all people, should know how some people view the wives of redcoats. They be seen as traitors, slaves to the Saxons and their king."

Brigid flared, "And so the Whiteboys impose their own notions of justice, and them not above robbery and the brutal violation of innocent women?"

"Now, now, those rapes were terrible, sure, but such tactics were never ordered by the central committee. One group got out of hand, that is all. From what I hear, some of those women were beautiful, and you know how Munstermen can be. Still, discipline has been restored, and such a thing will not be repeated. We are not animals."

"Oh, of course not." She nearly said something very cutting, but remembered her mission, saying instead, "All that aside, Uncle, will you speak to those you know, and convince them of their, *our*, innocence? Those women are as poor and desperate as any in Ireland, and deserving of pity, not menaces."

O'Brian looked down and sniffed in wry amusement. "Will I speak to them? Certainly, *a grah*. But can I convince them? That, I do not know. But will you now step into my house and share a meal? Your aunt will never forgive me if she does not hear of your children, and we will tell you of ours."

Corporal sensed a shift in the conversation, but only after looking up at Brigid and getting a nod of approval did he go forward to meet Michael O'Brian and receive a conciliatory scratch behind the ears.

*****

Catherine Cashman had been the housekeeper of the Lockwood family, and when she died, she had been grieved as if one of their own had passed. Brigid had never met Catherine's son, John, and while she knew of his affiliation with the Whiteboys, she was unaware of the very violent nature of his work.

Thus, when she returned to Doonasleen the next morning she did not know the granite-faced man who stood in the yard beside Cissy and Diarmuid Doolan.

Private Doolan was as incapable of grinning as any man on God's earth, but he nearly did so, as he introduced John Cashman to Brigid Lockwood.

"You see, Missus, John here is a friend of mine, and come to help fend off the Whiteboys, God curse them, if ever again they have a notion of stopping by to knock more poultry on the head. There is not a chicken on the island that is safe from their depredations, sure."

Brigid decided that Doolan had been drinking, and so turned to give John Cashman a graceful nod, saying, "I loved your mother, John Cashman, as good a woman as ever walked. It is good of you to come and help keep the peace, sir, but I wonder if perhaps you have some special knowledge of the Whiteboys?" She had a clever tilt to her head that told Mr. Cashman, Private Doolan, and Miss

Cissy Lockwood that she knew very well that Mr. Cashman was acquainted with the movement.

John Cashman looked her straight in the eye and said with a charming smile, "Oh, no special knowledge, I'm sure, Mrs. Lockwood. But I can tell the white ones from the black, and more important, I can usually tell which ones might be a shade of grey, and that makes all the difference. A grey fellow can be reasoned with. But those that are white to the core, well, those are the difficult ones, aren't they? Young Diarmuid and I shall deal with those as need be."

Tossing his head toward the ruins of a church, the ruin that stood at the edge of the Drombeg, Cashman went on, "You know, two hundred years ago my people prayed there." With a tone that mixed nostalgia with derision, he went on, "Teampall Ó gCaoinleáin, they called it, as certain of their God as the sun coming up in the morning. In honor of those simple people, I shall serve those who live in the shadow of the old church."

*****

The clan O'Falvey had once been the hereditary admirals of Desmond. But the glory of Desmond was long faded, their ships a distant memory. One branch of the O'Falveys had fallen to a desperate living, clinging to a handful of acres north of Clonakilty, but the memory of their past glory still burned in their hearts. While their resistance to the English was sporadic, it was tenacious.

While the O'Falveys were dedicated, few of them were especially bright. That trait rendered them ideal tools for Father McGlynn's handiwork. At the rise of the moon, eight O'Falvey men, fathers and sons, brothers and cousins, passed into a remote glen to meet the priest.

One of them stumbled over a rock, prompting his uncle, the imposing Darragh O'Falvey, to bark, "Will you not be more careful, you plodding fool?"

The clumsy man replied, "Am I not moving like a cat, this ancient darkness or no?"

The man's brother scoffed, "A cat carrying a hundred of bricks, sure."

The others laughed, far too loudly for men sneaking toward a secret meeting, but they had shared a bottle before they set out. They routinely drank before such meetings, to bond and to brace, for in truth they feared the priest. Over the years they had come to view him in a nearly supernatural light, and that night the priest did not disappoint.

The O'Falveys rollicked into the glen, and, as if by magic, Father Joseph McGlynn appeared amongst them. A sober man, well prepared, can amaze drunkards with astonishing ease.

They listened in rapturous attention when the priest told them, "You men have been doing God's own work, and one day, one distant day, you will all be rewarded a thousandfold in heaven. But for now, the Lord calls thee once again. At the next new moon you will go to Doonasleen, where spoiled filth defiles the holy ruin of Templequinlan. There you will cut three throats: men, women, children, as you please. No more, but no fewer. By killing just that number, you will attest to our discipline, and the precise power of the Cause."

Some of the more decent men recoiled at that, but McGlynn held up two priestly fingers and went on, more softly, "Do not quail before the task before you. It is prescribed to you, and so it will be done. You will shed the blood of Saxon slavers, and so make another step toward the freedom of the Irish and the salvation of your souls."

*****

An emerald green Irish field, dotted with white-clad figures on an achingly beautiful Munster afternoon. Most were military men, including the august personage of Major General Sir John Lambert, who stood waiting his turn at bat.

Eight years earlier, Lambert had commanded the 10th British Brigade at Waterloo. Each of the brigade's three battalions, men of the 4th, 27th, and 40th regiments, had suffered serious loss, but the 27th, the Inniskillings, had suffered most. One of the seven Inniskilling companies was commanded by then-Lieutenant James Lockwood.

In the following years, Lambert's career had carried him to numerous postings, that year bringing him to Ireland, as the newly appointed military commander of the southern counties. But no matter his posting, Lambert remained a devoted cricketer and an officer of the Marylebone Cricket Club.

Lambert stood in the center of a knot of elegantly dressed spectators. Brigid Lockwood approached with not a little apprehension. This was a very English game, and a very English audience. She had been careful in her selection of dress, as she needed something elegant to mark her as a person of means, and while she wished to look attractive, she had no desire to be alluring. Men could be such fools if they got the wrong scent. She had never played the coquette, and she had no interest in doing so now.

Sadly, Brigid did not care for cricket, being much fonder of a good hurling match. The speed and dash of hurling was so much more interesting than the interminable pace of cricket. All that passed through her mind in an instant, but without a blink she offered up the one bit of cricket tactics she could muster. "I beg your pardon, General Lambert, but I wonder if their leg-side boundary fielder is out of his normal position?"

Lambert looked off to that part of the field and said with some appreciation, "Oh, you are quite right, madam. Hopefully our batsman notes it as well. It could be critical in the coming moments." Then, turning to look down at her, he said, "That was well remarked, madam. Are you a student of the game?"

Without a blush she gushed, "Oh, my dear General, I am a most devoted follower."

"My dear woman, you are a pillar of hope in this island of ignorance. I have been playing since I was a boy, but here in Ireland I find rebellion the only sport, other than the occasional bout of peasants running about with sticks."

"As fond of the game as I am, sir, what drew me here was mention of your name. You see, sir, my name is Brigid Lockwood, and you perhaps recall my husband..."

"Lieutenant James Lockwood!" boomed Lambert with evident delight. "My dear Mrs. Lockwood, may I congratulate you on your choice of husband. He played a most valuable role in the Inniskilling's stand at Waterloo, an outstanding regiment, that. And if I may say, my brigade was critical in the victory, even if all the credit goes to the guards and the heavy cavalry." Lambert held up a finger and then went on. "I may have slighted your husband, madam. Do I recall seeing his name in the *Gazette*, a captain, now?"

"Captain Lockwood would be so pleased to hear you remember him, sir."

General Lambert was pleased, perhaps overly so. Mrs. Lambert then drifted over to join them and the general made the introductions. Mrs. Lambert was much younger than her husband, a plain woman who made no effort to be agreeable. Brigid decided to dislike her, especially as Mrs. Lambert wore a massive collection of diamonds around her neck, an *outré* accessory for a sunny afternoon's cricket match.

Mrs. Lambert moved on, and from the field, Brigid heard someone call General Lambert for his turn at bat. Brigid hurriedly said, "If I may, my dear General, mention a matter which merits your attention. There is a group of women, wives of the regiment, whom I have taken under my wing, and who are being harassed by a gang of Whiteboys."

"An outrage, madam! But I do trust you to understand my position, as I am new here, and find myself beset by requests at every turn, with so few resources at hand. A gentleman's house near Bandon was burned last week, and you can imagine the howls of outrage. Now, if you will excuse me…"

A young man ran over, calling, "Beg pardon, sir! Your turn at bat, please sir! Packenham has us up by fourteen, but got out on Major Brown's wicked googly. You're up, please, sir!"

Lambert snatched up his bat, and growled, "A googly, the rogue!"

He turned to go, still giving Brigid half an ear, as she said with some urgency, "Doonasleen farm, just east of Clonakilty, please, sir! Army families!"

Lambert trotted out onto the field, calling over his shoulder, "I shall look into it, madam! And do give Captain Lockwood my regards!"

Mrs. Lambert gave Brigid a glare that conveyed the obvious message—Mrs. Lockwood was not welcome. The glare was taken up by Mrs. Lambert's friends. Mrs. Lockwood, not immune to such pressure, beat a graceful retreat to the lane, where Liam O'Flynn of the Shannon Arms waited with the inn's inelegant carriage.

As Lambert took up his place at the wickets he muttered to himself, "Good old Lockwood. If any officer in His Majesty's service knows Ireland and the Irish, it is he. How I could use such a fellow!"

Chapter Fourteen

James lacked definite orders, a pleasing sense of independence rarely afforded infantry officers. As liberating as that notion was, he reminded himself that he had to maintain a veneer of decisiveness in front of his men. He caught a few questioning glances from the company. He thought of them now as his company, not as a draft, some collection of random men.

The mosquitoes had tormented them all morning, and now the rising heat added to their misery. The Irishmen were drawn up on the dusty dirt road that ran beside the Demerara River, the river to their backs, the low buildings of Georgetown a mile to their left. To their front lay a patchwork of fields, the jungle perhaps three miles beyond. On the Inniskillings' right, the river wound south, lined by an endless stretch of fields and groves, each plantation marked by a handful of buildings, some of them in flames.

The fields around them bore only the stubble of harvested sugar cane, though some fields in the distance held standing crops. James could see people dashing between the cover of those fields. If he were commanding the rebellion, he would have scouts hidden there, watching his potential opponents, and he suspected the slaves were sufficiently organized to have done just that.

"Sergeant Maguire, please ensure that the men have loaded their firelocks and see that their flints are properly mounted."

Maguire saluted and said "Yes, sir," but ventured to ask, "Shall I have the company fix bayonets, sir?"

"Oh, I think not. Things look rather quiet. I doubt we shall find the need to skewer anyone." James said that more loudly than necessary, hoping to calm them. Having loaded muskets was a matter of course, while fixed bayonets meant imminent close action.

James waited for Maguire to go through the ranks and then ordered the men to attention. They were still ragged. They had fought well aboard the *Halcón*, but the perfection of drill still eluded them.

The captain's voice boomed in the still morning air. "Inniskillings! It is our mission to restore order here! I do not know what awaits us, so keep your wits about you, and adhere to the word of command! To the right, road march, march!"

James took his place at the head of the column. He admitted to himself that he would have preferred to direct the column to the north, back to the security of Georgetown. But across the flat fields to the south he could see a bridge, perhaps two miles away, and every infantry officer ever born knew that possession of the bridges was key to any battlefield. That bridge would control passage up the only road into town from the southern plantations.

They marched south, and as they approached the bridge, James was surprised to find it a drawbridge, designed to allow large boats to be moved up the canal to the inland plantations. A large group of slaves, two or three hundred men and women, approached the bridge from the south. The slaves seemed intent on seizing the bridge—his opinion of the tactical acumen of the rebellion's leaders was confirmed. The slaves, however, were armed only with machetes, axes, and a few stolen firearms. When the well-armed redcoats approached, the rebels held back. All except one, an old man with one leg, mounted on a battered old mule.

A hundred yards from the bridge, musket range, James held up a hand to halt his men, then went on alone to speak with the man who rode slowly toward the bridge.

"Ah, Mr. Africanus. I hope I find you well?"

"You do, sir. I have asked my people to fall back, hoping that you and I might come to an understanding."

"What I understand, sir, is that you need to send your people home, and have them return to their duty."

Scipio Africanus scoffed and said, "Their homes, Captain? Those palm frond huts? Their duty? Seven days a week, dawn to dusk, endless toil and humiliation? You amuse me."

Lockwood frowned, folded his arms across his chest, and paused a long moment before saying, "Despite my personal, my wholly personal, sympathies for your condition, sir, my duty requires me to restore order. Order, in this instance, requires you and your people to return to your previous situation."

Africanus paused, eventually saying, "I spoke with the leader of our righteous rising. I will trust you with his name, the only obligation being that you do not share it with the governor and his minions. This is a black man offering his trust—do not betray it. Jack Lancaster it is, of Success Plantation, who leads our revolt. He tells me to say that he has no yearning to fight your soldiers, but will keep our people from work until our rights are recognized and guaranteed."

"I am new here, but from what I have seen of Governor McAllistair, I doubt he will tolerate any defiance. He will certainly muster every man at his disposal..."

Africanus held up a finger, and with the other hand he pulled a scrap of paper from his breast pocket and read: "As far as regular troops, McAllistair, have you two companies of the 1st West India Regiment and the full battalion of the 21st Foot? The government is slapping together a Marine Battalion of four hundred men, officers and seamen from the ships in the river. As to the militia: three battalions, if you include the Provisional Battalion, six hundred men, though most of those white fools are boys and old men and don't know one end of a musket from the other."

James shook his head and muttered, "You are remarkably well informed."

Tucking away his notes, Africanus replied, "The governor doesn't realize his house slaves are people, with heart and minds and ears, so he will say shit in front of them you wouldn't believe. He is an utter damned fool."

James did not argue that point, so Africanus went on. "Now, so far, McAllistair is keeping his men in town, sometimes sending out a few soldiers, mostly to the north, along the coast. On those plantations, every white boy afraid of his shadow is begging for troops, and McAllistair is obliging. So there been no real fighting as of yet, but soon enough you and I know that McAllistair will pick a fight, and real blood will spill."

"Mr. Africanus, pray listen to me. I have seen this type of rising in Ireland a hundred times and more, and the result is always the same: common people, poorly armed, with no organization, cannot face a large force of formed troops, no matter their devotion to a cause. Your people will be cut to pieces, and in the end their lot in life will be worse than before."

"I thank God, Mr. Redcoat, that such choices are not left to one-legged old fools." With that, Africanus turned his mule south, but before rejoining his people he called back to Lockwood, "As a favor, a gesture, I shall tell you this, Mr. Redcoat, and now you are in my debt: two men swam off that sweet little sloop of yours before she blew up. Two men, who swam to the west shore and killed two white men before robbing a group of my people of their clothes, and food, and drink. The two men then rode away, as if the devil was at their heels, a hard man with a head wound, and a fool of an Irishman."

James hissed, "Otero. God *damn* Otero."

Africanus rejoined the people who waited for him, receiving him with obvious kindness and respect. James studied them. So many of them, men and women, carried a machete, issued to cut sugar cane. Those lean black arms swung the heavy blades with deadly ease, prompting James to consider the tactics he might have to employ. He could not allow those strong arms to close with his company. If it came to it, he would have to employ his firepower to keep the mob at bay. It would be an exceptionally ugly encounter.

Some of the rebels looked furious beyond measure, but others looked thoughtful, and might be reasoned with. But as James was a soldier, not a diplomat, he motioned his company forward to complete the seizure of the bridge.

The Irishmen, who had been watching their captain with increasing unease, hustled forward and took up position across the north end of the bridge. It took a few minutes, but they managed to rig the pulleys and ropes to the rough capstan, and cranked up the bridge. James was pleased; a forty foot gap of water was an effective deterrent to any immediate clash. The soldiers stood, returning the glares of the rebels until Africanus waved his crowd away, off to the east. In the distance, the soldiers could see more rebels gathering, by the hundreds, but not challenging the tiny bridgehead. They moved off toward another bridge in the distance, miles away to the east.

An hour passed, and other than a few musket shots from further south and some heavier firing from far away to the north, very little happened. The heat grew steadily, relentlessly, , along with the stench rising from the stagnant water of the canal. Biting flies swarmed, and the Irishmen's regard for Guyana continued to drop.

"Sergeant Maguire!" James finally called. "The men will stand at ease. Have half of them fall out to eat and rest." James was thirsty, but preferred not to ask any of his men for a drink; the clean water in their canteens was likely to be a valuable commodity, and soon. He was, thus, surprised when Private O'Donnell stepped up to offer him an elegant crystal glass full of fresh water.

When the captain gave him a look of astonishment, O'Donnell said with a straight face, "You might remember, sir, we agreed that I'd take up the duties of your servant when we arrived in Georgetown. Before we left the *Halcón*, the poor dear, I took the liberty of visiting Otero's store room, so that I might pick up a few items."

James eyed the beautiful crystal and said, "You have a discerning eye, Private."

With a tilt of his head O'Donnell said, "I have long thought a man might as well be hung for a sheep, as a lamb, sir." Then, after rooting through his haversack, he went on, "Now, I have a good loaf, a lovely Brie, and a tolerable apple for your breakfast. Sadly, the dinner menu will be the same, but I did lay hands on a charming bottle of claret. Senõr Otero had a substantial pantry. It's the pity of the world that it's all at the bottom of that dirty old river now."

James waited for his men to eat before he did so himself. His respite did not last long—he had scarcely sat down in the meager shade of a spindly Awara palm before he saw a carriage trundling down the dusty road from a distant town. As he pulled himself to his feet, James noted that the driver was no hand at even that modest two-horse team. Further, the horses had obviously been harnessed by someone wholly unfamiliar with the intricacies of harness, as the wheeler was slowly being strangled by an imprudent application of the breast strap.

Captain Lockwood was more amused than surprised to find Mr. Read driving. That elderly gentleman scarcely needed to rein his team to a halt, as the two beasts gasped to a stop with discernable relief. A smiling James shook Read's hand and helped him down, saying, "You continue to amaze me, Mr. Read. A soldier, a diplomat, and a keen hand with a rein!"

Read stepped down, pale and stiff, and as James gave him an arm and helped him into the shade, the captain nodded toward O'Donnell and said, "The claret, if you please, Private."

Several of the men nodded in greeting, Read giving a weak wave in return. Private Moriarty, whose unflattering nickname in the company was "Ainnis" ("Wretched"), countered his miserable epithet by hustling forward to spread his blanket for Mr. Read's comfort.

After a nod of appreciation to Moriarty and O'Donnell, Read took a long drink of claret and said, "My dear Captain Lockwood, I am pleased to see you and your men were clever enough to evacuate the *Halcón* before her unfortunate destruction. At Camp House your deaths have been assumed, but the arrival of your boat's crew brought word of your wise move to defend this end of town. I might also mention that your women and children are safely ensconced in the barracks. Now, might you have any notion as to how your ship could have blown up in such a spectacular fashion?"

Lockwood gave the curious Privates Moriarty and O'Donnell a look that sent them hustling back to their friends. Quietly, he told Read, "I have word that Otero has escaped, perhaps in league with one of my men, one whom I had left to guard him."

Read digested that news for a moment, then muttered, "Senõr Otero is an enterprising fellow. He should be knocked on the head at the first opportunity."

"Believe me, sir, I intend to do so. I blame myself. If I had handed him over to McAllistair, the *Halcón* would still be afloat. It was my God damned petulance that allowed him to escape."

"For what my opinion is worth," said Read, "you were wholly in the right in your insistence on a trial, but, contrary to popular belief, doing right is rarely its own reward."

"I shall not be quite so neat next time." He spoke with an edge of rage, but, collecting himself, he went on. "But now to the business at hand. I wonder, sir, if you have spoken to the governor since the start of the rising?"

"I have. I had thought him a fool before this morning, but he now reveals himself a cowardly, violent, irrational fool. He rants, cowers and bluffs, issuing contradictory orders, howling for summary executions. He has no notion of command, or the Rule of Law." After draining his glass, Read added as an aside, "Say what you will about Otero, he had a nose for good wine. But I wander. When I could no longer bear McAllistair's idiocy, I proceeded to the inn, where I found the stable deserted, its staff in rebellion or in hiding. But, being a Northumberland man," here Read swelled with some pride, "I have an innate communion with *Equide Equus*, and so harnessed these honest beasts and struck out in search of you, sir, and your men, trusting in your martial skills."

James glanced over to see Private McNamara, who had served as an Athlone ostler in his youth, shaking his head and re-working the team's harnesses, the two horses responding with something like bliss in their eyes. James asked Read, "What is the situation as you know it, please, sir? I am acting without orders, and, while I believe this bridge to be key to the defense of Georgetown, I wonder if the governor will condone my decisions."

"I am no soldier, but I think no rational being would question your decision to hold this place; even if McAllistair should prove difficult, Colonel Leslie and Major Addis are not such sycophants as to ever disagree with your very prudent moves."

Sergeant Maguire stepped up, saluted, and said, "Beg pardon, sir, but there's a rider approaching from the south. He looks right agitated."

"Very well, Sergeant, pray have the bridge lowered and we'll see what this fellow is about."

The rider was indeed agitated. He galloped across the bridge and, reining in, screamed down at the soldiers, "For God's sake, what are you doing! Are you cowards, or fools? My plantation is overrun by the blacks, and you sit here at your leisure! What the hell are you about, you pack of redcoated..."

The horse was frantic, echoing its master's state. The rider allowed the beast to caper close to the big officer, the one with fury in his eyes. Captain Lockwood grabbed the fellow, pulled him from his horse, and threw him to the ground.

With one foot on the man's chest and one hand on the hilt of his sword, Captain Lockwood growled, "You will collect yourself, sir."

The man had little option but to do so, as he realized he had insulted and angered a very large man, plus a hundred of his armed followers. When James allowed him up, the man stammered, "Right sorry, please, sir. My name is Beckham, owner of Great Diamond Plantation. I have been the most kind and indulgent master, but my people have gone mad! I scarce escaped with me life... For God's sake, sir, will you not march?"

Beckham was an ugly brute, perhaps thirty years old; his clothes were finely tailored, but he spoke with a dense Cockney accent that James had last heard from a Marshalsea pieman.

"I have a hundred men here, Mr. Beckham. I am in no position to garrison every plantation between here and the Amazon."

Beckham was taken aback, finally blurting out, "It's just two miles from here! My family is being held captive! My wife and two little girls will be murdered by those black devils!"

Lockwood frowned, nodded, and folded his arms. Turning his back on the others he took a few steps toward the canal, looking off into the distance. Beckham made as if to interrupt him, but Read waved him back. Lockwood eventually turned back to them and said in a stern tone, "Corporal Shanahan, choose five men; you are with me. Mr. Read, I wonder if I might ask you to delay your return to town? Sergeant Maguire, you will take command of the company, but you will please consult with Mr. Read in any conversations with the rebels. You will fire only in defense of your lives, or the lives of the innocent. Mr. Beckham, you will leave that horse here. It is a damned fool."

"Christ, man!" burst out Beckham, "You'll need more men than that! There's darkies down there that'll..."

Captain Lockwood

Captain Lockwood would brook no discussion. He strode over to the waiting company with Maguire and Shanahan, leaving Mr. Read alone to rebuke Beckham. "Oh, do shut up, sir," he snapped.

Shanahan quickly pointed out his five men. Private O'Donnell, who had surreptitiously shared the last of the claret with his mates, ensured that he was one of the five. As the little party crossed the bridge, Lockwood told Maguire, "Sergeant, pray pull up the drawbridge behind us. We may be a while." ·

They marched in silence, Beckham at Lockwood's side, evidently stung into silence by Read's insult, but finally blurting out, "Can we not pick up the pace a bit, General?"

Lockwood did not bother to look at Beckham, saying only, "I am a captain, sir. Captain James Lockwood, 27th Foot."

"You are a brave cove, coming out here with six men at your back, Captain, but I know this colony, and I can tell you, these blacks respect force, and nothing else. You should have these men fix their bayonets and be prepared to shoot."

Lockwood was unaccustomed to explaining himself to anyone, especially civilians, and never to civilians who were damned fools. But he reminded himself of the politics of this place and the likelihood of this particular damned fool having the governor's ear.

"Mr. Beckham," said James, trying not to clench his teeth, "my men will keep their firelocks on their shoulders. We are not here to assault the rebels. I do not wish to pick a fight." Pointing to the cotton and plantain fields that lay less than a mile off, he went on, "There are hundreds of people out there, and it is likely many of them would be willing to fight if provoked."

"Then why be timid? You could have brought a hundred men! You're fuckin' redcoats!"

194

"A hundred men would likely be seen as a threat, and thus incite a violent response. My hundred men might kill hundreds, but an enraged mass would eventually overrun a hundred men like a wave. That has many times been proven in Ireland. No, sir, we shall tip-toe in, ever so politely, and tip-toe out with your family under protection."

They had passed more than a mile south, and as they came upon some tall grass that lined a section of the road, they were especially cautious. But there was no ambush, only a handsome young couple who peered out at the soldiers.

Beckham saw the couple, and vehemently pointing them out, he yelled, "Oi! I see you, Quoffey, and you, Yobbah!! Quoffey, you had best get back home before Mr. Blue finds you missing and takes the hide off your back! And Yobbah, you return to your duty, or there will be hell to pay! You listen, now!"

To Lockwood, Beckham explained, "Quoffey is from La Penitence, that's up between your bridge and town. He's been sweet on my Yobbah for a year or more, and many a Sunday I've had to chase him off, but I'm going to have her bred to Ned, my prime specimen. That's what comes of giving the blacks a day off. Fuckin' Methodies."

Quoffey expressed his opinion of Beckham by turning and dropping his pants, which drew laughter, hesitant laughter, from Yobbah.

Shaking with rage, Beckham muttered, "Oh, one word from me to Mr. Blue, and that Quoffey will be hanging in chains, just you wait and see. And I'll see to that slut Yobbah myself, oh, Christ, yes."

That rage kept Beckham quiet for the next mile, though they passed more and more people, some of whom were very close to the road, and while they eyed the soldiers, there was no obvious ill intent. James thought to himself that Shanahan had chosen his men well—there was no panic, no foolishness, and, in fact, several times they had ventured a small wave and a casual, "Good morning," although Private Darby's, "*Dia duit*," brought some puzzled looks.

The party eventually turned up the dusty narrow road that led to Great Diamond. Fifty men and women blocked the lane with machetes, axes and clubs in their hands. Beckham, who had walked at Lockwood's side since leaving the bridge, now hung back.

Lockwood halted his little command fifty yards from the rebels, telling Shanahan "Corporal, I am going to go speak to those people. Do stay here, firelocks on your shoulders. If this turns ugly, stay together and fall back to the bridge."

With a sniff of amusement, Corporal Shanahan replied, "If this turns ugly, sir, we had all best sprout wings."

Some of the slaves called out, "Come on, then, white men, and fight us! We will cut your throats for you!" but they were quickly silenced by one man, a stocky youth who stood confidently at the center of the road.

When Beckham saw who stood there, he called, "Billy Carrera! That's my best waistcoat, damn you! You've been in my wardrobe, you insolent bastard! I'll do you for that! These are king's soldiers, and they do what I tell them! Back to work, all of you, or they will kill every one of you!"

Captain Lockwood placed a hand on Beckham's shoulder, and, while not making it obvious he squeezed, very hard. "Mr. Beckham. If you speak again I shall turn you over to those people, and be damned to you. Do you understand?"

That threat seemed to cut Beckham deeply, and after turning decidedly pale, he nodded his understanding.

Lockwood then walked forward, doing his best to look as casual as a six-foot two-inch, fifteen-stone man with a scarlet coat and a sword on his hip could manage. Several of the rebels tensed, looking very eager to cut the soldiers to pieces. But Billy Carrera motioned them back and then walked forward, looking pleased to shake the soldier's proffered hand.

"Good day, sir," said James. "My men and I are here with Mr. Beckham to collect his wife and children, and we shall then see them back to Georgetown."

Billy Carrera gave a hearty, honest laugh, and replied, "He told you that, did he, soldier man? He has no family here. He has no family anywhere on God's Earth. God in heaven, you are a very gullible man to believe anything Beckham says."

In an instant Lockwood saw the truth of it. He paused half a beat, hissed a furious sigh, gave Carrera a slight bow and said, "I beg pardon for wasting your time, sir."

Carrera nodded and said, "You must never trust that man. He is the most vile toad in the colony, sister-son of the governor, and so there has been no law on Great Diamond. But now there is law, as I am master." There was no pride in that statement, only determination. "I lead here for as long as your white God allows. I am not a bad man. And so, I send a few of my people, my wiser people, to walk you back to the canal, soldier man."

As Lockwood turned back to his men he was pelted with verbal abuse, several of the slaves jeering and taunting, "Cowards! Soft old women in red coats! Come fight us, and we shall show you how men fight!"

Lockwood walked straight to Beckham and hissed, "Mr. Beckham, you have deceived me."

Beckham grinned and whispered, "I have six hundred guineas in gold in my office, and by God, I shall not let the blacks have them." Then looking past Lockwood to point at the people who had been his slaves, Beckham screamed so that both the soldiers and the rebels could hear, "Captain Lockwood, are you going to take that abuse, sir? Are you a coward? For God's sake, do your duty, damn you! Shoot them! I am the governor's nephew, his voice here, and I say, fire on those black devils!"

A handful of rebels broke from the crowd, running toward the knot of soldiers, screaming and waving their machetes. The Irishman instantly leveled their muskets, fingers on the triggers, screaming back at the onrushing black men, Beckham in their ears, calling, "Fire! Fire!"

Carrera dashed forward, ordering his people back, but still two came on. Lockwood whipped his sword from his scabbard, but he turned back to his men, roaring, "Shoulder your arms, damn you!" swinging his sword, he knocked the muzzles skyward, but still the two young men came on, heedless, panting and sweating and strong, heading for Beckham, who stood stock-still in terror. Lockwood managed to trip up the first man, who crashed face-first into the hard dirt, but in doing so the captain had left himself vulnerable to the second, who swung his machete with practiced skill. That skill, however, was built on stationary sugar cane, not a man who had trained and fought and killed for the past twenty years. Lockwood dodged the blow, and, with a deft flick of his wrist, he snapped his point up to the young man's throat.

For an instant James was tempted to kill the impudent young fool, but his reason prevailed. He kept the point just at the point of breaking the skin. The young man went very still, terror in his eyes. The taunting and jeering stopped; the mayhem on the road came to a halt. There was silence, all eyes on the huge soldier and the young man.

Then a voice came from the crowd, an older woman's voice, pleading in the still air, "Please, mister soldier, don't kill my Anthony! He's a good boy! Please, let me have him back!"

Lockwood's point did not waver, but he tossed his head toward the woman and told the young man, "Go to your mother, son. No more nonsense, now."

The chastened youth helped his friend to his feet, and with heads down, they slowly returned to the group at the head of the lane. Carrera and some of the older folks scolded the two with some vehemence, and the worst of the tension was broken. James had to use the lull while it lasted.

In as calm a voice as he could muster, James called, "Now that I think of it, Mr. Carrera, I wonder if your people have been read the Riot Act? Lacking that, my men and I have no authority here. As His Majesty's subjects, you have rights. Only after a magistrate has read the Act aloud can His Majesty's troops act against civilians, and even then we have to give them an hour to disperse. Think of Peterloo, sir."

Realization dawned on Carrera's face, and he gave Lockwood a wry smile. So, too, did many of his people understand what was about, and so laughed and jeered at Beckham, rejoicing in the notion that they were indeed people, with inherent rights.

Beckham was incredulous. "But they are rebels!"

Lockwood gave a theatrical shrug and said, "I have seen nothing from the governor placing the colony in a state of rebellion, no Proclamation of Martial Law."

"But they are God damned slaves!"

James spoke very loudly, deliberately throwing his voice. "Do not be foolish. Laws apply to all of his Majesty's subjects, slaves or not. I am intimately familiar with the Act, and I can assure you, it does not make any distinction regarding condition of servitude. This will not do." With a nod to Carrera, Lockwood ordered his men back to the end of the lane, Beckham skipping with rage in their wake.

Carrera sent a handful of rebels—calm, older people—to efficiently escort the soldiers back to the bridgehead. That escort twice needed to shoo off gangs of young men who were anxious to fight, but the redcoats' muskets stayed on their shoulders, and there was no real difficulty. At the bridge, the escort fell back, and Lockwood's weary patrol crossed back over the Inniskilling Bridge. They were welcomed back with open relief.

Beckham stalked to his horse, and with murder in his eyes, he spurred away toward Georgetown.

Mark Bois

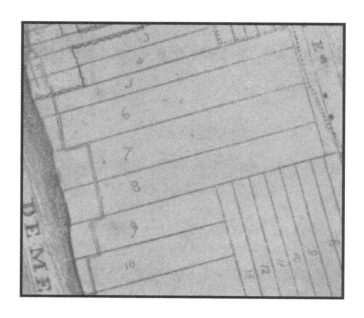

3 Werk en Rust

4 Le Repentir

5 La Penitence

6 Ruimveld

7 Houston

8 Rome

9 Velserhofd

10 Peter's Hall

11 Providence

12 Herstelling

Chapter Fifteen

General Sir John Lambert sat at his desk at the Cork Barrack. A stylish, and to all appearances unconcerned, captain of militia stood at attention before him.

"Captain Daniels, I am angered, nay, *outraged*, with the behavior of the men under your command during the recent weapons search at the village of..."—checking his notes and then butchering the pronunciation—"Aghabullogue. For God's sake, three of your men are charged with the murder of two residents there! The court martial is to be convened next week, and from what I have seen of the evidence, they are likely to be found guilty. Murder, sir! I spoke to them at the garrison bridewell, and all three men say that you, Captain, ordered those people killed. And though you will be called to testify at their trial, I ask you now, on your honour, sir, did you order those people to be killed?"

Daniels sniffed and casually replied, "Stuff and nonsense, sir."

A long reflective pause by Lambert was eventually followed by, "Very well. Point the second: the village priest asserts that you, Captain Daniels, sabered a man from horseback for no cause."

"Sink me, the fellow assaulted me, sir."

Lambert once again consulted his notes. "The wounded man is over seventy, and nearly blind."

The captain had a glimmer of amusement in his eyes.

Lambert eyed him for a moment before he went on. "Very well. Those charges aside, I am prompted to conclude that you are in a state of disdain, perhaps even of loathing, for the majority of this island's population."

The captain made no reply.

"Captain, it is not my intention that the forces under my command should act as a God damned occupying army! Our goal remains the suppression of rebellion, but the common people must be treated with something like God damned respect if we are to keep the whole God damned island from turning against government. And yet you and your ilk continue to act as if this country is your personal fiefdom. Is there not one king's officer in Ireland who has the sense God gave a rabbit? Is there not one, sir?" Still receiving no reply, Lambert gave the rigid captain a backhanded wave and a frustrated, "You are dismissed, sir, you are dismissed."

Lambert turned to look out his window, watching as junior members of his staff tossed around a ball in anticipation of their upcoming cricket match. The previous match had gone very well, and Lambert recalled the pretty woman who had spoken to him.

Calling his ADC from the outer office, Lambert said, "Tankersley, pray fetch Anderson—no, no, never mind, I shall write this letter myself. I mean to pinch one of Warren's officers, and he

203

is a touchy cove. A personal letter will strike a better tone. Pen and ink, if you please. And fetch that map of Cork and Kerry, won't you? I cannot bring to mind the name of a town down there. Damn this mind of mine—I must drink more, or perhaps less—but something must change. Do you recall a town with a name that has to do with kilts?"

*****

Colonel Simon mulled over Miss Lockwood's request for help for the women of Doonasleen. Clonakilty's fledgling police force, five men who answered to the mayor, never ventured beyond the town proper. The barracks on the north side of town housed a hundred officers and men of the Cavan Militia Regiment, red-coated infantry responsible for patrolling the rolling hills above town. But those men were commanded by a timid young lieutenant who rarely kept his men out after dark. The Whiteboys ruled the night across all of Ireland's rural west, and those hundred men could not contest that supremacy.

The nearest major military presence was fifteen miles away, at the Bandon Barracks, home to four additional companies of Cavans, three troops of the Muskerry Legion Cavalry and a troop of the West Cork Yeoman Cavalry. In truth, while Simon could suggest deployment of the other commands, he commanded only the sixty men of the West Corks. It was in his power to call up the rest of the regiment, five additional troops, but that was to be only as an emergency measure. The yeomanry was a tool of the Ascendency, and a rumoured attack on a group of wayward Irishwomen would in no way pose a crisis in their eyes.

*****

Father McGlynn possessed a remarkable voice, a distinguished bearing and a sense of theatricality. He could thus celebrate Mass with a nearly mystical skill, and while his parishioners strained under the apprehension that not to attend Mass was a mortal sin, so great was his appeal that they willingly flocked to him, some on a daily basis.

Of course, not everyone at Mass was a Whiteboy, but McGlynn required every Whiteboy to attend Mass. McGlynn was well aware of his ability to control the rebels through the enchantments of religion.

He was, therefore, infuriated when Darragh O'Falvey came to him after Mass to meekly suggest, "I do beg your pardon, Father, but some of my lads are not over... well, *keen*, on killing anyone up at Doonasleen. Their neighbors say that they are a decent bunch, keeping the place up, and their kids are as..."

McGlynn held up two ecclesiastical fingers, paused a powerful beat, and then said in a tone that gathered fury, "Are 'some of your lads' become slaves to the Saxons, my son? Do 'some of your lads' doubt the authority of Mother Church? Are 'some of your lads' resigning themselves"—building to a crescendo—"to the very flames of hell, and an eternity of torture at the hands of Satan and his demons?!"

O'Falvey quickly crossed himself, then, holding up his rough hands in submission, he said, "Ach, Father, now, please don't doubt them. They're biddable lads, but maybe they've spent too much time with their mothers. They just ask, and mind you, Father, it's them asking, not me, if it would do to just knock some folks around a bit? Draw some blood, scare them right thorough, and still make the point?"

"The *point*, O'Falvey? When His Father asked him to die upon the cross for the sins of the world, did our Lord ask what was the *point*? If you people will not do..."—the priest stopped abruptly, frozen in thought, and then in a tone of revelation, went on—"Of course. I must lead them myself. For all these years I have acted as the head and the heart of this holy cause. And now, as I grow in God's grace, I shall also serve as His hand. I shall lead your people in this action. I shall act as God's avenging sword. I shall strike down on that coven of traitorous witches. But know this, O'Falvey," concluded the priest with a blossoming madness in his eyes, "as God's vengeance shall strike down the witches, so too shall it strike down any of God's soldiers who may falter in his duty. God calls for a wave of blood, one which shall sweep away all who transgress against Him."

*****

For a fortnight Doonasleen had been guarded by an odd collection of sentinels. Every night, Corporal M'Vicar patrolled the east side while Private Doolan patrolled the west. John Cashman, meanwhile, slipped out each night to stalk the most likely approaches to the farm. All three were armed, and all had seen battles, great and small.

Cissy Lockwood had been determined to join her friends in standing the night watch, but her mother would have none of it. "*A cuisle*, it is time that you come to terms with the fact that you are the daughter of a family of means, a lady, with all the benefits and limitations that title brings. Diarmuid, Corporal M'Vicar, and Mr. Cashman are all military men, and we are fortunate in having them watch over us. You and I can best serve these families by working with everyone we know, so that we might ensure their safety and prosperity."

Cissy anticipated her mother's instructions and had prepared a defiant response, but she held back. She was maturing, and while she saw in her mother's face fear, indecision and, perhaps, a brief flush of weakness, she saw also love, protection and an enduring morality. And so Cissy did not contest her mother's instructions, though she retained a private passion to *act*.

Each night the doors of the farm were barred and every window shuttered, battened from within. There had been several rainy nights, but, even so, every available container was filled with water, in case the Whiteboys should resort to incendiary tactics, as thatched roofs were exceptionally flammable.

With each dawn, the three weary sentinels would lay down their arms to get what sleep they could. Like Cissy, Brigid lived at Doonasleen, spending her days watching over her charges while the farm went about its business. A threat of violence or not, the army wives displayed a knack for raising poultry, and, in turn, selling their eggs in town. They quickly turned a profit, and amongst the market regulars and the people of Cloghgriffin Township the army families were respected, and very nearly appreciated.

That reputation had not altered the Whiteboys' determination. Brigid carried a note in her pocket, newly arrived from her uncle: "*My words were in vain. They will come soon, a grah. For God's sake return home to sleep at Fáibhile Cottage, and let happen what must happen. You need not endanger yourself, or your daughter.*"

The next morning found Marie Hurley slowly walking up Templequinlan Road to offer further advice on the proper rearing of chickens. She did so every few days, not so much from necessity as from a liking for the people of the farm. She no longer had children in her life, and that gap in her heart was filled by the tumbling *leanaí* of Doonasleen.

That morning, her visit was a typical one, but for one hurried moment when she was alone with Cissy. The old woman grabbed Cissy's collar and hissed with a sudden urgency, "Quickly, now—do you know they will be coming soon, dear girl? You must protect these babies! For God's sake be on your guard!" And then Marie moved on, tottering toward home, little Honora O'Leary holding her hand as far as the end of the lane.

*****

Father McGlynn's education at the Collège des Irlandais in Paris had not included any coursework in military tactics, but that deficiency was rectified by a number of military treatises perused over the years. He could not, of course, keep such titles on his bookshelf, and so stored them beneath the altar, prying up a slab which covered the grave of a predecessor, one Father Mac Fhlannchaidh, who had been slain by Cromwell's men in 1641. Mac Fhlannchaidh's dusty remains offered no protest.

For years McGlynn had successfully directed his rag-tag rebels, employing the advice of authors as diverse as Sun Tzu, Tacitus, and Frederick the Great. That night he studied a new book, an obscure American work that listed the advantages of a night attack:

—*Darkness can conceal the movement of large forces.*
—*Physical and psychological factors favoring the attacker (shock, disorientation, and isolation) are easier to achieve— element of surprise is increased.*

The author also included a list of disadvantages, some of which caught his eye.

—*Command and control are more difficult.*
—*Terrain is more difficult to traverse.*

*—The attacker loses momentum, because he attacks at a
reduced speed in order to maintain the coherence of the unit.*
—Land navigation is more difficult at night.
—The risk of fratricide

The last on the list made McGlynn smile wickedly; nearly every battle in Ireland's long history had not just risked, but positively reveled in, fratricide.

He mulled over the American's points—they all rang true. With sudden inspiration, McGlynn rose and stalked back to the sanctuary to consult his almanac. In three more days the waxing moon would set at two in the morning. McGlynn decided to move his men in the moonlight and get them settled into their positions, but only after complete darkness fell would they attack, kill without mercy and retreat into the night.

As he returned the treatise to the tomb, McGlynn eyed the twenty French muskets that had lain alongside Father Mac Fhlannchaidh for five years or more. With sudden clarity, he knew their time had come: he would loose them upon God's foes.

Late that night the O'Falveys gathered in a secluded field outside Clonakilty to receive their orders. They were not surprised to hear that they were to attack Doonasleen three nights hence. Though they had, once again, been drinking, even two bottles of *eischa beatha* had not prepared them for what McGlynn did next. The priest led them down through the hedges and into the town, where anyone might see them, and then into the Chapel of Saint Brigid itself.

McGlynn had left that day's prayer candles burning, and in that dancing red light the priest distributed Charleville muskets to quaking Irish hands. The Whiteboys could rarely match their opponents in weaponry, but with a gift like God's own grace they now held modern muskets and received them with a fierce, reverent, determination. With such weapons in their hands, their hesitance to kill diminished.

*****

Sister Margaret was displeased with Sister Theresa. While the house of the Little Sisters of Mercy had voted to aid the army families of Doonasleen, Sister Theresa had become increasingly reluctant to do so. Margaret loved and respected Theresa, and only with the greatest hesitation did she decide to challenge her on the matter.

Theresa, however, had been summoned—there was no other word for it—to St. Brigid's to meet with Father McGlynn and Bishop Brady. Undaunted, Margaret discreetly followed her there, and then waited across the street in the doorway of Mary Fitzpatrick's bookshop to avoid the misting autumn rain.

Sister Theresa was an older woman, but when she stalked out the door of St. Brigid's, Margaret had to hurry to keep up with her. Theresa, angry and distracted, did not seem surprised to see Margaret there. As they hustled down the Western Road, Theresa pulled a sheet of paper from the folds of her habit, handling it as if was straight from Satan's desk. "Bishop Brady presented me with a letter from the archbishop, Sister. The archbishop! We are to restrict the focus of our activities. O'Connell's Catholic Association is about to ally itself with the Church, but such a union makes the Castle very nervous, so for the foreseeable future both the Association and the Church mean to look very passive, at least until the Castle is accustomed to the union."

"Passive!" cried the young nun. "Are we to allow the poor and sick to suffer while the great men play politics?"

With regret in her voice Theresa went on. "We shall continue our work with the weak and poor, Sister. But the Father, the bishop, and now the archbishop, all order that we do not interfere with what is going on over at Doonasleen. We dare not defy them."

Sister Theresa knew nothing of Father McGlynn's connection with the Whiteboys, and Margaret would not tell her, for fear of revealing her own knowledge of the movement, and likely betraying her uncle. But Margaret had been calling on Aileen O'Falvey, who had been ill for many weeks, and Margaret told herself "After I pray with Aileen, won't I find those two worthless sons of hers, and give them each a piece of my mind."

*****

Brigid Lockwood returned to Fáibhile Cottage in time to hurriedly dust her drawing room and prepare tea. She had invited some prominent people to tea, and was determined to keep up appearances. She expected Colonel Simon of the West Corks, Major and Mrs. Jackson of the Cavan Militia, and Major Gaye of the Muskerry Legion Cavalry. Brigid had long been a friend to Colonel Simon, and thankfully, it had been some years since she had found it necessary to fend off his attentions. She was acquainted with Major and Mrs. Jackson, as that lady was active in area charities. She had only once been introduced to Major Gaye, and although she had hoped to gather support from the local militia, she thought him a loathsome toad.

The little party was a disaster. Colonel Simon committed a breach of etiquette by bringing along his nephew, the uninvited Reverend Cyril Babcock. Fully aware of this social faux pas, Simon was unsettled and defensive. Major Jackson was pleasant but non-committal and Major Gaye took the opportunity to sit inappropriately close to Mrs. Lockwood. Only Mrs. Jackson's intervention prevented a very unpleasant scene.

If the military men were polite in their refusal to commit to the defense of Doonasleen, Reverend Babcock was less subtle in his opinions. "If I may be blunt, my dear Mrs. Lockwood?" He gave her one of his pastoral smiles; Brigid very much wanted to slap it off his handsome face. "If the natives desire to murder one another... well, perhaps we might allow them to do so? Let the criminal elements prey upon one another, and decent society benefits! Q.E.D!"

"Reverend Babcock, these are innocent women and children!"

"So you say, madam, but contrary to popular notions, women and children are not *by nature* innocent. Did not God burden us all with Original Sin? Article IX of the Thirty-Nine Articles, the foundation of the True Church, tells us, '*in every person born into this world, it deserveth God's wrath and damnation.*'"

When the miserable party finally broke up, Brigid was left with the dirty dishes and a realization that the Anglican establishment would do nothing to protect the families of Doonasleen.

*****

It was October, and that night was especially cool, although it looked to stay dry. Over the past three weeks, Diarmuid Doolan had worn a path into the turf west of Doonasleen. His musket was on his shoulder, loaded and with the bayonet fixed, as was the doctrine of the 27th Foot, if night action was possible.

The 27th Foot, however, had no tradition of beautiful young women accompanying the regiment's sentinels. Corporal typically slept at the foot of Cissy's bed, and she had to walk tiptoe to get past the snoring beast some time after two o'clock in the morning to surreptitiously join Private Doolan's watch.

"You know, girl, if your mother knew you were out here with me she would skin us both."

In the dim moonlight he missed her smile, but he heard it in her voice when she replied, "My mother would be pleased, though, if she heard I was out walking with an eligible gentleman. She so very much wishes to be a grandmother. Without news from Mary in France she depends on me, though thus far I am afraid I have proved a sad disappointment."

Doolan coughed the rough laugh unique to elderly Irishmen. "A bit of advice, *a grah*: if you are striking out upon a romantic stroll, do not carry a shotgun on your shoulder. Now, what type of load have you chosen?"

Cissy laughed the bubbling laugh that, in the past, had dented the heart of several young men, and said, "Any man who calls upon me had best be prepared for a woman of will. As to my load: I have opted to play the American, and loaded buck and ball."

Doolan muttered, "In the service we call them 'Jonathans.' Mad fools, the lot of 'em. But their buck and ball may be the very thing for a night like this. In this feckin' darkness a wide bite might serve better than a keen one."

*****

In that same faint moonlight, Father McGlynn gathered his command in a secluded field, and in the shadow of a hedge, he had each of them come forward so that he might hear their confession. That lull allowed the O'Falvey men to share three bottles of poteen, a gift from the good father. Confident of heaven, distinctly drunk, and awkwardly bearing their new muskets, those sixteen men formed up and followed McGlynn across the fields for the final mile to Doonasleen.

Captain Lockwood

*****

For the first hours of the night, John Cashman patrolled the stone fences and hedges east of Doonasleen, and finding the night quiet there, he slipped back to the farm.

M'Vicar was alert. "Tilly," he said, pulling back the hammers of his carbine.

"Goldilocks," replied Cashman. They used the names of the farm's chickens as sign and countersign. Tossing his head to the east, Cashman said, "It's quiet as a tomb out there—I'll go check on our redcoat."

With a nod of approval, M'Vicar said, "Quiet is fine by me, Irish. Tell Doolan that I think he's a miserable old ground pounder."

Cashman flashed a grin and walked across the silent farm yard. He scarcely knew M'Vicar; they shared only the regard tough men hold for one another. That tough old corporal carried his carbine and had his curved sabre slung across his back. Cashman had two knives in his belt, a double–barreled shotgun in his hands and another on his back; M'Vicar had not asked how he had come across such an arsenal.

A moment later Cashman and Doolan exchanged the names of chickens, which brought a smile to Cissy's face. As Cashman strode up, he appeared unsurprised to find Miss Lockwood with her light shotgun patrolling alongside Doolan.

Among themselves they spoke only Irish. Cashman quietly said, "M'Vicar's side is quiet, so I thought I'd wander over here to see if the devil is out tonight."

Doolan scoffed and said, "If he is, give him my regards."

"The priest will be here to make introductions, soon enough."

As Cashman slipped away to the north, silent as a cat, Cissy hastily whispered, "Do be careful, James."

214

From the darkness a shadow whispered. "is waiting for me at home, isn't she? If I get killed out here I'll never hear the end of it."

With that, the shadow slipped away.

*****

The moon had set, and it had gone very dark. Only a few stars illuminated the fields of Doonasleen. A rustling sound made Cissy look off toward Cnoc na Sióg, the fairy fort; she had thought herself accustomed to it, but she was Irish, and in that darkness she knew the low mound bled menace.

For a moment she doubted her senses. In the starlight she saw shadows emerging from Cnoc na Sióg, furtive and silent, rushing toward her. It was madness, surely, for her to see fairies, there were no fairies—the fiery plume of a shotgun split the darkness, split the silence. Another blast—the other barrel.

The firing came from the wall down by the pigs' field, firing at the fairy fort shadows. Cashman had spotted them, but too late. The Whiteboys were past him, but he had alerted the watch, and shouts and cries amongst the shadowy figures showed that Cashman had surprised, confused, and likely injured some. But still they came on, shouting, and then roaring.

Cissy hurriedly raised her shotgun to her shoulder, pointing at any shadow that caught her eye, but then a calm whisper was in her ear: Doolan, saying, "Don't betray your position—you have one shot —don't throw it away, *a cuisle*. Wait for one to draw close, make certain of him, and fire. Then drop your weapon and run."

From the field, perhaps fifty yards away, two muskets fired back toward the shotgun, the flashes silhouetting ten men or more running toward Doonasleen. "No, not yet," whispered Doolan.

A few seconds passed, her mad panic dropping, her nerve returning. Two more shotgun blasts, closer, now. Cashman was moving, hacking at the Whiteboys' rear.

Gasping, roaring shadows were closer now as Cissy's finger tightened on the trigger. Another Whiteboy fired at Cashman, a wild, foolish shot, and in its flash, Cissy saw a man—ten yards away, perhaps, and carrying a musket. She fired. The flash of the primer enflamed her cheek, followed by a roaring cone of fire and smoke and shot. The man fell, screaming, and then Doolan fired as well, his man just feet away, and from the darkness a voice—she thought it might be the priest—screamed, "Fire!" and ten or more Whiteboys fired, an organized volley, balls filling the air.

Cissy heard those balls whistle past her, and madly reached out for Doolan's hand so that they might bolt back into the farm for cover and to reload. But he was not there. In the darkness she reached out, desperately seeking him out, afraid to call for him as the shadowy Whiteboys came on. She finally found him lying in the grass, his blood hot and sticky on her hands, and he gasped, "Run," but she would not leave him. She threw her dark cloak around them, a tussock in the rich dark Irish grass, praying they would be missed.

The priest, she was sure now that it was the priest, screamed, "Charge! Take your revenge!"

The shouting Whiteboys pounded out the last yards toward Doonasleen. Cissy could hear them all around her, and with a heavy thudding kick, one running figure tripped over her. From his knees the panting, terrified voice of a very young man cried, "What the hell is that!"

Cissy could only make herself as small as possible, holding the cloak over the crumpled Doolan, who was very still.

216

A shot came from the farm, and the young man dropped. Corporal M'Vicar called, "Cissy! Doolan!" and Cissy nearly called for him, but more shots erupted, back and forth. She clung to Doolan in the cold wet grass, whispering, "Oh, please, Diarmuid *a grah*, you must not be badly hurt. Please tell me you're not badly hurt."

There were more shots, more shouting, and from very nearby Cissy heard McGlynn screaming, "Come back, you cowards! God commands you to fight these devils!" Encouraged, Cissy peered out. Just as she did so, the field was suddenly bathed in light. One of the shuttered windows of Doonasleen was thrown open, every lantern burning, a number of women silhouetted there. The remaining Whiteboys froze for an instant, just feet from the blazing light, and in thunderous flashes the farm's pistols fired, and three men around McGlynn crumpled, but, as if immortal, he stood unscathed.

From the window, Brigid frantically screamed for her daughter, and Cissy could not resist replying, lifting her head and calling for her mother.

McGlynn saw her, nearly at his feet.

McGlynn raised his pistol toward Cissy, crying out, "Die, harlot!" but then a shadow flew across the field, the dark form of John Cashman, a flashing knife in each hand, a shadow that passed over and swallowed the priest.

Chapter Sixteen

The men of the patrol gathered around their captain. "Well done, all," he said. "Get some sleep, now." James then considered the wisdom of getting some rest himself. At first, the question of sleep was a professional one, as he had not slept in thirty-six hours, but once he thought of closing his eyes, he realized how very tired he was.

Lockwood wiped the sweat from his face, the afternoon sun pounding through the scarlet broadcloth of his coat. When Private O'Donnell brought him a cup of Captain Otero's wine he drank deeply. Looking about, James was pleased with Maguire—the company was well in hand. Half the men were in their shirtsleeves in the shade, napping or tending small cook fires. The men on duty were in their coats and shakoes, but were allowed to sit in their ranks, quietly chatting.

James yawned, stretched his eyes, and muttered, "Christ but it's hot." Turning to the waiting Maguire, he said aloud, "Make your report, Sergeant."

"Things have been quiet, sir; we've had no contact with the rebels at all." When the captain turned to look for the carriage, Maguire added, "Mr. Read returned to Georgetown about an hour ago."

James motioned toward the cook fires and asked, "Whatever can they be cooking in this damned heat?"

With some pleasure Maguire said, "Some old folks came down from Georgetown to trade with us, sir. It seems that flour is terrible dear here, so the blacks think our old biscuits are like candy; it's all what you're used to, I suppose. A handful of biscuits got us bundles of these yellow things, plantains they're called, something like a potato, but sweet, like. Damned tasty! I believe Private McIlhenny is frying some up for you now, sir."

A number of Awara palms lined the canal, and while the larger clusters were populated by dozing redcoats, a small grove had been set aside for Captain Lockwood's use. In that welcome shade, James sat on a fallen trunk and set to the bottle of claret.

Private O'Donnell came over to bring a plate of fried plantains, which indeed proved a treat, pairing well with the claret. O'Donnell then laid out a blanket for the captain's bed, prompting that gentleman to say between bites, "I believe I ordered you to get some rest."

"Not to worry, sir. McIlhenny is frying me a couple of those plantains, and after my dinner I shall sleep like the dead, sure."

After a long drink of wine, James waved his fork at the private and said, "You seem to be settling into army life rather well, O'Donnell."

The soldier brushed some rocks and twigs from under the blanket and replied, "It's not so bad, is it, sir?

"All modesty aside, Private, you are fortunate in serving with this regiment." James found the wine going to his head. "It is my informed opinion that the 27th is one of the best regiments in the army, even if we are not especially fashionable."

O'Donnell hesitated for a moment, then took a seat on a trunk opposite his captain and said, "You know, sir, that prating cock O'Boyle won't shut up about the regiment at Waterloo. Is he right, sir, in saying that the Inniskillings were the bravest men on the field?"

James took another drink of wine and quietly said, "Waterloo? Well, none of our people ran."

"And so tell me, then, sir, why wouldn't a sane man run from such a place?"

"Well, out of fear, of course."

"Fear, sir? The lash?"

"Oh, no, not for fear of any physical punishment. No flogging is enough to force a man to face a hell like Waterloo. It was fear..." James took a long pull, and after an unfocused moment he frowned at God and added, "...of disgrace." Another long swallow. "Englishmen of my class believe they have a monopoly on honour. But I have been an officer of this regiment long enough to know that nearly every one of us, no matter his rank or birth, values the esteem of his brother soldiers more than he values his own life. A man does not risk his life for King and Country, and it is especially foolish to think an Irishmen would die for England, and an English king. No, a soldier, a true soldier, risks his life to protect his brothers, and to have them know that he is a man."

O'Donnell pondered that for a moment and then said, "Well, now, you say they stayed together out of fear, sir. And while I'm new to this business of soldiering, I have tasted a bit of fighting, and I wonder if a better word is 'love,' sir. I wonder if they stayed because they loved one another, with all the roses and thorns such a word carries."

As the captain stared into his wine, O'Donnell rose and went on, "Now, sir, I shall leave you to sleep a bit. And as long as we are speaking of love, I might mention that it has been a while since you have written anything to Mrs. Lockwood, sir, and you might think of a few lines to put down when you get a chance. You must keep writing to her, sir, as I keep writing to my people at home. Ties to home and decency, that's a good man's path. I wonder if that is the reason so many of the whites here in Guyana have gone so very bad."

James did go to sleep with thoughts of Brigid tumbling through his head, but not before pondering the depths of Private Conchobhar O'Donnell.

*****

Private McIlhenny shook him awake. "Beg pardon, beg pardon, sir, but there's a column of troops coming down from Georgetown."

James was instantly irritated. He had been dreaming of Brigid and resented leaving her, particularly for such an abrupt return to this hot, insistent place. More than that, as he came awake James could see the sun was low in the western sky, and he had meant to sleep only an hour or two. He should have left orders to be woken—he had been slack, and he cursed himself.

"Fucking hell," muttered the captain as he sat up. That nearly drew a grin from the young private, who was soldier enough to remain straight-faced as he turned to rejoin to his friends.

As he threw on his coat James barked out to Maguire, "Sergeant, the company will fall in!"

Captain Lockwood

As the men hustled to dress and assemble, James stepped out into the road to study the newcomers. The column had halted a half mile off, and looked thoroughly disorganized. O'Donnell stepped up, handed the captain his small brass telescope, and asked, "Brother redcoats, sir?"

Lockwood made an effort to swallow his foul mood. He studied the column for a moment before saying, "A militia regiment. Red coats do not a soldier make, Private. Their colonel looks to have ordered a reversal in their order of march, to right in front... A difficult transition on this ground... and haven't they made a cock of it." Smiling now, his eye still to the glass, the captain added, "Oh, the colonel looks to be a man of some temper. How he harangues them. There... the first company has regained its senses, and all's well that ends well, I suppose. They shall be joining us shortly."

The militia regiment advanced, its colonel at the head, looking furious and embarrassed, with another officer in a blue coat riding at his side. Lockwood and his company were smartly drawn up and snapped a salute as the column passed. The colonel, a potbellied man of at least seventy years, scarcely acknowledged the salute as his regiment passed over the bridge. James had been a soldier for twenty-five years, and beneath the fresh uniforms of the militiamen he saw a motley assortment of clerks, dock hands, and shop boys. Nearly every white man in the colony was enrolled in the militia, the only requirement being a white skin. Government was generous in supplying the whites to suborn the blacks: weapons, uniforms, and pay, a deliberate effort to segregate and intimidate.

The last company of militiamen detached from the column and clumsily formed line across the south end of the bridge, while the remainder of the regiment passed off to the south. James shook his head—no soldier ever born chose to defend ground with a bridge to his rear. In a flash James recalled how once Brigid, after having a bit too much wine, had used a coarse phrase he admired: 'Feckin' eejits,' and he had to stare off into the scorching sky for a moment to suppress his grin.

So intent was James on studying the militiamen that he failed to notice the officer in the blue coat, who had pulled his mount off to one side. That gentleman drew close to James, leaned over his horse's neck and said with a smile, "Really, Lockwood, I had thought myself worthy of at least a 'good day,' although perhaps your time ashore has erased your affection for the Royal Navy."

"My dear Quash!" cried the delighted Lockwood. "My dear fellow, how do you do? How do you come here?"

The smiling Captain Quash slid from the saddle, and after James had crushed his hand in an iron grip, Quash said, "McAllistair has snapped up my marines and most of my crew as part of some composite regiment. I shall command the battalion once it's formed, but that will be another day or two, so I thought to come see you. That lot," he explained, motioning toward the militia that continued over the bridge, "the Christchurch Militia Regiment under Colonel Amos Cowden, if you were wondering, is to relieve you here."

Tilting his head toward the militiamen, James said, "Your Colonel Cowden opted not to speak to me?"

"He was embarrassed, the poor old fellow. His regiment must look like stumbling amateurs to a professional like yourself, and he is a touchy cove."

James sniffed and replied, "His regiment is made up of civilians playing dress-up, but for this Cowden fellow to attempt complex maneuvers with such men, on this ground, makes the lot of them look foolish."

"Pray, what is the relationship between militia and line officers? We do not have such issues in the navy, as our service is superior in every way, but in the army, would you be forced to obey a colonel of militia?"

James frowned and said, "That is a matter of some contention, especially in the colonies, where militia and line regiments routinely bump heads. If Cowden pressed the point there would be no question of who was in command; while a line captain always supersedes a captain of militia, a colonel is another matter. Thus, a fellow who spends his days counting beans could dig a uniform coat out of his trunk and order a captain of twenty years' active service to sing 'Greensleeves' and jump in the canal."

They both went silent, cocking their heads, listening to scattered musket shots from off toward the south. James shook his head in mute anger, closed his eyes for a long moment, then muttered, "And a man who counts beans for a living can also order his people to shoot everything that moves."

Quash nodded solemnly and said, "They were ordered to recover Great Diamond Plantation. I hear that you have been there yourself?"

"I have. The rebels holding the plantation seem reasonable, but dedicated."

"Dedicated slaves?" said Quash. "They must have found a capable leader. Still, Camden's five hundred bayonets will likely scatter them."

For a moment James was tempted to argue, but exhaled and said only, "It will be ugly. These things are always ugly."

With regret in his voice Quash said, "I also carry orders from Governor McAllistair. You and your company are to return to Georgetown, where you will report to the governor at Camp House."

In a private tone he added, "I might mention, James, that the governor is displeased about the escape of our friend Otero, and has been further stoked into a state of agitation by Mr. Beckham."

Captain Lockwood grimaced, nodded, and said, "I had expected as much."

Quash gave a quick smile, then paused for such a lengthy period that Lockwood gave him a look of anticipation. Quash went on, "It is not really my place to say, James, but as I consider myself your friend, I feel warranted in sharing a bit of information that was disclosed to the senior officers of the colony. McAllistair has received confirmation that your regiment is sailing from Gibraltar and is expected to arrive here in three weeks or less."

James was unsuccessful in stifling a wide smile.

Quash raised his eyebrows in an affable manner and said, "I assumed that news would please you. The governor's conduct toward you may be tempered by the knowledge that the officers of your regiment will soon play a major role in domestic matters, but, more importantly, in relations with London. He is not so much a fool as to ignore your reputation in the service, and within your regiment. The next few weeks shall prove to be most interesting."

"I may have mentioned that my wife is an Irishwoman, one who is fond of a saying common among her people. I shall not attempt the Irish, but in English it is said, 'If your messenger is slow, go to meet him.' If the governor wishes to give me a thumping, perhaps I had best go and see him."

*****

The sun had dropped to the horizon as the Inniskillings marched back toward Georgetown, the last rays playing on the dusty column of twos. Captain Lockwood was at their head, accompanied by Captain Quash, who led his horse as the two officers chatted.

Quash took a bite of the plantain supplied by Private McIlhenny, saying, "These are quite good, aren't they? As I was saying, McAllistair called upon the merchant ships to land their crews for his provisional battalion, but Clapsaddle would have none of it. He took the *Dispatch* out, bound for Jamaica, though he asked me to tender his regards."

"Noble fellow. He fought like a lion when we boarded *Halcón*, you know." After a pause Lockwood went on, "I wonder, Quash, if I might ask your opinion on a matter which has troubled me in the past, as the situation here has brought it rather to the boil."

"Goodness, James," said Quash with a smile, but without looking at him, "this sounds quite serious. Are you perhaps contemplating selling out and taking up a life at sea?"

James sniffed a laugh and said, "You perhaps do not face such quandaries in the navy, but I find my duty increasingly at odds with my personal convictions." He was careful not to commit himself; he considered Quash a friend, but they did not, could not, share a bond that allowed complete honesty. James hesitated. He shared his innermost concerns with Brigid, of course, and dear old Tom Mainwaring... the list in his head ended there.

The discussion was curtailed by a scream from up the road, and after a moment, a young black woman darted from a sugar cane field, bare breasted, her clothing torn, two young black men in pounding pursuit. More voices erupted from the field, some roaring, some shrill, calling for help.

James sighed, shook his head, and said, "Sergeant Maguire, deploy first platoon."

226

Quash placed a hand on his sword hilt and said, "I am a tolerant man, but I have always found rapists to be unpleasant fellows."

The screaming young woman reached them, taking panting refuge behind Corporal Shanahan. Her pursuers drew up ten yards from the soldiers, at a loss, until a pudgy young white man came crashing from the field to stand beside them.

It took a moment for the white boy—he was every bit a boy—to catch his breath enough to say, "These men work for me, and that girl belongs to me, soldier boys! My father owns Werk en Rust, and he told me to gather our people!"

Quash sniffed in disgust. Lockwood stepped toward the boy and said, "There is a difference between 'gathering' and 'raping,'"—there was a noticeable pause as Lockwood lost his temper—"you insolent goddamned puppy. And if you call this company of His Majesty's soldiers 'boys' again, I shall kick your adolescent arse from here to Jamaica."

There was a growl of agreement from the ranks, and James heard someone, perhaps McIlhenny, mutter, "Let's skewer the blackguards."

Maguire growled, "Silence in the ranks, there. You lads will skewer only those the captain tells you to skewer, and no one else."

The boy heard all that, and his eyes went wide in shock and—not a little—fear. The young woman, clutching the rags of clothing remaining to her, still standing behind Shanahan, gathered herself to yell, "My sisters are in that field, please, sir! Don't you leave them to that Jacob Van Haanrade!"

"Sergeant Maguire!" growled Lockwood. "Second platoon will assume skirmish order and clear that field!"

The Irishmen rolled into the field, and after several minutes of yelling, crashing and thumping, four black men, somewhat the worse for the wear, were brought out to the road. Two battered women followed, cursing the four men with impressive fury. With more than a few kicks, Van Haanrade and his men were sent south and told not to veer from their course until they reached the Straits of Magellan. The three women were told to go home and stay close to their men, though Lockwood had little hope for their future.

The company continued north into Georgetown.

*****

A small, battered boat leaned into the brisk southwest breeze as she rounded Wakenaam Island, leaving the Essequibo River in her wake. At the helm was a tense, silent black man, one who expertly drew every bit of speed from his boat, eager to get these two white devils to the Oronoco, out of his boat, and out of his life.

One of the white devils was Private James Hogan, who lay in the bottom of the boat steadily snoring. In the bow crouched the second white devil, Captain Miguel Otero, a pistol in his belt, a long slender knife in his hand, its blade sparkling in the sun.

There was silence in the boat as afternoon wore on. Eventually the wind wore more westerly, and as the boatman fought to keep his course to the north-northwest the boat heavily shouldered the rising waves. Water broke over the gunwale, waking Hogan. He sat up blinking, disoriented, saying, "What the hell?" But then, seeing Otero, the knife, and the furious man at the helm, Hogan recalled the choices he had made and grimly sat, considering them.

Otero had a bottle. "Tell me, Senõr Edourd," he called back to the man at the tiller, "you seem to love this boat, this…"—tapping the gunwale he went on in a thick Irish accent—"…this precious blossom?"

"I do," Edourd said with restraint in his voice, but that restraint did not extend to his eyes and the hatred that lived there. "I worked for twenty filthy years to buy her."

"She's old, but she performs well. It is a pity we had to force you to carry my companion and me. But after all, when you return home you have two prime horses to compensate you for your time."

"What would I want with two stolen horses, white man? I am a free man, but the plantation men would have me in chains in one damned minute if they found me with stolen fucking horses. I am a free man, and I shall stay one. This boat is my life."

"You choose your words well, Senõr," said Otero with a smirk, "for in this instance your boat is indeed your life. I am seaman enough to know that the Oronoco is treacherous, and as you know this boat and these waters, I leave the helm to you." Otero took a long drink, then added, "See us to the Oronoco, and you shall be showered with fucking reward. See us not to the Oronoco, and I shall see you showered with fucking pain."

*****

The streets of Georgetown proved to be full of men in uniform, but the Inniskillings looked at them askance, as mere civilians playing at soldier. One militia battalion was dressed in dark green uniforms identical to those of the 95th Foot, "the Rifles," one of the premier light regiments in Europe. The Rifles had served beside the Inniskillings at Waterloo, and to see grinning militiamen playfully aiming Baker rifles at one another made Lockwood wince.

It was nearly dark when the Inniskillings reached Camp House.

Turning to Maguire, Lockwood said, "Sergeant, carry on to the barracks. Seek out the barracks commander, and request rations and a quiet place to bivouac. The commander will be a regular officer, but do watch out for militiamen. Remain polite and cooperative, but allow no disrespect."

Lockwood strode up the steps and was clumsily saluted by two militiamen. He had scarcely opened the door before Major Addis waved him directly to the governor's door.

With a significant cant to his voice Addis said, "The Governor will see you *immediately*."

Governor McAllistair did not rise when Captain Lockwood entered his office, nor did he acknowledge the Captain's salute. He continued signing a number of papers that lay across his desk. It was intended as an insult, but as Lockwood had expected such treatment, he used the pause to his advantage. He studied the governor—he seemed older, weaker, and his eye had developed a discernible twitch. James saw that the papers on his desk were orders of execution. The nervous old man did not even bother to review them before he signed.

Eventually the Governor turned and snarled, "Captain Lockwood, I have never had an officer in my service who has posed such a burden, nay, more, an absolute *obstacle*, to this colony's interests. First, your headstrong insistence on legal niceties leads to the escape of the pirate Otero and the destruction of a valuable schooner. Compounding that folly, you then failed to render aid to a propertied citizen of this colony, exposing him to humiliation and loss of property at the hands of a pack of slathering black mongrels!"

Lockwood, at strict attention before McAllistair's imposing desk, raised an eyebrow and asked, "Slathering, sir?"

"Yes, God damn it, sir, slathering!" The governor ran a hand across his face, breathing hard, sinking into a pensive fury. As he steadily stewed, Lockwood consoled himself with the thought that this regiment and its tradition of soldiering—*God damned professionals*, he nearly said aloud—would arrive in just weeks.

In a throttled tone, McAllistair went on, "It is my intention, however, Captain, to give you opportunity to redeem yourself. My personal safety is very much at risk, so I shall employ your company as my guard. You, sir, will be allowed to select a few men, a corporal's guard, but no more, mind you, and you will be transported to the mouth of the Orinoco. I shall loan you my best tracker, an Ingarikó Indian named Tarong. He is a foul brute, but in the past ten years he has retrieved nearly a hundred escaped slaves from all corners of this colony. Upon your arrival on the Orinoco, you will employ Tarong to track the pirate, Otero. You will apprehend Otero and return him to the judgment of this government for immediate execution. You fail at your peril."

*****

The company was scattered across the parade ground on Georgetown's eastern border, a few small fires keeping the night at bay. Slave women emerged out of the darkness, obviously exhausted but mute, bringing the troops some sacks of biscuit and beef, a firkin of rum, and bundles of firewood. When some of the Irish got to their feet to help them with their burdens, the surprised women flashed them looks of appreciation. As Private Rooney relieved an older woman of her burden he said, "*Go raibh maith agat, Máthair.*" She looked at him in fear, as if expecting a blow, until Private McCarthy explained, "He says, 'Thank you, Mother.'" They were rewarded with a golden smile.

A stiff breeze coming in from the sea brought some measure of relief from the heat and the insects. Some of the men had acquired the hardened soldier's habit of sleeping at every opportunity, no matter how brief. Others sat about the fires, chatting with their mates, occasionally cocking their ears to the sounds of scattered gunfire to the east. They had the sprawling parade ground to themselves, as the 21st Foot still occupied the barracks, and the militia, evidently, had no taste for sleeping outdoors.

Sergeant Maguire and Corporal Shanahan sat together near the gate, awaiting the captain's return. Maguire picked at the sparse grass, muttering, "Poor thin stuff, you couldn't raise a cow on ten acres of this shite."

Shanahan pried at the ground with his bayonet and added, "This soil is shite as well. They get plenty of rain, sure, but with this soil and this heat, even a man rich in land couldn't grow potatoes enough to feed himself, let alone a family." He sniffed in frustration, returned his bayonet to its scabbard and quietly added, "Why would anyone fight for such a place?"

When Lockwood strode into the firelight, the two NCOs jumped to their feet.

In a voice that brooked no discussion, he told them, "I have been detached to hunt Otero. Shanahan, you are with me. We need three more... Say, O'Boyle, McIlhenny, and O'Donnell. Draw biscuit for ten, no, twenty, days, and each of us shall carry three canteens. See that each man carries sixty cartridges—there is no telling what foolishness we may encounter. Roust them out and take them back to the barracks to draw whatever you need from their stores."

When Shanahan drew breath to comment, Lockwood intercepted him with, "Kick in the God damned doors if you must. See it done, Corporal." As Shanahan turned to go, Lockwood added, "Oh, I forgot I shall require a musket, pack and cartridge box, as well." Then, digging out his purse, the captain handed the corporal a guinea and said, "This is for the armoury sergeant, the customary present, damn him, but without it he would doubtless issue me some Dutch trade cannon from the last age. Insist upon a new Tower of London piece, a carbine, if he has one, though you needn't worry about a bayonet, as I shall keep my sword."

The corporal nodded and hustled off, barking orders in the harsh, sarcastic, instructive, unquestionable tone of veteran NCOs.

Lockwood turned to Maguire. "Sergeant, you will take command here. The company will serve as the governor's personal guard."

Maguire seemed very human for a moment, his sergeant's mask slipping as he muttered, "There's glory, sure."

James nearly laughed aloud, but caught himself, and said, "I am confident that you and the men of the company will conduct yourselves honourably." Then in a significant tone, he added, "I will confide in you, Sergeant, that the balance of our regiment is due here in Guyana in just weeks, perhaps days. Their presence should see things change for the better, I am certain. In any case, with luck we shall be returned from the Orinoco by then, Senõr Otero in tow."

Chapter Seventeen

The fighting was over. The windows and doors of Doonasleen stood open, each filled with frightened, determined women bearing pistols, knives, and lanterns. The light illuminated the dewy grass of Buaille, the milking place, and the shattered bodies lying there. The shadowy form of Cnoc na Sióg, the Hill of the Fairies, loomed in the darkness beyond. Of all the bodies, the priest's lay closest to the farm, hacked and shattered by the fury of John Cashman. A moment of panting silence was broken only by the sound of the surviving Whiteboys, crashing off into the darkness.

And then, in an instant the quiet was split by chaos. Wounded Whiteboys shrieked, calling for aid, for mercy, for their mothers. Cissy, too, screamed for help, pressing both hands to Doolan's chest, her hands wet and sticky with blood. Cashman ran to her, calling for M'Vicar. Brigid, too, came running, calling for Cissy, weeping to find her daughter whole but Doolan so badly hurt. Corporal dashed from the farm at Brigid's side, barking fiercely, frantic and confused. From inside the farm came the sounds of children, who were crying, as were some of their mothers, while other women ran out, to gather up the guns and prepare for the next assault. Margaret Hanahan McIlhenny, hugely pregnant and nearly hysterical, broke into a run, tearing down Templequinlan Road to get help, but Eileen Goodwin grabbed her, nearly tackling her into the wet earth.

Dawn was coming, and Brigid determined what needed to be done. She ran back to the farm, calling for bandages and hot water, and for the God damned bawling to cease. She pointed out Anthony Goodwin, the capable boy who tended the chickens, and said, "Anthony, you run down toward town. Any soldiers you see, direct them to come immediately to Doonasleen. If they doubt you, say that the wife of Captain James Lockwood of the Inniskilling Regiment tells them to stop mucking about, and that they had best tend to their duty. Off you go, now." But then, catching herself, she added, "But first, do tell your mother where you are going. We musn't have her worrying."

Caoimhe Leahy hurried from the farm carrying bandages and blankets, soon followed by Vera McGunn with two buckets of water. They joined Brigid, and the three rushed over to dress Doolan's wound. M'Vicar held a lantern aloft as they knelt in the grass around him. When in that sparse light Cissy caught sight of Doolan's ashen face she unsteadily got to her feet and backed away. She swallowed her fear and fought to regain her breath. Standing still at last, she looked about and noticed the sky graying to the east.

She went to where John Cashman stood watching over Doolan and pulled him aside to declare, "John, it will be dawn soon. You must go! You cannot be found here, cannot be questioned by the king's men."

Cashman reluctantly nodded his agreement.

In the shifting lantern light, Cissy looked down at the blood on her hands, but she gasped at the sight of John Cashman. "Dear God, John, you are covered in blood."

He slowly inspected his hands, his coat, his linen trousers, and grimaced. "No fear, *a grah*, "he said. "None of it is my own."

She motioned toward the farm and suggested, "Perhaps you should wash quickly, and we can find you a new coat."

Still staring down at himself, he said quietly, "The priest's blood, it is. I shall wash myself in the sea, and I shall be clean again."

*****

When full daylight arrived, so, too, did Colonel Simon and twenty troopers of his Yeoman cavalry. They trotted up Templequinlan Road and into Buaille, drawn swords shining in the sharp morning light, their horses' hooves throwing up clods of earth, most of the troopers looking frustrated not to find anyone to hack to the ground.

Colonel Simon reined in where Brigid, Cissy, and M'Vicar knelt over Doolan, who lay semiconscious and gasping as they dressed his wound. When Brigid looked up at Simon, she saw how the prospect of action, of violence, was a drug to the old fellow, putting a spark of energy in his eye that she had thought long past him.

"Good morning, Mrs. Lockwood!" cried Simon in a voice tinged with madness. "It appears as if the devil's minions are afoot!" Then studying the bodies in the grass, he went on, gleeful. "I count three enemy dead and four wounded, and you have, what, one man down? I salute you, ladies Lockwood—a great night's work! Pray, have you left any for us?"

Brigid Lockwood flared in rage, "Damn you, John Simon, have you no humanity left to you? You must fetch a doctor right bloody now!"

Simon was not put off. He had admired and, at times, lusted after Brigid Lockwood for many years, and for her to address him with such passion was fuel to his fire. With a wild smile he roared for one of his troopers, "Private Fox! Return to town, locate Dr. Kelly and escort him here. At the gallop, if you please!"

Private Fox, who in normal life owned an unsuccessful wallpaper shop, was disappointed of his opportunity to sabre the wicked, but did as he was ordered. He wheeled his horse and tore back to Clonakilty.

Still lacking anything like an enemy to hunt, Simon impatiently cried, "Corporal M'Vicar, make your report!"

Nodding to Miss Lockwood and motioning for her to keep pressure on Doolan's wound, M'Vicar slowly got to his feet. His age, exhaustion and the ebb of combat adrenaline showed in his face and voice as he stood upright and replied, "If you please, sir, the enemy mounted a disciplined night attack, but the defense was prepared and the enemy was repulsed. The last of the Whiteboys retreated to the northwest."

If Simon had his wits about him, he might have questioned how such an unlikely garrison had been so successful against a determined attack, but he was intent on his quarry and so turned his mount and spurred away, his enthusiastic troopers in his wake.

*****

The Yeomen galloped and hacked throughout the day, and were largely successful in tracking down the last of the Whiteboy band. They were, however, only the first wave of government vengeance. The militiamen from Clonakilty barracks were not far behind the

237

Yeomen, and soon, hundreds of men from Bantry Barracks were deployed, with orders to make Clonakilty howl.

The brazen strength of the Whiteboys, the involvement of a Catholic priest, and the plight of the families were soon trumpeted in every newspaper in Britain, and in Parliament itself, used as an example of the state of Irish affairs. That attention prompted a squadron of light dragoons to be deployed to Clonakilty, soon followed by a regiment of Fencibles.

In the manner typical of government retribution, the innocent suffered as well as the guilty. Many common people, innocent of any involvement with rebellion, were insulted, beaten, or forced from their homes. There were rumours of torture in the dark corners of the Clonakilty parishes. The panic of crisis allowed the law, always an elastic concept in Ireland, to be warped into the violent excesses of blind retaliation.

As Government reacted, so too, did the people. The army families, Irish and Catholic though they were, were nonetheless decried as foreign, as strangers who brought nothing but trouble. The O'Falvey Whiteboys, dead, imprisoned or in hiding, were widely regarded as fools, but they were part of the fabric of the community and the government's destitution of their families was seen as the fault of the women of Doonasleen.

The Church vehemently disavowed Father McGlynn's activities. Martin McGuinness, the Archbishop of Armagh and Primate of All Ireland, immediately excommunicated him. McGlynn was quickly and quietly buried in unhallowed ground, the grave unmarked.

*****

Two weeks after the attack, the Committee for Beneficent Works called a special session to discuss, once again, the women of Doonasleen farm. And, once again, Reverend Cyril Babcock insisted

238

upon meeting at the Customs House rather than Reverend Butler's home, citing convenience and the need for an 'impartial atmosphere.' That Saturday afternoon, the eight gentlemen arranged themselves around a massive table in the long, elegant, airy upper hall, while rain steadily tapped at the tall windows.

Reverend Butler was a man of God, but a man nonetheless, and sensing insult, he opened the meeting in a harsh tone unusual for him. "After the attack on Doonasleen there is no question of the army families remaining in Clonakilty. The blood of both sides has been spilled and vengeance is in the air. The safety of the women and children must be the prime consideration in our deliberations."

Reverend Babcock shrieked, "I heartily disagree, sir! My God, sir, have you no sense of Government's opportunity? These women serve such a purpose! A gang of Whiteboys has been drawn into the open, and cut to ribbons! And their leader, a Papist priest, exposed, and killed! A triumph for both our honoured government and our sacred faith!"

Mr. Beemish, who could never be called soft on Catholicism, frowned and said, "Come now, sir, surely you do not intend that we use these poor women as bait for rebels? Come now, sir, come now."

Mr. Boffut, whose waistcoat scarcely constrained his prodigious girth, did not look up from the table to quietly rumble, "And in all truth, the rebels were 'cut to ribbons' by two old men and one young woman, while the king's forces were asleep in their beds."

"Miss Lockwood..." flared Babcock, but he went no further.

"There never was such a young person of my acquaintance," said Mr. Jackson with an appreciative grin, very nearly a leer. "Such spirit! She rides, shoots and with such marvelous aplomb, such marvelous..."

Captain Lockwood

Jackson raised his upturned hands to make a gesture, likely an inappropriate one, prompting Reverend Butler to quickly insert, "Style! Yes, Mr. Jackson, the committee is quite unanimous in its regard for Miss Lockwood." Butler had called the meeting for early in the day, in hope that Mr. Jackson, typically his ally, would not yet have partaken of the grape; in which hope he was disappointed.

Babcock, who privately entertained an obsessive fascination with Miss Lockwood's boots—sweet Christ, how he lusted after those boots—cleared his memory, and his throat, and shakily said, "To return to business." Assuming an exultant voice, as if sharing a wonderful secret he went on. "Just two days past, while in Dublin, I was privileged to dine with Lady Grinstead. Imagine, gentlemen, then, my delight, my positive astonishment, to find myself at table with the Lord Lieutenant's own secretary! He deigned to speak to me, and after I partook in two glasses of wine, which is *so* unlike me, I assure you, I made so bold as to speak of our victory here in little Clonakilty. He was enthusiastic, nay, positively effusive, in his praise!"

Mr. Jackson, his head resting on his fist, sneered and said, "I am acquainted with the Lord Lieutenant's secretary, and he is the greatest..."

Butler jumped back in, "I am certain the committee—"

This time, however, Jackson would not be deterred, continuing, "...prig in all of Ireland, a strutting ass and a confirmed sodomite."

Babcock came to an immediate, shocked, halt. Looking around the table for support but finding none, he sputtered, but failed to find the proper response. There followed an angry, an uninterested or a drunken pause, depending upon each member's interest.

Finally, from the end of the table a hand was politely raised.

240

Reverend Butler, looking relieved, said, "The Chair recognizes Mr. Brown."

Mr. Brown was typically silent during their meetings, his membership on the Committee largely due to his generous contributions to the Relief Fund. He was a Friend, and, as such, was viewed with subtle suspicion by both the Anglicans and Catholics, but no one who knew him doubted his evident goodness.

"If I may, please, gentlemen," said Brown, obviously nervous, "offer a possible solution. The Society of Friends is undertaking an effort to aid the poor by establishing factories and employing those deemed most in need." Anxiously looking around the table and detecting at least a flicker of interest, he swallowed hard and proceeded. "My brother, Mr. Ezekiel Brown of Carrickfergus, is, even now, managing the construction of a linen mill, and I have taken the liberty of writing him, to suggest our army families as deserving of such employment. Just yesterday I received his reply, in complete agreement and support."

Mr. Beemish shrugged, and said, "An equitable solution. We are shed of these people, and your brother is ensured of free labour. They can be indentured for the cost of their transportation up north, and so he can do as he pleases with them. Those children could prove most useful in such a factory, their little fingers clearing tangles in the looms and such. They might require some beatings, of course, but if managed properly..."

Reverend Butler flared and roared, "We shall certainly not consign these people to slavery!"

Mr. Brown, growing animated, replied, "Goodness, gentlemen, please! The Society is determined to see the factories run by Christian principles! Fair wages, decent hours of work, and clean little cottages in which these people might live safe, and, please God, happy lives! The children taught to read!"

Reverend Babcock slapped a palm on the table and cried, "Madness! For such common people, such... Well, as a Christian I must not slander... I shall only reference the Duke of Wellington, who referred to their class as the scum of the earth. Now to be coddled in such a fashion, when they might remain here as kindling for battles between good and evil, battles which might spark even the Kingdom of Heaven?"

The meeting quickly broke into a roaring, gesticulating melee, but in the end, the committee voted seven to one in favor of proposing such a move to the people of Doonasleen. Mr. Brown was tasked with approaching Mrs. Lockwood with their offer.

*****

"Oh, go on, Missus, I'll be fine, won't I?" croaked Doolan to Mrs. Lockwood. "Jesus, with that Dr. Kelly and our Cissy to look after me, I'll live to be a hundred, sure." They spoke in Irish, an apt language for soft conversation.

Brigid was sitting in a chair at his bedside, and putting the back of her hand to his forehead she said, "That foul fever seems to have gone down. But you must promise, *promise*, Diarmuid, that you will remain in your bed until Dr. Kelly says otherwise."

Doolan gave her a grizzled grin and nodded weakly.

She squeezed his arm and wistfully said, "When Captain Lockwood returns home he'll want to see you healthy and strong, so pray do not disappoint him." Getting to her feet she went on, "I shall be back home in four or five weeks, as soon as I see our people settled. Mrs. Nelson is, once again, such a friend to these ladies. Mr. Brown's ship will carry us there, and so it will carry me home. Corporal M'Vicar will stay here with Cissy to keep watch on things."

She smiled and added, "The families are so excited, it would do your heart good to see them so. And I forgot to mention that Margaret had her baby last night!" With a tease in her voice she went on, "She has named her baby boy Diarmuid, by the way."

Brigid knew Doolan as well as anyone on earth, but she was surprised to see him tear up.

"Give them my dear love, the sweet people. And a new Diarmuid... God bless him."

She kissed him on the cheek, and said, "Rest well, knowing of their love for you, and so, too, of my love for you, Diarmuid *a grah*."

And so, she was gone. Diarmuid settled back into his bed in the little bedroom off the kitchen of Fáibhile Cottage. The smell of Cissy's own soda bread filled the house, and the lilt of gentle conversation from the kitchen was music to Doolan's ears, and soul. In truth he felt death drawing near, but he had never been so content in all his life.

*****

Cissy had been very young when she had first met Doolan, her father's soldier servant, and even then he had seemed very old to her. She had come to love him, and over the years her heart of hearts dreaded thoughts of his mortality, the day he might die.

The very day that Brigid left for Carrickfergus, the fever returned, and Cissy grew terribly afraid.

A week passed, and Dr. Kelly pronounced the situation grave, but Cissy would not relent. "We must certainly take him to Bath. Everyone knows that those waters have restorative properties." Kelly was disappointed but not surprised to see a degree of wildness, of irrational denial, building in her eyes.

"Miss Lockwood, a man in Private Doolan's condition is not to be shipped across the Irish Sea, and there can surely be no sense at all in spending a small fortune to..."

"We will not discuss the cost of what needs to be done, please, sir. What say you to Mallow? Mallow, of course. No sea journey would be required, only a brief carriage ride, and I have often heard that Mallow's waters are the equal to Bath, or Spa itself. Mallow, certainly, will do him a world of good. I shall take him there. M'Vicar will remain to watch over the house."

"Miss Lockwood... Cissy... you must prepare yourself..." but Cissy shot past Kelly with blind energy, calling for M'Vicar.

*****

The baths at Mallow had been fashionable fifty years before, and in their slow decline from prominence the bath house and the surrounding lodgings had grown shabby. Still, every day, attendants came and carried Doolan, thin and feverish, to the baths.

At first it seemed to be doing him some good, the warmth aiding his struggling body. Kelly came up every few days to confer with the doctor in attendance at Mallow, both of them shaking their heads as Miss Lockwood continued to press her case. But the power of the waters failed them. A week after their arrival in Mallow, Kelly noticed a marked decline in Doolan's condition. While the old soldier was with the Mallow physician, Kelly finally managed to corner Miss Lockwood for what was to be the most painful discussion of their acquaintance.

"It will be any time now," he said.

*****

No more trips to the waters; they were in vain.

At one point, Doolan drifted to the surface, saw his Cissy, saw her pain, and giving her his last smile, he whispered, "No feckin' tears, *a cuisle*. No priest. Soldiers, we are. My peace, at last."

She sat beside Doolan for so many days and nights that the notion of time no longer held much meaning for her. At some point in her stay in the little room in Mallow she had, however, noticed that the old clock on the mantle had stopped. Whether it had stopped that morning or ten years before did not matter to her, as it was dead, its period of animation over. The hands were stopped at 8:45 and she recalled that before they'd left home, the case clock at Fáibhile Cottage had also stopped at fifteen minutes before the hour.

She had time, time to muse over clocks, and springs, to ponder how 8:45 was an understandable time for a clock to stop, how even with its spring winding down, the hands, aided by gravity, might tick downward from twelve, but rounding six, they would find the going increasingly difficult. They might approach the horizontal of nine, but to face the laborious climb up to twelve would be quite beyond them.

She looked down into Doolan's face and understood that the mainspring of his life had wound down—he had reached his predicted time, his 8:45. His had been a valiant effort, but now it was at its close. Then, in her mind came the thought, the anguish of knowing how her father would mourn the loss of Diarmuid Doolan.

Cissy leaned over to kiss the old head, whispering, "Goodbye, my dear old friend." Doolan felt her there, and was comforted.

A moment of full clarity, of full release, came to him, too far away to tell Cissy, though he knew that she was right there beside him. His mind rose up and roared in joyous release, filled with vitality and a fierce capacity for love. No fever tortured him;

instead, the kindness which he had known as a child was now his all, and he found great peace.

*****

Cissy held her own private wake that night, alone, and drunk for the first time in her life.

Doolan was buried the next day in the graveyard of St. Mary's Church. After the traditional fee was paid, the Mallow priest performed the service with the sterility of one who was unfamiliar with the deceased.

The two doctors stood with Cissy, and a handful of people from the Baths, out of courtesy, all of them offering condolences. But such kindness was lost on Cissy: never weeping, but bereft of her innocence, quietly convinced that God had removed his sanction. All words of comfort, of faith, rang empty. There were people saying the usual things, but they did not register. She wanted only to be past them, her only impulse to go home.

After the funeral, Dr. Kelly escorted Cissy to new lodgings. "Miss Lockwood, I think it best that you remain here in Mallow for a few days, as you are badly in need of rest. The lady of the house is kindness itself."

Cissy sat in her new room for perhaps an hour before she went out, emotionless, and hired a local man to drive her home in a jaunting car. At dawn the next morning, they rattled south, out of Mallow, past St. Mary's graveyard and its freshly turned earth. Her last image of the place was of butterflies flitting about, joyous, detached.

The jarvey driver soon regretted his fare, as he and his horse were accustomed to local trips and Clonakilty was forty miles off. Worse, it was bad luck to carry a grieving woman, luck defied again when the stone-faced woman chose to sit on the bench facing to the right, in violation of long-standing tradition. That bad luck soon evidenced itself in the cold rain that began at Garrycloyne and followed them all the way south. The driver wrapped himself in his heavy hooded cloak, but the woman refused the cloak he offered.

Infrequently, he looked back to see her soaked, her tears mixed with the rain. She would take no comfort. Despite his entreaties, she sat sobbing in the rain, until he gave up and concentrated on getting her out of his rig, and her bad luck with her. It was evening before he pulled up his tired horse in front of her home, the woman soaked and shaking like a leaf. After handing her off to the scolding old soldier at the cottage, he crossed himself, slapped the reins, and galloped away.

Chapter Eighteen

It had rained in the night. Captain Lockwood woke to a foggy dawn, soaked and stiff. He lay in his blanket, disgusted with the weather, with the service, with the governor, and with himself. His inner voice swore horribly, but remembering how Brigid hated him to say such things he mentally repented.

He surprised himself by thinking, "I wish I were at home."

While on his long spells of Foreign Service he had disciplined himself and would not allow himself to dwell on such thoughts. Yet, on this occasion, he had been away for only weeks, and he allowed himself a few moments to miss his home, his children—but above all, he ached for Brigid's company. He was forty-one years old, and while inured to the physical costs of a soldier's life, he found himself weary of the moral costs, the threats to his notions of decency and, above all, the challenges to his honour.

He had a list in his daybook of the names of all the men who had died under his command. The list consisted of ninety-six souls, and he deemed it likely that the name of Private Leahy, murdered by Otero and O'Boyle, would have to be added. While James was determined to recapture Otero, he loathed a traitor before all else. He was certain every man in the company was with him on that point: a man who betrayed his brothers was reviled. They would kill or capture O'Boyle.

James struggled to his feet, feeling his age, knowing he had lingered in his blanket longer than he should have, and took measure of the situation. The sentries were at their posts around the parade ground, three shadowy figures fifty yards off, the fourth outlined by the fog brightening to the east. The rest of the company was stirring, most of them grumbling in the ageless manner of soldiers at dawn. One man from each mess was stoking a fire back to life, responsible for his mates' breakfast.

One fire, though, was already roaring, the men of the patrol around it, drying out their equipment and shoveling down their breakfasts. Their friends came and went, all looking concerned. Privates Rooney and Coughlin brought canteens back from the well, full and fresh. Private Toon, who had a genius for knapping, refreshed their flints. Private Colm, who had apprenticed to a cutler in his youth, brought a keen edge to their bayonets and knives.

James saw Colm begin work on a sword, and looked over to see his scabbard lying empty; O'Donnell had been tending to things while his officer slept. It was something Doolan would have done, and for a moment James wondered how the old fool was faring at home. Lockwood rubbed his face with both hands, a gesture familiar to anyone who knew him. He threw on his coat and strapped on his sword belt.

The men of the patrol, ready to set out for the Orinoco, shook hands with their friends. There was some clapping of shoulders, some admonishments to watch their asses, and James heard

Coughlin tell Hanahan, "Now, you watch out for those nasty old jaguars, boyo."

Hanahan, the young man sounding more and more like a soldier, laughed and said, "And you watch them colonists' daughters, boyo, you being a governor's guard and the glory of the world."

Shanahan came over to hand his captain a carbine and a cartridge box, saying, "A good weapon, I think, sir. May it profit you." Lockwood nodded his thanks, slung the carbine over his shoulder, and hung the box on his sword belt.

The diminutive Private Rooney shyly approached the captain. Placing a worn sealskin pouch into the towering officer's hand, he said, "*Chun tú, Captaen, a grah. Is é cré Gartan.*"

In the pouch was a ball of white clay, and Rooney began a long explanation of its purpose, in an Irish wholly beyond Captain Lockwood. Private Coughlin stepped over to help. "He says, sir, that it's Gartan clay. Magical stuff, it is; it will keep you from all harm, and see you home again. Rooney here got it straight from the hand of Cillian O'Friel himself, O'Friel being a hundred and ten if a day. You see, sir, only people of the O'Friel clan can pick up Gartan clay. If any other should be so foolish, he'd be stone dead in a day. Perhaps a week, but dead, nonetheless. Among Donegal men, Gartan clay is a prodigious charm."

Lockwood folded up the pouch and tucked it inside his coat. He shook Rooney's hand, saying, "*Go raibh maith agat, Saighdiúir,*" Thank you, soldier, with a passable pronunciation that brought a smile to the little fellow.

"*Ádh mór, Captaen, a grah,*" replied Rooney. Good luck, Captain, dear.

*****

Duty in the Customs Service of Guyana Colony was a thankless task. The service possessed just one boat, the *Vigilant,* a forty foot launch crewed by two men, though she often carried a handful of soldiers of the garrison to help enforce His Majesty's policies on taxation and slavery. She was rigged fore and aft, a traditional Bermuda rig, so she had just one mast that carried a broad mainsail and a respectable foresail on a bowsprit. Her only armament was a swivel gun in the bow, which by most standards of naval armament would scarcely count as a weapon at all. Still, it fired a cluster of thirty half-inch balls a hundred yards, and the *Vigilant* had applied it to good purpose, on more than one occasion.

That only one boat served such a lengthy coast was an indication of the colony's disdain for the king's policies. On that morning, however, she was to carry Captain Lockwood, his four men, and the tracker, Tarong, toward the mouth of the Orinoco.

The *Vigilant* was tied up at Government Pier. As Captain Lockwood stepped aboard, a gnarled old sailor knuckled his forehead and said, "Seaman Pigg, senior rating, at your service, Your Honour." Gesturing toward a younger fellow up in the rigging, Pigg went on, "That's Affleck, my mate, sir." That affable young man gave them a friendly grin and a wave.

As the rest of the patrol clambered aboard behind him, Lockwood returned the salute and said, "I am told, Pigg, that you are a man of some knowledge of the Orinoco. Once we are under way, I wonder if you might share some of your genius with me."

Pigg, whose person was as foul as his name suggested and thus unaccustomed to anything resembling respect, blushed beneath his deep tan and replied, "Thankee, sir, I'm familiar with the damper parts of that coast, as it were, as familiar as a Christian can be of

251

such a dark place." Motioning toward a dark man asleep in the bows, Pigg added, "That foul old Tarong is already aboard, the heathen, and as the tide is ebbing, we had best shove off."

At the mention of his name, Tarong sat up, looked toward the west, muttered, "Keymis," then, lying back down, he said no more.

Corporal Shanahan and Privates O'Boyle, McIlhenny, and O'Donnell settled amidships, staying as far away from Tarong as the small vessel allowed, but casting more than a few suspicious looks his way.

The tide carried them away from the oppression of the jungle and out into the Caribbean, but not before they passed Government House, where Mr. Read stood and raised his hat in salute. James raised his shako in response, and the men of the patrol all waved, fond of the old gentleman.

The sun gained strength as the warmth and the breeze pulled the last of the dampness from their clothing. As he basked in the fresh air and Caribbean sun McIlhenny muttered, "If only my Mags could see me now."

Once out into blue water, the *Vigilant* settled into a west-northwest course parallel with the land. James ducked under the main yard to sit by Pigg at the tiller, and, with his hair whipping to windward, James said, "Now, then, Pigg, tell me where we are bound. What is this 'Keymis' which Tarong spoke of?"

Pigg leaned over, farted, and, returning upright, replied, "Well, Your Honour, Keymis Planation is the nearest thing to a civilized place a Christian will find on the Orinoco. It's an odd place, do you see, where Indians and blacks and a few barking-mad whites cross paths. I've carried Tarong there a few times—as he has people there —when he's been tasked with chasing down some poor fool who has upset the great men."

Lockwood nodded and said, "I can read a map, Pigg, and the Orinoco Delta is a vast place. Can this fellow find a man like Otero, a pirate and a seaman? Otero will certainly seek out men of his own kind, in search of passage up to Isla de Margarita. I wager this Tarong has never trailed a hardened villain like Otero—he is not some frightened, half-starved slave. You are a seaman, Pigg, and you know of what I speak."

Pigg grew serious. "Oh, Your Honour, I know from pirates. Wasn't I a quarter-gunner aboard HMS *Tyne*, 28, under Captain Godfrey? Right hard service that was, Cuba and Puerto Rico, nearly all the close-up work done by men rowing in open boats, chasing those fucking pirates from cay to cay through shoals and reefs and into hidden passages through the mangrove swamps. One spell, we saw thirty days and thirty nights, without any kind of shelter, under Lt. Freeman, but we would have done another thirty for that man, without a word of complaint."

With some impatience, Lockwood said, "Then how are we few to find two men in all the miles of the Orinoco?"

Pigg hawked and spit over the lee gunwale, then went on, "The Orinoco delta, do you see, Your Honour, as big as it is, is no more than a mangrove swamp, with barely an acre of dry ground in a hundred miles square. No, sir, the Spanish tried to tame it, then the Dutch, and now a few of the more stupid English, but all they manage to do is cling to the few dry spots and try not to die, usually failing right quick."

Lockwood shook his head in frustration, and said with an edge, "And so you think Otero will seek one of these high spots? Why would he not take to the swamps?"

Pigg waved a stubby finger toward the big soldier and said, "There is swamps, and there is swamps, sir. Up north there is plenty of fresh water, fruit, and fish along the coast, and, hell, the pirates could lay up for weeks, hiding like rabbits in a burrow. But, do see you, Your Honour, the Orinoco is another kettle of fish altogether. Little fruit, few fish a man can eat, and the water as foul as Satan's piss. Some few desperadoes have set up shop there, small fry, not in Otero's class. Still haven't they, once or twice, come after my *Vigilant* and made me run like a hare?"

James looked over to see that his men were listening as well, and Pigg looked to be enjoying the attention. "No, sir, there are only a few places on the Orinoco Otero can run to, and that fellow there,"—he tossed his head at Tarong, still sleeping in the bows —"will use his dark magic, and will get us on the scent. But from what I've heard of this Otero, sir, when you get near him, I'd advise you to put some lead into him as soon as you lay eyes on him."

*****

Lockwood had great trust in his men, but in all his life he'd never been tasked to work with a man like Tarong. The tracker wore only a loincloth and a white coral necklace, and carried only a crude bow and a quiver of long arrows. He had black tattoos up both arms and on both cheeks. As the *Vigilant* steadily plowed to west-northwest, the soldiers tried to engage him, but when spoken to, or on the rare occasions when he mumbled a few words, the Indian did not make eye contact. He sat alone in the bottom of the boat, dozing, but then violently twitching awake to glare in hatred at the strange white men around him.

The soldiers had endured that glare twice since they had left Georgetown, but the third time it happened, Private O'Boyle put a finger in the Indian's face and said, "You can stow that shite, boyo, or I shall kick your arse from here to Thursday, and won't you wish you had kept a Christian look on that pagan mug of yours."

James watched closely, but chose not to interfere, as he knew that some kind of understanding, however rough and cruel, had to exist between the white men and the Indian. But even though directly challenged, Tarong did not make eye contact. He muttered a few words in a language unknown to the white men, then lay back down and paid them no further attention.

*****

Tarong had worked for the pink fools for many years, hunting the black fools across what the pinks called their colony. For all those years the fools of both colors had puzzled him, they with their violence and their wicked ways. He had, for instance, always maintained the ways of his people, never looking into another human's eyes, so as not to steal away bits of their soul, but still the fools kept up their rudeness, and it was only for the gifts they gave him—grain and salt and plantains—that he forced himself to bear their company.

He had great affection for his wife and four children, they being safe and sheltered at Waramuri, his village far off in the jungle. The pink men had never ventured far enough into the jungle to find Waramuri, and the few starving, frantic escaped blacks who reached the village were summarily killed. Secrecy and isolation was the Ingarikó way.

His world was the jungle; in their language his name meant 'bird,' a deeply personal assignment of identity. The birds were his soul, his connection to the gods. Tarong hated the sea, and hated the boats. Canoes on the rivers were natural, but the reign of his gods did not extend out to the salt waters. While he would never allow the fools to know it, he was desperately afraid to set foot in their boats, and he was certain that any moment at sea could mean his death, a death beyond the blessings of the birds and the gods.

255

When the pink fools looked away, Tarong studied their faces, and he saw that two of the redcoat soldiers had survived death's song. When one of those two cursed him, Tarong honoured the man, politely averting his eyes and offering a blessing on the fool's ancestors, but such courtesy was ignored, as the fools always ignored courtesy.

After he led these pink fools to the two fleeing pigs, Tarong intended to go home, and hoped it would be many days before he would be forced to do such things again, in the company of such people.

*****

By late afternoon the *Vigilant* had drawn into the brown waters of the Orinoco. The boat noiselessly rode the tide ten miles and more upriver, the channel still a brown half mile across. The jungle stretched from horizon to horizon, thick, swampy, and deadly.

Eventually Pigg pointed upriver to one of the few places where the jungle had been hewn back from the river. "Now, Captain, you see that patch there, off our port beam? I'm going to set you dry-footed there—Keymis, at last."

When they bumped against the Keymis dock, the place was, to all appearances, abandoned. The men aboard the *Vigilant* were silent and tense, oppressed by the sense of the place. The afternoon heat pushed down like a devil's dream, the air as still and damp as a sodden cloth.

O'Boyle whispered, "Rebels, pirates or the devils have swept this place like a Pharaoh's plague, sure."

"Steady, now, men," said James, not unkindly, though he, too, was struck by the eerie silence.

Like a shadow, Tarong slipped over the gunwale and up onto the dock. When Lockwood rose to join him, the Indian angrily waved him back, with no regard for rank or courtesy. For an hour or more, Tarong squatted at the end of the dock, still as the stagnant air, until he cocked his head toward a spot on the tree line, rose and trotted off into the jungle without a word.

When long minutes passed with no sign of Tarong's return, Captain Lockwood frowned and disembarked his men. Pigg and Carter remained at their posts, ready to beat a retreat to the open sea at the first sign of trouble.

Two hours passed. The plantation still showed no signs of life, and while James was curious as to what had happened there, he was in no position to investigate. He paced the sunbaked earth at the foot of the dock, although he allowed his men to relax. In his youth, Private Hanahan had developed a skill for whistling—mimicking the pipits, wrens and thrushes of rural Sligo. On that stagnant Guyana evening, he lay on his back, using his pack as a pillow, and entertained his mates by imitating the clicks and warbles of the jungle birds, uncannily copying their songs.

As he stalked the clearing, James's thoughts wandered, and he thought of Waterloo. He did not think of the victory, but only of the horrible loss. A distinct memory of that day floated into his consciousness, prompting him to turn back to his men and say, "O'Boyle, I saw a hatchet back in the boat; grab it and cut me a few stout green sticks, won't you?"

O'Boyle hesitated for a second, and then with a nod of agreement he hopped to his feet.

"Whatever does he want those for?" whispered McIlhenny.

"Tourniquets, mate, tourniquets," said O'Boyle softly, his mouth grinning, his eyes in pain.

Shanahan rose to stand over O'Boyle as he worked at the edge of the jungle, his musket at the ready, "In case of jaguars and lions and such."

As abruptly as he had left, Tarong emerged from the jungle. Three other Indians stepped silently out of the trees to watch him, until without a wave or word, they slipped back into the darkness of the jungle.

Tarong trotted toward the boat and made no acknowledgement of the white men, but then he suddenly froze in shock and emitted a muffled cry. Turning to Hanahan, who had unconsciously continued to whistle like the jungle birds, Tarong dropped to all fours and crept toward the shocked redcoat. When Hanahan stopped whistling, Tarong raised both hands, begging him to continue. Hanahan looked over at his captain, who raised an eyebrow and then twirled a finger, motioning Hanahan to go on. Tarong listened in rapture, finally drawing an elegantly colored feather from the pouch at his waist and reverently pressing it into Hanahan's hand.

Tarong rose and walked to stand by Lockwood's side. The tracker still did not make eye contact, and while his accent was thick, the captain thought he detected a tone of satisfaction when the Indian said, "We seek the old place on the Barima River where the Spaniard holy men were killed, and their magic with them. The Warao call it Towakaima, the Spaniards called it San Francisco de Alta Gracia."

Chapter Nineteen

If Brigid Lockwood had been fully immersed in the privilege of her class, she might have engaged a carriage to carry her from Ring quay to Fáibhile Cottage. As she was, however, at heart a product of her childhood, she left her trunk with Mr. Quaid, so that he might bring it up to the house when his horse felt up to it, and swiftly walked the three cool, misty miles home.

She had begun her journey home from Carrickfergus the day after receiving a letter from Cissy, telling of Doolan's deteriorating health. Brigid had been forced to wait a week for Mr. Brown's merchant ship to load up for its return journey south, but she had not been overly concerned, confident of the old soldier's tenacity. But, through every moment of her journey back down the Irish Sea, she had grown less confident of what she might find. She strode away from Ring quay fearful but dry-eyed, although, by the time she walked the final quarter mile up McCurtain Hill, she was nearly running, nearly weeping.

She had not yet reached the end of the garden wall when Cissy came running out the door, weeping as well, calling for her mother, and Brigid knew the truth of what her heart had told her.

*****

The day after Brigid returned home, Cissy stood looking out a rear window, worrying about her mother. Brigid had gone out to assess the state of the kitchen garden, once the pride and joy of Diarmuid Doolan, but left unattended for the weeks they'd spent at Doonasleen. Cissy watched as Brigid strolled the garden, shaking her head at the state of the lazy beds. Brigid suddenly turned her head, as if someone had called her, and Cissy saw her mother walk hesitantly to the tall hedge that bordered the rear of their garden.

Brigid spoke with someone through the hedge and then, nodding her head, she returned to her inspection of the garden. When Brigid came back into the kitchen, she did not mention her furtive visitor, and Cissy, not wishing to play the spy, did not ask.

Two nights later, the thinnest sliver of a moon rose, well after midnight. Brigid went out very late and very quietly, but not so quietly that she escaped Cissy's attention. Cissy heard her mother slip out the kitchen door, Corporal trotting out at heel. Cissy very nearly threw on her clothes to follow, but she instead contented herself with slipping on her robe, making tea, loading her pistol and anxiously waiting.

Eleven hundred years earlier, a family band of Irish farmers, weary of their neighbors' depredations, had constructed a ring fort atop a low hill. That little fort was the home of their clan, for hundreds of years to follow, overlooking the land they knew as *Cloich na Coillte.*

By that dark August night in 1823, the ring fort was little more than a low circle of stone and soil. Still, the two people who walked into the ring were children of the clan. As Brigid walked slowly into the ring, a shadow rose up, a shape in the starlight, a wraith rising from the memory of soil and stone.

She spoke in Irish. "Do you wish to kill me, Uncle?"

"Do you wish to kill me, Niece?" Nothing more was said for a long moment, until Michael O'Brian sighed and spoke with regret in his voice. "When I was young I loved my little sister as deeply as anyone in all the world. And now, she has gone to the angels, and I say such things to her own daughter. The gates of hell shall swing wide for me, sure. How are you, child?"

"The shame is mine, Uncle, may God bless you and keep you. I am well, thank you."

With a smile in his voice, O'Brian said, "I see you brought your pony." Corporal left Brigid's side to trot up to O'Brian, who bent to give him an affectionate thump. "Christ, but I love a good dog. Now, come and sit beside me, woman."

Settling on one of the great hewn stones that lay there in the starlight, he said with a frown in his voice, "Christ, these stones have the chill of the dead in them."

He took off his coat and laid it out for Brigid to sit.

"You have always been the most gentle of men, Uncle."

O'Brian sniffed and said, "Not so gentle these days, Brigid Ní Brian, Ban Uí Lockwood. When you and yours put an end to the priest, you made me the chief of the Clonakilty Whiteboys. Now doesn't every government lackey in Munster want to turn me in for the bounty, the creatures. The attack on Doonasleen was none of my doing, by the way, that being the madness of the priest. The Central Committee has denounced that attack on innocent women and children, and ordered no retribution toward you or your Cissy, the dear child."

"And there shall be no retribution toward our friends, Uncle? Is that understood by you and your Central Committee?"

"Those two old soldiers? One of them is gone now, I hear. The other? I suppose we have no grudge with him. Michael Cashman, though? He has betrayed his comrades and the Cause, and if we lay hands on him we shall be the death of him, sure."

"Ach, Uncle! Can you not let the man be? He saved our lives!"

"I suppose no thinking man can argue with *what* he did, but he shall be damned by *who* he was when he did it. The world is an irrational place, as you doubtless know, woman. Christ knows, we Irish are mad to cry treason, and howl for revenge as quick as we breathe."

*****

Two of the Cork Whiteboys, each with a knife and a pistol in his pocket, watched the people queuing up to board the *Albion May*. She was an aging merchantman, tied up to Queenstown's Fitzpatrick's Quay, bound for Boston. Her manifest called for her to be laden with four hundred souls, emigrants in search of any life, other than their own.

The quay teemed with downcast passengers, their sparse belongings in their hands and on their backs. There were a thousand or more people there to see them off, though many already had been waked away, as America was far away, past Tir na Nog itself, and the prospect of return was beyond imagining. Such a departure was as great a separation as death.

As the grim passengers boarded, the May's first mate checked their names off the passenger manifest. Yet to board was the McCarthy family: three young girls, Catherine, Agnes, and Cecelia, their mother, Mary, and her new husband, John. The Whiteboys knew him as John Cashman.

John kept his family well back from the crowd, watching from Chapel Hill Street above. While Mary distracted her girls by pointing out the place where the bishop hoped to one day build a great cathedral, John studied the mass of people below.

When the crowd looked to thickest, he gave Mary a significant nod, and cheerily told the children, "Time to go, now, my loves."

They did not go straight down King Street to the quay, but instead cut to the east, down Harbour Street, still well above the shops and hotels that lined Beach Road. The family passed a well-dressed gentleman who noted that Mary and the girls each carried a piece of baggage, but the man of the family, a large, tough lout, had only a large pack on his back, his hands free. The gentleman sniffed in derision as he passed, but John paid him no heed, his eyes active.

There was one gate in the stone wall that lined the road to their right. John tried the latch, and, finding it locked, he gave it a subtle shoulder. It popped open, revealing a narrow stairway that led steeply down to the back garden of a hotel below.

He turned to his family. "Isn't this a treat, now? A secret passage down to the sea! Let's go now, shall we? Careful, now, poppets."

John led them down the steps and through the small garden. Throwing open the door into the hotel kitchens, he startled two women working there, giving them a smile and saying, "Pardon us, please, dear women."

The kitchen workers might have raised a fuss, but the three little girls who followed the man into their kitchen gave them a wave and a smile, followed by their mother, who gave them an apologetic, nervous grin.

The McCarthys passed down a narrow hall into the front hall of the hotel, where the owner instantly surged at the sight of them.

John pointed a finger at him, his eyes howling a threat, and the owner spun on his heels to closely study the key rack.

The family quickly herded past the front desk, though the youngest girl piped out a polite, *"Dia duit, mháistir."* God be with you, sir.

They came out into the bustle of Beach Street. A bend in the shopfronts allowed John a covered position from which he could study the road to their right, a mere hundred yards separating them from the quay.

A few seconds passed, the passing bodies blurring the faces, until with a nearly audible click, he locked eyes with a familiar face, then another—two of the Cork Whiteboys. Tough bastards, both.

John turned to his family and paused for a moment to smile down on them; Mary desperately worried, the three girls as happy and innocent as the Christ Child.

"Go along to the quay now, won't you, my dears? I need to speak to a couple of old friends, and I shall join you in a moment."

Mary put on a brave face and herded the girls out into the street, down toward the quay and toward the ship that seemed so very far away. John, too, stepped into plain sight, and trading an obvious look with the two Cork men, he walked across the road into a weather-beaten warehouse.

The warehouse was a low, shabby building half-filled with barrels and boxes. An old man there rose from a stool and raised a hand to protest the intrusion, but when the intruder, as tough a lad as ever he had seen, handed him a shilling and said, "Go and get yourself a pint, won't you, Father?" he did so.

The two Cork men entered the far side of the warehouse, silent, their hands deep in their pockets, their eyes alight and studying every corner.

They drew close, and John said, "God and Mary to you both, Matthew and Liam."

"God, Mary, and Patrick to you, John," they both replied.

"No trouble, then?"

The taller Cork man said, "Ah, that eejit David O'Toole was to stand watch with me today, but his cow took ill, the poor creature. Perhaps some wicked brute fed her *buachalán buí*, the Devil's own ragwort. So O'Toole had to beg off, and happily our dear friend Liam here was next up on the duty roster."

"Well, I thank you both. Things might have turned ugly if the committee had some of their new boys out here today."

"We've been through too much together to deny you a chance to be on your way with that lovely Mary and her lambs."

"You're good friends, sure."

They shook hands, said their farewells, and John said, "I had best go." He turned to rejoin his family, but then turned back, and in a flash he had a knife in each hand. He deftly flipped them so that he held the blades, and offering the handles to his two friends, he said, "A parting gift, brothers. I'll not need them again. I shall soon be John Cashman again, an American, a fisherman, and a family man."

*****

The ladies Lockwood attended Mass at St. Brigid's, Cissy out of a sense of obligation to her mother, Brigid out of a sense of piety and a fervent desire for the Church to shake the onus of Michael McGlynn. The new priest, a Passionist named McDevitt, was a young man who exuded an air of genuine kindness. Brigid like him immediately. Cissy liked him well enough, but rather pitied him, as she was certain that God had washed his hands of humanity, and was now watching only from a distance.

McDevitt was especially kind at the end of the service, greeting and blessing each of the congregants on the steps of St. Brigid's. But when Brigid and Cissy went into town, there were widows in the background, staring, their black shawls drawn over their heads, their dark eyes following wherever they walked. In those ancient, relentless eyes, the blood of the Whiteboys would never be washed from the hands of the Lockwood women.

The Committee had ordered that no vengeance was due them, but the Committee held sway over the men. The great mass of the local women kept their own council—the Lockwood women, once disliked, were now widely loathed.

As they strode up the Western Road in the mist, Brigid took Cissy's hand and told her of the meeting with her uncle, concluding her summary by saying, "As we are not to be murdered by one Committee, let us call on another, shall we?"

Cissy had seen a great deal in her twenty-one years, and said with some bitterness, "Every committee of which I have ever heard is designed solely for the purpose of allowing certain men to dominate their neighbors."

*****

The Church of Ireland, Ross Diocese, Committee for Beneficent Works convened in Clonakilty's Linen Hall, their session once again marked by rain drumming against the windows.

Reverend Babcock submitted a motion that he should replace Reverend Butler as Chair of the Committee. A heated debate ensued, in which Reverend Butler's friend, Mr. Jackson, referred to Mr. Beemish as an inconstant goubermouch, an insult which certainly would have required Mr. Jackson to call for an explanation, when Brigid and Cissy walked in.

All attention turned to the ladies, and Mr. Brown, who, as a Friend, was immune and vehemently opposed to the gentlemanly requirements of dueling, saw relief wash over Mr. Jackson's face.

Brigid and Cissy had left their wet cloaks downstairs, but after the brisk walk down McCurtain's Hill in the rain, their cheeks were aglow and the hair that framed their smiling faces was coiled in charming damp ringlets.

They were, in short, in looks, so when Brigid asked, "I wonder, please, gentlemen, if my daughter and I might address the Committee?" most of those gentlemen leapt up to welcome them and pull more chairs to the table. The only exception was Reverend Babcock, who flipped through his notes, looking displeased, and occasionally looked up to mutter, "Most irregular... Most irregular."

When the ladies had been seated and the gentlemen returned to their places, Reverend Butler said, "I believe the members will agree that we might delay the discussion of the previous motion in order to cede the floor to the esteemed ladies Lockwood."

There followed a nearly unanimous rumble of, "Hear him, hear him."

Brigid nervously squeezed Cissy's hand under the table; Cissy returned the squeeze and gave her mother a nod of encouragement.

"Esteemed Gentlemen of the Committee for Beneficent Works, In light of the chronic poverty and hopelessness crippling the lives of so many of our neighbors, and the misguided acts of rebellion that such poverty and hopelessness provoke..." A few rumbles rose around the table, as that point was a common source of disagreement between the Butler and Babcock factions.

Brigid paused and tilted her head ever so slightly. The rumbling gentlemen were sufficiently well bred to recognize that the lady was in the right, they were in the wrong, and so instinctively and instantly went silent.

"...the Lockwood family has determined to contribute 100 pounds to the Committee's funds, to enable its good works."

As that sum neatly doubled the annual budget, there was a generally approving rumble, as nothing gratifies gentlemen of any ilk more than the control of specie.

Benefiting from that positive note, Brigid went on brightly, "Further, as the Lockwood family is so thoroughly impressed by the composition and ability of this body, it is my intention to join the Committee."

There followed a lengthy and confused pause, as no one had quite expected such a suggestion. Reverend Babcock rallied first, saying with barely concealed amusement, "The Committee is, of course, Mrs. Lockwood, most appreciative of the generous financial gift to enable God's work here amongst the Canaanites, but perhaps we might be so bold as to suggest to Mrs. Lockwood that she await her husband's return? Though that may be some time, I think, as Captain Lockwood is, I believe, wielding God's sword of holy justice by suppressing murder and revolt amongst the slaves. Righteous work, indeed, as Luke 12:46 to 47 tells us, 'And that servant, which knew his lord's will, and prepared not himself, neither did according to his will, shall be beaten with many stripes.'"

Babcock looked around the table, secure in his knowledge of verse to cow the faithful. With a satisfied smile he went on. "While it is not my place, and certainly not my intention, to instruct Mrs. Lockwood, I am prompted to add in no uncertain terms that, while many of the Committee's activities are executed by the ladies of the best families of the town, its *direction* is the realm, the exclusive realm, of this select body of *gentlemen*."

While some of the gentleman squirmed in their seats, none countered Babcock. Cissy Lockwood, though silent, looked to be containing her anger. Her mother looked wide-eyed, innocent, and clearly taken aback. Brigid politely said, "Oh, I do beg your collective pardon, gentlemen, if I have overstepped my bounds. Perhaps I have misunderstood the Committee's charter." Then, pulling a folded paper from her bag, she went on. "The committee's founding charter, however, published in the London Gazette, on 22 March, 1820, seems quite clear on the point of membership: 'All local Gentlemen of means or their surrogates are invited to join the committee.' As you so kindly mentioned, Reverend Babcock, Captain Lockwood is away on foreign service, but he was kind enough to leave me with..."—she pulled forth more carefully folded documents—"his Power of Attorney, allowing me to act in his stead in all matters, as I act for him here, today. I have also taken the liberty of bringing along income statements from our man of business, as I was unsure what level of income rendered one 'a gentleman of means.'"

There then followed a few whispered conversations between neighbors, steadily building to yet another loud, increasingly acrimonious, discussion. As the din built, Mr. Beemish reached over and slid the income statement closer. After giving it a quick review, he raised his eyebrows, gave a nod of affirmation to those around him, and slid the sheets back to Mrs. Lockwood with a slight, seated, bow.

The discussion droned on. Several motives were at play. Reverend Butler desired to find another ally on the committee, many of the gentlemen held considerable respect for a serving officer, and several were covertly pleased to be anywhere near the ladies Lockwood. Behind all other motives lay the inescapable fact that Babcock, for all his sway, was a loathsome toad.

The tide of the discussion shifted wholly in favor of the ladies. Babcock, seeing himself outplayed, grasped at one point, crying out, "While Mrs. Lockwood might, on the most indecently extended point of law, be allowed membership in this august body, no other person"—he shot a poisonous glare at Cissy—"can be allowed to attend. Is this a committee of serious concern or a ladies' social club, where we allow ourselves to be overrun by feminine prattle?"

Brigid held up a finger and once again referred to her notes, saying, "I do apologize, Mr. Babcock, but the charter does state 'surrogates,' in the plural, you see, and while my daughter and I will certainly quality for only one vote on the committee, I believe we shall both attend, if for no other reason than the pleasure of this good company."

Soon, the ladies were asked to step out, a cup was solemnly passed around the table, and when it returned to Reverend Butler it was found to hold nine white marbles and only one black. Fortunately, the committee's voting process did not rely upon the rules common to Gentleman's Clubs, so the one black ball did not trump the positive nine.

The ladies were politely invited back to the room to be welcomed with considerable good will. The one exception, of course, was not ready to rest his case.

Babcock sat sullenly with his arms crossed and then finally flared, leaning forward and exclaiming, "I cannot but object, gentlemen, most vehemently object. *In extremis*, I turn to the ultimate source, the definitive guide to our behavior. Scriptural tenants, gentlemen, God's own laws, which require that men and only men, be tasked to rule." Turning deliberately to Miss Lockwood, he went on, "Genesis 3:16, 'And *he* shall rule over *you*.'"

Cissy's familiarity with the Bible was fleeting, though the night previous she had pulled the ancient and shamefully dusty Lockwood copy from the back of a bookshelf and excavated two arrows for her quiver. She fired both. "Proverbs 14:1, Mr. Babcock: 'A kindhearted woman gains honor, but ruthless men gain only wealth.' Psalm 92:6, 'A brutish man knoweth not; neither doth a fool understand this.'"

"Well said, Miss Lockwood!" roared Reverend Butler from the end of the table, banging his hand on the table, drowning Babcock's stuttering response. "Well done indeed, chapter and verse! That put paid to you, my dear Babcock, put paid indeed!"

Mrs. Lockwood smiled and drew forth more heavily written pages from her bag. "If I might submit for the committee's review a few notes on how our funds might best be applied to aid the poor. I also include a proposal to engage an attorney to act *pro bono* on behalf of the tenant farmers in their relations with their landlords, as the traditions and laws of the Conacre system, gross abuses, the most flagrant injustices, are being perpetrated on a daily basis. These widespread evictions are wanton, cruel, and not only morally indefensible, but also economically ruinous. I particularly wish to draw the committee's attention to a report from the Parliamentary Select Committee on Agricultural Stability," she said, passing over another sheaf of papers, "which I propose henceforth be the basis of our operations."

Mrs. Lockwood went on for some time, to the delight of some of the members and the chagrin of others, although nearly every member took secret delight in Babcock's sudden and complete defeat.

Chapter Twenty

Otero had never sailed the Orinoco Delta, but in the cantinas of the Isla de Margarita he had heard penniless but ambitious pirates drunkenly proclaim their plans for Santo Francisco de Alta Gracia. Otero had paid them no mind, as they were lowly criminals, not professionals such as himself. Those lowly men, braggarts without ships, were trying to recruit men to join them in the Orinoco, close to the rich shipping around Georgetown. They hoped to lunge from the shelter of the delta swamps in small craft, to overwhelm the fat merchants and become rich.

Otero had dismissed them, but he remembered the name of the place they'd planned to go, and as Edourd steered them into the delta, Otero patiently played him. The pirate was not without charm, and Edourd slowly relaxed. Otero asked about what had happened to all the Spaniards, and Edourd spoke of how, farther up the Orinoco, the Spaniards had their empire in place, African and Indian slaves in an endless hell, their masters in a scarcely better state. Upriver, where the ground was firm, stood many towns and plantations, but in the choked, sodden delta, the native peoples still held sway. The Spanish priests had established their missions among the swamps, but they had died of despair, disease and Indian arrows. Edourd ticked off the names of Spanish missions which had failed in the delta, perhaps proud to display his knowledge... La Purisima Concepcion del Caroni, La Divina Pastora, while up the River Cuyuni there lay the ruins of San Miguel del Palmar. And then, pointing up a narrow brown ribbon of river far to port, he mentioned Santo Francisco de Alta Gracia, pointing up a narrow brown ribbon of river far to port, at the mouth of the narrow Amacuro River.

Shortly thereafter, Edourd made the mistake of turning his back on Otero to clear a grommet, and the pirate, with a flick of his knife, ended the boatman's hard life.

Hogan had been asleep, but leapt up and cried out, "Ah, shite, why'd you do that, ya prick? He was all right, him!"

Otero very nearly murdered the Irishman as well, but thought better of it, as he needed someone to help him handle the boat, now that its owner was face down, twisting away in the choppy brown water.

Instead, the pirate lunged across the boat and viciously punched the cowering Irishman, over and over, crying out, "You think this is a game, you pig? I will survive this, and you are either with me, or in my fucking way! Decide which, you cringing fool!"

Otero, wild-eyed and elated, rose to take the tiller and turned the boat to port and the mouth of the Amacuro.

*****

Captain Lockwood consulted Seaman Pigg, and it was decided that the *Vigilant* would spend the night anchored in mid-stream. Fewer mosquitos would torture them there, and the wisps of sea air that found their way up the Orinoco would make the heat easier to bear.

Tarong, however, was not fond of such a plan, and pointing back to the east he said, "Santo Francisco de Alta Gracia lies at the death of the Amacuro, on the sun-rise edge of the mighty Orinoco, that way! Let us go there, now, find the evil men and be done!"

Despite the tracker's protest, the *Vigilant* coasted out into the open water. She turned into the wind. Affleck lowered the mainsail and the anchor was dropped. For a moment, the boat drifted with the current, until the anchor cable went taut.

Affleck looked content, and called back to where Pigg stood in the stern. "Good holding ground, mate!"

Satisfied, Pigg sat beside Lockwood with a battered chart. "We passed the Amacuro on the way up here, sir. It's about twenty miles back downstream, little more than a creek, but deep." With a fat finger he pointed it out on the chart. "That's it there, sir."

"No," said Tarong, pointing insistently downstream, "the Amacura is *there*, not on foolish paper!"

Pigg shook his head, gave Lockwood a look, and said, "Bloody heathen. At any rate, sir, the only two tributaries along that stretch of coast are the Amacura and the Barima, just a few miles apart."

In the failing light Lockwood studied the chart, which showed the mouths of the two rivers, though inland it read only "unexplored." Then, turning to Tarong, he said, "Tracker, what can you tell me of this coast, where the two rivers drain into the Orinoco?"

With some pride, but without looking into their eyes, Tarong said, "Barima is a proper river, from three and ten mothers, far above, where only Arawaak people can go. But Amacura is a bastard of bastards, with not even a mother—most foolish of rivers, narrow as a snake, it rises in the east and runs west, a foolish river, contrary to the gods' laws."

"Very well, then," said Lockwood intently, "are you certain the renagadoes are there?"

"So say the Arawaak who are known to me. Eight moons ago, white men who carry no flags returned to Towakaima, to piles of stones left when the Spaniards were killed. The Arawaak hate white men but are too weak to fight—too many lost as slaves to the Spaniards up the Orinoco, or to white men's sickness. And so Arawaak watch, and wait. They have seen a small boat come with two more white men, one of them in a red coat."

Lockwood flared and hissed, "Hogan still wears our coat, then. We'll see to that soon enough."

The captain pressed Tarong for more information, but he shared little more. Lockwood especially wanted to know how many pirates occupied Santo Francisco de Alta Gracia, but Tarong only shrugged and said, "Some." He then went to his spot in the bow, curled into a ball, and went to sleep.

Pigg and Lockwood lingered over the chart for some time as the rest of the men ate, spread their blankets, and settled in for the night. The white men slept well, but as each of them took a turn on watch, they noted that Tarong slept fitfully. He was not accustomed to the pink fools, their boats and their insistence upon counting, a most unnatural practice.

James woke early, when the stars were just beginning to fade, and he took the leisure of lying still and thinking about the men in the boat. Tarong was, and would likely remain, a mystery to him. Pigg and Affleck were sound, and could be relied on. Those three men were useful, and he would do his best for them, but he did not love them. In his innermost heart he had, however, come to love the four red-coated Irishmen sleeping amidships. He was proud of them. Honest, honourable men, all four had acquitted themselves well when they had taken the *Halcón*. Shanahan might have a good future ahead of him, sergeant's stripes, at least. O'Donnell, the former bounty thief and deserter had surprised his captain, and likely himself, by becoming a fine soldier. James had known O'Boyle at Waterloo, and felt a special bond with him, his only true veteran. And then there was the boy, McIlhenny. James questioned his decision to bring him along on the patrol, but the lad was working hard to learn his trade, and James wanted to give him the opportunity. Beyond that, he liked having McIlhenny about, as did the others. Brigid had asked him to keep an eye on the young father, and, resolving to do so, he crawled upright, stiff and sore.

As the dawn took hold, the soldiers fell to their normal routines, tending to their equipment before seeing to themselves. In those conditions, the weapons took priority, as the dampness could swell the wood and bind the action.

Corporal Shanahan looked toward his captain and asked, "Permission to dry fire and reload, sir?"

Lockwood nodded his permission. Seeing the soldiers loading their weapons, Tarong clapped his hands over his ears, drawing grins from the soldiers. The unleaded shots were fired over the side, each report making Tarong wince. The firing also caused hundreds of startled birds to erupt screaming from the jungle on either shore, their distress obviously painful to Tarong. As they reloaded their muskets Private Hanahan made amends by whistling a few bird songs, earning a grin of appreciation on that distant, stolid face.

Captain Lockwood pulled the men together and explained his plan, concluding, "There's no telling what kind of fight this will be, so look sharp. If it looks like too tough a nut we'll sheer off, but by

God, Hogan and Otero have to pay for what they did to O'Leary. We'll leave our shakoes off, but we will fight in our coats—the heat be damned. We live or die like soldiers, Inniskillings, for better or for worse."

Hearing that, Pigg remembered something and hustled back to pull a bundle from a low chest in the stern. He thumped forward to raise a white naval ensign, limp but visible on the main mast.

Almost bashfully he said, "We're only sixty feet, but we're a king's ship, damn it anyway."

The air was still and the sails lay limp, but as soon as the anchor came up, the tide pulled the *Vigilant* back downriver, toward the Amacura. They followed the right-hand shoreline, hoping to approach the pirate camp unnoticed.

Pigg ceded the tiller to Affleck and took up position behind the *Vigilant's* pivot gun.

The captain posted his men in the bows—sharp-eyed, their muskets bristling over the gunwale.

The Amacura slowly came in sight to their right, a narrow snake of brown in the all-encompassing green, the jungle a tunnel of emerald on either side, reeking of decay. The tiller came over, and they came into the Amacura. On the south side of the river there was a small clearing and the ruins of a stone chapel.

Without a word and with scarcely a sound, Tarong slid over the side and dog-paddled toward shore, his bow on his back.

Lockwood hissed, "Where the hell is he going, the..."but, swallowing his rage, he snapped his attention back to Santo Francisco de Alta Gracia.

A few more seconds of silently gliding up the Amacuro, with its tide now pushing against them, way coming off the *Vigilant*, as more of the clearing came into view. Crumbling ruins, some crude huts, a couple of canoes, a small fishing boat, but no movement. Pigg, peering over the iron sights of the swivel gun, waved Affleck forward to drop anchor, so that they would not drift astern.

A man, a white man in a red coat, came running from behind the ruin of what once was the church, wildly waving his arms, splashing out into the water, crying for joy, "Hello, the boat! I'm marooned here! Thank God! I'm saved!"

From the bow, Shanahan whispered, "Hogan. Fuck me, but it's Hogan."

In that same moment, the traitor saw the red coats aboard the boat, and a look of terror crossed his face.

Wide-eyed and shrieking, he turned and splashed back toward shore. Shanahan and McIlhenny, eager as hounds, leapt into the water in pursuit. They half-swam, half-ran in pursuit, trying to keep their muskets free of the water, but it was obvious that Hogan would reach the trees and escape.

Still Lockwood said nothing.

Private O'Boyle looked up from his musket and said, "Sir?"

Hogan was allowed another few steps. Finally, in a voice devoid of emotion, Lockwood said, "Fire."

O'Boyle and O'Donnell fired, but their shots were lost in the bark of the swivel gun. Clouds of dirty white smoke, jets of fire and lead—the foliage at the edge of the jungle was flayed, and in that instant Hogan was swatted face-first to the ground.

Shanahan and McIlhenny reached Hogan, their muskets raised. They slowly lowered them. Shanahan called back to the boat, "Still alive, sir, but just!"

James scanned the clearing, and seeing no other movement, he said, "Seaman Pigg, pray reload and keep an eye open. Be ready to haul that anchor up, as we may be returning in a damned hurry."

Carbine in hand, the captain hopped over the gunwale into the waters of the Amacuro. O'Boyle and O'Donnell hurriedly finished reloading and jumped in after him. They went ashore, looking all about them, their muskets at the ready, but the rough huts that stood among the ruins of the mission were deserted.

James found Shanahan standing over Hogan with a look of hatred, but young McIlhenny knelt over Hogan with tears in his eyes. McIlhenny rolled the gurgling body onto its back and looked up to his captain with a pleading look on his face.

Shanahan dispassionately said, "A ball clean through his spine, sir. He'll be gone shortly."

Lockwood knelt beside McIlhenny at Hogan's side, but there were no tears in his eyes. He took Hogan by the collar and hissed, "Where has Otero gone?"

Hogan muttered, slightly amazed, "Can't feel my legs, can I?" But then with a flicker of his eyes toward McIlhenny he went on, "It was just me what freed Otero. I did it."

An equally brief but very real flicker of gratitude crossed McIlhenny's face.

The worn brick red of Hogan's coat rapidly grew thick with blood, and his eyes grew dim. Lockwood gripped fiercely and shook him. "Where is Otero, man?"

Hogan returned long enough to gasp "Yesterday. Overland. Boat... on the other river. I hid." With a ghost of a smile he whispered, "Confessed... die clean."

"How many men are with him?" Two more hard shakes, McIlhenny looking away, but the other soldiers eagerly leaning in. "Damn you, you traitorous bastard, answer me, how many?"

Hogan surged, his eyes wide, and with his dying gasp he said, "Fuck King George."

Hogan was dead. The soldiers rose from around the body, all but McIlhenny, who looked stunned, and was still kneeling.

Captain Lockwood thumped the boy on the head, not unkindly, and said, "Stand to, son."

Then to Shanahan he said, "Corporal, have the men search the camp."

It was then they saw Tarong flitting through the trees at the edge of the jungle, once again in his element, an arrow knocked in his bow, a shadow in the trees. After a few moments he emerged, and looking back into the trees he said, "No others here."

Gesturing toward Hogan, Lockwood said, "Before he died, he said that the renagadoes have gone up to the Barima."

Tarong looked offended and said, "I know that. Did you not know that? A child knows that." Pointing across to the north shore he said, "Canoes dragged up on that bank yesterday, heavy footprints, white men. There is nothing that way for white men but the Barima."

Lockwood scoffed in frustration and said, "Very well, then, Tracker, what else can you share? How many men? How long would it take them to reach the Barima?"

Tarong shrugged, and, turning away, he said, "Some. Half a day." He then cocked his head as if hearing something, and, without a word, trotted back into the jungle.

Lockwood shook his head and walked back toward the waiting *Vigilant*. "Seaman Pigg! How long to the Barima?"

"It's only five or six miles, sir. We can use the end of this tide, and there looks to be a bit of a west wind building. An hour or so, with the blessing."

Tarong returned with two natives, their tattoos and dress marking them as from a different tribe. The two others hung back, but Tarong approached the big officer to say, "The Arawaak beg to have their canoes and paddles returned to them, as they were stolen, and two women raped by the white men with no flags."

"Well, certainly they shall have them back, with my compliments. By way of compensation, they shall have whatever they please of the pirates' camp."

Tarong scoffed into the distance and muttered, "Even the Arawaak have no use for such foolish things."

As the tracker turned to go, Lockwood distractedly added, "And tell them that if they come across any of those villains, they should feel free to knock them on the head."

Tarong made the slightest gesture to the two Arawaak. Without a gesture of acknowledgment, they trotted down to two canoes on the south bank, while another handful, mostly old men and boys, appeared from the trees on the north bank to reclaim the canoes there. In a twinkling, all the canoes were being skillfully paddled or towed upriver, the outgoing current having no effect on their remarkable speed.

The four enlisted men joined their captain. Shanahan reported, "Not much to the camp, sir. Just filth, rats and fleas. But we did count sleeping spots, and we figure ten or twelve men. Filthy brutes, sure."

Shanahan hesitated a moment, then went on, "And we'd like to ask permission to bury Hogan, sir."

McIlhenny, head down, quietly said, "He was my mate, once."

For a moment James belled his cheek with the tip of his tongue, then said, "For what he was, very well, you may bury him. But quickly, now." But then in a flash of anger Captain Lockwood snapped, "But not in our coat. He'll not face God with anything like honour. Damn him, he will not wear our coat."

Chapter Twenty-One

With a cup of tea at her elbow, Brigid sat at her desk and wrote a letter to her husband. She was in good humour, and very conscious of the fact that her previous letters would have caused James considerable concern. Over the past weeks, she had told him of the plight of the army wives, given a slightly filtered account of the fighting at Doonasleen, and imparted the heartbreak of Diarmuid Doolan's death. She was determined to share the hope she now felt.

Taking up her pen, she told James of her membership on the Committee for Public Works, and that, while Reverend Babcock had been a stinker—that was the word she used, "stinker"—Reverend Butler and some of the other gentlemen were pleased to hear her suggestions on how best to help the common people.

Brigid was thrilled to tell her husband that Cissy had a gentleman caller. Dr. Kelly had made the introductions, sending a note by the boy from the Shannon Arms: *Dr. Kelly begs the honour of calling upon Mrs. Lockwood tomorrow at two o'clock in the afternoon, and begs also the privilege of introducing his new colleague, Dr. Colm McNamara.*

Kelly was considering retirement and had engaged the services of Dr. McNamara, newly graduated from Trinity. Kelly, newly married himself and suddenly a devotee of romance, had been impressed by the young man, and soon thought of Miss Lockwood's happiness.

After that initial visit, Brigid judged McNamara a kind, intelligent gentleman, but perhaps not the most handsome of men. While putting away the tea things, she had voiced that opinion to Cissy, and was surprised to hear Cissy say that she thought Dr. McNamara to be perfectly handsome, especially when one considered his determination to help the common people *pro bono*, which was a prerequisite for anyone desirous of Miss Lockwood's company.

Signing her letter with great affection, Brigid looked out the drawing room window to check the weather, and finding the sky nearly sunny, she put on her bonnet and pelisse. She then called upstairs to tell Cissy that she was going to the post office, and set off down McCurtain's Hill.

Posting a letter at the Clonakilty post office was rarely a quick affair. The postmaster, Jasper Hobgood, chatted up every client, regardless of age, class, gender or religion.

Eight years earlier, Mr. Hobgood had earned Brigid's lasting friendship, as he had shown her great kindness when reading the *London Gazette* from the post office steps, the *Gazette* which bore the list of the officer casualties from Waterloo.

On that June day in 1815, Hobgood's reading of the *Gazette* had broken the terrible news. Two weeks later, her anguish had been magnified by a formally addressed letter from Inniskilling Regimental Headquarters, sealed with their black-ciphered wafer, officially informing her of her husband's severe wound. The letter carried bureaucratically phrased wishes for Lieutenant Lockwood's swift recovery, but for efficiency's sake the letter had also included the steps for her to follow, to apply for his pension, if he did not.

But all that was behind her. As Hobgood collected Mrs. Lockwood's 6d. to post the letter to Captain Lockwood (a letter to a private soldier cost only 1d. postage, a rare government benefit for the rank and file) they discussed the weather, politics and the states of various pregnancies, marriages, and the sometimes awkward timing inherent in such matters.

Girvin McMurtry, an unpleasant old crank who lived out by Deasy's Quay, entered the post office, obliging Mrs. Lockwood and Mr. Hobgood to cut short their chat. Glancing outside, Brigid was surprised to see heavy rain drawing near. She was making her hurried farewells to Mr. Hobgood when his assistant, Mr. Reilly, came hustling out from the back.

"I thought I heard your voice, Mrs. Lockwood!" Reilly said, smiling. Handing Brigid a letter, he added, "This arrived in this morning's bag. Here it is, then, and we can save our Sullivan a stop on tomorrow's route."

She gasped, and nearly cried out, being caught so unprepared: a formally addressed letter from Inniskilling Regimental Headquarters, sealed with their black-ciphered wafer.

Chapter Twenty-Two

Captain Lockwood stood in the *Vigilant's* bow, his hand shielding his eyes from the growing sun as he studied the coast ahead. A west wind was building, carrying the cutter on a north-northeast course up the coast. Once again they hugged the densely jungled shoreline, hoping to surprise whomever they might encounter once they reached the Barima.

Affleck clambered up the mainmast with Pigg's glass to scan the mouth of the Barima. Long minutes passed as the soldiers took position around their captain, doing their best not to look anxious. They re-checked their priming, propped open their cartridge boxes along the rail and loosened the bayonets in their scabbards.

When Tarong went to the starboard side and looked deliberately into the jungle, Lockwood looked back, pointed at his tracker, and said sternly, "This time, you stay aboard until I say otherwise. Do you hear me, there?"

Tarong frowned, exhaled loudly, and sat in the bottom of the boat, thoroughly put out.

Captain Lockwood

The sun was gaining power, but the building sea breeze carried freshness, pushing back the reek of the jungle. More minutes passed, the wind and the sea spray filling their senses. Their eyes intense, their minds filled with what might happen and what might be expected of them, they scanned the banks for movement.

"Sail coming out, mate!" came Affleck's urgent voice from above.

Hurriedly Pigg waved to O'Boyle to take the tiller, handing it over and slicing with the flat of his hand to indicate their course. "Just so, soldier, just so." The sailor then scrambled up to take Affleck's place in the top.

Pigg studied the strange vessel for a moment and then called down, "Captain Lockwood, sir, a galiot coming out of the Barima! I wager those are the gents we're looking for!"

He clambered down, and after a quick consultation with Affleck he took the tiller and bore away back toward the northwest, as close to the wind as he could hold her.

When Lockwood looked back toward Pigg with a fierce and questioning expression, Pigg called, "We need to get some sea-room, or that brute will pin us against the shore!"

The *Vigilant's* motion was wildly different now, as she bucked against the wind, shouldering her way through the waves, spray flying back from her prow. Lockwood was very nearly forced to crawl as he went back to join Pigg.

"It's an old galiot what's coming out, sir," Pigg said, "built by the Dutch in the last age, I'd wager. Twin-masted, square-rigged and a damned odd duck, seventy years old, if she's a day. But good for a pirate's business—in a calm, she can put out her oars and take any merchantman in sight. And since she has a flat bottom, she can be hauled up on shore and hid as quick as kiss my hand."

Lockwood nodded his understanding and said, "Otero will be aboard, trying to make his way back to the Isla de Margarita. So the question is, Pigg, can we take her?"

"Well, sir," said Pigg, rubbing his stubbled cheek with an open palm, "We have the legs of her, of course, and we can turn much quicker, but she has a great ugly bite."

Handing his glass to Lockwood, Pigg went on, "You'll see that gun in her bow, sir? Likely a twelve-pounder, which is far too much gun for such a craft. Thirty-eight hundred pounds—I've never seen the like, the pretentious bastards. I wager she's two strakes down at the bow. With a four-pounder she might handle well enough, but with a flat bottom and all that weight forward, she'll turn like a Tyne collier." In a softer tone he said, "Still, goodness knows what that gun could do to our little *Vigilant*."

Lockwood, the glass still at his eye, said flatly, "I make out fifteen or sixteen men."

Pointing toward the red-coated Irishmen who had come astern to listen, Pigg said, "If you're determined to try her, sir, I'll ask to press a couple of your lads to help with the braces. We'll have to jig like a hare to stay out of the way of that nasty old gun. We'll need to work our way down her sides, where our dear swivel will teach them some fucking manners."

Lockwood was no naval tactician, but he felt, he *knew*, it could be done. A reliance on feelings was irrational, so he tried to calm himself to measure the odds against them. And then his men interrupted him.

"No worries, sir, we'll do for this lot like we done for those *Halcón* bastards," said Shanahan.

"Just like before, eh, sir? Feckin' Marines, us," said O'Boyle with a mad grin, drawing a chuckle from his mates.

With equal measures of pride, excitement and concern, Lockwood said, "Make no mistake, she'll be a tough nut. We'll have to taste that bow gun of theirs until we can close in alongside."

"Shite, we didn't come all this way to turn tail, Captain, *a grah*," said O'Donnell, nearly scolding.

"Let's get those bastards, sir," said McIlhenny, and that settled the matter.

Captain Lockwood picked up his carbine, drew back the hammer, and said, "All right, then, sharp's the word and quick's the action."

"Baltimore, brothers, Baltimore," said O'Boyle with hatred in his voice, in his soul.

After hearing such madness Tarong said, "No, no!" and pointed toward shore, wanting no part of the pink fools' fighting on the godless sea.

Lockwood put a big finger in the tracker's face and said, "Yes, yes, sir, and if you do not wish to have those men with no flags kill you and drop you into this endless water, I suggest you buck up directly."

"Fuck," muttered Tarong, to the infinite delight of the others.

Lockwood and Pigg sat together, finalizing their plans as the enlisted men sat amidships. His friends around him, O'Boyle said in quiet earnest, "Ya know, boys, when I was born, an old woman who lived alone in a cave, a witch of the first order I can feckin' tell ya, came to my mother's side and said that her baby boy would one day come to the place where danger awaited him. Seems the old bird was right."

"But not alone, O'Boyle, not alone, she didn't tell your ma that, eh?" said Shanahan, grinning from his place on the rail.

"Nah, not alone," said O'Boyle, looking about. "Ma would have liked you lot, right villains you are, but loveable as a basket of kittens."

That brought barks of laughter, but they grew serious when they saw Tarong rise from his place in the bow. The Ingarikó Indian was resolved, and staring across the water toward the men who were his enemy, he pulled a knife from his belt and ran it across his forehead. Trickles of blood running down his face, he drew no more smiles. Tarong, terrible and committed, strung his bow, slung his quiver, and readied himself.

Jerking a thumb toward the tracker, O'Donnell said, "A fuckin' warrior, him. No more songbirds, McIlhenny. Eagles for that boy, now."

McIlhenny screamed like an eagle, and the four enlisted men joined him, laughing and shrieking, then too, the sailors, with Captain Lockwood smiling broadly. Tarong stood erect, holding bow and knife aloft and howling a challenge to his enemies.

Pigg threw the tiller over, and they bore down on their enemies.

*****

There was panic aboard the *Dikkehoer*. The captain, a young Dutchman named Van Hofwegen, was the first to sight the English cutter to the south-southwest. He ordered the helm to be put over, and for the *Dikkehoer* to retreat to the shelter of the Barima.

"No, you fool!" cried Miguel Otero. "It's just a fucking boat! Let's kill those fools and press on to the Isla de Margarita!"

Some of the crew responded to Van Hofwegen's orders, some heeded Otero and ran to gather their weapons, and some stood motionless, too drunk or too stupid to decide which of the orders to follow.

Pointing to the ensign at the stranger's masthead, Van Hofwegen looked at Otero and yelled in a thick Dutch accent, "You didn't say shit about the fucking Royal Navy being after you! This was no part of our bargain, you son of a whore! An easy trip, no fighting, and a pile of gold, is what you said!"

Otero pulled a horse pistol from the helmsman's belt, stuck it in Van Hofwegen's face, and blew the captain's head off.

The crew was not entirely shocked; they had recognized Otero's ruthlessness from the moment he stepped out of the little fishing boat. They switched their allegiance in the second that Van Hofwegen died.

In the time-honoured way of the pirate, Otero was now captain, and he hurriedly assessed his command. As the *Dikkehoer* plowed into the waters of the Orinoco, he was already aware of the shocking leeway the galiot made. With the wind anywhere but dead astern, she wallowed to windward, nearly as far as she went forward. For a moment, Otero calculated the myriad factors at play, then, pointing out men from the disordered mass of seamen, he screamed, "You four, aloft, pull in the sails!" Pointing to a black man who seemed capable, Otero ordered, "Man the gun, draw that damp charge, and reload with double-shot." Then to a drunken Englishman who had Royal Navy tattoos he said, "Make sure every musket aboard is ready to fire, or I will do you like I did Van Hofwegen. You other slothful dogs, mount the oars. You'll row, fight or die!"

He had 21 men, and he would let every one of them die to ensure his passage to the Isla de Margarita, and his return to glory.

*****

The wind remained in the west, and the pirates lay directly to the *Vigilant's* east. Her fore-and-aft rig meant that her best point of sailing was a broad reach, so she cut off to the east-northeast at a brisk pace.

Pigg placed ropes into the hands of O'Boyle and O'Donnell, telling them "Pull like furies when I give you the word, mates." The other soldiers lined the windward rail to stiffen her as she built up speed. Pigg took the tiller as Affleck went forward to ready the swivel. Tarong stood in the bow, the congealed blood on his face a frightening mask, as he howled curses and challenges at the pirates.

The breeze was freshening, the *Vigilant* showing what she was capable of. The galiot was pulling nearer on the starboard bow when Lockwood called back to Pigg, "She's lowering her sails! What is she about, Pigg?"

"She means to play the galley, sir! She'll rely on her oars to pivot, and keep that great gun of hers pointing at us. A good play, but if this breeze keeps up, we may foil her yet."

From half a mile away, the galiot fired. Both balls skipped across the *Vigilant's* bow, the spray of the second coming aboard. Several of the men traded a look, and Captain Lockwood silently whistled.

Pigg ruefully wagged his bushy eyebrows at Lockwood and said, "Neat practice, sir. They look to have a gunner aboard."

*****

Aboard the *Dikkehoer* there was a cheer as their shot skipped just in front of the English boat. Otero put an end to that, screaming, "Reload, you sons of whores! Grape shot!"

Otero continued to calculate the variables. The wind was stronger, bringing the Englishman 300 yards closer every minute. The black gunner knew his business, but the rest of the gun crew were fools. If it took two minutes to reload, they might get off two more shots before they closed.

Captain Lockwood

The Englishman continued working to their starboard side. But, as the *Dikkehoer* pivoted to keep her gun bearing on the Englishman, the wind caught her bow and spun her head wildly to the north.

Otero had never seen a ship behave so badly. He screamed to the oarsmen, "Port oars, back water! Starboard side, pull, damn you, pull!"

Only hard work at the oars kept the flat-bottomed *Dikkehoer* from wallowing broadside to the wind. When at last the gunner waved back to Otero that he was ready to fire again, the new captain called, "All oars, hold water! Keep her steady, you bastards!"

The gunner peered over the long barrel of the twelve-pounder, the smoldering linstock in his hand.

*****

Lockwood studied his pocket watch. He looked over to Pigg and said, "Two minutes."

Pigg yelled, "Hang on, you lot!" and threw the tiller hard over. The *Vigilant* spun to port, most of the way coming off her, and an instant later the pirate fired. The twelve pounder's shot was again well laid. Grapeshot, now: six two-inch balls howled across the sea in a tight pattern, through the space that the *Vigilant,* by rights, ought to have occupied. The jibe had done just enough. The shot howled past her starboard bow.

Affleck directed the Irishmen to haul the sails back into order. Pigg turned the *Vigilant's* head back around to the east, but she was slow to respond, as the wild jibe had brought her nearly to a halt.

As the cutter slowly gathered way, Lockwood muttered to Pigg, "Otero will not fall for that again."

"No, sir, he will not."

*****

Every man aboard was a slave to the gun or was fiercely handling an oar, as the *Dikkehoer* lurched in the brisk wind. They could just keep her bow pointed at the Englishman, but they could make no head way, and every minute pushed them further back toward the bar at the mouth of the Barima, now just a few hundred yards astern.

Otero roared in fury when the cutter's jibe saved from his attack. The Englishman had guessed his reloading time, but the Englishman did not know that Otero had been raging through the crew, finding two skilled gun crew among the rowers, and that Otero himself now captained the gun.

In a minute and a half, the gun was reloaded, the cutter less than three hundred yards off, still steering an easterly course, still looking to get past the *Dikkehoer* to the north. The oarsman held water, the Englishman kept on, and Otero fired.

*****

The *Vigilant* was just preparing to turn sharply to starboard. By steering directly to the south they planned to pass the pirate's port side before the galiot could bring her heavy bow back into the wind. The *Vigilant's* crew was tensing for Pigg's order when the pirate's grapeshot flailed them.

In action, Lockwood often felt as if time was slowing. The creeping perspective he had known at Waterloo came to him once again. In a slow sequence, holes appeared in the sails, a stay parted with a snap, and Affleck's head was suddenly gone, leaving only a pink mist. A ball struck the gunwale, and razor-sharp splinters sliced through the air. O'Boyle slid down to the bottom of the boat with a long piece of oak sticking out of his leg. He lay next to

McIlhenny, who clutched a long wound across his face, the boy steadily screaming in agony.

That feeling of altered time also allowed Lockwood a sense of rational detachment; while his inner man was horrified and panicked, his outer man remained an officer of the regiment.

In blind anguish, Pigg abandoned the tiller, howling and weeping, to crawl toward Affleck's twitching, spurting corpse. The *Vigilant* raced on to windward, and the Barima bar.

Lockwood rushed across to take the tiller, and roared, "Hard a-starboard!"

Affleck's tutelage and their soldiers' discipline proved sufficient. Shanahan and O'Donnell trimmed the sails, and as their captain turned the tiller, the battered *Vigilant* answered and bore heavily to the south.

Tarong kicked Pigg aside and rolled Affleck's body over the side. The tracker then turned to see to the wounded, and, with real skill, tended them both. Lockwood screamed for Pigg to man the swivel, but the filthy creature clung weeping to the rail, grieving for his mate.

Leaning steeply to windward, the *Vigilant* bore down on the galiot.

*****

Otero saw his shot strike home, but it was not enough. The Englishman whirled like a dancer and came cutting down his *port* side.

The Englishman was hurt, moving more slowly now. Otero quickly calculated and realized he'd have time to reload before the Englishman was on them. But the *Dikkehoer* was nearly broadside to the wind, still rolling steadily back toward the bar. The sweating men at the oars would have to bring her bow sharply back to port if they were to get the gun to bear.

"Port side, back water! Starboard, pull, you bastards, pull!" Otero joined the rowers, throwing himself onto a starboard oar, their combined strength bringing the bow back into the wind. Looking up at the boat bearing down on them, Otero saw red coats, and in a surge of hate, he recognized Lockwood and his Irishmen.

*****

Lockwood threw the sobbing Pigg back to hold the tiller. Shanahan gave his captain a nod and manned the swivel. Gritting his teeth, O'Boyle grabbed his musket and crawled up to take his position beside O'Donnell at the port side.

Lockwood grabbed his carbine and joined his men at the rail. Tarong left McIlhenny to take up his bow and quiver, and Lockwood waved him over to join them in the shelter of the rail.

Tarong, however, took position behind the narrow mainmast. Still refusing to catch Lockwood's eye, he tapped the mast and said, "Ingarikó fight from behind trees."

They were less than a hundred yards from the galiot. With growing horror, Lockwood saw the pirate's bow coming around. He stared down the barrel of the heavy gun, knowing what was to come.

*****

The gun was loaded, and looking up from his oar with grim satisfaction, Otero saw that it had been brought nearly to bear. One more stroke from the starboard oars would do it. Each of the oars had two men on them; Otero pulled beside a little bald Frenchman.

"Pull you dogs, pull for your lives!"

Pull they did, especially the two massive brutes just behind Otero. They pulled like fiends, hoping to impress this new captain. But their oar broke with a sharp crack, throwing them to the deck, and most of the starboard rowers with them. Confusion, a mad tangle of men and oars, the port rowers stopping to stare, Otero screaming in rage, kicking and punching the men back into their places, but in those few moments the relentless wind pushed the bow back to the north, their chance lost.

The Englishman had drawn very close, but the great gun was now useless. Otero screamed, in a voice that brought blood to his throat, "Small arms! Small arms, damn you! Man the port rail!"

Small arms were stacked amidships: muskets, blunderbusses, musketoons, boarding axes, pikes, cutlasses, even an ancient crossbow. The pirates scrambled to grab their weapons.

*****

It was if the angels had reached down to push aside the gaping mouth of the twelve-pounder. In just seconds, the *Vigilant's* crew went from the certainty of death to a fierce determination to overcome their enemies.

There was chaos aboard the galiot, but aboard the *Vigilant* the men were steady and resolved. Pigg gathered himself enough to steer the cutter close to the pirate's side.

The last seconds passed, and as they ghosted alongside the galiot, the *Vigilant* loosed hell.

Lockwood, O'Boyle and O'Donnell fired their muskets, taking down three men opposite. At such close range, firing into such a confused mass of men, it was difficult to miss. Tarong's arrows were light, made to bring down small game in the jungle, but he was deadly accurate. Two pirates shrieked in pain, the barbed points buried deep. Lockwood saw a knot of men gathered amidships, pulling weapons from a pile, and he turned to point them out to Shanahan at the swivel, but there was no need. The closely packed pirates looked up in horror to see Shanahan grinning at them from behind the swivel gun. He fired, and ten men were torn to pieces.

And then the two craft had passed. Lockwood looked astern, and saw Otero. The pirate screamed a curse and fired a pistol, the ball thudding into the gunwale beside Lockwood. Lockwood bent to pick up McIhenny's musket, but in those few seconds the range had widened, and Otero was gone. He did make out the name *Dikkehoer,* roughly painted across her stern.

Lockwood grabbed Pigg's shoulder, and yelled, "Come about for another pass! Quickly, now, before they can rally!"

Pigg, sobbing, ashen and distraught, muttered into the bottom of the boat, "Haven't you had enough, you bloody minded bastard?" Lockwood very nearly struck him, but then Pigg looked up, and said more clearly, "No room to leeward, or we'll be up on the bloody bar. We'll have to tack. Here, take the tiller and bring her around when I say. I'll get you on her again, and be damned to you."

And so, the *Vigilant* tacked, clumsily, awkwardly, but she once again bore down on the *Dikkehoer*, as the soldiers reloaded their weapons, their eyes ablaze.

*****

The *Dikkehoer* rolled wildly, broadside to the waves with no one at her helm, her sails furled, her oars all ahoo, abandoned and tangled, as the wind pushed her further toward the Barima bar, now just two hundred yards to windward.

Across her decks lay fifteen dead and wounded men. In the bottom of the galiot lay seven desperate, heavily armed pirates, criminals and outcasts, waiting for their moment, knowing they were about to fight for their lives.

Captain Lockwood

The *Vigilant* hove-to alongside the *Dikkehoer*, perhaps twenty yards off, a creaking silence as the two craft rolled in the waves.

Three muskets lined the *Vigilant's* rail, an arrow was knocked at her mainmast, and forward, the lethal swivel gun was manned and ready, but no targets revealed themselves. All the while, both vessels drifted closer to the sandy bar.

Frustrated, Lockwood finally pointed to the galiot's hull and roared to Shanahan at the swivel, "Sink her!"

When the next wave exposed the *Dikkehoer's* rotting bottom, Shanahan fired and blew a foot-wide hole into her. As the *Dikkehoer* rolled back to port, water poured in and she began to founder.

Shanahan hurried to reload the swivel, but the pirates knew their chance and took it. They rose and took aim.

Tarong's bow twanged and a pirate took an arrow through the hand. The three Irish muskets fired, one pirate dropping dead with a ball to the head, others dropping back into cover. But the rest of the band drew a bead and fired.

Pigg sat at the tiller and made no effort to take shelter. He took two balls to the chest and rolled silently overboard, relieved of his grief.

Otero leapt up and fired a blunderbuss, the full load striking Corporal Shanahan, exposed at his post behind the swivel. The young NCO dropped into the cutter's bottom, his vacant eyes to the blue Caribbean sky.

For a moment, Captain Lockwood's detachment failed him. He stared, shocked and grieved, his breath clenched in his chest. His decisions, his orders, had brought that young man to his death. But as he had done since he was a boy, James Lockwood choked back his swelling emotion and maintained his façade.

There followed a deadly exchange of musketry at close range, a cat-and-mouse game of loading and firing from what little cover the two craft could offer. Just yards apart, both the *Dikkehoer* and the *Vigilant* drifted until at last the foundering *Dikkehoer* struck the sandy bar broadside and lodged there.

Thee Irishmen's fire had killed and wounded several pirates, though they had been hurt in return. O'Donnell was hit in the arm, and Lockwood had felt a ball whisper past his cheek, an angel's kiss.

The *Dikkehoer* was grounded, and the *Vigilant* continued to drift toward her. Lockwood knew the pirates' numbers would likely overwhelm them if it came to a boarding action, so he leapt up from the rail to finish reloading the swivel.

A mad thought ran through his mind: Brigid would have been very unhappy if she had seen him expose himself in such a fashion. But, while several balls flew past him, he was untouched as he primed the piece and brought to bear on the galiot.

And then Otero rose from cover, roaring. He fired at Lockwood as the swivel fired in reply. Otero's shot missed, while Lockwood's did not.

Otero was blown back like a rag doll, riddled with shot.

When Otero fell, the rate of fire coming from the *Dikkehoer* slowed—his death took the fight out of the remaining pirates. There was no thought of their surrender, of course, as they would be hanged, out of hand, if captured and taken to Georgetown. The few survivors crawled from the sinking galiot, splashed out to the bar, and broke for the shelter of the jungle. Many of them were slowed by wounds, but Lockwood could do nothing to stop them. The exhausted, bloodied men of the *Vigilant* could manage only a desultory musket shot or two before the surviving pirates were out of range. In the silence that followed, the wind continued to push the battered *Vigilant* toward the bar, until she, too, went aground, just yards from the *Dikkehoer*.

The soldiers turned to care for their mates. Lockwood tied a rough bandage around O'Boyle's leg, Tarong once again tended to McIlhenny, and O'Donnell rolled a rough bandage around his own forearm. The Inniskillings occasionally raised their heads to ensure that the pirates did not rally, but the survivors had had enough, and disappeared into the trees.

It was with amazement, then, that Lockwood and his men saw those same survivors come tearing back out of the jungle. The explanation soon revealed itself, as twenty or more Indians followed in close pursuit, long spears and wicked war clubs in their hands. They quickly overtook and killed the last of the screaming pirates.

Tarong then patted McIlhenny on the head and said, "You will heal, song of the birds. Now, I will fetch a gift for your governor." With that, the tracker went to the rail and hopped into the narrow stretch of water between the battered craft. He clambered aboard the *Dikkehoer*, and after a moment, he reappeared, dragging Otero's body over to the galiot's shattered rail. He pushed it overboard, then waded back to the *Vigilant*, towing Otero's corpse.

It took a moment, but when Lockwood realized what Tarong was about, he went to the rail and reached a long, powerful arm to pull him back aboard. They then used a boat hook to drag the bloody corpse over the gunwale. The body of Captain Miguel Otero rolled into the bottom of the boat.

The Arawaak spent some minutes despoiling the bodies of the pirates, but then formed again and moved toward the boats, yelling and pointing at the white men there. Tarong rose and gave them one long wave, with both arms fully extended. The Arawaak went silent, lowered their weapons and returned to the jungle.

"Jesus," muttered O'Donnell, lowering his musket.

"The Arawaak hate white men," said Tarong, as if explaining the obvious to a child.

They threw a piece of sailcloth over the pirate's torn body, but Corporal Shanahan's body was reverently wrapped in their blankets and laid in the bow.

In the hours that followed, they ate, drank, slept and wept at Shanahan's side. The day wore on. The men remained in their shirtsleeves until late afternoon, and the high tide came. The wind had come around to the south, and, with more water under their keel, the awkward sailors freed the *Vigilant* from the bar.

As they floated clear of the *Dikkehoer*, Lockwood peeled off his shirt and boots to swim across and set the galiot alight. Her hull was breached and the hold full of water, but her grounding had left the main deck above water. He intended to spend just a moment at it, but when he climbed aboard the galiot, he found one man still alive among the corpses and gore. A black man, shot in the chest, gasping for breath, unable to speak, but with pleading eyes, reaching up a hand to the soldier.

James tried to ignore him. He cut open a cartridge from the twelve-pounder and sprinkled the powder across the deck, then found a whale-oil lantern and poured it over a pile of rags. Pulling a striker and flint from his pocket he nearly struck the fire, but he paused and muttered, "Oh, damn it all, anyway."

Tucking the flint back in his pocket, he went to the wounded man, took his hand, and examined the wound. On a dozen battlefields, large and small, he had seen such wounds, and he knew the man was dying, but he could not leave him to the flames, or roll him into the sea to drown.

Despite O'Donnell's and O'Boyle's best efforts, the *Vigilant* was drifting further and further from the *Dikkehoer*, and Lockwood heard them calling, "Captain, come on, sir! Hurry, sir!"

The pirate was fading, yet Lockwood still kept his hand, saying softly, "It's alright, mate. Just let it take you. Easy now, it's alright."

The man slipped away silently. The big soldier sighed, rose slowly and struck the fire. As it roared across the deck he dropped back into the warm water. The *Vigilant* was a hundred yards off, his men shouting for him, but he had never been a strong swimmer, and he was tired.

The fight had worn him, and he sensed his Waterloo wound seizing his lungs as he struggled. The relentless surf kept pulling him down, and he was very near his limit when he thumped against the hull, and his men eagerly reached down to pull him back aboard.

They had raised only the most rudimentary rig, bearing northeast, when the galiot's deck magazine blew up, and, with it, the last of the pirate presence on the Orinoco.

Chapter Twenty-Three

Brigid Lockwood fled the post office with the letter from Inniskilling Regimental Headquarters stuffed deep into her bag. She hurried home with her head down, forcing herself to think of anything but what news the letter might carry.

She dashed through the front door of Fáibhile Cottage and across the slate hall to the drawing room, and dropped onto the settee. She pulled the letter from her bag, and stared at it.

Cissy came in from the kitchen, paused for a long moment, and asked with quiet surprise, "Mama, whatever is the matter?"

"A letter from the regiment. But I shall not read it."

Going to sit beside her mother, Cissy cajoled, "Ah, and so you think it holds ill news, then? But perhaps it might bring good news, Mama."

"It is foolish, I know, to think such thoughts, but I cannot help myself. What if your father is hurt? Or ill? Major McLaren warned us about the Guyana Colony—so many soldiers lost to disease. God, what can this mean?"

"We shall read it together, Mama. For good or for ill, we are together."

They hesitantly opened the cover, and then with relief and growing delight, they read:

> *To Mrs. James Lockwood*
> *Fáibhile Cottage*
> *Clonakilty*
>
> *Inniskilling Regimental Headquarters*
> *Enniskillen Castle*
>
> *Our Esteemed Mrs. Lockwood,*
>
> *It is with particular shame that the regiment must admit to a grievous error in its clerical responsibilities, to wit, the status of Margaret McIlhenny, née Hanahan.*
>
> *The marriage certificate of Miss Hanahan and Private Kerry McIlhenny, dated July 27, 1823, was received by the regiment, but through an inexcusable lack of attention, Mrs. McIlhenny's name was not registered in the Married Roll.*
>
> *That error has now been corrected, and as you were compassionately involved in the recent settlement of the regimental wives, it was deemed appropriate to notify you.*
>
> *I remain, madam, your most devoted, etc.,*
> *Major Blair McLachlan*
> *Depot Commander, 27th Foot*

Brigid was very tempted to dance around her drawing room, but she was determined to act her age, and so she only smiled in relief, and with tears in her eyes she patted the letter and said, "Dear Major McLachlan... such a kind man, to see to Mrs. McIlhenny's needs, and then to think to inform me. Yes, a true gentleman. Your father is quite well, of course. I was so silly—he is quite well."

Brigid was unsure whether to laugh or cry, and so did both. Cissy, who had inherited some of her father's ability to mask emotion, had also inherited some of her mother's spontaneity, and so she laughed and cried with her mother without a hint of restraint.

Chapter Twenty-Four

There had been some talk of burying Shanahan at sea, but it was decided that, as a soldier, he merited burial in soil. They spent that night anchored on the Orinoco, none of them sleeping, the wounded men suffering in silence, but suffering nonetheless. Lockwood felt himself growing feverish, and by dawn he was violently sick over the rail. When morning came, they cautiously set sail to bring the *Vigilant* home, two dead men aboard, Shanahan honoured, and Otero reviled.

By late afternoon, the *Vigilant* neared Georgetown. Lockwood had no intention of attempting anything resembling a nautical maneuver to end the patrol. He steered the cutter to within hailing distance of a Royal Navy brig and called for O'Boyle to drop the anchor. As O'Donnell roughly pulled the mainsail down, Lockwood hailed the brig and howled for their surgeon.

The brig responded, their first lieutenant and surgeon coming over in the launch, with ten capable seamen. The navy men boarded the *Vigilant* wide-eyed; the cutter's battle damage, her bloody sides and her dead and wounded earned the redcoats instant respect.

The surgeon quickly evaluated Privates McIlhenny, O'Donnell, and O'Boyle, approved the dressings that had been applied, and ordered them to the garrison hospital. The surgeon then eyed Lockwood, took his pulse, and said, "You are pale and feverish, sir. I think it best you accompany your men to the hospital. Dr. Patterson has an excellent store of Jesuit's bark which may prevent this fever from getting out of hand."

The stresses of combat, of command, of responsibility, began to wane. With an inkling of relief edging into his mind, and while feeling as sick as he had in all his life, James asked the lieutenant, "Sir, might I ask that my tracker be escorted to Government House, along with the body of the pirate Otero? He must claim his bounty. Tarong of the Ingarikó people has served well, and deserves our respect."

The lieutenant, impressed, said, "It would be my pleasure, sir, to attend to the end of such a rogue as Otero. But, surely, the honor should be yours? The death of that fellow is quite a coup."

Lockwood shook his head, saying, "Thank you, no. I shall see my men to the hospital." Tarong deserved his fee, but James wanted nothing to do with Governor McAllistair, who would certainly have Otero's corpse defiled, in the manner reserved for traitors and pirates.

The lieutenant called across for another boat, and as the Irishmen were helped into the launch, Lockwood, suddenly furious with himself for forgetting, called back to the naval officer, "Will you see to my corporal, sir? I beg you, see to him as he deserves!"

Reassured that the dead soldier would be taken ashore with all due honours, Lockwood, a blanket across his shoulders despite the heat of the day, slumped against O'Donnell.

Tarong and his odious prize were taken aboard the brig's jolly boat. As the two boats were rowed away to different parts of town, from beneath his bandages, McIlhenny whistled a goodbye to Tarong, a long, glorious bird song, earning a long, unguarded bark of laughter from that stoic face.

Once ashore, the soldiers were met by a young militia ensign, a brash young man carrying a claymore far too heavy for him. His command consisted of a single-horse cart, driven by a strong young black man, a slave, spiritless and broken. The face of the black man told James all he needed to know about the state of the rebellion.

Once the soldiers had been trundled aboard the cart, the ensign learned that the pale captain had not heard of the rebellion's collapse. "Oh, sir!" he excitedly squeaked, "The 21st and the West Indians marched out, and there was a great battle with the rebels out at Bachelor's Adventure! Two thousand against three hundred! Two hundred blacks killed, buckets more wounded, and only one man of the 21st got a scratch! What a victory! Ain't it prime! My regiment was not allowed to leave town, us being such stout defenders, but I die thinking of how I missed all the fun!"

*****

The hospital's Dr. Patterson evaluated and dispatched Privates McIlhenny, O'Donnell, and O'Boyle to beds in the Enlisted Men's ward, and sent Captain Lockwood to a private room in the Officers' ward, where he was prescribed both Jesuit's bark and laudanum. Lockwood's Waterloo wound had given him long experience with laudanum, and he steadfastly refused the doctor's dose, to that gaunt gentleman's annoyance.

Even without the laudanum, Lockwood's exhaustion and the luxury of sleeping in a real bed gave him a long, restful night's sleep, and in the morning he felt well enough to tip his much-loved quip about "Jesuit's bark being worse than its bite," to Dr. Patterson's further annoyance. He also felt well enough to ask for pen and paper, and wrote a concise, carefully crafted report to the governor, regarding the recent actions on the Orinoco. Three drafts later, he was content, and an orderly was dispatched to Government House.

Lockwood then determined to rise and visit his men, but was dissuaded of that course by both Dr. Patterson and by the swirling dizziness he felt upon standing. Eventually, Private O'Donnell was allowed in, to inform the captain of the well-being of his men, and of their delight in sleeping in beds with crisp, clean sheets.

By afternoon, a letter from the governor was brought in by a pimply ensign. The letter's contents were as Lockwood had suspected.

The Governor acknowledges the death of the pirate Otero and the destruction of the pirate dinghy and its crew, but the governor is shocked that in doing so, Captain Lockwood has been so profligate with both the lives of both his men and the lives of the men of the Revenue Service. Further, the extensive damage to the Revenue Service cutter Vigilant is estimated to exceed £200, and the governor questions how Captain Lockwood had allowed such a diminutive pirate vessel and a handful of incapable felons to cause such extensive damage to one of His Majesty's prized vessels. Lastly, the governor is amazed at Captain Lockwood's, caution, nay, timidity, in abandoning the pirate base, won at such cost in lives and matériel.

Governor McAllistair commands Captain Lockwood to gather at once, the one hundred men of his command and to reclaim the pirate base known as Santo Francisco de Alta

Captain Lockwood

Gracia. This mission is of the utmost urgency, and thus every man must be mustered, including any malingering in hospital. Government will, at great expense, provide a merchant vessel to return Captain Lockwood and his men to the Orinoco. It must, however, be understood by Captain Lockwood that, due to the ongoing State of Emergency in the Colony, only the most basic of supports can be offered to such a distant post, and it is hoped that Captain Lockwood will not trouble government for excessive and puerile demands for food, water, medical supplies, etc., etc.

Finally, it must once again be explained to Captain Lockwood that protection of trade and industry, the Empire's life blood, are not to be sacrificed to the reservations of junior officers of liberal tastes, and that those pillars of empire must be defended at all costs, including the expenditure of the lives of His Majesty's soldiers, who are honour-bound to obey the orders of their superiors.

John McAllistair, Governor

*****

A steady rain fell on Georgetown as Captain Lockwood and Mr. Read sat in Lockwood's dimly lit hospital room. Slatted shutters covered the windows, giving the room an especially intimate feel. Overhead, a ceiling fan, propelled by an old black man sitting out on the porch, slowly stirred the warm, damp air. The man was a slave, but Lockwood paid him a sixpence every morning.

Read and Lockwood were sipping dark rum and had been doing so for some time, so what little reserve their relationship had yet to overcome, was now gone. The aged Read reached for the decanter, needing two hands to lift the leaded crystal. He topped off their glasses and said, "You know, James—goodness, I do not believe I have yet asked your permission to address you by your Christian name—I trust I do not give offence?"

Lockwood, who had been discharged from the hospital only three days before, grinned from his comfortable chair and said, "I would consider it an honour, sir."

"I should be honoured if you would refer to me as Gordon, by the way. To continue: I have yet to ask after the health of your men, especially young McIlhenny. I trust they are quite recovered after your adventures on the Orinoco?"

"They are doing well, thank you, though McIlhenny will lose an eye."

Read gave Lockwood a significant look. "That renders him unfit for further service, does it not? He shall be returned home?"

"I am trying to arrange it before we depart for the Orinoco. I thank God for this fever—an odd thing to say, is it not?—but I cannot justify this delay much longer; McAllistair continues to press."

Read stared into his glass and said, "Both Dr. Patterson and I have applied to McAllistair regarding your health, but he is determined to do you harm. Patterson takes his profession very seriously; he told McAllistair in rather forceful terms that to post a company of newly-arrived white men on the Orinoco during fever season is a death sentence." Then after a painful pause he went on, "James, have you considered other options? Might ... well, might you not go home?"

James sniffed in frustration and said, "Yesterday I met with Colonel McDonald of the Royal Scots, and he very kindly agreed to carry that very proposition to McAllistair: I would sell out and go home if he would keep my company here in Georgetown.

MacDonald returned quite shaken. He was ashamed to carry such a reply, but he said that if I sell out, McAllistair would consider me a coward, and post my company to the Orinoco, regardless."

There followed a long pause, both men thinking, until they directed their conversation elsewhere, wandering across numerous topics, as conversations between men of experience and intellect often do. Read eventually got around to saying, "A bit of business, now, please, James. As you well know, on the morrow I embark on my return to London. A brig, I am told, the fastest thing afloat, though when I saw it in the harbour this morning I thought it a tiny thing, the merest skiff. I dread the thought of being at sea in such a diminutive craft, facing the seasickness again, and, in this instance, without your valued company. But, I do so look forward to reporting back to the Colonial Office. I have spent long hours preparing my report, regarding the state of this Guyana Colony, and I shall give the current regime such a beating, such a beating!"

Lockwood set his glass aside and said with great earnestness, "A great deal depends on you, Mr. Rea—I beg your pardon—Gordon. Only pressure from London can bring about anything like change to this vile place. Since our arrival in Guyana, I have become fully aware of the evils, the God damned misery, of slavery. I am ashamed to have given it so little thought before. I beg you to write to me on any matter in which I might be of aid to you."

"I thank you, James. McAllistair is aware of what tone my report shall carry, of course, and so will use all of his parliamentary influence to keep slavery alive. Many of the men in Parliament grow rich from colonial slavery, though they will never admit it."

Read then pointed a bony finger at James and went on, "Slavery is the chief of his worries, but McAllistair will also attempt to erase evidence of his numerous, wholly illegal, abuses of power. The

English people, despite their violent, vengeful pig-headedness, still take the right of trial by jury most seriously, so McAllistair knows he is in jeopardy on this matter, as well as countless others."

*****

Over the following days, Lockwood's fever returned, spiking to such a degree that he was wholly confined to his bed. He lay sweating and restless, but finally resolved to perform the task he had been avoiding since their return from the Orinoco. He pulled some sheets from his Day Book—the list of the men under his command who had lost their lives. He worked to steady his hand as he added the names of Private Eamonn Leahy and Corporal Paul Shanahan. He fell asleep with tears in his eyes.

A morning finally arrived when he felt well enough to get up and open the shutters of his room. He looked out to see transports gliding into the Georgetown anchorage. The First Battalion, 27th Regiment of Foot, the Inniskillings, had arrived.

*****

The men of Lockwood's company were drawn up at the end of the quay to salute the arriving Inniskillings. They were pleased to see their captain, looking pale but determined, striding down from the hospital to join them. He inspected them in much the same manner as when he had first met them on the parade ground of Enniskillen Castle, just weeks before. But they were all soldiers now.

Lockwood saw Private McIlhenny, his face still heavily bandaged, standing at stiff attention beside Sergeant Maguire.

Without looking at his officer, and scarcely moving his lips, the sergeant said, "He's not discharged, yet, sir."

313

Captain Lockwood

Lockwood looked at McIlhenny with what little kindness a company parade allowed and said, "No, Sergeant, he is not."

Governor McAllistair and his glittering retinue arrived in two open carriages. As they dismounted, they stood well away from Lockwood and his men. McAllistair did, however, shoot Lockwood a look of pure hatred, a look that Lockwood noted, as did many of the others gathered there.

The first boat brought ashore the battalion's senior officers and the ten company commanders: Lieutenant Colonel Stephens and fourteen officers in their best uniforms. The requisite formalities ensued. After several minutes of salutes, bows, introductions and pleasantries, the colonel joined the governor and his party, to be whisked off to Government House.

The company officers were left behind and quickly relaxed, as Lockwood dismissed his men back to their barracks. None of the current officers had served with Lockwood at Waterloo, but some knew him and came over to chat. None of those men, however, was his closest friend, Captain Tom Mainwaring. The distracted adjutant, his roster book tucked under his arm, eventually hurried over and handed Lockwood a letter from Mainwaring, dated a month earlier. Lockwood stepped away to read:

> *My dear James,*
> *I dash off these lines to tell you of my astonishing change in plan. You will forgive me celebrating a bit—the wine here in Gib is cheap and strong, as you may recall.*
> *My news: last week I was bored with Gib, and so crossed over into Spain (with whom we are, at last reading, still at peace) for my constitutional. I was crossing a stony patch of parched grass to have a look at an old Moorish*

tower when I was accosted by a furious shepherd. You may recall my Spanish being rather threadbare, but after a few minutes of the shepherd's blathering, I came to realize that he was accusing me of having to do with his sheep!

As I was in Spain, I was, necessarily, in civilian clothes and without my sword, but I had that lovely old blackthorn stick you and Brigid gave me (pray forward her my dear love. A fine woman, that) and so I gave him a right good thump and sent him on his way, the cheeky fellow.

Thinking that he might go and gather his fellow guardians of quadrupedal virtue, I deemed it best to beat a retreat to friendlier environs.

Imagine my surprise, my utter astonishment, to be the next day button-holed by the adjutant of the garrison, and placed under arrest! I immediately applied to Colonel Stephens for relief, and he, quite rightly, made umbraged inquiries on my behalf.

As the regiment was to sail in just days to join you in Guyana, it was assumed that any charges, foolish, politically motivated, sheep-incited charges, would be quietly dropped, but Governor White is such a dolt as to insist that the regiment sail without me!

Well, as you can imagine, that decided the issue, and right quick. I am selling out and going home. I finish this letter in a great hurry, as the regiment sails in minutes, and my ship for home (HOME!) sails in just hours.

I return to Leister and Julia, not wealthy, but able to travel as we please, rather than at the pleasure of King and Country.

Captain Lockwood

I do beg your pardon for not joining you in Guyana, but I hope my story explains my situation, and I trust you know that I remain your most loyal, devoted, and affectionate friend.

—Tom

James smiled wryly and tucked the letter inside his coat. He was surprised at how disappointed he was. How very different his life was when in the company of people he loved!

He told himself once again that, perhaps, he had seen enough.

*****

As soon as he was able, James made ready to call on Lieutenant Colonel Stephens. As the captain's best uniforms had gone down with the *Halcón*, O'Donnell did his best to patch up his officer's one remaining coat, but the captain made less than a striking impression.

Lockwood was not acquainted with Stephens, who had purchased over from the 33rd Foot. They had hardly been introduced and seated in the colonel's new office before Stephens burst out, "You are playing a rather neat game, Lockwood, hey, what! A meal-ticket wound at Waterloo, prolonged sick leave away from the regiment, then these weeks scampering about Guyana, feats of derring-do and tweaking the governor's nose, and now that the regiment has caught up with you, you are off again! A neat game, sir, a neat game indeed!"

Lockwood closed his eyes for a second, the fever's effects still lingering, not completely trusting his senses. With a shake of his head he asked, "Beg pardon, sir, but how am I to be off again?"

"Come now, sir, don't be coy! You've been pinched! Aide-de-camp to Major General Lambert, commander of His Majesty's forces in Southern Ireland! A bold stroke, indeed, sir! You've played your cards well, sir, very well!"

"I beg pardon, sir, but in all honesty and upon my honour, sir, I have no idea how this came about."

"Your orders are clear, sir, there is no room for argument." Stephens handed across the orders, and as Lockwood scanned them, the colonel changed his tack, and in a conspiratorial tone said, "In truth, sir, this works out better than we might have hoped. In all honesty, Captain, the governor is determined to see you broken. Broken! From what I hear of the Otero matter, there is, of course, no question of your conduct. You behaved as a professional, and an honourable officer of the regiment."

The colonel looked toward the door and then went on in a harsh whisper. "The governor had ordered me to post you and the men of your draft to the Orinoco as a permanent garrison, sir—searching the jungle for escaped rebels and preventing any pirate incursions... It's a death sentence, of course, bloody murder, and I could not defy him, but then, hey presto, I present him your secondment orders! Even a colonial governor cannot defy Horse Guards! This can be our only course: we shall see you safely and honourably away from his attentions. Home, sir!"

Lockwood roughly rubbed his face with both hands, his mind a confused spin of hesitancy, relief, and sudden, glittering joy. After a long pause he said, "But what of my men, sir? I must know they are seen to."

"As to them," said Stephens, pulling some papers from a drawer, "once you have gone, there will be no more talk of this posting to the Orinoco. They will be spread among the companies as required, but, in standard practice, we shall do our best to keep mess mates together." Then, referring to a sheet, he went on. "I understand the men who accompanied you to recapture Otero behaved very well. So, I have a plum for your... damn, what's his name?... Private O'Boyle. In salute to you, Captain Lockwood, Private O'Boyle is to be made corporal in the Grenadier Company. There might normally be some resentment in the ranks about that—a man from the depot coming in to take such a coveted spot—but hearing he is a Waterloo man will stop their gobs."

Wearily, resigned, Lockwood said, "Privates O'Donnell and McIlhenny, might they accompany me to Ireland?"

"Your servant, and the boy who is to be discharged? Yes, of course, that will not pose an issue. But there is one further order from the governor which I have no option but to obey: he orders you to leave the colony immediately."

"Oh, come now, sir! I have my men to address... matters to attend to..."

Colonel Stephens briskly slapped the folder closed and said, "I am, this minute, to see you aboard the *Oriole*, one of the foul little tubs which carried us here. She sails on the next tide, and we must... but come now, Lockwood, you are gone quite pale. Stay in your chair, man." Then out the door Stephens yelled, "McCauley, there! Fetch the captain a brandy! He is quite unwell. And pass the word for Dr. Toon!"

*****

Darkness had fallen, and only a few lanterns illuminated a panicked crowd at Government Quay. McAllistair had ordered, too, that a dozen unwelcome Baptist and Methodist missionaries were to board the *Oriole*, banished from Guyana Colony. One of their number, the Reverend Jones, had been imprisoned, charged with

318

inciting rebellion, and so the other missionaries and their families gathered on the quay in a hurried, disordered panic. Three militia officers and a platoon of their men herded the missionaries into boats with rough disrespect toward the whites and curses and surreptitious blows to their free black congregants.

Circles of flickering light illuminated that emotional mass of humanity, to which was added a four-horse carriage carrying Colonel Stephens, Captain Lockwood, and Dr. Toon, who was attempting to administer the alcoholic tincture of laudanum to the captain. Again the captain refused such treatment, so Dr. Toon contented himself with taking a few surreptitious nips of his own.

In the darkness, noise and commotion the horses grew frightened and misbehaved, and as the coachman tried to rein them in, the off-side leader danced sideways in the traces, knocking a militiaman to the ground. The enraged militiaman got to his feet and struck the horse across the face with the butt of his musket. The horse screamed and kicked, and pandemonium erupted. The coachman leapt from his seat to trade blows with the man who had struck his horse, while the uncontrolled horses continued to wildly dance and snort, the carriage lurching as the three Inniskilling officers dismounted. Dr. Toon was stunned into glassy-eyed silence, but Colonel Stephens roared orders, and Captain Lockwood was only slightly less emphatic in telling the militiamen to form up and quit their damned nonsense.

Many of the milling civilians were crying, yelling or both. The militia officers, who appeared to be in drink, stood and laughed, while from the darkness some of the militiamen boozily taunted, "Teague officers are still just teagues!" and "Fuck the line!"

Outraged, Colonel Stephens stepped forward and grabbed the nearest militiaman by the collar. Far from cowering, the militiaman

319

resisted, and his rough mates surrounded the colonel. Stephens reached for his sword, some militia hands reached to prevent him doing so and things were on the verge of growing very ugly, when Captain Lockwood roared, "Sergeant Maguire! First platoon will guard the colonel! Second platoon will disarm the militiamen!"

Lockwood's company came trotting in, from the darkness into the lantern light, with their bayonets lowered, their faces set, silent, disciplined, and very angry. They fulfilled their orders quickly and with professional skill, but with obvious disdain for the God damned amateurs.

Colonel Stephens pointed out some of the militiamen and directed Lockwood's Inniskillings. "You, sir, place that fellow under arrest! Well done! By God, Lockwood, these men of yours are worthy of the regiment! Private, grab that fellow as well! Lay hands on a colonel, will you, you militia devils? I'll see the hide flogged off the lot of you!"

Sergeant Maguire, much more the NCO than when they had left Enniskillen, stepped up to salute his captain, and said, "When word came for O'Donnell and McIlhenny to pack up and come down to the quay, we figured you were to return home, sir, and so I took the liberty of calling out the company to salute your departure."

"Well done, Sergeant," said Captain Lockwood as he unsteadily took a seat on a missionary's trunk.

The Inniskillings quickly restored order and assisted the last of the missionaries in getting themselves and their luggage across to the *Oriole*. As they did, the enlisted men each took a moment to stop by to bid their captain farewell. Lockwood had no choice but to go and the men showed nothing but genuine affection in wishing him the best, but through the filter of his fever, Lockwood was ashamed to be leaving them, all the same.

The last of the missionaries were aboard. The *Oriole's* boat returned to the foot of the quay, calling for any last passengers. Colonel Stephens took Lockwood by the arm and hurried him along, saying, "Come now, sir, honour has been served, and orders must be followed. You're off!"

Privates McIlhenny and O'Donnell had their packs on their backs, looking excited, ready to go, when Colonel Addis of Governor McAllistair's staff rode up. He did not deign to dismount, only calling out: "Colonel Stephens! I am instructed to inform you that by order of His Excellency Governor McAllistair, due to the ongoing state of emergency in the colony, no enlisted men are to depart for the next sixty days." He handed a copy of the order down to Sergeant Maguire, and then spurred away, not a little ashamed.

Stephens held the order up at an angle to catch the lantern light, and as he read he muttered, "Petty, vicious little bastard, is he not?" Then, shrugging, he gestured McIlhenny and O'Donnell back, away from the boat, and told the pale Lockwood, "There is nothing for it, sir. You travel alone, Captain, and good luck to you."

*****

The *Oriole* plowed into the Atlantic with an awkward pitch and roll. Nonetheless, the sea air and the release from the stagnant decay of the Guyana coast were a blessing. The cabins had gone to the married missionaries, so Captain Lockwood was relegated to a stuffy little closet with a cot far too short for a man of his stature.

Every inch of the *Oriole's* cabin deck was hot and reeked of vomit. James had the impertinence to wonder if the Methodist faith required its celebrants to be subject to nausea. Their wives were either bilious or preachy, though one of the younger wives, a Mrs. Taylor, plain but buxom, made it clear that she was less than fond of her husband, that seasickness would keep that pious gentleman confined to his cabin and that any attention from the gallant officer would be well received.

James, honestly taken aback by the notion that a woman other than Brigid O'Brian Lockwood would determine to pursue him, found it necessary to spend most of the journey in his cabin, feeling mildly ill and entirely dissatisfied. There were more than three thousand miles between Guyana and Madeira, and with every mile the *Oriole* faced storms, heat and relentless illness. Weeks passed with James Lockwood in his cabin, clutching his aching head and avoiding the increasingly obvious, increasingly buxom, Mrs. Taylor.

Chapter Twenty-Five

A chaise pulled up in front of Fáibhile Cottage. The gentleman within hesitated to emerge, as the house was in an obvious state of chaos. Despite the cool autumn air, all the windows stood open, the curtains flapping in the breeze. The front door, too, stood open, where a woman in bare feet and rolled up skirts was fiercely mopping. Several other persons were visible through the windows, all wildly active, and the noises that emerged did nothing to entice him.

He made out the sounds of chatter, squabbling, and scolding. The daily stresses of domesticity had always made him uncomfortable. Somewhere inside the house a dog, likely a very large dog, was barking—the gentleman had never cared for dogs. From further within came the sound of voices singing—the gentleman had never cared for music.

The coachman, unaware of the gentleman's reservations, pounded on the coach roof with the butt of his whip and called down, "We're *here*, sir! Fáibhile Cottage!"

The gentleman slowly, achingly climbed down, straightened his coat, and told the coachman, "You will please return for me in an hour's time. I have a ship leaving on the next tide."

As the coach rattled off, the gentlemen looked at the wild disorder of the house and told himself, "I may have erred. I ought to have told him five minutes."

He waited for the charwoman to toss a bucket of dirty water off into the roses and then went to the door to inquire, "I wonder, my good woman, if Mrs. Lockwood is at leisure."

The woman looked up at him, and the gentleman noticed she had a clay pipe clamped in her teeth. The gentleman had never cared for women who smoked.

An elderly woman emerged from the drawing room, her hands full of fabric and her mouth full of pins. She tilted her head toward the gentleman and muttered a question in Irish.

The charwoman pulled the pipe from her mouth and told the seamstress, "He wants to know if Mrs. Lockwood is at leisure."

Both women laughed, the seamstress returned to the drawing room, and the charwoman told the gentleman, "There hasn't been leisure in this house for a week, sir, a solid week, as aren't we working like fiends to get dear Fáibhile ready for the Lockwood's fancy company?"

From the drawing room came the sound of two men banging on the walls and loudly arguing in Irish. The dog which the gentleman had feared, as large and as black as he had imagined, galloped through the kitchen door with a bun in his mouth. It skidded to a halt, glanced up at the gentleman, saw him to be a stranger, and paused to decide his course. Opting to shirk his duty and carry on with his devotion to sin, the dog clamped the bun more tightly and dashed past the gentleman, out into the yard, just seconds ahead of a young woman, a young lady, who was calling out, "Corporal Lockwood, you naughty brute!" As the young woman watched the dog's galloping escape she muttered something in Irish which made the charwoman grin, blush and return to her work. Through the open kitchen door the gentleman saw a young man in an apron, happily kneading dough and singing.

The gentleman offered his card to the young woman. She was dressed very simply, her hair was tied back, her hands white with flour, a charming streak of white across one cheek, and she was achingly lovely—the gentleman had always appreciated lovely women. He bowed in a manner which could only be described as nervous, and said, "My name, Miss, is..."

The young woman smiled kindly at him, a charming young woman, but she did not read the card, only hurriedly saying, "Oh! You must be Mr. François with the wallpaper samples. My Mama is so glad you could come to the house." She took the gentleman by the elbow and steered him across the wet slate floor toward the stairs, speaking quickly. "Do come upstairs, won't you? Mind the puddle, sir."

As it took some time for the old gentlemen to climb the stairs, she had the opportunity to rattle on, "Mama is in the front bed room with Mr. O'Donovan, our painter, discussing the right shade of yellow, and we would so value your opinion in matching it to your samples. We are expecting a visit from Captain and Mrs. Mainwaring, dear friends of my parents, and..."

As they reached the top of the stairs a woman emerged from a sunny doorway, another lovely woman, and the younger woman said to her, "Mama, Mr. François is here. Shall we compare our yellows?"

The old gentleman paused at the end of the hall as a puzzled expression crossed the older woman's face—their visitor was certainly *not* Mr. François. His guide grew puzzled as well, finally saying, "Oh, I do beg your pardon, sir. I thought you were ... Oh, how very rude of me."

The two women stood together in their upstairs hall, nonplussed, painted in the soft sunlight, and the old gentleman was now pleased with the notion of an hour in such company. With a smile and a bow which he typically reserved for court, he said, "My name, ladies, is Read. I hold a post in His Majesty's Colonial Office, and am newly returned from Guyana by way of Horse Guards. And I have some news which may please you."

Chapter Twenty-Six

Madeira itself was scant relief. The *Oriole* passed on toward England, and so James Lockwood was finally shed of the vomitous missionaries and their desperate wives, but he was now forced to waste endless hot, humid days waiting for a ship to Ireland, yearning to be on his way, to be home, to be whole again.

He spent a shilling of his dwindling funds to buy a copy of the London *Gazette,* where he was saddened and wounded to see an article about the resolution of the Guyana Slave Revolt.

LIST OF THE INSURGENT NEGROES
Who were Tried by Court-Martial, held at the Colony-House, with their Sentences, &c.
Those marked thus [*], are still confined at the Colony Jail.

This mark [†], points out insurgents who were decapitated, after being taken down from the gallows. Their heads were affixed on poles within the Fort.

An extra feature of the article was a map, which showed 'Places along the Public Road where the rebels, or their heads, were hung *in terrorem.'*

Name	Plantation	Sentence	
Attilla	Plaisance	Death	Executed
Adonis *	La Bonne		Respited
Austin	Cove	Flogged	2 years in work house
Alexander	Lusignon	Up the Coast	
Achilles	Beterverwaging	Death	In Chains
Billy ↑	Ann's Grove	Death	Executed
Beffaney. ↑	Success	Death	Executed
Britain		Respited	
April*	La Bonne	Under Sentence	

James studied the list of punishments, a grimace of disgust locked on his face. He forced himself to trace his finger down the long list of names and the savage abuses meted out. He found the name of Carrera, the young man who had behaved so decently at Great Diamond. The young man had been executed in chains, and his head displayed on a pike. James turned quickly way from the paper, a sudden taste of bile in his mouth, and sat staring for long minutes.

He returned to the paper, searching for the name of Scipio Africanus. With a small sense of relief, he observed that name, at least, was not listed. He hoped the old fellow had had a better turn of fortune, but he would never know.

James carefully tore the lists, three pages long, from the paper, folded them, and tucked them into his Day Book. He would honor those people in that small way, although he felt—he knew—he should have done far more.

Far back in the paper was a small advertisement calling for 'Persons of Virtue' to join the 'Society for the Mitigation and Gradual Abolition of Slavery Throughout the British Dominions.' James sniffed, doubting his credentials, but he read the Society's goals with attention and then tore the advertisement from the paper and tucked it into his Day Book.

*****

Another ship at last, after endless days of delay, discomfort, illness and frustration, but James Lockwood finally stepped ashore on Queenstown quay. His baggage consisted of just one valise, the few things O'Donnell had managed to gather for him before he left Guyana.

How very different was the climate in Ireland. It was raining, it was cold and he had a long walk to the Admiral Nelson, the little inn the Lockwoods always frequented when in Cork. Once there, the usual innkeeper was not to be found, and the new man was sullen and of no help: they had no guest named Mrs. Lockwood, they had no letters for a Captain Lockwood, they had no rooms, and if that gentleman wanted dinner, he would be disappointed, as every table was booked by a party of merchant officers.

James stepped back out into the cold rain, telling himself "It was too much to expect, I suppose, for word to have reached home in time. Still, I feel a bit flat."

In the waning evening light, he pulled his cloak closer and passed through the streets to call on three other inns, but there was no room. It was growing colder, and the rain kept on. The streets were nearly empty, though there were whores on many of the corners, bedraggled and sodden. He assumed their lives were especially hard, now that the wars were over.

One painfully young woman stood shivering in a doorway and caught the tall soldier's eye. She reached down with one hand to hike up her skirts, saying nothing, but pleading with her eyes. Lockwood stopped, hurriedly pushed a few coins into her hand and scolded, "For God's sake, girl, go and get yourself something hot to eat." He went on in the dark rain, finally finding a room at the shabby King's Crown.

The next morning, he went out in search of a chaise to carry him home. He had at first planned on taking the Mail, but on that foggy morning he thought, "It will be worth it, I think, to play the great man at least once."

The clerk at the post office was the picture of accommodation. He said that one advantage of the hard times in Ireland was a ready supply of chaises, and after accepting the captain's three pounds, four and six he guaranteed a four-horse chaise at the Crown in one hour.

Four hours later, the captain was trying to decide whether to order his dinner or return to the post office to dismember the clerk. When the chaise did finally rein up in front of his inn, the sullen driver claimed to have no idea he was late. Lockwood growled, threw his valise up to the idiot footman, and climbed into the carriage.

In his hurry to be on his way James had forgotten to bring anything to eat, an omission he soon regretted. He felt the familiar twinges that marked the approach of one of his headaches, so in a soldierly manner, he resigned himself to hunger, put up his feet, folded his arms across his chest, and went to sleep. The ride through Cork Town allowed him that luxury, but soon the road going south and west grew potted, the lurching chaise threw him awake, and further rest was rendered impossible.

All that afternoon the chaise pitched along, but late in the day it made a final deep, grinding, tilting lurch, and ground to a halt. The cursing coachman climbed down, came to the window, and reported, "A broken wheel, please, sir, and aren't we in a bad spot for it." Looking up and down the muddy track he went on, "I'll have to send our Jimmy back to Ballinhassig to rouse their smith, and a wheelwright, if ever they have one, but it'll be morning or later before we are rolling again."

The big soldier sighed in frustration and said, "Very well, then, is there an inn in Ballinhassig?"

The coachman averted his eyes and evasively said, "Well, pardon me for saying so, your honour, but a fellow in a red coat might not be over welcome there, sir, if you understand me. Not that I have aught to do with those Whiteboys, but one hears rumours, as it were. No, sir, if a fellow was determined not to spend the night in the chaise, and him being a gentleman in a red coat, I might suggest he go on to Innishannon and the Golden Harp, but that is seven miles or more, and this rain is a misery, sure."

Captain Lockwood did not balk at the notion of a seven-mile march, cold rain or no. He wrapped himself in his old oilskin cloak, pulled his shako onto his head, and strode down the road. The coachman called after him, promising to find him in Innishannon as quick as he might get his wheel repaired.

The first mile went well enough, and James took some pleasure, albeit a chilly, damp, pleasure, in being in his home country, the brisk air clearing his head wonderfully. But soon the wind rose, cutting and cold, and he grew foul tempered. The road wound down into a little hamlet, where three local toughs sat out of the rain under the eaves of a low shabeen.

Those worthies got slowly to their feet when they saw a lone man coming down the road, and, seeing the shako, they decided to rough up the soldier for amusement. When the soldier came nearer, they noted his size, his confident stride, and the sword that hung beneath his cloak, and after trading a look they sat back down.

Two hours in that rain rendered Lockwood irritable; another thirty minutes of stumbling through the inky darkness of Innishannon, looking for the Golden Harp, pushed him to near fury. The streets were deserted, and it was only the kindness of yet another sodden whore, one who politely gave him directions, that kept him from sleeping in a doorway.

While the keeper of the Golden Harp went off to check on a room, Lockwood poked a spoon into something that he had been told was stew. He mulled over the goodness of whores, in comparison with the balance of humanity, until with a sniff of frustration, he pushed the plate away. Taking a drink from his glass, he decided that the Harp's wine could best be applied as rat poison, and so called for beer.

In his red coat and flashing epaulette, he drew some surly glares from the locals, though no one went so far as to express disrespect. He removed the cover from his shako and subtly but deliberately placed it on the table so that the shining brass plate was legible in the firelight. He intended for the three-castle emblem and the bold "27" of the Inniskilling Regiment to make it clear that he was not some bumbling militiaman, but rather a professional soldier and no one to be toyed with. He ensured the hilt of his sword was free of encumbrance, and seeing himself eyed by a hulking brute at the bar, he mused, "Perhaps I should have brought my pistols as well."

Eventually, the hustling innkeeper came back to the captain's table to say, "It's as I feared, sir, our Mary has booked our last room. But if you don't mind sharing with another gentleman, sir, a Mr. Haythornthwaite, a cattle buyer from Derbyshire, he is willing to split the fare."

After viewing the room, the bed and the cattle buyer, James opted to drink two more tankards of beer and sleep in the snug.

*****

He woke on the wooden bench stiff, sore, and bad-tempered. He should have known better than to sleep with wet boots on, after a long march.

Breakfast was a stale biscuit that a rat had likely been at, a bit of cold, fatty ham, and no eggs, as the Harp's cross-eyed cook explained, "Maggie's our only bird, isn't she, and this morning she does feel put upon, mmm."

"She's not the only one," grumbled the big soldier. The Harp had no newspaper more current than the previous century, so he went out in search of something to read. He hobbled through the muddy streets in vain, eventually returning to the inn, convinced that Innishannon was the least literate place in Ireland.

After weeks of discomfort, delay, and inconvenience he was nearly mad with frustration, just twenty miles from home. In a flash, he recalled the morning, twenty-odd years earlier, when Brigid and he were newly married and she had lectured him on the difference between an Irish and an English mile. He recalled how that young Brigid Lockwood had been wearing nearly nothing, as she sat up in the narrow bed, lecturing him on that rainy morning. He reveled in that memory for several moments, but then found it necessary to distract himself by calculating that twenty English miles equaled about sixteen Irish miles—only that far away from the woman he loved.

It was noon before the chaise pulled up in front of the Harp. After paying the innkeeper's felonious bill, Lockwood saw the post boy sleeping on the roof of the chaise, and the coachman bleary-eyed and grinning.

Lockwood growled up to him, "Are you in drink, sir?"

"Christ, no, sir. I shall see you to Macroom directly."

Lockwood pointed up and hissed, "If you see me to Macroom, coachman, I shall see you drawn and bloody *quartered*. We are bound for *Clonakilty*. Clonakilty, sir!"

Fear and the resultant adrenalin gave the coachman sufficient sobriety to see them safely through Bandon, but then a wrong turn at Oldchapel Village and a stubborn resistance to admitting his error carried them miles out of their way. The driver had to go as far as Clashavoon to find a place to turn around, which displeased his passenger to no end. The horses, too, seemed displeased to re-do the miles back to Oldchapel, finally turning left, and back onto the road toward Clonakilty.

Once he was sure the driver had at last found the right road, James tried to sleep. It was the one remedy he could use to avoid the haunting headaches, and he very much desired to be at his best when he reached home. They were just a few miles away. So long as the chaise maintained a moderate pace, he could rest, but when the driver slapped the horses into a trot, a sudden lurch slammed his head against the door, and his mood shifted into a state of instant rage.

James was prepared to pound on the roof and curse the driver, but he heard a racket from behind, and turned to look out the small oval window at the rear of the chaise. A stylish yellow phaeton with a fine pair of grays in the traces was trying to pass them. Despite the drizzle and the threat of rain to come, the phaeton's top was down, so James could clearly see the driver, a young buck in a light blue coat, who was roaring for the chaise to pull aside and let him pass. The attractive young woman sitting next to the buck was equally emphatic, waving and calling for the chaise to clear the road. The chaise driver was not about to oblige them.

That stretch of road was narrow, winding, and muddy, so the chaise's driver would typically keep a cautious pace, as he had no desire to break another wheel and risk another dose of the big soldier's wrath. But the driver was a prideful man, so when the young pup in his fancy rig came trotting up from behind, he gave his horses a snap, to show this newcomer how a professional coachman handled his rig.

The newcomer, however, was having none of it and pressed his horses to keep hard on the chaise's heels. The road straightened and widened as it sloped down toward the Arigideen, and the phaeton swung wide to pass on the left. The chaise driver put his four horses to a solid trot, and the race was on.

James pounded on the roof of the carriage, as he knew something that the chaise driver, and evidently the phaeton driver, did not know: at the bottom of that gentle slope there was a sharp turn to the right, then another sharp left over the Lisselane Bridge.

It had been the site of numerous accidents, and after all he had experienced, James had no desire to die, four miles from home.

In the excitement the chaise driver did not hear, of perhaps did not heed, the warning from his passenger. He was, however, not a complete fool, so when he saw the road ahead disappear off to the right he quickly tried to rein in his team.

As the phaeton drew even, James looked over to see the young woman looking back at him. She positively stuck her tongue out at him; his response was to give her a fatherly frown and an emphatic gesture toward the road ahead. He then slid to the bottom of the chaise in anticipation of what would likely happen next.

The chaise driver was still pulling hard to slow his team, but the phaeton driver was late in seeing the turn. He was nearly past the chaise's leaders, but not quite past, when he pulled his team in a panicked turn across their path. The high right-rear wheel of the phaeton struck the chaise's left-hand leader, and while the wildly leaning phaeton and its screaming passenger made the turn, the chaise did not.

The four very unhappy chaise horses, one of them especially so, careened into the right-hand ditch, where after a moment of screaming, roaring, and jolting, they came to rest with yet another broken wheel, a broken yoke, tangled harness, and the chaise nearly on its side in mud a foot deep. The horses were unhurt, but frightened. The driver and the footman rushed to tend the horses, leaving their passenger to climb out of the steeply canted chaise. Without a word, the soldier waded and rolled in the muck to retrieve his valise, and then strode off down the road.

As the big captain stalked past, the coachman looked up from the wreck of his chaise to ask tremulously, "I wonder, sir, if you'll be needing anything further?"

Lockwood growled and went on. Spectacularly dark clouds were rolling in from the west, but he was just four miles from home.

Chapter Twenty-Seven

Fáibhile Cottage was overflowing with happiness. Mr. Read had shared the news, the wholly unexpected, joyously received news, that James was homeward bound. Captain Lockwood was aboard the *Oriole*, destined for London, where he was to be met by an official from the Colonial Office, who was to carry him to meetings with Lord Rathbone and General Lowery Cole. Captain Lockwood's input regarding the state of affairs in Guyana was to bolster Mr. Read's damning report, which would likely bring about wholesale change in the management of the colony.

Brigid could thus estimate that James would arrive at Fáibhile Cottage in two weeks, sufficient time to plan a celebration, both of his return home and his appointment to General Lambert's staff. After Read's visit she had written a note to the general, to thank him for the return of her husband, a note she asked Cissy to edit, as her disdain for punctuation nearly betrayed her once again.

General Lambert's prompt, polite, friendly reply shared more delightful news: in light of his long, honourable, and valued service, Horse Guards had it in mind to grant Captain Lockwood a brevet majority. While he was in London, General Cole himself would bestow the honour.

Captain, Brevet Major, James Lockwood's return celebration would also be marked by the presence of his dearest friend, Tom Mainwaring, and his wife, Julia. They had planned to visit at any rate, but the news of the James's return was an especially happy coincidence.

The ladies Lockwood and the Mainwarings had only to wait the two weeks until James's return, which seemed an unduly long while, but in the meantime, they had one other's company to enjoy.

*****

Four miles. It would have been six if he had followed Bandon Road down into Clonakilty proper, then back up McCurtain Hill Road to Fáibhile Cottage, but he knew where to cut across the fields, taking delight in the familiarity of each fence and tree.

The coming storm made that midafternoon as gloomy as dusk. Halfway across Mr. O'Leary's pastures he laughed aloud, drawing the attention of O'Leary's otherwise impartial cows. He saw Fáibhile Cottage, a light burning from every window. He would have run the rest of the way if he had not been so very tired, and his cloak and boots, his very being, so caked with mud.

He hurried across the fields, but his final steps toward the house were hesitant. After all he had seen and experienced, he saw his house, his garden and the beech trees towering overhead. From his dark place, he could see the brightly illuminated interior. Through the windows he could see his family and friends, active and happy. It was if an ornate play had been staged and he was the sole spectator.

He stared at Brigid for long moments, elegant and beautiful and kind. He studied Cissy, his dear daughter, a woman now. There was a young man there, too—James struggled to remember the name of the young doctor whom Brigid had mentioned in her letter. When Cissy went to a dimly lit corner to pour another cup of punch, her companion followed her, where they touched hands and shared a smile. He might have been tempted to kiss her, the rogue, if she had not danced away with a laugh, elegant and beautiful. James Lockwood decided that he liked that young man.

For a moment he watched Tom and Julia. She was so lovely, laughing and chatting, holding Tom's hand. He was so comfortable, so at ease, so alive, his handsome features marred by the horrid scars of his Waterloo wound. James did not see Doolan, wondering where the old fool had got to, though a dark shadow of worry grew in the back of his mind.

He felt too dirty, strangely unworthy, to pass through his own front door, and so slipped through the shadows to the rear and the intimately familiar kitchen door. Passing into the warmth and gentle glow of the peat fire, it was Corporal who first welcomed him home, ecstatic at his master's return. There was no sign of Sergeant, and with an ache of perception, he knew the old dog had passed. Looking into the little room behind the kitchen, he saw it standing empty, and in his heart he knew that Doolan was gone as well. Time had passed, cutting its ugly, unrelenting path through their lives. But he was home now, and he would not waste the time remaining to him. He would revel in the company of those he loved.

The kitchen door opened, and he saw Brigid.

His heart leapt, it was she, her face, her voice, her hair, her sudden presence striking him like a physical blow. She clasped both open hands to her face in a shock of joy and surprise. Three thousand miles and as many deep horrors had passed since he had last seen her. He had come from a far hemisphere; every mile he had traveled was marked in his face. He did not hesitate again, but went to her, lifting her from the doorway in a mad, spinning kiss.

She laughed aloud and said, "My dear James! You must never, ever leave me again."

He smiled down at her and replied, "Must I not? Very well then, *a stor*, I shall never roam again. Never again."

Cissy came to the door, standing for a moment to drink from that cup of joy and relief, and then ran to her father. He held her for a long moment of honest, open joy, but soon she coughed a sob and murmured into his chest, "Father, we have lost Diarmuid."

"I know," he whispered, kissing the top of her head. "It will be all right, my dear, everything will be all right now."

In a moment, the kitchen was teeming with people, with laughter, embraces, hurried explanations, introductions and news. A letter had arrived the day before, from Private O'Donnell—he was escorting Private McIlhenny home to Enniskillen and would then make his way to Clonakilty. While his promise of "no more pear-making" had puzzled the family, it brought a sparkling laugh from the muddy captain.

But in the end it was all about the two of them. Propriety be damned! In that warm glowing place of remembrance and future hopes, they ignored the storm raging outside and clung to one another in kisses and smiles and laughter and kisses.

The End

About the Author

Mark Bois

    In 2006 Mark Bois fulfilled a long-time ambition and returned to school to earn a Master's degree in history. His Irish ancestry and a fascination with military history prompted him to write his thesis on the Inniskilling Regiment and their bloody stand atop the ridge at Waterloo.

    Amongst the dusty rosters and letters in the British National Archives, and then in the artifacts and records of the Inniskilling Regimental Museum, he found what he needed to write his thesis. He also discovered the fascinating personal stories that inspired *The Lockwoods of Clonakilty*.

    As a happily married man and the father of five, Bois finds it interesting to tell the stories of families. He thinks it especially important to share the stories not just of soldiers, but also of those who wait for them to come home, and the burdens they bear alone, and together.

If You Enjoyed This Book

Please write a review.
This is important to the author and helps to get the word out to others.

Visit:

PENMORE PRESS

www.penmorepress.com

All Penmore Press books are available directly through our website, amazon.com, Barnes and Noble and Nook, Sony Reader, Apple iTunes, Kobo books and via leading bookshops across the United States, Canada, the UK, Australia and Europe.

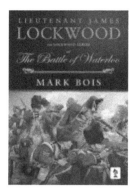

Lieutenant James Lockwood

By

Mark Bois

"Captain Barr desperately wanted to kill Lieutenant Lockwood. He thought constantly of doing so, though he had long since given up any consideration of a formal duel. Lockwood, after all, was a good shot and a fine swordsman; a knife in the back would do. And then Barr dreamt of going back to Ireland, and of taking Brigid Lockwood for his own."

So begins the story of Lieutenant James Lockwood, his wife Brigid, and his deadly rivalry – professional and romantic – with Charles Barr. Lockwood and Barr hold each other's honor hostage, at a time when a man's honor meant more than his life. But can a man as treacherous as Charles Barr be trusted to keep secret the disgrace that could irrevocably ruin Lockwood and his family?

Against a backdrop of famine and uprising in Ireland, and the war between Napoleon and Wellington, showing the famous Inniskilling Regiment in historically accurate detail, here is a romance for the ages, and for all time.

"... Bois' meticulous research and command of historical detail makes this novel a must read. He sets the standard for research and understanding... and the audience will demand more novels from this new author. Historical fiction welcomes Mark Bois with open arms." – Lt. Col. Brad Luebbert, US Army

PENMORE PRESS
www.penmorepress.com

KING'S SCARLET

BY

JOHN DANIELSKI

Chivalry comes naturally to Royal Marine captain Thomas Pennywhistle, but in the savage Peninsular War, it's a luxury he can ill afford. Trapped behind enemy lines with vital dispatches for Lord Wellington, Pennywhistle violates orders when he saves a beautiful stranger, setting off a sequence of events that jeopardize his mission. The French launch a massive manhunt to capture him. His Spanish allies prove less than reliable. The woman he rescued has an agenda of her own that might help him along, if it doesn't get them all killed.

A time will come when, outmaneuvered, captured, and stripped of everything, he must stand alone before his enemies. But Pennywhistle is a hard man to kill and too bloody obstinate to concede defeat.

PENMORE PRESS
www.penmorepress.com

The Lockwoods

of Clonakilty

by

Mark Bois

Lieutenant James Lockwood of the Inniskilling Regiment has returned to family, home and hearth after being wounded, almost fatally, at the Battle of Waterloo, where his regiment was decisive in securing Wellington's victory and bringing the Napoleonic Wars to an end. But home is not the refuge and haven he hoped to find. Irish uprisings polarize the citizens, and violence against English landholders – including James' father and brother – is bringing down wrath and retribution from England. More than one member of the household sympathizes with the desire for Irish independence, and Cassie, the Lockwood's spirited daughter, plays an active part in the rebellion.

Estranged from his English family for the "crime" of marrying a Irish Catholic woman, James Lockwood must take difficult and desperate steps to preserve his family. If his injuries don't kill him, or his addiction to laudanum, he just might live long enough to confront his nemesis. For Captain Charles Barr, maddened by syphilis and no longer restrained by the bounds of honor, sets out to utterly destroy the Lockwood family, from James' patriarchal father to the youngest child, and nothing but death with stop him – his own, or James Lockwood's.

PENMORE PRESS
www.penmorepress.com

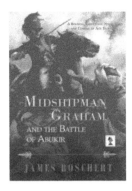

Midshipman Graham and the Battle of Abukir

BY

James Boschert

It is midsummer of 1799 and the British Navy in the Mediterranean Theater of operations. Napoleon has brought the best soldiers and scientists from France to claim Egypt and replace the Turkish empire with one of his own making, but the debacle at Acre has caused the brilliant general to retreat to Cairo.

Commodore Sir Sidney Smith and the Turkish army land at the strategically critical fortress of Abukir, on the northern coast of Egypt. Here Smith plans to further the reversal of Napoleon's fortunes. Unfortunately, the Turks badly underestimate the speed, strength, and resolve of the French Army, and the ensuing battle becomes one of the worst defeats in Arab history.

Young Midshipman Duncan Graham is anxious to get ahead in the British Navy, but has many hurdles to overcome. Without any familial privileges to smooth his way, he can only advance through merit. The fires of war prove his mettle, but during an expedition to obtain desperately needed fresh water – and an illegal duel – a French patrol drives off the boats, and Graham is left stranded on shore. It now becomes a question of evasion and survival with the help of a British spy. Graham has to become very adaptable in order to avoid detection by the French police, and he must help the spy facilitate a daring escape by sea in order to get back to the British squadron.

"Midshipman Graham and The Battle of Abukir is both a rousing Napoleonic naval yarn and a convincing coming of age story. The battle scenes are riveting and powerful, the exotic Egyptian locales colorfully rendered." – John Danielski, author of *Capital's Punishment*

PENMORE PRESS
www.penmorepress.com

Penmore Press

Challenging, Intriguing, Adventurous, Historical and Imaginative

www.penmorepress.com